blood and silver

blood and silver

blood and silver

erotic stories

patrick califia

CARROLL & GRAF PUBLISHERS
NEW YORK

BLOOD AND SILVER
Erotic Stories

Carroll & Graf Publishers
An Imprint of Avalon Publishing Group, Inc.
245 West 17th Street, 11th Floor
New York, NY 10011

AVALON

Compilation copyright © 2007 by Patrick Califia

First Carroll & Graf edition 2007

"Mercy," "Too Much Is Almost Enough," "Blood and Silver," "Love Sees No Gender," "Incense for the Queen of Heaven," and "No Mercy" were originally published in *No Mercy,* copyright © 2000 by Pat Califia, published by Alyson publications.

"Big Girls," "Daddy," and "What Girls Are Made Of" were originally published in *Melting Point,* copyright © 1993, 1996 by Pat Califia, published by Alyson Publications, Inc.

Library of Congress Cataloging-in-Publication Data is available.

ISBN-13: 978-0-78671-809-2
ISBN-10: 0-7867-1809-9

9 8 7 6 5 4 3 2 1

Printed in the United States of America
Distributed by Publishers Group West

Contents

Contents

Big Girls

Once there was a bar called Jax. If the drag queens haven't taken it over or the vice squad hasn't closed it down, it's probably still there, giving decent lesbians a bad name.

Jax was in a strange part of town. The neighborhood wasn't bad, exactly. When middle-class white people call a neighborhood "bad," they mean poor black people live there, and Jax was not situated in a residential neighborhood. It was in the middle of an industrial zone full of warehouses, produce wholesalers, sheet metal shops, places where you could rent forklifts or buy several tons of green coffee beans, a recycling center, some union halls, a marina, and a couple of freeway on-ramps. There were also a few oddball shops whose owners couldn't find affordable space elsewhere and whose customers wanted their unique merchandise enough to make the trek— an art gallery that was so progressive, the vice squad attended its openings; a store that sold bones (animal and human) and lizards, turtles, and tropical snakes; a tattoo parlor; and an excellent Italian restaurant.

This location was part of what made it possible for Jax to be a cross between a seventies gay male leather-bar-with-back-room and a fifties working-class dive for dykes. Jax could never have stayed open in the thin strip of the barrio that white dykes were busy gentrifying because those women didn't drink enough (in public, anyway) to keep up payments on the lease. If Jax had been located closer to downtown, where the gay bikers and other butch thangs in black cowhide tried to keep eros alive despite AIDS and the Alcoholic Beverage Commission, the men would have squeezed out the women. Anywhere else in town, the owner would have catered to a straight clientele and made a hell of a lot more money. But here, he was content to have any customers at all, even if they didn't look anything like the Lusty Ladies of Lesbos who almost let their tongues touch on the cover of his favorite X-rated video.

This part of town was, however, surrounded by bad neighborhoods, so cabdrivers didn't like to go there. A gypsy cab company called Black Pearl serviced the area. Black Pearl hired mostly Rastamen and an occasional dreadlocked sister. The dented, crippled cabs were redolent with ropy green smoke, and the drivers didn't care what the oddly dressed women in the backseat got up to as long as they didn't bitch about how long it took to get them home. A city bus came within four blocks of Jax, but it stopped only every two hours or so.

From the row of Hondas, Nortons, Yamahas, Beamers, Kawasakis, and the rare Harley parked outside, you'd think everybody got to Jax on a motorcycle. But on any Friday or Saturday night, the place was too jammed for that to be possible. When the image-conscious drove a car to Jax, they parked it a block away and evaded questions about their mode of transportation. Four-wheelers and pickup trucks were the only things with steering wheels that were butch enough to get parked within sight of the bar's front door.

A few skinny, tattooed punk girls—artists, strippers, welfare mothers, musicians, dealers—who had lofts in the neighborhood just walked to the bar. Black dykes from the shell-shocked parts of town around Jax also turned up regularly, and they formed their own coterie within the rest of the bar's kinky, mostly white clientele. They appreciated the intense sexuality of the white girls, recognized it as a valid reason for being there, but envied the excesses some of them committed with their appearance and disapproved of the thoughtless way they squandered their resources. Many of the white girls who frequented Jax lived on the edge, but if their survival was really threatened, they had somebody to call for a plane ticket home to Orange County or Long Island. They did not know what it means to live without that safety net.

The black women at Jax were mostly into fifties-style butch-femme, but a few of them were there because they were interested in leather or white girls or both. And not all of the butch-femme couples were necessarily vanilla. They just didn't put their stuff out where everybody could take a look. Even in a dyke bar, some things remain your private business.

The sex workers—strippers, phone sex operators, professional dominants and submissives, call girls, and hookers—held the whole mix together. They were the sharpest dressers, the ones who spent the most money, and the white ones were the only Caucasian women who didn't hesitate to cross the color line when they wanted to buy somebody a drink or find a dancing partner. They did this partly because their work rewarded them for being bold and aggressive hussies, and partly because black dykes gave you less shit about being a whore. In their capacity as outcasts and go-betweens, they were the first ones to greet newcomers, loan people money, or perform at benefits, and they knew everybody's secrets. They stopped at least as many fights as they started and reunited as many estranged couples as they blew apart.

The regulars—women who showed up every weekend and at least once during the week—were another important social caste at Jax. The regulars had certain privileges—playing dice with Kat or Lolly, the bartenders, occasionally getting to stash a coat or a purse behind the bar, a free drink when business was slow, running a bit of a tab. One of them might be drafted to fill in behind the bar if Kat or Lolly called in sick, or get screamed at to please clean off some tables and bring the empties up front when there was an insane, crushing crowd. Kat and Lolly looked the other way if they saw one of the regulars slipping little white paper envelopes under the tables in return for a few folded bills. What the fuck, the State Liquor Authority never came here anyway. (The owner had a Sicilian surname.) In addition, the regulars got first crack at interesting newcomers. The bartenders usually didn't trick with anybody the regulars hadn't screened first.

Other women besides Kat and Lolly sometimes used the soda gun or shoved swizzle sticks into mixed drinks, but they came and went faster than the pretzels. Kat and Lolly seemed as much a part of Jax as the scratches on the floor or the scorched wallpaper in the men's room. They were big girls, picked for their popularity and their ability to run roughshod over a crowd that got rowdy even for a bunch of drunk and horny lesbians. The pay wasn't great, but the tips could be good. When push came to shove, Kat and Lolly knew they were lucky to have a job that let them look the way the Goddess made them. It would have taken more than a make-over from *Cosmopolitan* to turn either of them into anything other than bulldaggers. So if the tips didn't stretch their wages enough to make ends meet, the bartenders concentrated on tail. Sex is never free, but at Jax, women didn't have to pay cash.

Lolly was at that stage in a slightly older bar dyke's life when she forgets exactly how many anorexic, pink-haired girls with eight earrings she's slept with. She was kind of afraid to admit, even to herself, that she couldn't even remember exactly how many of them she'd lived with. Did it really matter? Every single time, it was true love. Lolly had short black hair she kept in a DA and a few crude tattoos done in india ink at juvenile hall. She couldn't hold her liquor, so she let customers who insisted buy her a drink out of her own bottle, specially labeled, which Kat filled with iced tea just before they opened.

When Lolly fell off the wagon, she fell hard. She cleaned out the till, picked the best-looking woman in the place, hollered, "Somebody ought to treat you right, sweet thing," carried her out bodily, perched her on the back of her bike, and laid scratch out of there to go on a binge that didn't end until the money had all been spent on bad booze and sleazy lingerie, and Lolly's new mama could hardly walk to the bathroom.

In her younger days, Lolly had extended these benders by shooting up speed. She would supplement her cash flow by soliciting contributions with a .38 from gas stations and convenience stores. But she found out that prison time goes even more slowly than juvie, and the thrill of having a crude design etched into her body with a sewing needle had disappeared with adolescence. Being held in the daddy tank with the other diesels was not her idea of a good time.

Now she puts the brakes on before that can happen. She picks a fight with the "sweet thing," tosses her out, throws all the ripped and soiled lingerie she can lay her hands on after her, and comes crawling back to Jax just before it's time to open, bitching about her hangover and ready to lick Kat's boots in public ("Shit, I'll even kiss your butthole, buddy!") for covering up for her. Occasionally, the sweet thing puts her pretty finger to the wind and splits first, usually after hacking up her erstwhile daddy's dick.

Lolly had been doing pretty much the same thing for (ahem) years, but she was still convinced that someday the love of one good woman was going to save, redeem, and reform her. "Too bad you can't sing," Kat jeered at her. "You're just a country-western singer who missed her calling, girl. You better come to Jesus or just admit you're nothing but a run-around tramp with a military haircut. Too bad you can't sell all those thirty-day chips back to the AA store, honey. You'd have enough money to retire."

Kat, a six-foot-tall, broad-shouldered woman with big hands, feet, hips, and heart, and blonde hair she shaved herself with poodle clippers, was more complicated. She was too young to be a straight-forward bar butch. Oh, every now and then, she got an itch for some wildcat in a leather miniskirt and spandex leotard and handed Lolly her bar towel so she could take Miss Lucky out the back way. There was a sort of patio out there, a fenced-in place with a locked gate where Kat and Lolly left their bikes. She liked to stick her tongue down the drunk girl's throat, pull her top down and push her skirt up, and destroy as much underwear as necessary to get access to her cunt. Kat wasn't much good at foreplay. If being dragged outside with Kat's big paws around her throat wasn't enough to make a girl's pussy overflow, she was liable to find her-self slinking back inside, unscathed and unsatisfied. The clientele at Jax kept track of such things.

Kat fucked hard when these frenzies took her. She wanted all the way in, right fucking now. And she wanted them to stand up for it, no matter how tall their heels were. Those pretty girls shimmied on Kat's fist and screamed loud enough to be heard inside over the jukebox and the pinball machines and the video games, the crack of pool balls and the beehive hum of a hundred women jammed in denim-crotch-to-leather-clad-butt, satin-cleavage-to-leather-jacket-lapel, talking about everything but their jones and usually drinking too much to do anything about it anyway.

One of these prize felines, an unusually slender dancer by the name of Sage, who floated around the bar on heels high enough to be illegal, had long hair bleached to white and a meaner attitude than most. Once spirited outside, she took the intentionally quick and brutal fist without complaint, and proceeded to walk up Kat's thighs, fucking herself while she stuck her tongue out at the big woman whose quads were being tenderized by her steel-tipped heels. "Show me everything you got," she panted. "Show me something I haven't had before. Do you think you can do anything to me I haven't done to myself already? Damage is my middle name." And she showed Kat the scars on her arms. "Lick them," she demanded. "See if you can lick them off me, big girl."

That bitch got laid out on the seat of Kat's bike and fucked proper, at leisure, until the bartender was completely wrung out and hoarse, and both of her hands were as wrinkled as prunes. The mighty sounds of impact and thankful flesh awed the whole bar into silence. Kat's forearms were so sore from satisfying the white-haired, sharp-hipped dancer that she let people pour their own beers the rest of the night.

After that, she was Lady Sage as far as Kat was concerned. She wouldn't mind having at that fierce little witch again sometime, if she ever showed up wearing the right outfit and the moon was full. But the rest of them she forgot as soon as she let them fall to the concrete. The ones who tried to sit on her boot and suck on her 501s got kicked aside. The last thing Kat wanted after messing somebody up and making her come a hundred times was to get messed up herself. "Gotta get back to work," she would grumble, if she said anything at all.

These quasi-consensual episodes gave her a sort of high, made her feel big and mean and good-looking, and confirmed her position at the top of the fuck circuit in Jax. But it also left the taste of something missing in the back of her throat, and it was such a lonely and bitter flavor, she couldn't imagine making a whole meal of it by taking one of these fancy sluts home to leave her hair in Kat's sink, her nylons under the bed, and the dirty dishes from her attempt to prove she was a good cook piled up in the sink for Guess Who to wash.

Time was when Kat had lived with girls who were a bit like her fuck-bunnies, although a little less wild. She took lovers who were legal secretaries or cocktail waitresses, while she had a dirty job someplace working with men who were usually shorter than she was and never as good at keeping the machines running. If it had an engine, Kat had an immediate, intuitive understanding of how it worked. Broken machines seemed to tell her what was the matter, like old ladies complaining to their doctor, and her capable hands always made it right.

When Kat went home, whichever of these girls she was currently living with would immediately tell her to wash up. The bathroom was always full of nail brushes and Lava soap, and there was a can of mineral spirits or kerosene underneath the sink. One of them had even said to her, over the dinner which Kat had cooked, "For heaven's sake, you never get clean. Can't you wear gloves at work?"

Kat had helped her move out a week later. The bitch (by then, Kat had taken to calling them bitches when they weren't around) wound up with an ambitious and successful feminist attorney who never came home in time for dinner and had beautifully kept hands with long, pearl pink nails. Every time Kat thought of those sexually disabling claws, she smiled and figured there was a little justice in this world.

These straitlaced femmes loved Kat for what she did to them in bed, and for what they hoped she would become after they got her to go back to school. Most of them thought she was not as bright as they were—overlooking the pile of technical journals on her side of the bed, the books by women authors she was always reading, and her subscription to the Sunday *New York Times*. It wasn't hard, usually, for Kat to find out how to make a woman's toes curl and her face get red. She liked seeing her prim lovers rip up the sheets. But they never seemed to be able to perform the same kind of divination for her. Usually they rolled over between her legs and expected ten minutes of mouth-work to send her to the moon. She wouldn't stand for that. So they would roll away and express some sympathy about her being a stone butch, voice some hope that she would "work on it," and fall asleep.

None of these girls was bad-looking. Kat liked fine, presentable women with good legs and pretty faces. When she went out to dinner with them or took them shopping, they made an obvious couple and a striking one. She would look impassively at the men who noticed her partner and feel grim satisfaction when they dropped their eyes and took their prick energy elsewhere. Being big had its advantages. She had an aptitude for violence, but she wasn't addicted to it. Fighting hadn't been much fun for Kat since she got shot. She was just minding her own business, walking down to the corner store, when the barrel of a gun came out of the window of a passing car, and her shoulder stung. It didn't hurt at all. Passersby had to force her to lie down on the grass and wait for an ambulance. At the hospital, they told her she was lucky—the bullet barely missed an artery.

Having a chunk of lead put in you for no good reason certainly reminded you of your own mortality. After that, Kat lost her patience with two-faced foxes who got themselves hot by setting up two butches to fight over them. If you got killed by hitting your head on a table or having a broken bottle rammed into your throat, you'd be just as dead as a crumpled body in some neo-Nazi's crosshairs. Why should she assault another butch, another woman who was humiliated and frustrated by the simple desire she felt for her own kind, unless the woman was out for her blood or didn't want to pay for her drugs?

When she left her last femme behind, Kat found herself making this speech: "I never let you doubt the fact that I love you. I always held you and defended you. But how do I know that I am loved? Who holds me? Who defends me?" Her ex said impatiently, "How am I supposed to get to work every day if you keep the car?"

Kat couldn't imagine having to make that speech to another butch. She became what she called "a faggot"—a butch who was interested in other butches. She figured there weren't too many vantage points for spotting rough trade better than her post behind the bar at Jax. While she mixed drinks and measured out shots, she kept one eye open for women who rolled their own cigarettes, women who worked out or had a belt in karate, women who rebuilt their own carburetors and put in their own transmissions, women cops or truck drivers, women who carried knives and shot straight, women who had been in the service, women who had bulging arms and calloused hands and stood tall.

It was a preference that a lot of people—including Lolly—didn't understand. "You're some queer kind of queer," Lolly once said to her best, maybe only, friend. "Those kinda girls aren't gonna be interested in you. Whatchoo gonna do anyway, bump pussies?"

"You think that doesn't work?" Kat said, smiling, and put her cigarette out on Lolly's left hand, Lolly yelped and jumped around like she'd been napalmed. "Shit," Kat swore, "I'm sorry, good buddy. I'm gettin' old and blind. Gotta quit drinkin' that sterno. I was aiming for your twat."

It was none of Lolly's business what she did with other big girls. Not that Lolly wouldn't understand, in her gut, what Kat's kinks were all about. Lolly was just down on sex in general these days. The last joyride baby had left deep, angry red scratches on Lolly's cheek, cut her leather jacket into fabric-sample swatches, and broken her heart so completely that Lolly was probably going to be able to stay sober till spring while she nursed on the pain of it. Kat thought the pain of it was the whole point. But Lolly saw her own suffering as an act of God, a Greek tragedy, not as a self-inflicted ritual. Kat thought simple sexual masochism had a lot more dignity. And she honestly didn't think she could listen to a sermon about the healing power of true love without punching Lolly out. So she kept quiet and let it alone.

A baby butch or two sometimes came into Jax, looking for a daddy. If Kat was in the mood, she might oblige. If you had muscles, she liked to see them under stress, in restraint, and covered with the kind of sweat you break out in when you're scared you can't take it and don't really have a choice. The young studs who weren't stupid or resentful sometimes got a little of their own back. Making them satisfy her was another kind of workout Kat liked to put them through. But receiving sexual service—even honest, enthusiastic homage from the fist and shoulder of a delighted and respectful "boy"—wasn't what she really wanted.

When you are a big girl, you have to prove yourself over and over again. You go out to buy groceries and some asshole has to challenge your right to exist. You try to order a beer and another asshole won't let you drink it before you take his face off. Try and get back to your beer, and you have a whole house to clean. Men are the worst, but women are often not much better. You go to somebody's house for dinner, and she wants you to move the refrigerator, fix the washing machine, and insulate the attic. If you spend the night, you better mow the lawn in the morning. If there's something dangerous, exhausting, or dirty to do, you are supposed to volunteer. And the little women seem to think those jobs don't scare you, hurt you, or wear you out if you're big. If you can't handle it, that just goes to show you aren't as bad as you look.

Given how angry that made her, Kat would be damned if she could understand why she had an erotic appetite for being put to work, terrorized, tortured, and fucked until her ears bled. *But if we wait for things to make sense,* she told herself, *the closest we'll come to having sex is standing around with our thumbs up our asses.* Every now and then some big, bad, mean woman would come along who would look her up and down, like what she saw, and take it. When that happened, Kat didn't care if there were cameras rolling and every eye in the place was trained on her ass. She would have crawled over broken glass to follow a tall, authoritative woman out the door, and if some fool didn't recognize good luck and guts when she saw them, well, life's a bitch and then you die.

None of this prepared her for meeting somebody who was extremely mean, imperious enough to be the Empress of the Amazon Nation, and . . . short.

Granted, it had been a while since a superwoman had stalked up to the bar and slapped Kat with her gloves or poured beer all over her. So, Kat told herself, appetite, denial, and the blazing scream of the full moon's wide-open mouth were surely responsible for the weakness in her knees and the buzzing puddle in her leather pants when she heard a slap and identified the party who was responsible.

She was playing liar's dice with a misspent youth named Mick who put too much grease in her hair and made jokes about sucking dick in the boys' bars to keep gas in her bike at the end of the month. It was a Saturday, but it was pretty early, so it wasn't too crowded to see everybody who was there and what they were doing. Mick drank too much, and Kat told herself that penny-ante gambling with the child wasn't going to make her get sober. Right now she was swilling tequila because she was crushed out on Kat, and Kat wouldn't take her home again.

Should she, Kat wondered, give Mick another chance? Fuck, no! The last time she'd broken one of Kat's leather bondage cuffs, and in the morning she'd sneaked out and removed her own distributor cap so she'd have an excuse not to leave. She wouldn't say "sir," she couldn't take a decent beating, and she wore cheap men's cologne that gave Kat a migraine. Still, she was awful young to be after her own liver in such a serious way. What if she spun out on the way home? Mick never wore a helmet. Kat sucked in her cheeks and thought, *Sometimes I'd rather work at the SPCA.*

She was on the brink of taking the chain off her boot and dropping it between them to see if Mick could come up with an interesting, or at least a respectful, response when that slap rang through the bar, and somebody started choking and apologizing. There are a few noises that get you instantly hot if you're a perv—

the roar of a Harley that's just been stomped into life, a beer bottle breaking on the brick corner of a building, a .45 Magnum going off like a cannon, the deceptively soft thud of a slim arrow hitting the bull's-eye, metal striking sparks off of metal as a barbell hits its stand, a cold switchblade sliding open, ready to do more evil than a woman's sharp tongue, a bullwhip cracking from the stress of going faster than the speed of sound, a kicked-over table loaded with glassware, and a face getting slapped. You have about as much control over your whole body's response—goosebumps, sweaty palms, dry throat, and hard clit—to a moment like this as a piece of steel has over its own melting point.

Kat slammed her dice down on the bar and panned the crowd. She couldn't tell who had done it. Nobody looked the part. Then this four-eyed, redheaded pipsqueak in leather put one hand on her hip and drawled, "Who told you to sit down, snot-face?"

This kid was talking to somebody Kat recognized but couldn't put a name on—a brown-haired, brown-eyed, sweet-faced jock who moved slow and smiled whenever she was confused, which must have been most of the time because she always looked happy. Wasn't she on the softball team for one of the other women's bars, the largest one, the one in the barrio that played nothing but disco and salsa? She hadn't been in here before, but then, neither had that myopic dwarf dressed up in dead cow. Kat snorted. She wasn't partial to redheaded women.

"I'm a winner! I beat you!" Mick was crowing.

"Not on the best day of your life," Kat said under her breath, and shoved all the pennies on the bar into her opponent's lap. "Go play on the freeway, Mick," she said in a normal tone of voice, and used one hand to move the bad boy out of her line of sight. This needed keeping track of. There might be a fight. It'd be difficult to keep Lolly from breaking it up before the impudent squirt got her epaulets twisted off.

But there wasn't a fight. The woman who had gotten slapped was pulling out a chair. For her trouble, she got slapped again. "Don't try to buy your way out of this by making meaningless gestures," the diminutive domme sneered. "Apologize!"

When Artie—yeah, that was her name, Artie—went down on both knees, went down on *her face,* and told the floor she was sorry, Kat's jaw dropped so hard she almost hurt herself. Artie was wearing tight, very faded jeans, and Kat wished with all her heart the seam down the middle of that muscular butt would split wide open. By the time she yanked herself out of this vision, the tiny redhead was putting her hand in Artie's mouth—all of it—and Artie's eyes were closed in bliss. My God, how could a whole hand—well, if you had hands that small, they probably fit just about anywhere.

Kat blushed. So what? You probably couldn't hardly feel a paw that tiny anyway. (But a whole hand that's put inside an orifice, say, up the ass, just for example—not that Kat knew anybody who fantasized about such a thing—even if it was a small hand, would probably feel much more intense than a big hand that couldn't get all the way in. Hmm? Shit, no!)

In the back of the bar, where the green oasis of the pool table floated under a fake Tiffany lamp, one of the reigning mocha divas rocked herself out of her latest conquest's lap. Her name was Chambray, and she was wearing a knee-length dress made out of long red fringe. She now proceeded to shake those fringes out, a maneuver that created a small fan club which wistfully maintained a respectful distance because of Chambray's proximity to the Shark. You don't try to steal somebody's woman if she's recently walked out of the bar with half your paycheck in her pocket. You think about it, of course, but then you bend over the table and work on your game.

Shark had successfully defended her place at the pool table against a string of seven challengers before Chambray's scarlet dress and slim hips lured her away. "If I knew you were going to take off so fast, I wouldn't have thrown the game," she grumbled. "Not that it's any pleasure to kick her ass around the table," she added, and grimaced at Mick.

That worthy youth was using too much elbow to chalk up her cue and grinning idiotically at a plump blonde girl in a leopardskin Lycra dress who had brought her own cue, which broke down into three parts so it could be carried around in a zippered canvas bag that bore the Uzi logo. This zaftig wench was about to take exactly as many shots as there were balls to clear the table, and then teach Mick the meaning of good sportsmanship. As usual, Mick was too busy perfecting her 'do with a pocket comb to see the sucker punch coming. If you want to grow up to be a wise old stone butch, you got to beware of femmes who tilt their adorable little hats to the left.

Chambray ran her fingertips over Shark's high Cherokee cheekbones. "Gotta make my rounds," she sighed. "Make myself some money, take you out to an all-night diner where you can sate your appetite." She leaned forward until her breasts were almost entirely visible, and Shark's hands came up to greet them. Chambray had anticipated this, and caught her by the wrists. She pushed the bold, brown hands down and away. "Keep it warm for me," she said, and briefly cupped Shark's crotch, then stalked off, throwing one molten parting glance over her shoulder.

The touch and the look went through Shark like a burning spear, and she resolved to keep nothing but her own hands in her lap until that fine, hard, round ass got planted there again. My Lord, that girl knew how to shake her—well! It was enough to make your clit poke a hole in your acid-washed jeans, and it was plenty good enough to wait for, yes it was!

Chambray took her time working her way to the bar, where she ordered a Remy Martin three times from Kat before she got it—in the wrong kind of glass—with a twist! "I'm gonna report you to the tavern guild," she laughed. "We ought to take up a collection and send you to one of those bartendin' schools I see advertised on match-books. What kind of brandy snifter is this supposed to be?"

Then she saw that Kat's eyes were glazed over, and if she'd had a sleeve, she would have laughed up it. Like the little shit-disturber she was, Chambray picked up the quarters in her change and headed for the jukebox. Kat had three favorite songs, and she punched up every one of them twice. It was music to be subverted by. Let that iceberg woman melt down both of her legs and fill her boots. She was pretty with her mouth open.

Somebody else had her mouth open, too. Artie was still on the floor, and the woman standing over her was twisting her fist slowly, working it just behind Artie's lips. Spit and mucus were dribbling out of Artie's mouth, and she was wringing her hands behind her back, where she'd been told to keep them. Every now and then she mewed a little when her nose got blocked up and made it hard for her to breathe. The redhead was hissing something at her, close up and private, and whatever she said made Artie rub her thighs together like she was trying to start a fire.

And me without my Polaroid camera, Chambray thought. *What a show! Go for it, girl, punch your fist right down that throat.* An itch spread from her fingers up to her elbow, an urge to feel wet flesh close around as much of her hand and arm as she could coax down over it. *How'm I going to go back to Shark in this kind of mood?* she scolded herself. *This is not at all what I been promisin' that champion. I wanted to kick my heels at the ceiling tonight, until five minutes ago. Well, shit, I am a first-place trophy myself and I better not forget it. Everybody wants to take Chambray home. On the top or on the bottom, I always win my race. If the Shark can't deal with it I always got my cab fare tucked in my garter.*

She sailed back to the pool table, dispensing enough merchandise along the way to keep her promise to take Shark out to dinner. Much as she liked seeing Kat's wide-stretched mouth tremble and one hand struggle with the other beneath the bar, she had fish of her own to fry.

Now the redhead had Artie up over one of the silly round tables and was taking off her belt. It was a long piece of leather made weighty with chrome studs. She didn't pull Artie's pants down. There was no need. The belt came down with enough impact to render a mere layer of denim quite meaningless.

Lolly pushed by Kat to help some women who had been waving money at her for so long they'd forgotten their orders. "Caught many flies?" she hissed, and trod on Kat's toes. Her coworker gave her a dazed look. Lolly sighed irritably. "Thought you swore off Quaaludes," she said, and drew a deep breath in preparation for preaching at length from her diaphragm about the evils of artificial stimulants.

Kat lurched into action before the sermon could be delivered. She came out from behind the bar, stumbled over to where the redhead had pinned Artie down on the table with a hand on the back of her neck and was still strapping the daylights out of her. She put a hand on the sleeve of the woman's jacket and said, "Hey—"

The small woman turned and threw off her hand—no, Kat corrected herself, she repelled it. It felt a little like grabbing an electrified cattle fence. Her eyes were gray, the color of fog, the color of . . . steel? Her tongue had been sticking out, but it slid back into her mouth behind a pair of very pink lips, lips that tightened now into a thin line of disapproval. Kat almost blurted out an apology for touching her, then remembered that apologizing was what had gotten Artie into so much trouble.

"You gotta knock that off," she said instead, speaking too loudly and without taking counsel with her wiser self. "We don't allow that kinda stuff in here."

Reid looked around the crowded bar, taking her time, inviting Kat to look at the other patrons with her. Artie, confused by the absence of pain, said, "Reid?" Her voice was muffled, and the other women both ignored her, although Reid briefly squeezed the back of her neck.

Shark and Chambray were locked in a hard-core carnal embrace on the dance floor. Two of the other dancers, big women with enormous tits, had taken their shirts off. At one of the tables, a woman in a three-piece suit was getting a shotgun hit off a blimp-shaped joint from her date, who was wearing a sequined cocktail frock. At another table, three hookers in Cher wigs, halter-tops, miniskirts, fishnet hose, and high-heeled boots sat close together, kissing and fondling each other's breasts, while a fourth woman, on her knees under the table, went down on one of them. Her hands were busy underneath the other two women's skirts. Somebody in a baseball jacket was studiously cutting up coke on the jukebox. She lifted her head to protest when the two topless giantesses, who had stopped dancing and started struggling, bumped into the machine. She grabbed her mirror just in time to keep its contents from being scattered all over the floor as the giggling combatants crashed into the jukebox so hard they jarred the electrical connection loose.

Chambray shimmied over to the wall, pulling her dress down, and kicked the plug back in. The sudden return of the music was deafening. Flashing colored lights illuminated the loser's face as the victorious Sumo wrestler turned her over the glass and smacked her ass with a fist the size of a small ham. Meanwhile, the door of the ladies' room was shuddering as if somebody was taking a battering ram to it.

The lock broke, and it became clear that the battering ram was Mick, who flew through the abruptly opened door and sprawled on the floor, a sodden, sniveling mess. Her face was slathered up with lipstick, and she reeked of piss. "You can't do that to me!" she blubbered. The leopard-girl leaned on the splintered door frame, posing like a plump Jean Harlow. Then she pounced on Mick, took her under the shoulders, and threw her back into the bathroom. "If anybody has to take a leak for the next little while, you'd best use the alley," she smirked before she slammed the door shut again, and Mick began to wail in earnest.

"Oh?" Reid said, turning back to Kat. "Really? Exactly what is it that you don't allow here?"

The bartender barely heard her. Kat was lost in those eyes. The thick lenses distorted them, made them seem deep and enormous, all out of proportion to the other woman's face, like the huge, compound eyes of a bee. They were the color of the ocean in winter, an ocean that was brewing up a storm. Kat felt like somebody had arrested her mind and was patting it down. If she let this kid hold her gaze for one more second, Reid was going to know what she had eaten for breakfast and when she last changed her underwear.

"Well, uh—" *Jesus,* Kat thought, *I sound like some dumb buck private getting chewed out for calling his sergeant "sir."*

Reid shook her head and started to laugh. The laugh put goosebumps on the backs of Kat's hands and made her blush red as a baboon's behind. Nobody laughed at her. *Nobody.* Then the redhead put her little white hand in the middle of Kat's chest, right on the heart chakra, and pushed her away. "If you don't want to help me, get out of my way," she said, turned her back, and resumed taking care of business.

The push sent Kat onto the dance floor, into the arms of Chambray, who was grinding her butt back into the Shark's hungry pelvis. "You tryin' to join the space program?" the girl teased, wrapping her arms around the embarrassed bartender. "What's your hurry, sugar, don't I look good enough to spread on your sandwich?"

Kat let Chambray rock her and tug her around, and tried to regain her composure. That wasn't easy with Shark and Lolly both throwing lethal looks at her. When her breathing calmed down a bit, she made her excuses and got back to work. Things had gotten real busy—frantic, even. But damn, it was hard to make change and remember how to make a Bloody Mary when the crack of that belt kept wiping her mind clean.

She was about to announce that for the rest of the night, mixed drinks would be sold only by the pitcher when Reid dragged Artie off the table, pushed her onto all fours, and climbed atop her broad, bent back. She had wrapped her belt around Artie's head, and was using the two free ends like reins. "Crawl," she must have said, because that is what Artie did, through the entire crowd, toward the patio that Kat considered her personal fucking precinct.

Reid did have the courtesy to give Kat a mock salute as they passed. Then she gouged at Artie with her boots, and Kat saw the wicked flash of spurs. Maybe it was the belt that was stretching her lips wide, maybe it was endorphins, but Artie didn't make a sound of protest. She didn't balk or try to dislodge her rider. She just took Reid where she wanted to go, carrying her carefully—maybe even with pride.

At least out there Kat couldn't hear or see what went on. But some of the less-hung-up patrons were already clustering around the back door, which they kept open with a chair. "She's got a knife!" somebody yelped. Shark and Chambray looked at each other and laughed.

"Who let the tourist in?" Shark said contemptuously.

"You run a magnet through this place, it'll come out with more blades than a Swiss army knife," Chambray chuckled.

"One of my women don't need to carry her own protection," Shark scowled.

"Then you better stop messin' with black girls, honey. Ain't you heard we all carry razors in our shoes?"

"I hear you got a razor in your panties," Shark grinned.

"Is that what's keepin' you from getting your hand in there, you afraid I'll bite?"

Shark got both of Chambray's hands behind her back, and the lithe dancer twisted up against her as she peeled a triangle of wet red satin off her hips and rolled it down her long, muscular thighs. "Bite down, maybe," Shark said, her free hand doing teasing things under the fringed dress. "Talk back, definitely."

"You keep doing that, and I'm going to stop talking to you at all."

Shark laughed and kept on stroking her. Then Chambray said, dead serious, "Take me someplace where I can spread myself out for you," and she stopped laughing. It took her ten seconds to find their coats.

They left together and didn't come back. Kat didn't even see them leave. But she did notice that Reid and Artie didn't return. They must have gone over the fence and home—if the alley fish hadn't chewed them up into little pieces. By the time Jax closed, Kat had a headache that made her stagger. The neon beer signs behind the bar had been making her wince with pain. She had a nasty fight with Lolly about dividing their tips, which meant Lolly left without washing the rest of the glassware or telling her that the toilet had backed up. By the time she got the place locked up and was outside pulling on her gloves, Kat was snorting fire and brimstone.

There was a note on her bike, tucked between the seat and the gas tank. It was a phone number, written in large, shaky letters. She harrumphed, then folded it carefully and tucked it into her breast pocket. It wasn't until she got home and retrieved it for another look that she realized it had been written with a finger . . . or with a knife, in blood. Ha ha. Some joke.

Kat woke up in the middle of the night with a pounding headache, a throbbing bladder, and a telephone in one hand. In her other hand was the bloody number. What the fuck—what time was it? She couldn't call somebody now! Kat slammed down the receiver. She needed some aspirin and a catheter with a long tube. She tucked the note carefully under one of the phone's rubber feet, then headed for the bathroom, shuffling so she wouldn't accidentally step on one of Jezebel's kittens.

The next morning, she had a sore throat, a stuffy head, and felt as bad as the other guy usually looked. She picked up Jezebel, who had come up onto the bed to avoid the kittens she was weaning and demanded, "What did you do, beat me up all night long?"

The tortoiseshell cat made an indignant noise that Kat interpreted as meaning, "I hope the fact that you are ill does not mean you intend to neglect my very important feeding schedule."

"I'm not sick!" Kat roared, and carefully put the mama cat down. It took forever to get Jezebel fed (the babies kept trying to help) and longer to get coffee on. Once she'd dumped some food outside for the differently abled marmalade tomcat who lived under the back porch, the three black-and-white cats from the gas station, around breakfast, she staggered back inside and propped herself up against the counter to watch Mr. Coffee take a tinkle.

When the coffee was finally ready and Kat sat down with a cup of it, she realized it looked and smelled terrible. What she really wanted was a nice cup of English breakfast tea with milk in it. *Bleeech.* That did it. If she really wanted to drink a cup of tea, she was sick, and she didn't just have a cold, she had the flu.

She called Lolly and gave her the good news. "Okay," her buddy said curtly. "Means more work for me. Doesn't matter. Get more than my share of the tips anyway."

"Aw Lolly, don't snarl. My head hurts. I know I was a horse's butt last night. I must have been coming down with this bug."

Then Lolly turned into the Lesbian Crisis Center and wanted to come over and make her some soup. "I hate soup," Kat snarled. "That kind of slop is for puppies and old people. Besides, you can't cook. That's why you keep falling in love. If it wasn't for those worthless wenches you keep dragin' home, you'd never get fed."

That made Lolly laugh. Kat's head was feeling worse and worse. She had to lie down. How was she going to get off the phone and keep Lolly in a good mood so she would definitely remember to show up at Jax on time, do two people's work, and not get both of them fired? "Hey honey," she shouted into the phone, hoping the old, reliable gag would work, "why d'they call you Lollypop?"

"Because I got me a big sucker," Lolly shouted back, and laughed like a hyena.

Kat hung up. *Glad I'm not a Catholic,* she thought, *or I'd go to church and say a novena to St. Jude. That woman's a hopeless cause if I ever met one.*

She had some tea and dry toast and a handful of aspirin (fuck the ulcer; fuck the bills that are going to come in today's mail; fuck your mother if she gets in my way), and went back to bed. Jezebel was already there, taking a nap on her pillow. She eased into the other side of the bed, but the orange-and-black beauty woke up anyway and padded over to knead bread on her. Her claws were nice and healthy, and stuck decent-sized holes in Kat's chest through her pajamas. Kat lifted her up, pulled a blanket between them to buffer her tits from Jezebel's sharp toes, and fell asleep petting her, tracing the vibrations her purr made across her silky flank.

Kat jolted into wakefulness hours later, covered with sweat. The blinds were dark. It must be late afternoon, almost evening. Her heart was pounding. She had been having horrible dreams about being smothered by bears. Her mouth has been—was!—full of fur. She pried Jezebel off her neck, said, "Be grateful my gloves don't need relining," and levered herself up to go answer the door, which was banging and ringing and just generally having a party all to itself. Most annoying for and inanimate object to get busy like that.

On the stoop was Chambray, still wearing her red-fringed finery from the night before. Kat's head was thick with sleep, and she assumed that the usual thing had brought this dark and lovely woman to her door. "You picked one hell of a time to get amorous, darlin'. I'm sick," she said. The she realized that Chambray had a black eye. Oh-oh. Better duck and cover.

"I didn't come here to crawl into bed with you," Chambray said contemptuously, kicking the door open. The veneer panels obeyed her pointy-toed shoe like a john from Walnut Creek bring urged across the floor. "This place is a mess," she added, strolling over dirty laundry like a queen walking to her throne. "You live in a hovel, big girl, and you gonna be raisin' livestock soon, the kind you can't see with the naked eye."

Sick as she was, Kat got a grip and stopped Chambray's pacing with a hand on her shoulder. Moving carefully and slowly, for both their sakes, she turned the irate girl around and gently titled her head to the light. "Who hit you?" she said softly. "Do I need to take some serious drugs and strap on my six-shooter, or can they wait a coupla days to get skinned alive?"

Chambray just glared at her, her full lips locked together. So it wasn't a client. It was somebody they both knew. Probably Shark, that asshole. Kat sighed. She offered her arm, and Chambray tentatively rested the tips of her fingers in the crook of Kat's elbow. "Come sit on the bed and have a cigar," Kat said, offering the one thing she knew Chambray could not refuse.

Her visitor consented to sit by Jezebel, who was visibly miffed at having competition for her lackey's attention. When Kat presented Chambray with a thin, brown cigar, the cat uttered an obscenity and jumped to the floor. Kat knew the smoke would make her head spin, but she went to sit on the other side of the bed anyway and used a turkey wing to fan it away from her face.

"You ought to smudge this place more often," Chambray said, finally breaking the silence. "Oya would smile on you if you paid her more attention."

"All this African magic is such shit," Kat scoffed. "You're just a nicotine fiend like the rest of us mere mortals, Chambray. And you're goddamned lucky you got a note from your orisha says you can smoke in my house."

Chambray smiled. "Your house is about as chem-free as Spam. The only twelve steps you are ever gonna get will be the tap dance I do on your head. Tobacco is a purifying agent. It is also a powerful poison. And a stimulant. Like most good things it can be addicting. But you got to watch yourself, Kat, my friend, because not letting yourself have the thing you want can be as habit-forming as getting too much."

Kat didn't have anything to say to that. She just kept fanning nice and slow, like the ladies who sat in the front row of the church. In July and August, there was no way Kat could keep awake in church, no matter how often her grandma pinched her, no matter how loud the choir sang. The windows would be wide open and you could hear the bees buzzing in the lilacs outside, and that soft droning just . . . made you . . . zzzzzzzz.

When she woke up, Chambray had undressed herself, and they were naked in bed together. The smooth feel of female skin against her own automatically stirred Kat to action. She rolled over just enough to get her nose into Chambray's armpit. She smelled like tobacco, Thai spices, and a clean cunt that's starting to get sexy. Kat licked all around that armpit, despite the squirming girl who had come awake around it, and descended to her breasts, snuffling and kissing, using her tongue like a big, wet sponge, while Chambray shrieked and flailed around like a mad parrot hanging upside-down from its perch. Kat kept sliding down, leaving a snail trail across Chambray's flat, brown belly, making tuba-noises by blowing into her muscular abdomen. The tip of her tongue barely grazed Chambray's clit as it divided her sex. But she didn't even slow down. By the time she reached Chambray's feet and put those wriggling toes in her mouth, sharp nails were raking down her ribs and the backs of her legs, wherever Chambray could reach. Kat turned around and sat beside her, reached between her legs.

"Don't do that," Chambray moaned. She turned her face away a little. Kat wondered if she did that to make the black eye less noticeable, and had to fight off a wave of anger and nausea to continue.

"Why not, honey?"

"Damn all, are you as stupid as you are big? You saw who I went home with last night. What do you think we did, bake cookies? Woman has a right arm like a jackhammer."

Kat tut-tutted and slid one finger in. "Tell me if this hurts. Promise I won't move." Chambray did not tell her to stop. So she slid in one more finger. "This isn't much of a stretch for you," she said. "Is it? Is it?"

"Nooo. Oh. No."

"So if I don't move around, if I don't push hard, if I don't fuck you like a jackhammer, you should feel no pain. Isn't that right?"

"Oh. Oh. Oh."

Kat went up on her knees so she had more leverage. "Just want you to know I'm there, that's all. Can you tell I'm there?"

"Yesyes, yesyes."

"Wanna tell me something else? Wanna tell me if this is enough?"

"Don't—don't—don't—"

"Don't what? Don't put this other finger in here, this way? Don't push up a little bit to make sure it fits? Don't wiggle the tips of my—"

"Don't tease me you bitch, you bitch, don't make me scream it in your face, spell it out for you, be my horse, be my horse, I ride you, I ride you—on, oh—on—on—on you!"

Kat fell forward, lying across Chambray's belly, and gritted her teeth as she moved slowly but with lots of pressure, trying to give the girl what she needed without making her sorry later. It was difficult to stay in control with that silky skin rubbing against her feverish, too-sensitive body. Waves of the erotic perfume of a woman in heat kept coming up in her face, inciting her to riot in this flesh. But the tissues under the pads of Kat's fingers were swollen and abraded. No amount of lubrication could make the surface entirely smooth. Chambray threw her hips harder and harder, cussed at her, and clawed her shoulders. Kat got a bit dizzy. Maybe this wasn't going to work. Maybe she had started something she wasn't going to be able to finish. Dammit, she didn't want to frustrate—

Then Chambray put her hand on Kat's rump and eased two fingers between her labia. "Turn just a little, big girl," she said, and as Kat adjusted her position, she slid in.

The muscles under Kat's fingers smoothed out, the lubrication became thicker, Chambray's movements became more rhythmic and less desperate. So Kat endured the distraction of penetration, allowed it, and was just beginning to enjoy it when the girl underneath her came. So she pulled away, off the invading hand, assuming it was time to cradle the other woman and stroke the sweat from her body.

But Chambray did not assume they were through. She did not want to let go of Kat and tried to come up off the bed after her. Without thinking, Kat pinned her down. Quick as a snake, Chambray turned her head and bit Kat's forearm hard enough to bruise the bone. The big woman hollered and let her go. "What the fuck?" she cried, staring at her injured arm.

"What I give you I give freely, but don't you ever try to ravish me," Chambray hissed. "I am my own woman. Not your slave."

"I could tell you the same thing!"

"Didn't have to tie you down for it, did I?" Chambray snapped, getting out of bed. "What you think your pussy's for, girl, preaching gospel? Got your life savings up your snatch? Is it my fault you're too stupid to hold still and get fucked long enough to make you come?"

"Don't talk to me that way, Chambray."

"Don't talk to you that way? What do you know about being bad-mouthed? Nobody says nothin' to you but what you want to hear. It's all, would you please Kat an' by your leave Kat an' you're so funny, strong, an' sexy, Kat. Makes me want to puke sometimes to watch them fawn over your fat ass while you make a fool of yourself. Seems to me that's about half of your biggest problem, girl, all those drunk bitches you let follow you around with their noses up your crack."

Chambray bolted out of bed, and Kat followed her into the kitchen. She was smarting from Chambray's tart comments, but she was also worried that Chambray was going to do something a lot more serious than running her mean little mouth. The black woman was throwing cupboard doors open and slamming them shut. "Quit makin' all this racket," Kat said. "You're scaring my cat. Ssh, baby, nobody's mad at you, princess. The booze is over there, you rampaging harridan. Pour us both a shot."

They sat and drank together, silently, until Kat finally said, "What are you doing over here anyway? If Shark just turned you inside out you didn't need to scratch my back. Did you guys have a fight?"

Chambray just shook her head and reached for the bottle. Kat took it out of her reach. "No, now. I know that look. Don't bullshit me. Something upset you besides me playing hard to get. We been friends too long to let this go."

Chambray started to cry. It was an ugly sound that put Kat's teeth on edge. For decency, she went over to the sink and turned her back. She ran some water she didn't want into a glass, touched it to her lips, and poured it out without drinking any. By the time she sat down again, Chambray had put herself back together.

"Shark says," Chambray began, getting her voice under control, "the Shark says I should quit letting white girls like you treat me like a piece of meat."

Kat almost hit the table. But for once in her life, she had the sense to keep her temper. This was delicate stuff. The two of them had never talked about color. They pretended that being friends had somehow settled all that. And they didn't talk about sex, either. When one of them got horny, she would drop by the other's place and see what happened. They didn't date. They would never be lovers.

"Shark wants to be your one and only?" she said, trying to keep it light. It wasn't. She would miss Chambray badly. But there was a lesbian code that said it was so hard to find a mate that you did not come between a friend and her lover, even if your friend sometimes slept with you. Lovers, even potential lovers, had to come first—even though the friendship would usually outlast the romance. And (at least in the beginning) you don't tell your friend anything bad about her lover, even if you know their story can't have a happy ending.

"Maybe. She wants to tell me what to do. She wants me to want her. She wants to be my only choice. An' if I do all that, who is to say if she will love me or laugh at me? The woman wants to be a hero, an outlaw, some kinda romantic movie-star pimp and pool-hall champion. She is a certified public accountant, Kat. She lives with her mama, who has arthritis so bad she hasn't been able to work for years. If I can get out of her bed as easy as I get in, don't it just remind her she is nobody special, never going to shake things up, never going to be famous for what she does best? It's what they do to us. How we do each other. I hate it, and I hate us."

"Chambray," Kat said, and cleared her throat, "nobody has the right to make you feel bad about what we do together. I don't treat you like a piece of meat. I am very damn fond of you."

"But if I was a white girl, would you make me take my hands off your body?"

Kat did hit the table then. She also shouted. Chambray tried to leave the house, and Kat got between her and the door. "Don't go!" she cried. "Please." She slid down to the floor and put her arms around Chambray's knees. "This is not about color, it's about power. It's about who I let close to me. I haven't let anybody make me come for so long that I just . . . forgot about it somehow. I am begging your pardon for pushing you away tonight. Don't go. Or you'll never come back, it will never be the same, and I can't stand it. To have you even wonder—Chambray, it hurts me like a knife in my heart. What can I do, what do you want me to do—crawl into the bedroom?"

"For starters, yes."

Kat froze. She was being called on her grand gesture, and she just didn't have the guts to walk it like she talked it.

"Don't tell me you don't want to," Chambray said vindictively. "I saw the drool runnin' down your face when Reid slapped shit out of Artie and rode her out of the bar. Everybody in Jax could smell what was runnin' down your legs. Why do you think this love stuff is always a one-way street? All the girls you've dragged out of Jax by their nipples know your story, Kat. They know what you really want. Me an' Lady Sage an' everybody else, we laugh at you and take what we want from you because you are too gutless to get down on your knees. But someday somebody is gonna get you good for all of us, Kat. We're all waiting and wondering when it's gonna happen. As far as I'm concerned, it can't be a moment too soon. You can play pony for the whole damn world then and I'll just laugh my sweet ass off."

Kat was pinned to the floor by her fury. She could not speak. She couldn't even raise her fists. Chambray's words would pass right through them. All she could do was wait it out. The last time she'd been in an earthquake was a lot more pleasant.

"Well, I guess I know where I belong now," Chambray said, turning on her heel. "I got somebody who's waiting for me who isn't ashamed to spread her ass or tell me she can't come unless I pull her hair real hard." She paused for one last salvo. "And how dare you think it was the Shark who gave me this black eye, you racist motherfucker? I walked into a door." The slam that accompanied her exit was so loud that Jezebel and her kittens sank to the floor with their ears back as if a gale was passing overhead.

Kat finally let her breath out and took in some oxygen. Now her soul felt as battered as her body. But, strangely enough, she didn't feel feverish anymore. Her head was completely clear. Without letting herself think about it or hesitate, she went over to her bedside table, turned Reid's bloody calling card rightside up, and dialed the number that had been written there in somebody else's pain.

Reid sat in front of the TV with a plate of Chinese takeout and a Coke. She handled the chopsticks carefully. The fingertips on both of her hands were raw from the overly enthusiastic manicure she had given herself for Artie. She had a bad headache from spending the day outside in the sun, drinking Khaliber that she'd lugged to the field herself because concession stands never sold nonalcoholic beer, and watching Artie pitch a no-hitter. She hated fake beer and Softball about equally, but knew what you had to do after a scene to keep things friendly with a butch bottom. You had to acknowledge who they were in the real world, and make them feel successful and important, or you might make yourself an enemy who had some dangerous stories to tell about your most intimate habits.

After the game, Artie had been surrounded by her jubilant, dusty teammates, Las Estrellas. Artie asked her if she wanted to go celebrate with a few "brewskies," and Reid shook her head. "I've got three tapes I have to transcribe for a client by Monday," she lied. "Great game, though."

One of the other players butted in, a copper-colored woman with a mop of long, curly hair. "Who's your tiny friend, Artie? Hey, honey, what sport do you play—midget wrestling?" Her Spanish accent made Reid's cunt tingle even as the words made her hackles rise. She liked long-haired butches and (in a slightly different way) boys who wore earrings. But she recognized that tone, and she didn't like girls who assumed they could use it on her without getting slapped.

Nevertheless, this was Artie's turf and Artie's day to be the hero. So Reid tried to keep her sense of humor. "Yeah, you gotta watch out for us little people, we might walk off with your kneecaps."

But the pumped-up jock didn't want to let it go. "I think maybe you're a cheerleader. Where's your pom-poms? Want me to take you back in the locker room and help you look under the benches?"

Reid got a little pale. She was always too full of herself after a scene. It was hard to let go of a vision of yourself as lord of the universe, completely powerful, immediately obeyed, feared utterly. The world was collapsing into a tunnel, and this woman's broad, nasty face was at the other end of it. "Those the same benches the coach gets your ass up on?" she hissed. "Maybe that's where we oughta go looking for pom-poms."

"Uh, Reid—," Artie sputtered. "Barbara—hey, guys—"

"Listen, Artie, I don't know what you see in this pipsqueak, but if she doesn't want to help you celebrate, we can just carry her along for you. Our first-string pitcher oughta have whatever she wants on the day she shuts out the Shamrocks. Bet she'll fit in the trunk of my car." Barbara took one step toward Reid, and Artie grabbed her.

"Quit being an asshole," Artie said. Baseball diamond dust ran in streaks down her chalky face. "C'mon, let's go. Everybody's gonna leave us. Reid, I'll call you, okay?"

Reid sighed, took her hand out of her jacket pocket (leaving the knife behind), and waved goodbye. "Sure you will," she said softly. Goddamn novices, she could never tell them no when they came on so hard and seemed so sure about what they wanted. But they inevitably withdrew after the first scene, getting a little freaked out about the fact that they really could do all those things they'd been jerking off to for so long. Not to mention the shock of encountering somebody who had cooked up a few ideas of her own.

The TV picture went bad for a second. The gay boys upstairs must be running their dishwasher. Reid sighed and rubbed at the bunched-up muscles in her neck and shoulders. This apartment building was okay. It was nice to have faggots for neighbors. They didn't complain about all the thumping and humping that went on in her bedroom. But she missed the house in the suburbs with its carefully kept yard, and she missed Nikki, the woman who owned it. It was easy to forget how much she had hated the long drive to get into the city for leather events and the claustrophobia of living with a trust-fund baby who didn't understand why life couldn't be just one long scene.

Reid sighed again. Annoyed with the old-lady sound of it, she bit her tongue. The room over the garage that was supposed to be her office had never gotten remodeled. Nikki couldn't understand why Reid couldn't write the great American novel on her kitchen table. Her word-processing business fell apart because she kept missing deadlines. When Reid's bike finally quit running because it needed major repairs, her lover refused to spend what had suddenly become "her own money" to fix it. Reid knew what that triumphant smile across the class barrier meant. It meant, "I've got you. I've got control and revenge and I own your ass." It took Reid a week to sell the bike for parts, take the bus into the city and find her own apartment (the deposit came from an advance on her last viable credit card), and call an old friend who had a truck and needed to be strung up and beaten so badly she would just haul Reid's stuff away without gloating about how stupid Reid had been to think true love could ever work out with a chick from the suburbs.

But is all this fucking around any better? Reid asked herself. *Do they respect me the next morning?* Unfortunately, she had no idea what the two triumphant athletes had said to each other on their way to the parking lot. If she could have overheard that conversation, it would have made her feel a lot better than musing over love gone wrong.

First, Artie had put Barbara in a half nelson and faked breaking her neck. "Quit horsing around," she had said grimly, "or I'll have to hurt you."

"You're gonna hurt me? Promises, promises."

"I better, or Reid will, and then you'll be really sorry."

"You have got to be kidding."

"I am not kidding. I finally found out what this S&M shit is all about."

"Stop, you've only been whining about getting into leather for the last six months. And now you're holding out on me. I want to hear all about this. What did she do to you?"

"Not until you learn a little respect, Barbara. That's R-E-S-P-E-C-T. No, dammit, don't start singing the fucking song, I *know* the fucking song. Christ, somebody better teach you some manners before you hurt your silly-ass self."

Artie and Barbara didn't make it to the victory party, but they did drink a champagne toast to Reid sometime in the wee hours of the next morning. It's amazing how much fun you can have with ice cubes, the terrycloth tie off your bathrobe, and a Ping-Pong paddle.

Ignorant of all these ripples, Reid ate the last mouthful of shrimp fried rice, turned off the TV, and went into her bedroom. Unlike most S/M dykes she knew, she kept all her equipment out and instantly available. She couldn't afford a big enough apartment to turn one whole room into a dungeon, but her bedroom was the next best thing. She started to clean up, piling soiled trick towels into the laundry basket, carrying dildos into the bathroom and dropping them into the sink, scrubbing them with hot water and Betadine, going back to the bedroom to toss used condoms and rubber gloves into the garbage, hanging her whips back on the wall. A couple of things (a blade, a cane) needed to be wiped down with alcohol. Her chaps needed to be sponged off and oiled.

The familiar work of putting her tools in order calmed her down, and took the edge off her post-scene depression. Determined to preserve this improved mood, Reid resolutely did not look at the three chain collars that hung together on one hook. Each of them had once been worn by women she'd had contracts with. One of those contracts had been broken by cancer, one by an overdose, and one by dishonorable behavior on the part of Reid's property. She did not use these collars on anyone else. They were in permanent retirement. Reid knew she should probably just pitch them out, but she kept them to force herself to remember, to learn from the things that made her grieve.

For a novice, Artie had not been bad. Actually, for a seasoned player, Artie had not been bad. For the first time since breakfast, Reid smiled. The look on that nosy bartender's face when they rode by playing horsie was just too much. You could live on looks like that. *There* was a woman who never had to ask anybody for anything. Probably just took out a cigarette and didn't even wait for somebody to light it, just knew it would be burning by the time she took a puff. That was a weird little scene she had pulled, getting in their faces about bringing down the tone of Jax. Jax, of all places. Why, that hellhole would make your average longshoreman start cryin' for his mama. After getting all that static, she wasn't sure why she'd left her phone number behind. Hmm. Well, there had been too much blood to let it all go to waste (Artie bled real pretty), and she liked upsetting people. Liked it almost as much as she had liked looking for a hole in Artie's body that her whole hand would not sink into, with enough patience and Probe. Mmm-mmm.

She was sorting all her tit clamps out (pairs on chains hung on the pegboard, little plastic ones in bright primary colors went in the Tinkertoy can, rubber-covered wire ones went in the wooden Dutch Cleanser box, alligator clamps got dropped in the see-through plastic box from Radio Shack with all the handy little compartments) when the phone rang. She answered it without letting the machine pick it up—it was so late, it had to be either a wrong number or somebody she knew. "Sexual Compulsives Anonymous," she chirped.

There was dead air on the other end of the phone. "Put out or fuck off," Reid said politely.

More dead air. Then—"Will you give a person a chance to say hello?" someone said. Someone querulous. Reid knew she ought to recognize that voice. The tone was so familiar. Wait a second—"We don't allow that kinda stuff in here." Bingo.

"That was your chance," Reid said, and went to hang up the phone. A loud squawk erupted from the receiver, and she brought it back to her ear. "Is someone interfering with you, Miss?" she asked solicitously, in her best *Masterpiece Theatre* British accent. "Shall I call in the Yard?"

"Will you shut the fuck up for just a second?" Kat said. "What is wrong with you?"

"You're extremely rude, so I'll try to be brief. Number one, no, and number two, I don't think I want to talk to you long enough to explain that."

Kat did a very quick mental shuffle. She wasn't used to women who played with language this way. If you wanted people to think you were bad, you used short words and pronounced them emphatically. But Reid's whimsy was more intimidating than a truck driver's curse. *I don't think I'm smart enough to keep up with her,* Kat thought. She had to force herself to respond. "That's true. I was rude. Uh. There's no reason why you should explain anything to me. Uh. Uh. Is there any way we could start this whole thing over?"

"It does run counter to policy. Nothing personal, you understand. But I don't give second chances, and right now you're looking at your third."

Kat recognized that ploy. She knew how to be charming when a girl tried to give her a scolding. She ducked her head, even though Reid wasn't there to see how endearing it looked, and whispered, "I'm in big trouble, huh?" She thought she had managed to put just a tiny quiver in her voice.

"Afraid so."

"But I don't even *know* you." *That was good,* Kat thought, letting her voice crack at the end of the sentence.

"Bullshit," Reid said firmly, and was surprised to discover how much she meant it. "You know every thing you need to know about me. The only question is, what are you going to do about it?"

Now Kat was pissed off again. This woman must eat bricks for breakfast and shit out mortar. How could anybody be so impervious to her tact and diplomacy? "Confrontative little fucker, aren't you?" she snapped.

"You're the one who dropped the dime, big girl."

A very satisfactory kind of silence followed that comment. It lay at Reid's feet, glaring and sweating. Reid looked at herself in the mirror above her bureau. She was smiling.

A muffled cry of pain made Reid crinkle her eyebrows. She had no way of knowing that Kat was on the brink of tears. "What is this—phone sex?" she asked, sounding like a schoolteacher accepting a wormy apple.

"I need to see you," Kat choked.

"Ah. Yes. I am sure you do."

"What do I have to do, take a number and wait in line?"

Reid hissed. It was a really nasty noise. Emitting it made her feel like a rabid mongoose.

Kat finally decided to shape up. "No!" she panted. "Don't hang up! I'm sorry!"

"Do we know our *p* word?"

"Please. Please. Please."

"Yes, all right, don't get maudlin. You understand that if I agree to see you, it's only because we have unfinished business. You were a churl, and I don't overlook slights of that magnitude. If you agree to come here, you must understand that I will brook no challenges to my authority. And if you don't show up, I may very well come and fetch you. You owe me, bitch, so don't come over here planning to be coy or jerk me around. Knock the chip off your shoulder and come prepared to pay up like a decent chap. Wear old clothes, and bring a spare set."

"Okay. Just say when."

"The *p* word?"

"Please."

"The *s* word?"

"Sir."

"Shall we go for a complete sentence?"

"Sir, please tell me when I can make myself available, sir."

"I am pleased to note that your descent into loutish incivility is far from complete. Tomorrow. Nine sharp. Memorize this address."

"Thank you, sir," Kat said, writing it in the dust on her bedside table.

Reid did not reply; she just hung up.

Kat put the phone down and looked reproachfully over her shoulder at Jezebel, who stopped bathing one of her babies long enough to give Kat a level emerald stare of disapproval. "Don't be maudlin," she parroted. "You were a churl. I don't overlook slights of that magnitude. I will brook no challenges to my authority. The *p* word. Loutish incivility. Shit. She talks as crazy as a bag lady in a tinfoil bonnet. I'm goin' off to see a nut case." She locked her front door and went back to bed.

The next day, Kat was surprised to find that she seemed to have recovered completely from the flu. *Fighting with Chambray must have burned the virus right out of my system,* she thought as she rang Reid's doorbell. She had only the vaguest memory of what she'd done that day, but she was on time, wearing her oldest, greasiest T-shirt and a ripped-up pair of jeans, and carrying a gym bag with a change of clothes in it, so at least part of her brain must have been functioning.

She was buzzed into the building, climbed two flights of stairs, and rang again at the apartment door, where she was buzzed into a dark hallway. The lights suddenly went on. Reid was at the other end of the hall, wearing a pair of chaps and a plain motorcycle jacket. Under the chaps she wore a leather jock that bulged a little from the cock she was wearing. She was utterly unselfconscious about packing. Kat liked the set of her hips, the way she carried herself, her shoulders, her tool. You could call it having guts, you could call it having gonads, but what it really was, the girl had balls. Taking responsibility for your desire, wearing it where other people could see it, being defiant about your deviance—it was the kind of butch signal, like a shaved head, that Kat recognized and loved, that made her knees get weak. You had to flaunt it. You couldn't change it. You didn't really want to. Because even if you hardly ever get what you want, knowing what it would look like and trying to get it was so much less crazy than believing the lie that you wanted what everybody else wanted, that there was nothing else, no choice. *Fuck that,* Kat thought. *Oh, Reid. You little stud. Fuck me.*

They were the same leathers she had worn to Jax. Kat silently approved of that too. Leathers should be worn frequently, broken in, given a chance to absorb your sex and sweat, get some worn-in spots, bags and creases. She hated the twits who seemed to have a different outfit every weekend. Their stuff always looked brand-new. She was not into patent leather.

"Kneel," Reid said. She had suddenly gotten very close. The top of her head came up to Kat's breastbone. Then a searing pain hit Kat in the arm, and she went down. That buzzing noise was familiar. Yep, the woman was carrying a dog trainer, a silver, battery-powered wand that was sold in leather shops as a "cattle prod." Kat knew that a real cattle prod would have knocked her through the door. Little masochistic sprouts growing up in the country find these things out. On bad days, Kat used to go to the far side of the pasture, where nobody could see her, and try to climb the electrical fence. The memory made Kat smile, but she didn't think Reid would appreciate that, so she wiped the grin from her face.

"First lesson," Reid said. "Unconditional and prompt obedience. If you stop to think, you're taking too long. If you didn't hear me, it's your fault. So pay attention. You're about to get real busy."

A switchblade clicked open under Kat's left ear. "Chuck the jacket," Reid said. She was putting the dog trainer back on her belt. She got it into the leather carrying loop without looking. Before Kat's jacket hit the floor, Reid had grabbed the front of Kat's T-shirt and punctured it with the knife. Her booted foot kicked the kneeling woman's denim-clad knees apart. She took her time destroying the T-shirt, making sure Kat got a taste of the blade's fine edge while being careful not to cut her.

"I have a notion," Kat said, screwing her head around to follow the knife, "that we're supposed to be having a conversation right about now. Something about limits and safe words."

"Really. Well, if there's anything you think I should know, by all means tell me now, while you can still talk."

Kat was nonplussed by this flat invitation to spill her guts. She wanted to be prompted, drawn out, fussed over a little. But all she could think to say was, "I need this," and Reid rewarded her honesty by dragging the edge of the knife along her ribs. Kat's air came out all at once, and she thrust her torso into the thin line of pain.

"God, I'm glad I'm not the only one," Reid grinned. Rags that had been a T-shirt were bunched in her fist. Kat was naked to the waist. Reid whistled and used the point of the knife to trace the patterns on Kat's skin above her breasts, stepped close enough to look at her back, and scraped the switchblade over the skin between her shoulder blades. "Scars upon scars upon scars. Fine silver lines and nice fat white ones. You're just a whore for a sharp edge, aren't you, darlin'? Up."

Kat was getting the hang of her style, and was on her way to her feet. Reid's boot toe caught her between the legs anyway, just a little incentive to be quick about straightening her knees. For a moment

Kat saw red, and Reid snapped, "Put your hands behind your back." Kat threw her hands back hard and fast so she wouldn't kill the little motherfucker. At the base of her spine, she clenched her fists, reciting silently, *Whodoesshethinksheis, whodoesshethinksheis, whodoesshethinksheis,* while the knife chewed through her jeans. The thick denim came off in chunks. She was so used to Reid cutting nothing but cloth that the sting of a sweeping cut across the front of both legs made her gasp and tip forward. Reid was behind her and quick to take advantage of this minor loss of balance. She kicked one of Kat's heels forward, and kept her moving through the kitchen, into the bedroom.

The room was lit with candles and some track lights with red bulbs turned down low. It was hard to see details, but every wall seemed to be covered with hooks or shelves or pegboards full of equipment. There was only one picture, a life-size photograph of a Japanese woman with a full-body tattoo. She was fighting with sais, short-handled steel tridents. She had been wounded. Blood dripped from one of her arms to the straw mat on the floor. Only the shadow of her opponent's kimono and naginata, the spear-shaft tipped with a crescent blade, fell within the picture's frame.

Kat was so enthralled with this image that she barely noticed when Reid tumbled her to the floor and pulled off her boots and socks. It felt kind of good to be thrown around this way. When you're big, people don't try to propel you in a direction they've selected. Because she liked it, she didn't mind helping. Things sure were happening fast. Then cold metal went around one of her ankles, and Reid was sitting on her stomach, screwing in the key. The bitch didn't bother to take any of her own weight on her own two legs, just sat on Kat like she was a beanbag chair. *Well, okay,* Kat thought, *fuck you, I can take your weight. I could carry two of you around under my arms. It'll take more than this to crush me.* She would have liked to see what the little twerp was doing to her feet, though.

Reid came off her and turned around. Kat had time to see that there were steel circles around both of her ankles. Then Reid sat on her again and grabbed one of her wrists. Kat pulled back. Reid applied enough force to keep her hand in midair. They hung that way in space, eye to eye.

"I'm not a pushover," Kat said finally.

"Really?" Reid said dryly. "You're not a novice, either. So what is your excuse?"

"Fuck you," Kat said, and surrendered her hand.

"That's going to cost you," Reid promised, and put the cuffs on. These were hinged steel bracelets about an inch wide with a hasp that could be locked. She breathed a little easier now that Kat was almost in four-point bondage. Part of the thrill of playing with big girls was the risk that they'd lose their minds and turn on you. Might as well try to calm down a rampaging elephant. Now she felt secure enough to needle Kat a little. "Surprised they fit?" she asked, putting a little sneer into the question.

Kat just glared at her, resenting the way her thoughts had been divined.

"Well, don't be. You aren't the first big girl who found out how far it is to fall to my feet. And you won't be the last one either. Did it ever occur to you that this is probably never gonna happen again? So you'd better show me your best side, badass. I don't particularly care that we don't like each other much, but it seems a damn shame to waste the whole night. I can call you a buncha nasty names, slap you around some, maybe slap you around a lot, fuck you senseless, and then call you a cab. Or I can just call you a cab. You decide. Now."

Kat didn't say anything.

"Silence will not be accepted as evidence of consent. Later, maybe, but not now. You ask me nice or do without. Now!"

"You're a real ball-buster," Kat grimaced.

Reid laughed. "Yeah, I do that, too. Don't try to change the subject."

"You think I would have let you put these on me if I didn't want you to?"

"Okay, that's fair. You in for the duration?"

"Do your worst," Kat said through clenched teeth.

"Oh, darlin', darlin', you do not know what a temptation you are to me," Reid said, and kicked her to her feet, kicked her over to the bed, and shoved her onto her back. The bed had four eight-foot-tall posters and was braced with chains and turnbuckles. There were screw eyes all over the wood frame. A person could get into a lot of trouble here and not be able to do much about it. Kat shivered. If she'd had some rope, she would have been tying herself down.

"See, this isn't about who's tall, is it, darlin'?" Reid said. "It's about who needs it worse. How long you been doing without anyway?" She reached for some chains, started locking them to fetters and manacles.

"Damn you, don't you do me any favors!"

"Oh, I don't feel sorry for you. Not at all." Reid took up some of the slack in one of the chains. Kat felt the pull in her armpit, and realized she was going to be stretched tight as a drum skin across the surface of this bed. "Think I've never been lost in the desert? If we're still speaking to one another in the morning, we can tell each other all those stories, I'm just chewin' on your ass. If I didn't want you, big girl, d'you think I would have interrupted one of the hottest scenes in recent memory to write down my goddamn phone number for y'all?"

"You're lucky I found it."

"I'm lucky I'm alive. You feel lucky yet? No?" Reid chuckled. "Move around for me."

"How?"

Reid pulled both of her nipples straight up and twisted them. Kat found that she could indeed move. Reid took up some more slack in one of the leg-chains. Now there was a steady pull in Kat's groin muscles and down both sides of her chest. The weight came off her lungs, and Reid left her. She actually missed the little creep. Kat thought that was interesting. And she was vaguely worried about what Reid might find to implement her cruelty, out there in this strange room. *I'm alone and helpless with someone I barely know,* Kat thought. Why did she feel so calm and happy?

Reid was suddenly aware of being tired. The hours she'd spent with Artie had taken a toll, and so had all the stage fright she'd felt getting ready for Kat's arrival and wondering if she'd have the guts to keep her appointment. It was important not to get distracted by all the equipment and forget the person it was supposed to be used on. Reid didn't want this to be a perfunctory performance. Kat deserved a more personal effort. So Reid took several deep, slow breaths and hoped the energy she needed would keep on flowing.

"Anybody know you're here tonight?" she asked Kat.

Shit, Kat thought, *you have no right to keep pulling things out of my head.* "Yeah," she said, a little too loudly.

"Paranoid, weren't we?"

"Careful."

"Paranoids always are. Keeps 'em so busy they don't notice when you sneak up behind 'em."

What Reid came back with didn't make Kat feel any less paranoid, that was for sure. It was a black rubber gas mask. It had big bug-eyes of clear plastic, and the curved snout had the look of a pig.

"In for the duration, you said," Reid reminded her. Damning her own weird sense of honor, Kat didn't let herself say a word as Reid tucked her chin into the mask, stretched out the elastic straps at the back, and pulled it over her head. But she couldn't keep herself from breaking out into a cold sweat, and Reid scraped some of it off her flank and rubbed it into her own face.

It smelled awful in there, like rubber and something else, some chemical. The eyepieces weren't very transparent, and they distorted Reid's face. Kat was terrified of getting them fogged up. She tried to draw a breath and realized that the mask fit so tightly, it formed a seal around her face.

Reid said something.

"What?"

"Sorry." The other woman's voice was louder now, the enunciation more precise. "I said, don't gasp. If you draw slow, shallow breaths, you'll get enough air, but if you start to pant or gasp, you'll cut off your own oxygen."

Jesus. That was weird, to smother just because you were trying to breathe. Kat lay there, pretending she was perfectly calm. Maybe it was Sunday morning and she had just barely waked up, wasn't really awake yet—

The chemical smell she had noticed earlier flooded the mask. It was poppers. Goddammit! She did not like that stuff. The way it made her heart pound and the taste it left in her mouth were too much like terror. But Reid was touching her. She had on a pair of black leather gloves, and she was just touching her, gently, all over, it was sort of a massage. Kat didn't want to respond, but she felt her body melting anyway, yielding to those wise hands.

What a treasure, Reid thought, running her hands over the woman chained down to her bed. *So much muscle, and so much heart. Smart, too. Wish she wasn't so goddamn antagonistic. Well, whatever it takes to crank yourself up to go through with it. Bottoming like this would scare the shit out of me.* Reid shook her head, then corrected herself. *Bottoming like this has scared the shit out of me.*

When so many people in the community were obsessed with finding "a real top," it was too easy to forget your own history. Reid spared a few seconds of silent homage for her nervous, awkward, but determined younger self who had been willing to go under for just about anybody. She didn't want to waste any time being angry about the ridicule, abuse, and injuries she had garnered by wearing her keys on the right. It was better to remember the scenes that had been hot, and not add up the price. But she also thanked the Goddess for the naughty girls and obedient boys who had urged her to get on the other end of the riding crop. *I hope,* she thought, *I have treated all of you better than I got treated.*

Reid could tell that the poppers were cresting and the ride was getting smoother because Kat's pelvis was coming up off the bed in little, rhythmic waves of need. She rubbed her sex the way you rub a cat that arches its back at you. Kat rubbed back. She was wet. That was a good sign. Reid realized she wanted to fuck this big, hard body and see how many changes she could put it through. There was something addicting about having someone tough and well built at the end of your arm. It was a test of your own stamina, but it was more than that, more than just a challenge. Reid had always been told that she felt too much, wanted too much, had too much passion and lust and energy. When she was with a woman who was really big and strong, she felt as if she had a place to pour all that intensity without destroying the vessel. Slender, fine-boned women made her afraid that all of her good stuff would overflow and wind up in a puddle, just wasted on the floor.

This wasn't what usually happened. She didn't often want to fuck the people that she topped. Usually it was like being a windup toy. Only she had to wind herself up, and then they got to watch it wear off. All the time you wondered if they would even remember your face if they ran into you at the grocery store tomorrow. Being a top was like being a public utility. But even public utilities have their limits. Reid drew the line at going through the motions of sex unless she felt something for them between her own legs. Or unless they paid.

It was too soon to do that, to turn the scene sexual. But it wasn't too early to inform Kat about her desire. So Reid slid down Kat's body, sat between her legs, and thrust all her fingers between the slick and furry halves of her sex. She pushed slowly, up to the biggest part of her hand, before she felt any significant resistance. Not that there was no response—the poppers were still circulating inside the mask, making Kat's breath come short and sharp. Her nerve endings were raw. The muscles along her torso stood out as she tried to come down on Reid's hand. "This is for me," Reid crooned. "Dessert. For later." She wiped her hand on the bulky thighs. "I'll help you keep it wet," she promised, and slid back up Kat's body to confront her face-to-face.

After tripping alone for so long, it was very odd for Kat to see Reid's determined little face, wearing those stupid glasses, just inches from her own eyeballs. "I know all about you," Reid said, and for the first time, Kat thought maybe that was almost true. "If I do anything you don't like tell me to stop. If you get to me before the beast comes out, I will. But you aren't going to say no to me. You've been looking for me for a long, long time. Let's not waste any time pretending we don't understand one another. You need to be hurt. I need to hurt people. You don't think anybody can hurt you enough, and I'm sure you're wrong. I just want to feed you, darlin'. Till you just aren't hungry anymore. Are we having fun yet? I am. I am. I am."

The first time Reid said, "I am," she covered the snout of the gas mask with her palm. Suddenly, there was no air at all. Kat's whole body thrashed the way a fish out of water flops, and for exactly the same reason. Then Reid gave her life, gave her air. "I am," she said again with devilish glee, and took it all away. Kat's life was literally in the palm of her hand. Then it was back, sweet air, cold air. Kat's face, her whole body was hot under freezing sweat that melted and ran down her sides, pooled beneath her. "I am," Reid repeated with terrible conviction. Kat struggled with the chains, the hooks they were welded to, the wood the hooks were embedded within. But all she could really do was turn her head from side to side, and Reid had no trouble at all keeping the small opening in the mask covered. She kept it up a long time until Kat's field of vision swam with black mist. Then she let her go and leaned in closer still.

"Don't you hope I'm an ethical and compassionate human being? Aren't you glad you're too big to stuff into the trash compactor?"

And she hit the mask again, covered the hole, deprived Kat of the most important thing in the whole world. Oh, it was wicked, wicked, Reid thought, wanting to do this to somebody else. The temptation to take more than Kat would willingly give beat in her cunt like a hard-on that wouldn't go away. Sometimes Reid found that fighting that temptation was more of a challenge than getting the bottom to have a good time. The restraint she had to place on her own sadism had to be stronger than any chain that locked somebody else to her bed.

When Reid let Kat breathe again, it was only to give her more poppers, and when the air left after that, it was even more hellish. Kat's pounding heart demanded more oxygen, she *had* to have it, and it just wasn't there. She was sobbing and pleading, but the medium she needed to form words had been sucked out of the mask. There was only the threat of unconsciousness, Reid's looming face (which didn't look silly at all anymore), and all the things that had been taken away from her that she had thought she could not go on without. Kat felt two small, sharp tears gathering at the inside corners of her eyes. This was not like losing a job or a lover, it was not even like going without a meal or two. It was like dying, it was fucking awful, and Reid was not going to stop, she knew, until—

Reid stopped.

She pushed the mask up off of her face. Kat said, "Thank you, sir" before she could stop herself. She ought to be pissed, she ought to be resentful and wary of this woman, but this was the person who had saved her, who had let her live. The fact that it was also the person who had put her in jeopardy was too confusing to deal with. Frightened people need to feel safe, and they will turn their jailers into saviors if that is all the hope they can devise.

"How you doing?" Reid asked. Kat noticed that there were tiny wrinkles around her eyes. This was not a kid. This woman was her age—maybe older. She was certainly experienced. Had, uh, some exotic tastes. Yes. Because this was her idea of an appetizer. A warm-up. And she, Kat, had invited Reid to do her worst. The extent of her own stupidity appalled Kat so much that her next remark was a little too tart.

"Is that what you call getting lucky?"

The joke took Reid by surprise, and she felt her hackles rise. Was Kat going to be one of those ingrates and hypocrites who pigged out on pain and humiliation, and then just had to find a way to deny their own pleasure and make it look like you, the top, were the pervert, and they had been victimized? Reid broke one of her own cardinal rules and lost her temper. "Look, you don't get to fill out my report card. It's obviously a mistake to lighten up on you for even a few seconds." The defensive sound of this outburst made Reid blush. She had to get off the bed to cool her face off and simmer down.

"No—," Kat moaned.

But Reid was gone. She had left the gas mask on the bed, and by stretching her hand to the limit, Kat could just barely touch it. She had to, there were things she expressed by touching it that she would never be able to say out loud to Reid. Somewhere out there, Reid made the red track lights go off. There was only candlelight now.

Reid came back with a black plastic wand in her hand. It looked a little like a vibrator. She was fitting a glass attachment shaped like a mushroom into one end of it. She bent to plug it in somewhere by the side of the bed, and turned a knob on the bottom. The smell of ozone burned through Kat's dried-out nasal membranes. But she barely noticed it, because purple sparks were shooting out of the mushroom. "This is an ultraviolet wand," Reid said. "Smart girl like you's probably seen a million of them. But I do like to hear myself talk. It generates a field like static electricity. So I can use it anywhere on your body. Except the eyeballs. Oh, well. Here we go."

Every time she used an electrical toy, Reid chided herself for being lazy. But her lower back was sore from flogging Artie and sitting in front of the keyboard today. Besides, the three women she'd called to get the dish about Kat had all told her that the bartender was also a mechanic, maybe even an engineer. A technical girl like her ought to appreciate these warped machines. She ached to lay leather across Kat's back, but told herself that would have to be the evening's grand finale.

Reid stroked the hollow globe full of hissing, glittering magic up the inside of one of Kat's thighs. The leg threw itself out and went rigid. Kat said, "Hmm. Goddammit!" The sensation was very odd, almost impossible to describe to herself. There was prickling, and it made a sizzling noise, which probably made the prickling feeling more intense. But it also felt like little needles being driven into her flesh, needles that melted and left tiny seams of molten metal buried in her body.

Reid turned the UV wand up. The purple color got darker, reflected off her glasses. There were more sparks, and they shot further. "Hold still," Reid told her.

Kat could not. Chained in that position, there was nothing she could do to avoid contact with the glass mushroom, but she could not help flinching anyway. The noise of frying was ugly, and the feeling was too peculiar. She could not categorize it with the simple pain she got from a whip, and she could not build sexual tension out of struggling against and then yielding to it. It just made her tense and irritable.

"Hold still," Reid repeated. "Dammit, I mean it, now, pay attention. Do you feel that?" She ran the sparking attachment over Kat's belly, keeping it firmly in contact with her skin.

"No. I, uh, I don't. Not really. Should I?"

"No, idiot. But you feel this, don't you?" And Reid lifted the wand, put it down, lifted it again. Each time the glass surface left Kat's skin, sparks arced from the wand to her body, and there was that buzzing, prickly, piercing feeling.

"The moral to this story," Reid said, "is refer to lesson one. By not doing what I told you, you've inflicted a fair amount of discomfort on yourself. And I'm not sure I should have even told you. It's so much fun to make you jump." She repeated the lesson a few more times. It didn't really help. Kat set her teeth on edge and vowed not to knuckle under to something that wasn't really hurting her. Except that it did hurt. Only she didn't like it. But did she ever?

Luckily, Reid broke in on this introspection. "Well, that's interesting," she mused, "but it's not quite the thing, is it?" Kat turned her head and watched as the glass mushroom was replaced by a little steel pointer.

"This is the same but different," Reid warned. Of course, the first thing she touched was a nipple. Holy smoke! It was, Kat reckoned, about as close as you could come to being struck by lightning if you didn't live on top of a flagpole. The metal point concentrated the purple sparks into a single bolt of pure energy that was excruciating but compelling. The sensation left her speechless. Reid smiled, and began to apply the metal point to other parts of her body. Kat knew she was headed for her clit, and couldn't help but bend her neck and watch. It was a sickening sort of fascination. As the stabbing pain went through her again and again, Kat thought that this was not the kind of thing she was used to at all. You'd think these gadgets would just be distracting. It was like being in a very sick amusement park that was also a sort of prison. *I could get to like this,* Kat thought. Then added, *What the fuck am I saying?*

Then Reid put the metal point at the top of her inner lips, and Kat thought she was going to piss or go blind. That hurt more than anything else she could remember or imagine. She cursed with fervor, but (oddly enough) did not inveigh against Reid.

"Payback time," Reid said. "Remember the incident of the withheld wrist? How many seconds do you imagine you resisted me?"

"Seemed like forever. Five minutes?"

"Well, at least you're honest. If you'd said five seconds, I would have cauterized your clit. But it was probably more like a minute, even less. We'll make it sixty just to be on the safe side. And divide that into threes, that's twenty for each nipple and twenty for down here. In sets of five, I think. You're going to count and ask me for each shock, and then thank me."

It was the kind of thing that would have sounded boring on paper. But counting to sixty can be very dramatic when it is accompanied by intense (if brief) suffering. And the ritual of repeatedly calling Reid "sir," making a polite request to be hurt, and then thanking her for it put Kat back in the submissive mind-set she had acquired when Reid pushed the gas mask off her face. Being rescued was so much more important than asking why she was in trouble in the first place. And if she could not stop what was happening, at least it had some meaning. If Reid said it did.

And what Reid said was astonishing. She got especially eloquent whenever she hurt Kat's sex. "Bet your cunt hurts most of the time anyway" was one of the things she said. "Hurts from not getting touched. Aches to be hurt, huh? Bet you don't like getting fucked unless it hurts. But you like getting fucked a lot. Partly for the pain of it. So how is it to have pain without the fucking? There will be fucking later, but there isn't any now. I bet you could come on this. Shall I make you come on this?" Kat found herself begging Reid not to do that. She didn't want to know if that could be true, she didn't want to be exposed that way.

So of course Reid told her she couldn't help it, she would come the next time she felt the pointer touch her clit, and she did. It wasn't the kind of come that makes you feel finished, done with sex, and ready to go home. Still, it was intense enough to be embarrassing— the kind of thing that makes you feel like somebody else has dirty pictures of what you did in a motel.

Kat looked humiliated. Reid wanted to defuse that. She put her hand on Kat's mound, not to arouse her, just to steady her and draw off the shame. Kat's ability to come from pain filled her with awe and tenderness. Masochists were so amazing. They took her need to hurt and made it beautiful. "Have you played much with electricity?" Reid asked Kat, unplugging the wand and banishing it somewhere off-camera, along with the gas mask.

"Is that what we're doing?" Kat wondered.

Reid laughed. "Oh, yes. That's what we're doing. I have something else here I want to try. This is wonderful. It can hurt so much you'd just cut off your right arm to make it stop. And it can feel so good, like the fastest tongue in the world flickering on the most sensitive spot. Too bad you don't have rings in your cunt. It makes it easier to attach the electrodes. But these will do."

She had a pair of metal clips, trailing electrical wire and plugs, in her hand. "These are alligator clamps, but I've bent the teeth out and sprung them a little. They're just snug, they don't pinch."

"Awww."

"Don't be a smartass, I've got a pair that I left the teeth on. But those are for another time. You're just a baby, I have to be careful with you." Reid put a dab of ointment inside each of the metal jaws ("conducting jelly," she explained) and then placed a clip on each of Kat's inner lips. As she had promised, their grip was firm, not painful.

But Kat was too busy clenching her fists to pay attention to that. Whenever she started to relax, Reid would say something that got her back up. Kat was damned if she would back down from anything the little redhead could do with the radio-sized black box that she plugged the clips into. It had three silver rheostats and a little red button. After Reid turned it on, she held the red button down. It made a noise like a miniature klaxon. "That tells me how fast the pulse is," Reid said. "You don't feel anything yet, do you?"

Kat just shook her head. She didn't want to talk.

Reid turned dials. "Tell me when."

Kat screamed.

Reid turned dials back a tad. The pain subsided to a dull roar. "You were supposed to tell me when you felt anything at all, not when you were in agony. Of course, if that's what you wanted to get out of this—" She flipped one dial all the way to the end of its rotation. Kat cried for mercy and yanked on her chains until the posters of the bed creaked. She didn't even think about it, she just did it. She had never done that spontaneously before, begged for something to stop. Come to think of it, had she ever stopped a scene? Usually she just toyed with the idea, teasing herself with it, and before she made up her mind, the woman who was working on her had run out of ideas or steam and quit. She wondered if she had even had a real scene before. Reid's formality and formidable arsenal of equipment made Kat's previous experiences look like rough sex with a few fancy touches. It had taken a lot of manipulation and provocation to get most of her other partners to use a belt or tie her hands behind her back.

"Listen to me, now," Reid said, and Kat focused on her face. She looked so serious, like a well-meaning schoolteacher. Kat had a soft spot in her heart for all the sweet, solemn young women who had tried to keep her in school. She had gotten a few of them to take the pins out of their buns before she discovered wilder women whose hair and hearts were free, and had left school for good. But she still remembered how to paste a sober look across her mug and pretend that this time she really meant it; she was going to change her ways and try much harder.

"You've got to get over this macho idea that I can't really hurt you," Reid said. She knew that some of the anger she felt wasn't really Kat's fault. It was old stuff, accumulated whenever somebody tried to help her lift something she could handle on her own, patted her on the head, or tried to pick her up off the ground without her permission. When you're under five-foot-six, other dykes just don't take you seriously. They think you don't know how to change the oil in your own damn car, they assume that any shelf you put up is not going to stay on the wall, and they are always telling you you're "cute" when you're sweating over something difficult and don't appreciate comments from the audience. Anybody who wants to hassle dykes figures you're a safe target. Reid thought that was scary enough without the additional burden of the big girls' ignorance about how quick and mean a little dyke had to be to survive.

Reid dug a fingernail into her palm to bring herself back into the present. "Stop smirking at me," she told Kat sharply. "You look like a juvenile delinquent who's trying to get out of doin' detention. Don't you understand how hard I have to work to make myself behave and keep within some reasonable limits here? If you don't pay attention and help me, I'm going to start playing just to please myself. I know you're big and bad and mean as hell, but I can break you, Kat, in about five seconds, without even breathing hard. So tell me when it is just barely perceptible."

Kat nodded, panting. Reid inched the dial over. "There? Okay. We'll leave the intensity there for a while, and just play with the speed of the pulse and the shape of the wave." She twirled other buttons. "See? Feels different, doesn't it?" Kat was white-lipped, clutching at the sheet. "Oh, you like it slower. Okay. How about this? Yes, I thought so. Now, isn't it like it's just happening inside you, these regular pulses of pain that well up from your cunt, like lubrication? Couldn't you get used to that and start to expect it and even like it? It's a very seductive pain. It's so intimate. And inescapable. Relentless, even. Makes you want to squirm, huh? I bet it does. I can see it does. Oh, darlin', don't blush, I could make a four-star general tell me how to start World War III with this little black box. You're already taking more than most of the little pussycats I lure to my lair. If it makes you purr and grind around, that's a good thing. I told you, I recognize your stuff. You're a masochist. And that's okay, because I'm a sadist, and I like what you've got. I just want to hurt you severely for a long period of time. It'll make me very happy. You too. You too. You too."

She spun the intensity control over each time she said, "You too." It was like the gas mask. Kat couldn't breathe while it was happening. She said something about that, so Reid got the mask and put it back on her. She had been wrong. The two experiences had nothing in common. And together they were devastating. "I wish I knew how to start World War III," she croaked. Reid laughed so hard, Kat thought she would piss. "You're very funny," Reid said. "But you're thinking too much."

She changed something on the box. At first, Kat thought she was just changing the amplitude, but eventually she realized Reid was just turning the intensity up a little at a time. And she was still getting off on it. It was starting to feel like getting fucked, only there was no penetration, just the same kind of throbbing you got after somebody with really big hands stayed in just a little too long and banged around a bit too much.

"You're still hungry, aren't you, darlin'? Yeah. What's going on down here, where this evil little black box is humming away? Ain't 'run out of batteries yet. Eveready. That's you, huh? Ready now, anyway."

Reid released her ankles so Kat could lift her legs. She had not realized how cramped her calves and thighs were. When Reid saw how Kat's face twisted up as she worked out the kinks, she leaned forward and undid the locks on the wrist cuffs as well. Kat shook herself, putting joints back in place and driving blood into muscle groups that had been operating on less than a full supply. When she had limbered up, Reid handed her the black box, and laughed at the look on her face.

"I think we understand each other a little better now," Reid said. "If I thought you were going to turn it off, I'd never let you have it. I know what you're going to do with it. You don't know yet. But I do." While she was talking, she completed the awkward process of removing her leather jock. It took a lot of digging into her chaps and tugging on straps and snaps. Kat didn't crack any jokes or even smile, and Reid was grateful. Packing made you so damn vulnerable to other women's approval or ridicule.

Reid lifted Kat's legs, put them on her shoulders, and went in, fat and long. Kat forgot for a while what she held in both hands; she was too busy grinding back and grinning.

"Feels good?" Reid asked.

"Yes," she growled.

"Have at it, then," was the invitation, and Kat accepted. Reid had to dig both of her knees into the mattress and clamp her hands around Kat's hips to keep from being bucked off the bed. She could barely reach Kat's nipples, and she knew that messing with them would only increase the buffeting she was taking, but she couldn't resist the temptation to twist those dials. Fortunately, Kat wasn't about to let that spoon slip out of her sugar bowl for a long time. She wrapped her legs around Reid's butt and locked her into place. It took a couple of comes (well, more) to take the edge off the hunger that Reid had created in her. What the hell was Reid saying about a one-woman rodeo?

When Kat became aware of her surroundings again, Reid was softly urging her to check out the buttons on the box. So she started twiddling dials, feeling silly. But what happened to her cunt wasn't silly at all. It was dramatic. Having somebody fuck you while this other thing was going on could be habit-forming. She was terribly curious about how many different ways it could feel. She played with the frequency, she played with the amplitude. And always, always, that dial that governed the intensity of the current seemed to creep up until she had it all the way over to the right and was dammitall shouting at Reid to really fuck her, not bullshit around, put it in, motherfucker, and Reid pulled out her dick and slick-slammed her fist in there, and punched it out and punched it out and made it happen just right, while somebody said, "Come home, come home, come home."

And she did.

When Kat opened her eyes, there was a somewhat greasy and very short person with red hair grinning like a maniac and wiggling her ears. The electrodes dangled from Reid's hand. "Damn, you're good. I'm not bad, either," Reid said. She shoved the electrical box off the bed. "Roll over. I want to beat you."

"What?"

This bleary-eyed question made Reid's heart leap with glee. So it was possible for her to wear this big girl down. "Are you deaf? You didn't think we were done, did you?" Reid was tired of wires and dials. She wanted to move, jump, dance, kick ass, flex her muscles, throw her weight around.

"Well, the thought had crossed my mind, but I can get amnesia at a moment's notice. Hold still. You're makin' me dizzy."

"Uh-uh. Get amnesia now. Do I have to tie you down?"

Kat wondered where her pride had gone. With somebody who was in her own weight class, she could always hide behind the illusion that she was being made to do things she didn't really like. Now she wouldn't even have the excuse of being in bondage. Her resistance dissolved, and she found herself blushing at the thought of how much she craved Reid's severe attentions. She went cold and hot at the thought of giving it up to somebody who didn't look to be her match at all, and she ached to lay her big head on Reid's perfectly shined, little-boy boots. Apparently the old proverb was right. The size of the dog in the fight had nothing to do with it.

"Not if you don't want to," she mumbled with her head down, her mouth against the mattress.

"I'd rather not."

"Okay, but, uh, you can't hit my ass."

"Fine. Nothing on the butt, then." Reid trotted off, no doubt to return loaded down with whips, like a leather Santa Claus. She hadn't asked why Kat's ass was off-limits, and Kat was thankful. Really, now, how many fucking reasons could there be for somebody to hate getting hit on the ass? It wasn't because you loved your dear old dad. She intensely disliked explaining all that old shit to people. "Oh, that's terrible," they would say, and their eyes would get all misty. "I know just how you feel. I'm an addict and an alcoholic and a codependent adult child of alcoholic parents and an incest survivor with terrible food allergies." It made her want to pop them one right in the mouth. Nobody knew how she felt. Not ever. She wouldn't mind telling Reid all about it, sometime, but not right now. They were having too much fun.

Sure enough, the jolly old elf was back, tossing whips onto the bed. One, two, three, many.

"There's only one of me," Kat warned.

"I know. But there's enough of you to make a lot of hamburger. Grab those chains."

At first, Kat kept her head turned so she could see what Reid was using. There was a leather slapper, a riding crop with a very large but rigid flap of leather on its end, and a short whip with many flat strands. Then her neck got a crick in it. She had to straighten out her spine and lie flat. That meant she couldn't see, but Kat decided it didn't matter. It was easier to just close her eyes and let Reid whale on her. She could look later. All she knew was that her back felt as if it was heating up and swelling, rising like bread. She was relaxing and tensing, relaxing and tensing, as if one long muscle controlled her whole body. There were deep, thudding blows and wide blows that landed mostly on the surface. There were sharp, stinging, cutting, burning, and crushing blows—every feeling you could get from a whip. But it wasn't confusing, somehow. Each change soothed the pain from the previous bout and lifted her up another level, into acceptance and excitement. Both of them made occasional silly remarks, kept each other laughing. Kat was purring, rolling from side to side and wanting to be fucked again, but not wanting the whipping to stop.

Reid put one hand on the small of her back, slid it down. Kat's ass came off the bed to soothe itself along that hand. It patted her, and the tips of the fingers barely cupped the crack of her ass. Kat had no fear that Reid would suddenly take a notion to smack her butt or stab a finger into her asshole. This amount of touching was just pleasant—making her aware of her whole body again.

Then Reid shifted position, put both her hands on Kat's shoulders, and swung a leg over her. Her shoulders felt enormous. The slabs of muscle there were swollen and heavy from the whipping. Her skin smarted under Reid's hands, the abraded skin reacting to the salt in her perspiration. The weight on her ass was reassuring, pressed her back into the bed. She was not going to float away. Reid was not done with her.

The switchblade clicked open, the tip of it resting within her ear. It tickled. "Hold still," Reid said, and cut her from shoulder to shoulder. Kat bucked. "Goddammit, don't push up at me!" Reid snapped, alarmed. She slapped the open wound. But Kat couldn't help it. The pleasure and pain were too intense not to roll up and greet them. Steel parting flesh was her favorite sensation.

"Do me again," she hissed, and Reid cut below the first line of blood. At Kat's urgent request, five molten ribbons were laid across her back. The flowing blood seemed to release some big knot that had been buried in Kat's gut, and she began to cry, happy to be freed from its weight. Reid stayed on top of her, hanging on to her shoulders, rubbing her face in Kat's blood and growling softly.

"You smell good," she rumbled, and Kat felt as if she could go to sleep and never wake up again.

Then the air in the room seemed to freeze. Everything was suddenly different. Colors were brighter. The world was back in focus. A sharp, musky odor hit Kat in the face. Was that Reid? "Roll over," Reid said.

Kat hastened to obey. The tone of voice was flat and cold. She looked up. This was not the jolly old elf. No, this was another person entirely, twirling a cane, tipping it end-for-end from finger to finger. She took a closer look. Reid gave her a very unpleasant grin. Why were her canines so big?

"The better to tear your throat out with, darlin'. But not yet. Not yet. What's wrong? Don't you recognize me? You've been calling me out for the longest time."

What had Reid said earlier, something about the beast?

"Oh, yes, it's me. The other face of passion. You're afraid now, aren't you?"

"No," Kat lied.

"Then lock yourself in."

Kat cursed herself for a fool. The headlines would read, "Big Girl Found Murdered in S&M Sex Den." But her hands were already shackling her ankles, using the open padlocks that Reid had left hanging from the links of the chains. Those hands were shaking, but they seemed determined to do their job. She watched what was happening, wondering why she could not stop it. How could she be so frightened? Reid wasn't threatening her. There was no bluster. But there was still something violent in the air, like an apparently peaceful neighborhood that's about to erupt into a riot. Kat locked down her left hand and held up the right for Reid to fasten down.

Their eyes met. Reid licked her lips. Her tongue seemed to loll. The fingers that circled Kat's wrist and put it down onto the chain were very strong. "I need this," Reid said, and Kat heard the echo of her own voice in the hallway, felt again the searing path of Reid's blade across her ribs. Need. A need so bad it could make you take your bike through a red light at eighty miles an hour or get you into a fight you couldn't win, unless you learned how to let it out quietly at home with a razor blade or a lit cigarette or a needle full of smack. Well. This was something she was familiar with, after all. Probably. Maybe. She warily eyed the circling cane.

"Give me this," Reid said, and it was a completely selfish demand. Tops do not usually make such demands. Or if they do, it is only for a mouthful or two of what they really want. Reid was asking to be fed a whole meal. Kat swallowed hard. Her thighs were shaking.

"You can have whatever I've got," she said. "I might need a little help is all."

"Help?" Reid laid the cane across her thighs, sawed it back and forth. "Oh, yes. You mean you don't want to have a choice. But the chains are real, and I'm real, and you really can't just get up and go home. Not until I'm through with you."

She hit her lightly, rapidly, the cane bouncing with dreadful flexibility. There was a rhythm in this that made it a little less frightening. It acquired a predictability. Even if it was getting harder and harder, Kat knew it was going to be just so fast, so many beats per minute. The harder Reid hit her, the slower she went. Just before the blows got difficult to handle, she stopped entirely and told Kat to take a deep breath. Then she brought her arm down. The curve was beautiful, and Kat saw the welt come up before she felt a thing.

That was a good trick. But she was a little too busy to be full of admiration. This was devilish. The sensation started on the surface, went deep, expanded, contracted, and all of it was awful. There was simply no standing still for this. She was really glad Reid had chained her down.

The arm went up again. Kat took a deep breath, released it, and there was the welt oh God where is the pain where is the pain this is going to be bad—there! The pain! *Shit! What was I in such a hurry for?* Kat cursed to herself.

Reid gave her four more strokes, changed sides, and did six from the other side. "I'm a traditionalist," was all she said. Kat had no idea what she was referring to. She had never been caned before. It was not something anybody she knew would do. Maybe if she were British, she would have some memories or some fantasies that would make this easier to take. But she did not. So she fell back on Reid, the look on her face, the perfect concentration, the set of her shoulders, that look of a prowling wolf that was hunting because it had to, because the only way to get what it needed was to go out and find prey and overpower it. She kept making herself say, "Yes, sir, do me again, sir," and that helped some. So did the breathing. Relaxing when she saw that arm go up was an ordeal, but the one time she got hit on top of tensed muscles convinced her it was necessary.

There were deep red and black lines across both of her legs. The marks came in parallel sets. Where the tip of the cane had gone in, it was outlined in red, with a deep blue bruise around it. Some of the cane strokes had bitten deep into the tender inner thigh. One stroke had glanced off her cunt.

"You're so good," Reid murmured, and it was like being blessed. Kat had thought she was doing lousy. So there was hope. This could not last forever. And Reid said she was good. She would be good. All she had to do was stay here, breathe, relax, stay here—

"I beg your pardon," Reid said, "but this is something I really have to do."

The descending arm was too fast to follow. Just as the cane touched Kat's flesh, Reid pulled her arm straight back, so the blow both crushed and cut. Kat screamed so hard she thought her guts would come out of her mouth. But Reid went on until she quit screaming. Then the cane snapped. And Reid instantly stopped, dropped the broken cane, and sat down heavily. Her hands felt like she was wearing concrete mittens, but she managed to fumble the

locks open and let Kat go. Then she put her arms around her and collapsed on top of her. "I'm through," she said to the big woman's neck.

"You're not," Kat said. "Let's fuck. Me first. My turn." She rolled
on top of Reid, and was surprised to find out how well the small body
fit against her torso. She half-expected Reid to bite or slap her and
make some pompous statement about never letting herself get
flipped. It's true Reid put up a fight, but it was the kind of lazy
struggle that a girl makes to turn herself on. It was a covert way of
feeling Kat's muscles. Kat knew all about that dance and liked her
part in it. At first, she tried to go a little easy on Reid. After all, she
was ten inches taller and at least sixty pounds heavier than the other
woman.

But Reid didn't want a walk in the park on a sunny day, she
wanted a steeplechase. Reid got fucked the same way she topped,
with her teeth bared. "Talk to me!" she insisted, digging her strong
thumbs into Kat's biceps. "Tell me what this is, tell me what we're
doing. *Talk to me.*"

Kat snarled, "Now you know how big I really am, because I
really am on top of you, I really do have your hands pinned down,
and you really can't get away until I'm done with you." At that, Reid
grabbed Kat's ears, wrapped her thighs around Kat's forearm, and
came, damn near pulling off all three appendages.

"Your turn to catch," Reid said when she got her breath back.
"Gimme the Probe."

"I think the bottle's empty," Kat said apologetically.

"It better not be, or I'll shove it up your ass." Kat growled, and
Reid laughed. "With your kind cooperation, of course," she drawled.

"That'll be the day, even for you, Miss Wonder Dwarf. Wouldn't
it be easier to just let me get in my bag and give you my extra bottle?"
Kat scooted off the bed and went to find her duffel.

When she got back, Reid accepted the new lube with a little bow.
"Nice to know how you expected the evening to end," she said.

"Fuck you, Reid."

"No, I'm afraid it's your turn now."

Later, while they ate some Top Ramen (Reid had scrambled an egg into it, saying, "I need some protein," and Kat thought it looked disgusting, but she ate it anyway, trying to be polite) and drank nonalcoholic Coors Cutters (which really made Kat gag), Reid told her the story about Artie's obnoxious teammate. Kat grimaced. "Where can I get my season tickets for midget wrestling?" she asked.

Much later, after they had shuffled around the topic of sleeping arrangements and decided Kat would stay over and sleep in Reid's bed, the big girl said, "How can I thank you?"

Reid said, "You can take me to dinner tomorrow night. I'll wear my strapless black velvet sheath."

"Oh, fuck all," Kat said. "There is no Goddess. There can't be, because I'm in more trouble than even She could think up."

"But not more than you deserve," Reid said.

"Close."

"Not even close."

Daddy

I'm getting dressed for my daddy. She is waiting for me in the living room, sitting on the couch, drinking shots of Jack Daniel's and chasing them with beer. She just got here a few hours ago. Because we live so far apart, we only see each other two or three, times a year. Of course, if we quit spending so much money on long-distance telephone calls, we could probably pay for a few more plane tickets. All that aside, now that she is here, this apartment has become our world. We probably won't go outside until I drive her to the airport. For the next few days, we will talk, have sex, and eat. We will do all three of these things as if we were starving. I already feel a little crazy: confined, determined to get under her skin even though the end result is that I will lose her, and angry because I know this is as good as it will ever be for us. Our story will not have a happy ending.

What a big suitcase that word "daddy" is. It's jammed so full of stuff that I can never seem to get it closed. There's no time to unpack the whole bag now, but the most important things, the ones I use the most often, are close to the top. A few of them have toppled onto the floor, and they demand to be recognized. I have to name them before I can put them away and play. (Play? I don't think I do anything more important than this, or more serious.)

At the age of twelve, I stopped calling my male parent "daddy" and referred to him only as "father" and "sir." It was my first attempt to get revenge by following the rules just a little too closely. Since he overtly demanded nothing but respect and subordination from me, I gave him that, and worked hard to withhold the trust and affection that he also wanted, but could not ask for. That was difficult. My father is a very charming man. He is funny, flirtatious, expansive, and generous; tells great stories; makes perfect strangers fall in love with him. It was hard to be at war with him. As an adolescent, I didn't understand why I couldn't keep sitting on his lap and giving him mashed-potato-and-gravy kisses. I wanted to ask his advice, tell him my secrets.

But my father has no control over his temper. When he is angry, he throws whatever he has in his hand, slaps the closest person (sometimes more than once), and says something caustic and crushing. If he knows anything about you that will wither your ego or deflate your self-esteem, it comes out then. His rage is terrifying. It comes without warning, for no good reason. My father selected me for a target because I fought back, I fought well, and because I deliberately put myself in his path to keep him away from my mother and my younger brothers and sisters. I was not very old when I realized that I wanted to kill him. I had help figuring this out. Because after we fought, we would make up by going downstairs to the family room and cleaning his rifles and pistols together. He always made sure I knew which bullets fit which guns.

I knew my father would kill me, if he could make a suitable accident happen, because I would not submit to him or get out of his way when he needed to terrorize somebody. On some level, he probably realized that having a hard-on for me meant that he was turned on to something queer, strange, and masculine. I never went deer-hunting with my father. I never went driving with him alone. I never turned my back on him.

I wanted to be grown-up so I could take my mother away from him. He thought this meant I did not love him. And it's true, my love for him was very hard to see. But if I pretended to be more her child than his, it was only camouflage. I hated my mother's religion, her prudery, her shyness and rigidity. Of the two of them, she was less crazy, but only marginally so. He punished me for no good reason, but she wanted to squeeze all the joy out of my life to prevent God from punishing me later, forever.

I knew this whole situation was really her fault because she married him and she stayed with him, and I had utter contempt for those choices. When she was angry with him, she would try to seduce me into thinking I was her best friend, her only friend, her boyfriend. When she decided to forgive him, I was supposed to shed this adult, male identity and become a subservient, compliant, ignorant girl-child. These flip-flops were every bit as dangerous as his rage. My mother taught me how to figure out what women really want, and she showed me how vicious people can be when you tell them their own truth. I also learned that I have no control over my desire to protect others. Even if they are stronger than me, even if there is no way I can win, even if they don't deserve my help, I have to try to put my body between someone who is hurt or frightened and the thing that threatens them.

I did not want to take my mother away from my father for her own sake. I wanted to possess her because I understood that would make me like him, his equal, another man. And then, I thought, we would be able to touch each other again and our house would not be full of anger and sexual tension. I blamed my tits and pubic hair and pimples for giving me a sex and driving my father away from me.

My mother was not the one I wanted to come to my room at night and teach me what to do with the desire that shook my adolescent flesh. She was not the one I wanted to show me how someone else's hands could make me feel. He was my hero, the strong one, the

one who risked his life every day by going to work so far under-
ground, setting off dynamite and digging tunnels in the treacherous
earth. I learned how to touch other people by giving my father back-
rubs when he came home from work, slipping my hands under the
light, one-piece garment that all adult Mormons wear to remind
them of their temple vows. I ignored the way my mother rattled pans
and slammed the oven door in the kitchen while I loved his muscles
and inhaled his Old Spice cologne.

Now I am older, and so is he. Just four years after I left home, my
mother finally found her backbone because of my father's unre-
lenting cruelty toward her youngest son, my baby brother, the sissy.
She told him he could get a divorce if he wanted one because he was
not living in her house anymore. So he married a tart-tongued, busty
woman my age who is half-Mexican and half-Basque. When she's
angry with him, she makes Mexican food that's too hot for him to eat.
She never goes to church. She matches him drink for drink and won't
give up her job. They read each other *Penthouse Forum* in bed. There
are no more children in his house. He's happy with her, I think. She
doesn't add to the load of guilt he began to accumulate when his own
father abandoned him, his mother, and his sister in the middle of
winter, and he was not old enough to work the farm by himself and
keep them all fed.

I do not see him very often. But he is with me every day. Sometimes I think all of us are incest survivors, because we take both of our
parents with us every time we go to bed. I don't believe my father ever
came to my room at night. But I sometimes wonder if it would not
have been easier if he had put an end to my fear and simply done what
we both knew he wanted to do. Every time I flirt with a waitress or
buy a woman a drink, I am doing what my father taught me. Does
that make me a rebel or a collaborator?

After the beatings I took from him for being queer, no gay
basher can make me turn aside from another woman's hips. And I do

not intend to let the desire I felt for him go unnamed or wasted. I deserve a daddy who needs and wants and admires me. I deserve a daddy who will touch me until I come. As one of my friends who is a convert to Christianity told me, "I need to have at least one loving male figure in my life."

So here I am, getting dressed for someone who is not afraid of me or my desire, someone I can trust with my life and my back and my sex.

I wad up the white knee socks, cram my feet inside, and unroll them over my calves. I hate them. I want to wear nylons, but Daddy won't let me. Daddy says I'm trying to grow up too fast. So I have to wear these stupid, thick socks and oxfords instead of high heels. He says, "The nuns wouldn't let you wear high heels to school anyway." But I'm not going to school right now, and I think excessive consistency is bad for sexual fantasies. Hot with resentment (and nothing else, do you hear me?), I pull up white cotton briefs, eager to cover my shaved pubic mound and outer lips. The thin fabric rasps delicately across my clitoris, which is exposed, unprotected, always getting bumped and rubbed.

Daddy says I'm not old enough to wear a bra, so I tug on an undershirt. My breasts make it bulge, so I hurry to button up my shirt. It is plain cotton, white, with one breast pocket. In the pocket I put a folded hanky. The pleated wool skirt that I drop over my head is a cream, green, and brown plaid. I used to wear a cream-colored cardigan with it, but Daddy found a green wool jacket for me in a thrift store. On the left breast pocket it says, "Holy Name Academy." The motto is embroidered below: *Serve and Obey.*

There are cigarettes inside the jacket. I don't smoke, but Daddy put the cigarettes there along with a handful of rubbers, so there they stay, next to the catechism booklet. I have not memorized today's lesson. But it's too late for that. I fasten a gold chain around my neck. It has a little gold cross dangling from it, another gift from my daddy.

Because I am angry about the lesson, I march into the bathroom and slather some lipstick onto my mouth. Daddy won't like that at all.

When I present myself in the living room, Daddy ignores me. This makes me bite my nails and study her; try to figure out how much slack I will have tonight. If Daddy's other girls, the grown-up ones, the hookers, have been making their quotas, I can expect to be humored a bit, allowed a few mistakes. But something is usually going wrong in Daddy's life. The fences take too big a cut, the cops are greedy, the goddamn car needs repairs—and I am the safety valve. Which is why I don't feel safe at all. Steam is about to whistle through me, and I am going to get scalded. I am not tough enough to take this. That's why I got the job.

My daddy has short black hair and is wearing slacks, a man's shirt, and a tie. A black leather trenchcoat, suitable for concealing a sawed-off shotgun or a boosted carton of cigarettes, has been thrown across an armchair. I want to sit down and wrap myself up in that long coat, but I'm not allowed to use the furniture unless I'm told to sit down.

On the coffee table is a shot glass and a bottle of Jack Daniel's. On the floor is a dog dish. Daddy pours and drinks a shot of whisky. The dish on the floor is empty.

"My little girl," Daddy says, and I am very frightened. This is not an endearment. "Get over here."

I do not come quickly enough. Daddy grabs my arm and pulls me, hard, so I fall. There will be a thumb-shaped bruise above my elbow tomorrow. I stop myself with my hands, but the floor is still hard against my knees. I spend a lot of time on the floor when my daddy is around. I remind myself that getting there is the hard part, that once I get used to it, I am going to want to stay on the floor, and it is going to take another sharp yank to get me up on my feet again. Still, there is a part of me that dreads the whole evening. If I can get through this scene, I promise myself, I will never do this again.

"Wipe that shit off your mouth," Daddy says and slaps me in the face with his cock. While I was giving myself that pep talk about overcoming my resistance to kneeling, I noticed his fly coming down, the hand (that hand that can be folded in half lengthwise and go impossibly deep into me) fishing within Daddy's trousers. It was what made the pep talk work, probably.

So there it is: the reason why I am here. Not my daddy's dick (which is, after all, dispensable), but my need for it. The need that makes me open my mouth, tongue the rubber head, and try to get as much of it down my throat as I can before it is taken away. Sucking a dildo is so perverse, evoking a series of emotions and images that ought to be confusing, but that make perfect sense at the time. I am sorry the instrument that moves in my mouth is not flesh, because then I would be able to give my daddy pleasure beyond the visuals, the way it makes him feel to see me choke, cry, and struggle to expand my physical capacities to accept him. I am also (more selfishly) sorry because a real cock would come long before my daddy will get tired of this game and withdraw. Then I would be off the hook.

On the other hand, I am glad this is a dildo and not a cock, because I don't have to worry about STDs and because its presence means I am with a woman, which is consistent with my sexual identity, allowing me to sample the pleasure of oral violation without violating my sense of myself. And I strive to make this act as physically pleasurable as possible. I know the base of the dildo is riding against my daddy's cunt, and the hand that I have wrapped around the shaft of his cock is there to manipulate that point of contact as well as to keep me from being smothered by my own enthusiasm and Daddy's hands on the back of my neck. Then there is the point in time where I lose awareness of my daddy's gender, or even my own. It is an infantile state. I am sucking and this is what I must do to live. It is all that life is.

"You're such an incorrigible slut," Daddy says. "Advertising that pretty little mouth. Trying to get yourself thrown out of school? Who's that lipstick for, huh? The boys? You got a crush on some pimple-faced high-school dropout who's going to take my baby to the drive-in movies and pop her cherry on the backseat of his car? No way, honey. Your daddy takes better care of you than that. Doesn't he? Don't I?"

The shaft in my throat is gone, and I miss it. I try to find it again (my eyes blinded by tears), but I am getting slapped, and this ruins my sense of direction. Snot, spit, and tears fly off my face beneath the glancing blows from my daddy's hand.

"Answer me!" Daddy says.

"What's the question?" I squeal, shamed by my weakness (I hate pain), my undignified, wobbly voice, my inability to remember the simplest thing.

"Doesn't your daddy take better care of you than any of the local punks?"

"Yes, Daddy, you love me best of all."

"Do you have a boyfriend?"

"No, Daddy, I'm your little girl."

Daddy reaches under my skirt. My belly arches, and I make it easier for him to hook his fingers under the crotch of my panties and feel me. I want to be touched. It means no more hitting. (Although I wouldn't enjoy this respite if I thought that meant no more hitting, ever again.)

The shaved flesh is smooth; the cleft and its protruding inhabitants are wet. "That's why I keep you shaved," Daddy says, "to remind you that until you're all grown-up, you belong to me, and you have to do what I say. You have to take good care of your daddy." Then she slaps me again, a really hard blow that makes my head snap. "So I don't want to see any more slutty red paint on your face. If you're going to act like a whore, I'll have to treat you like one. You may think you're ready for that, you might think you'd like it, but I know better."

The tone changes from nasty to wheedling. "Come and sit here by your old man."

Daddy slides over a little, and I sit as far away from him as I can get. For that, I get slapped again and dragged over to the other end of the couch. "You're not going to make this difficult, are you?" Daddy says. "Don't tell me you've forgotten everything I've taught you. Do I need to teach you a lesson?"

Daddy unbuttons my jacket, "finds" my cigarettes and condoms, and shakes his head. "Lipstick. Smoking. Rubbers, even. Ready for anything, aren't you? You're hanging out with the wrong crowd. I haven't been strict enough with you. From now on, you have to come straight home from school. Here. Where I can keep an eye on you. You're grounded for a month, young lady."

This tirade sounds pretty middle-class, coming from my nonnuclear-family dad, and for some reason the lack of obscenity in it makes me really mad. I know that isn't the end of my punishment, but there's nothing I can do to hurry this up or delay it. Daddy is the only one who knows the script for the evening. I have to just sit here and play my part.

My green wool uniform jacket has been removed. Daddy pours and drinks another shot. Now he is unbuttoning my blouse. His cock is still exposed. I want to touch it. I do not dare. My daddy wants to touch me now, and I have to let him.

"I'm so good to you," Daddy says, feeling me. "Showing you what to expect when you grow up. Showing you how to make me happy. Taking care of you." Those long fingers have found my nipples and are making them a curse. How can something that goes on so far away from my cunt make it awash in sensation? "Don't pretend you don't like this," Daddy says, close to my face. I smell whisky and hair oil. I wish Daddy smoked. I like the way cigarettes smell.

"I do like it," I whimper. It is the line I have been taught to say, and I learned it quickly because it was true. Is true. No one will save me from this. The only person I can tell the truth to will use it against me.

"You're getting so grown-up. Pretty soon all the boys will be chasing you. Touch me," Daddy whispers.

He exposes my breasts and begins to suck on their tips, pushing them together so the nipples nearly meet. My breasts are so big that he has to push hard to squash them together this way. They ache inside from being shoved together. I want to cry, so I do, a little, and pick up my daddy's cock. I stroke it. "Do you remember when we used to play this game, when you were little?" Daddy says.

"Yes, Daddy," I gasp. I want to spread my legs. I want the thing I am handling to be shoved inside of me. But I can't stop handling it, not yet. And I have to keep my knees primly together.

"But we play other games now, don't we?"

"Yes, Daddy."

I am pushed off the couch and land on my rump, skirt awry, blouse tugged out of my waistband, undershirt wadded up in my armpits. A rude word almost issues from my lips, but I bite it back.

"Get on your hands and knees," Daddy says. I comply. "Pull down your panties." I comply. "Spread your legs." A moment before, I longed to do just that. Now I hesitate. I hear Daddy's belt leaving its loops. I don't know whether to obey now or not, since spreading my legs will make it easier for him to hit my poor shaved pussy. Of course, after I have been hit (only six times, that is all I can stand, I really have no willpower at all), I spread my legs and get hit there anyway, which makes me really cry.

"I hate you," I say, knowing it is not wise.

"I know," Daddy says. "Hand me the doggie dish, since you're going to be such a bitch."

"Fuck you," I say, getting dumber by the minute.

Daddy takes the dish. "You know I don't like it when you use bad language. Turn around and keep your head down."

I know Daddy has dropped her pants and is pissing in the dish.

"If you'd been a good girl, this would be Jack Daniel's instead of nasty hot piss," Daddy says smugly. That will be the day. I know little girls don't get to drink hard liquor, unless you count what comes out with the piss.

The bowl waits for me. I imagine there is a little steam rising from its rocking surface. Maybe I could drink her piss with my mouth up against her cunt. It would be an extension of cunnilingus. But I can't do this. Can't and won't.

"Aren't you thirsty?" Daddy asks, sounding concerned, and straps my ass before I can answer. Oddly enough, the beating does make my throat dry, perhaps because I am howling like a monkey. It takes a while before being belted seems worse than drinking piss out of a dog bowl on the floor. As I lower my head and stick my tongue out, I hear the click and hiss of the Polaroid. Another picture for our family album. The liquid surrounding my tongue is salty and bitter, but luckily still a little warm. Could anything be more revolting than cold piss? Then Daddy's boot comes between me and the bowl, and it slides away.

"The fact that you're willing is enough," she tells me. She is speaking out of role, in a kind voice that recognizes who we are when we are not steeped in these alternate personas. She has a knack for this, knowing when to back off and go easy on me. She is not this nice to the full-time bottoms (most of them butches or female-to-male transsexuals) who are always tugging on her jacket.

Sometimes I wish I were a masochist. Other people might think they're sick, but nobody snickers at their scars. Submissives embarrass even other S/M people. It's ironic that the kind of scene we're doing now—butch top, femme bottom—which is probably the most common kind of play is also the one that leather dykes talk the least about. Very few of us admit that we want a daddy, and an even smaller number of us can say out loud that we want to be Daddy's little girl. Even perverts think if you put on a skirt, you must be a candy-ass.

I'm lucky to have a daddy who isn't put off by my closet full of evening gowns and my drawer full of bustiers and black stockings. The gleam in his eye has mended my broken heart. My mother was wrong; the queer-haters who call me an ugly dyke are wrong. I'm capable of being a pretty girl, and I don't have to give up my feistiness to do it. I know that most people can't see any power in putting on a dress or makeup. Most people would laugh at me right now, or go off and be sick. But the only thing that really matters is how this makes me feel, and how it looks to my daddy. I have to concentrate on that.

"No, it's not," I say, full of a quiet fury about all of this. "Just being willing is never enough." I stalk across the floor (if someone can be said to stalk while she is on all fours) and chug the contents of the bowl the way my daddy throws back his shots. A masochist's pride is based on their ability to turn any extreme physical sensation into pleasure. A submissive's pride is based on their ability to obey any difficult order without hesitation. "You have to live out the things in your heart, or you don't deserve them," I tell the floor, speaking a little too loudly for somebody in my position.

"Then come over here and show me what you've got," Daddy says. Her tone of voice is lazy, but I can tell I made my point. I turn around and scoot across the floor to where he is reclining on the floor with his head on a pillow. Once he is sure that I am looking at his dick, he rolls a condom over it and lubes it up. I wish that dick were just a half-inch shorter. When we do it this way, it goes in just a little too far.

We've only played this game a few times, but I know what parts of it excite my daddy too much to be left out. I know I will be made to fuck myself. Daddy likes making me work for what I want. Sometimes I have to sit on my daddy's lap, facing him, so he can hurt my nipples while I rise and fall upon his dick. But tonight I have to kneel on the floor, and my tits bounce against my thighs as I rock on the shaft that I have coveted all night. Now I ride it with a fury to be rid of it. My daddy likes fucking me when I am angry. He likes knowing I can't do anything about it except come.

But before I am allowed to come, I am penetrated again. Daddy sinks two, then three greasy fingers into my ass. Now I will say whatever it takes to get this woman to keep on being my daddy, to keep my daddy fucking me until I come. I believe I would do anything to make this continue. I do not care what it looks like. I do not care what somebody else in the room might think. And this freedom from my ambivalence, my self-consciousness, is as precious as the physical pleasure of being perfectly fucked and mind-fucked, the treasured object of my daddy's amusement and contempt and cruelty, only a toy, but an irreplaceable, priceless toy.

Daddy says, "You dirty girl, you're dirty here. And you don't care, do you? I think you like it this way. With your ass full of shit." Then I am coming the only way I know how to come and be finished, done, spent, satisfied.

Of course this is not enough for Daddy. Daddy has other plans. The night is young. There is still the matter of the cigarettes, the catechism lesson that I have not memorized, and the lipstick. Daddy grabs me by the elbow, twists my arm painfully behind my back, and marches me into the bedroom. I am told to take off everything. On the bed is some black underwear. On the floor, high-heeled shoes.

"Since you want to be a whore, I'm going to train you to be one," Daddy tells me. "But I still love you too much to put you out on the street. You'll have to be my whore, my own sweet, private fantasy."

Daddy dresses me. First he puts me into a black bra. I am speechless with admiration. She has so much patience, this woman I love, to painstakingly dress me in these fragile and intricate garments, just so she can have the pleasure of removing them later. It is a reassuring ritual, proof that she likes to see me this way as much as I like being seen. It is also a way to preen and get petted without Daddy having to be sucky and sentimental.

The bra has an underwire that holds my breasts up. It fastens in front, to make it easy to take off. There are black panties. They fit funny, and I tug at them, trying to adjust them, until I realize they feel different because they are crotchless. I imagine her buying these things for me to wear, and I blush. It took guts as well as good taste. I know how tacky the clerks in lingerie departments can be to butch dykes. There is a garter belt, stockings with seams. Daddy brushes my hair out, then holds my face with one hand and paints it with the other. I sit on the bed with my legs akimbo, feeling relaxed, luxurious, and doomed.

"Whore," Daddy says. "That's what you'd like, isn't it? You'd like to be out there letting everybody stick it to you. But I know what would happen to my baby out there. It's better for you to get it from me. I can show you things nobody else can. I only want to do what's best for you. Besides, this is my pussy. I made it. So it's mine. I can do anything I want to it. Including fuck it. Or hurt it."

"No, Daddy!" I cry when I see the clothespins. I clap my knees together.

"Don't tell me no," Daddy says and forces my legs apart. In between the shaved lips, my clitoris is prominent, easily pinched up between his fingers and placed between the jaws of the clamp. There are three of them. My sex is painfully compressed. The clothespins protrude through the crotchless lace panties. I cannot bear to put my legs together now, nor can I bear to be used.

Daddy takes me to the bathroom. I have to crawl. Crawling hurts my cunt. It hurts my pride, too. I have an unreasonable amount of pride. It keeps coming up, like the national debt, distracting me when I want to do other things. In the bathroom, there is an enema bag. A series of nozzles have been laid out on a towel. The smaller ones are there to make the last one look even bigger. It is black, and has a rosebud tip on it. Daddy puts it in my mouth.

"Get it wet," he says. "Daddy doesn't want this to hurt when it goes in. Do you remember? This is how Daddy taught you to suck on things, to let me put things in your mouth, so you could get them wet before Daddy put them in you. When you were little, you were naughty a lot and wouldn't go every day. I had to put you on a schedule. I had to train you. It's important not to forget your training. I don't want to spoil you."

Daddy withdraws the fat nozzle from my mouth and jams it into the hose on the bulging red enema bag. The clamp on the hose responds to his thumb, much like my clitoris. He inserts the nozzle into my mouth again and lets a little warm water squirt against my tongue. His voice is persuasive. "Suck it. Drink it. Taste it. You'd like to suck my cock, wouldn't you? You'll get it later, little-girl whore. Suck this for now. You'll do whatever I tell you to do with that pretty mouth. Do you like your lipstick now? Do you? Then tell Daddy thank you. Thank Daddy for making you be his pretty slut."

I repeat the ritual. It's much better than reciting my catechism, although there are some odd similarities. But no amount of verbal acquiescence can prepare my bottom for the cold KY, the invasion of an enema nozzle that is very nearly the size of a penis. I imagine water flowing into me before any is released, and yelp. "Crybaby," Daddy reproves, and lets it gush.

Once again, my resistance is shattered. No matter how I plead, the entire bag is emptied into my bowels. As soon as I can, I must rush to perch on the bowl. There isn't even time to get myself into trouble by asking Daddy to leave the room. I can't help myself, I have to empty my cramping belly. Daddy hugs me because my stomach hurts and rubs my shoulders while I whimper. Then he flushes for me, removing some of the smell from the room, and lets me wipe myself. Somebody who would stay with me through all this, see me this way, must love me.

I feel giddy, but Daddy has refilled the bag. It's time for another trip to the floor. This time the nozzle goes in more smoothly, and the

water disappears quickly. My ass is plugged, and Daddy crops me. I
scream, but only because it hurts. I am not really fighting now. I know
if I scream really well, Daddy will only hit me a dozen or so times. And
I like the way it feels a few minutes after each blow. My ass feels hot,
big and hot, and I want to rub it up against something, anything.
Every now and then my thighs bump the clothespins between my legs,
and I mew. But I can barely feel them unless they are touched directly.

Daddy fixes that. He has me position myself with my thighs
apart and uses the clothespins to jerk me off. I am instructed to come
on the pain. When I do, I am surprised and pleased. Then I have to
extrude the butt plug and drop my water. Daddy lets me do this in
private. After I wipe with paper, Daddy gives me a wet towel. I stand
up and clean myself carefully.

Now I am positioned on the bed, on all fours again. My hands are
cuffed together. Daddy works his cock into my ass. The head sliding
past the sphincter seems to make a popping noise, but it is probably
only in my mind. Being considerate, Daddy holds still once he is in,
to let me get used to this awful urgency. I am the first one to move.
Of course. I have no self-control. That is why my daddy is always
restricting and punishing me. I can't seem to learn my lesson. I just
can't seem to behave myself.

"Can I come, Daddy?" I beg. "Let me come, please."

"Take off one of the clothespins."

"No!" I shriek. Daddy has been handling my welts. Now his
hands dig into them. I do not heed the warning. Several hard slaps on
my butt make the crop marks burn. I take off one clothespin, yell,
and cry. Daddy hacks me harder. I want to come, I think I might
come even without permission. But Daddy knows this and stops
moving. "I'm not going to start moving again until you take off
another clothespin," he says. I know he means it. Still, it is several seconds before I can nerve myself to revive the sensitive flesh of my sex
by taking all the pressure off it. It is so terrible I think I will die, but

then I do not, so of course I forget about dying and try to come again. "You can come as you remove the last clothespin," Daddy says, and I say bad words, but do as I am told.

Good girls do what they are told, but good girls are never told to do the things my daddy tells me to do. I don't care, I would rather be a very bad girl, being fucked this way, even after I've come, my clitoris feeling as if it's been cauterized, lucky girl, dirty girl, I love my daddy, I do, I do.

It is the kind of sex that makes you feel as if you will never need to have sex again. I imagine that all I want to do is curl up with my head on her shoulder and go to sleep. I shed what remains of my finery and creep in between the covers. Then she stands up and undresses and takes off the dildo and the leather harness, and I discover that I may need to have sex again sooner than I thought. Much sooner. She slips into bed beside me and shoves my head down, toward the foot of the bed.

I know her clit will be so hard it will seem ready to burst, her vagina so wet I will hardly need to add lubricant to my fingers. And this is what makes me love her as well as want her. When she brings her cunt to me and puts it in my face, I know that this scene, the fantasy characters we've lost ourselves in, are as hot for her as they are for me. She demands that I make her come. She does not let me lie around in my sweat and get lazy or paranoid. She puts me to work, fucking and sucking her, and lets me earn my keep.

Do we sleep? Do we eat? If we do, I don't remember, because it doesn't matter. I feel myself changing inside, energy shifting, my fantasy selves shuffling themselves like a pack of wild cards and jokers, trumps and Greater Arcana. I am becoming someone else. It's time to change reels, but it won't be the same movie.

My boy has gotten dressed for me. Maybe it's the following night. Maybe it's just later in the same day. But I have issued instructions, left the room, and transformed myself. Now I am back to see how well my orders were followed.

These are the clothes I always ask for: a white T-shirt, faded 501s, black cowboy boots. No belt. Those pants aren't going to stay on long enough for him to need anything to hold them up. Under the jeans, there will be no underwear. I know this because my boy takes these details seriously. There is something touching about this. He has good reason to distrust all putative masters. Still, he has certain ideas, certain standards—a code. And in his heart, he has kept faith with it, despite many disappointments. I am also moved by this complete shift of role and attitude. Nobody can make my boy ashamed of what he wants, and he would never resort to the cheap tricks of bottoms who try to provoke a top by being lazy or rude. His position is, *If I am going to do this thing, I will do it right, to the letter, perfectly.*

Tonight I am a sadistic daddy. I've been many different kinds of dads for boys of all ages. Sometimes I take little boys to ballgames, barbecue hamburgers for them, and put Band-aids on their hurt knees. Sometimes I take older boys to that house on the edge of town where young men lose their innocence, introduce them to the madam, and remind them to use some protection when they get the girl they've chosen up the stairs. Sometimes I beat the snot out of young bucks who've gotten too big for their britches. All these daddies have one thing in common—an unmanly willingness to give unqualified approval and affection. I can't be somebody's daddy if I don't love them.

I have other ways of being a top, but they are more clinical and much less sexual. When I'm Daddy, I want to get my dick into something hot and tight. I want to show that boy what his cock and his butt are for and fuck the come out of him. If a boy needs to be thrashed before he knows I love him, I'll wallop his ass until he cries. But then I want to take him in my strong arms and ride him till I'm coming dry. So many dykes grew up longing for rites of passage, ways to test their courage, systematic training in how to be strong and capable, scrappy adults. When I am Daddy, I take care of that need. Unlike most real daddies, I never make a boy feel ashamed of being afraid or queer. Good daddies turn out boys who can be brave and strong as well as excellent cocksuckers.

But this particular boy doesn't want a daddy. (At least, not yet.) While he was away from me, he gave a lot of women pleasure, but he didn't get much back. It's hard to define the quality in a bottom that makes a top reluctant to undress or get off. It's probably not a rational decision. I'm sure I've turned down bushels of orgasms, just because a whisper of a chance existed that I might hear about it later in a less-than-kind tone of voice. God knows even a charity fuck might be less demeaning than some of the hot sex I've had—we've both had—with the psychos and losers that our cunts decided they had to back into. When I refuse to let a bottom get in my pants, I'm not sure if I'm protecting myself from sexual shame or perpetuating some of its foundations. All I know is, we won't put out if somebody doesn't scare us and yet somehow convey the message that it is safe to let down our guards.

The part of this boy that is willing to say it needs anything is buried deep. Deprivation has turned into denial. If I tried to comfort him now, he would mistake it for pity, and bolt from the room. My job is to break him down. Get him to confess to being human. But before this boy will accept any warmth from me, I have to be a mean son of a bitch. Masochists are often like that. Most people need to be tenderized with arousal and sensual teasing before they can accept any pain. Masochists don't really like being caressed or entered until they have been hurt in the particular way they prefer, for as long as it takes to convince them you mean business and will not abandon them or judge them. I will not be able to get or give much tenderness to this boy until I remind him that I can make him suffer for every sin he even imagined committing. I wonder if I can make this work.

Having someone else's body and soul under your hands is terrifying. It's so easy to make mistakes. Do I still have what it takes?

He is waiting for me in the middle of the floor—the exact middle of the floor. This is a task I give every new boy, to go and place himself in an appropriate position in the exact center of the floor. Very few of them figure it out. This one looked up before I had even left the room, saw the light fixture, and knelt smoothly below it. I like that kind of intelligence. Most of the people I play with are just smart enough to get themselves into trouble. This one is smart enough to get me into trouble.

So I tell the daddy part of my persona to be patient for a while and pour my distilled need and attention into the sadist. Colors get brighter. My hearing seems sharper. I swear I can taste new smells on the air. My body feels quicker, more precise, more obedient to my will. I pause for a moment after entering the room and examine the raw materials I have to work with—the strong ropes that hang at each corner of the bed; the whips, restraints, clips, knives, dildos, and a dozen other kinds of toys; the boy. Under those jeans is a pair of long, slender legs. I've never seen those legs in black seamed stockings (and I probably never will), but I know they'd look perfect. Those fashion-model legs give her a height that I find very attractive. They also give her a mean and accurate kick. Always I see her with this strange double vision, the elegant and severe woman who exists at a tangent to the young male rebel.

We don't deal with her female persona very often. The lady inside her is street-weary and knows only one thing to do with sex— trade it for money. I've seen a picture of her, and she's very beautiful, but her eyes are mad and vacant. She doesn't occupy her body unless it's been flooded with enough junk to make it seem safe to be there. The only reason she's alive is because she never trusted anybody. As far as she's concerned, people who make promises are pimps, dealers, users, and con artists. It's hard to argue with that experience. But sometimes, if the sex is really good, I can say a few words to her, in between strokes, just enough to feed her and keep her alive. I want to let her know I'm out here waiting if she ever feels like coming out and letting me touch her. She has closed a lot of doors between us, but there must be peepholes in every one, because I feel her watching me, trying to figure me out, hating me and wanting me at the same time. But I know this is not her night. This is just one more round in a long fight to prove myself worthy of an audience with that chilly, regal, lonely bitch.

Anyway, I don't believe in the phony equality that says, *If I wear a dress, you have to wear a dress.* We do what's hot for each of us. Our needs are not identical. There's no way I could cope with the terrible things I'm about to do to this woman I love. So she doesn't inflict them upon me.

Then I stop thinking and start kicking and slapping. My boy has been waiting for me for a long time. Being down on his knees is not intrinsically exciting for him. Being shoved around and forcibly put someplace is. I hate to think what would happen to my nose if we ever got into a real fight. But we're doing this together. So he avoids me, twisting to make sure my kicks land on muscle instead of on joints, and he puts his hands up so I have to knock them aside to strike his face. He only tries to get up once, but I am quick enough to snag him by the hair and slam him back down to the floor. Now we are both breathing hard. A little sweat is starting to sprout on our upper lips, under our arms. This is a good place, loose and almost out of control.

I kick him in the crotch, letting the top of my foot catch the fleshy part of his cunt. It makes a nice, solid noise and sends a shock up through his torso that rattles his teeth. "What's the matter, boy?" I say. My voice is distorted because I'm out of breath and low because I'm so horny I hurt. I swear that each kick brings the smell of her cunt up into my face, even through the thick denim of the jeans. "You wouldn't be trying to get away from your old man, would you, now? You know that's not a good idea. You know that's not allowed."

My fingers are folded over the handle of my knife. I don't remember taking it out of the sheath, but I transfer it to my left hand so I can slap him again, harder, daring him to hit me back. It's so difficult to sit still and let somebody hit you in the face. It's the kind of thing that makes you want to spit and lunge at your tormenter. I couldn't get away with it if he didn't know that much, much worse things could—and will—happen. "Be grateful it's just a slap," I say, and we both know what I am talking about. "Take off your boots, you dumb shit. You know you aren't allowed to wear any boots in here." In fact, this is a new rule I just made up, but his lack of protest is evidence of how quickly and surely the scene has gotten off the ground. He reaches behind himself, with those long, pale arms that are almost double-jointed, and slides the cowboy boots off, kicks them into the corner.

I drag him up on his knees with one hand twisted in the front of the white T-shirt. It's so old and thin that it tears, making an injured sound. I put the knife away and shred the shirt with both of my bare hands. It's a ridiculous, Hulk Hogan kind of gesture, but he knows that T-shirt is a substitute for flesh, and it makes his eyes go wild.

The half-naked body in front of me is too thin. All those years of junk, methadone, lithium, Elavil, and whatever medication she's on now keep her looking starved. I don't usually like angular women. But it looks right on her. The bone so close to the surface reminds me of the connections between death and pleasure—how the imminence of death drives us to pursue oblivion, bliss; how our pleasures kill us. The clear outlines of her skull remind me that we don't do recreational drugs; we don't have casual sex.

"You been working out," I say, touching the exposed chest. The skin is vampire white. "That's good. I like thinking about you throwing those weights around." There is absolutely no subcutaneous fat. The chest muscles are so hard, they seem to be made out of plastic or stone, not living tissue. I move away for a minute so I can take my jacket off and arrange it on the bed. When I come back, I test his upper arms, grasping them hard enough to bruise, and hoist the boy onto his feet. I turn him around, get his pants unbuttoned, and somehow manage to simultaneously strip them off his butt and legs and throw him backwards onto the bed.

There are cuffs waiting to be molded around wrists and locked in place, then locked to chain. I will start out tonight with my meat on its stomach. His torso rests on the cool, slick surface of the armor that I wear every day to warn people to keep away from me unless they really want my attention. He puts his face into my jacket and refuses to watch me imprison his limbs.

Sometimes I omit the ankle cuffs because it's fun to watch them kick, but tonight I want to see him stretched out on this bed tight as a deerhide being scraped clean for tanning. So I buckle on the padded ankle cuffs, and I drag him down and chain him up so snugly it makes him gasp. That's perfect. It makes me giggle when people assume that bondage is somehow lighter than other kinds of S/M, or isn't about pain. Good bondage is stressful, and the bottom has to struggle with their own discomfort to endure it.

I am wearing my boots, my chaps, and a black T-shirt. Underneath the chaps, I have on my dick and my jockstrap. Some of my friends wear fake mustaches and strap their tits down with Ace bandages or plastic wrap and tape to do this kind of scene. I'm impressed and turned on when somebody's makeup and drag is good enough to get them into a gay bathhouse or allow them to use the men's room. But I don't like being restricted that way. I associate compression of my torso and an inflexible waist with wearing a corset, not having cut pecs and a hairy chest. Any illusion of manhood I create is based on my stance and voice. Being read visually as a man in public is less important to me than administering the proper combination of blows and threats in my own bedroom.

A few of my friends are taking male hormones and using male names full-time. Sometimes it's tempting to follow them. I love their big muscles, deep voices, and furry faces. Sometimes it seems to me that being a man would make my life a hundred times easier. I know that some of the people I sleep with don't like my ambiguous gender and wish I would choose one side or the other. But I'm not a man or a woman. Sex reassignment would be as crazy for me as aversion therapy for homosexuality. The things I hate about being female come from outside of me, not from within. I don't want to be a little dude with a big ass and a dick that doesn't work right. The thought of giving up my tits makes me nauseous. I cling to my female body, even in the middle of this genderfuck fantasy.

My trussed-up victim looks so good, I just *have* to reach under the tight-stretched banana-shaped curve of my jock and squeeze the hard shaft inside it. He is watching me, head turned to the side, eyes in slits, fists clenched. "Don't start thinking about dessert before you've had your main course," I caution. Then I throw a leg up onto the bed and lower my body onto his. My cock presses into the back of his thigh. I have my teeth hooked in the rim of his ear. Black hair, full of pomade, curls in a perfect juvenile-delinquent DA under my hands. This is a smell I will remember later, when I'm jacking off, after she is gone.

"Do you know who you are?" I whisper.

I get a vigorous shake of the head.

"You're the punk that gets beaten and fucked on my jacket. That means you belong to me, asshole. And if you're worried about fucking this up, don't bother. Because I am not going to allow you to be anything less than perfect. Tonight I get what I want. And what I want is to see you in pain. In pain and then stuffed full of cock. So get your shit together." I have my fist in his hair, and I gently raise his head and mock-slam it into the mattress. "Better grab that jacket.

Hang on tight. Bite it if you have to. Because right now that jacket is
the only friend you've got."

I move away, stand up, and go to the wall to select my first whip.
I have three flat, unbraided cats I like to use to start a scene. One is
very short and lightweight, another is short but weighs a little more,
and the third is long and heavy.

I pick the easiest instrument and start lightly circling it above his
back. His hair is so full of greasy kid's stuff that it doesn't even move
in the breeze I'm making. It's hard to tell exactly when the whip
makes contact. I want this to be slow and careful. All I want is to
remove a few dead skin cells, get the blood circulating, wake up the
body and its appetite for struggle.

"It's been a long time," I say, and he groans and pushes his hips
into the bed. "If you've forgotten who you are, maybe you don't
remember me either. Do you know who I am?"

He turns his head and shows me his teeth. He is impatient for the
whip. All these questions make him nervous. He doesn't want to talk,
he wants to get beaten. But I shake my head. I will not let the whip
land until we finish this conversation. The last time we were together,
I visited the city where she lives. And I noticed a few things there that
I want to use now.

"No," he drawls, to see if insolence will hurry me along. "Who
do you think you are?"

"I'm the person who's going to make you scream and try to get
away." He grunts cynically. "Oh, believe it. I will. But I'm more than
that. I'm not just your jailer. I'm not just your master." I lean down
to whisper in his ear. "I'm your daddy."

This evokes a wordless wail of protest. The bed creaks as he
thrashes around. I am relieved to see that all the screw eyes remain
sunk deep in the wooden frame of my bed. The chains hold. He gives
me an indignant look that says silently, *You betrayed me.*

"Don't try to bullshit me," I say contemptuously. "It's not hard to figure out what you really want. Did you think you could just keep it to yourself, that I'd never notice or try to make you say it out loud? I met your friend Jackson, remember? You took me to his shop. But I think you wanted to look at more than a new motorcycle jacket. What is he, fifty? I saw you take off your keys and shove them in your pocket. I saw you scrambling to find something—anything—that you could do for him, whether it was get him a fresh cup of coffee or sweep up the scraps on the floor. I saw him looking at your butt, wondering why his dick was hard. He really cares about you, even if the only thing he dares do about it is squeeze your arm or make you hang around and try on vests and harnesses and talk about bikes. Jackson is never going to beat your ass. Wouldn't you rather have a real daddy, somebody who would let you suck his dick?"

He does not answer. I hit him a few times with the whip. It's not very long or heavy, but I make the blows count. "Answer me," I insist.

I get my response, but she will not look at me. "All I want is for you to beat me as hard as you can for as long as you can. If you want to make up stories about what you think it means, I can't stop you. But I will never ever call you . . . that. You can't make me."

Because she will not look me in the eye or even say the offensive word, I know I am on the right track. "We'll see," I say.

I've been gently whisking the surface of his back, butt, and thighs. Now I let a few strokes land harder. I get an affirmative grunt. So I stop the circling motion and strike overhand and down instead, a simple thudding chop that makes a fair amount of noise and hardly stings at all. I pause to run my hands over the skin. I already want to fuck him, shove my cock between the ass cheeks that are flexing in doubt. *Is this what I really want?* I hear him thinking. His body hasn't had enough time to get its endorphins circulating. I sympathize. Neither one of us is very good at taking pain without chemical assistance.

I don't want to leave him alone with this anxiety or let him get impatient. He's had too many aborted scenes with tops who chick-

ened out at the crucial moment, threw down the whip, and pleaded
to be held. That's such a rotten thing to do to a masochist. Being a
whip tease is every bit as bad as the other kind. I hope there's a special hell for people who make carnal promises that they can't keep. I
am old-fashioned about keeping my word. You could call it a fetish.
And I have promised this boy quite a drubbing.

So I take the whip in a circle around my head and bring it down
hard, flicking my wrist so it sends a wave down the blades that peaks
on the right side of his ass. I keep on doing this, taking a breath
between each stroke, until the ass and shoulders are uniform sheets of
red. A white belt of untouched skin rings his kidneys and lower back.
I haven't missed once. Good for me.

"You're beginning well," I say. I separate the cheeks and spit, let
my finger follow the white bubbles down the crack. I spit again and
apply the blob of water and slime to the sphincter. His hips are
absolutely motionless. This lack of response makes me feel bitchy. I
shove three fingers up his cunt and gently frig his clit. This gets a rise
out of him. He slams the bed with his fists, and his upper body curls
up in protest. He really wants to be fucked, but I haven't hurt him
nearly enough. What a dilemma.

"Let's get serious now," I say. I skip the other warm-up cats and
select a whip with a long, braided stock that splits into two tails. It's a
combination quirt and blacksnake. It's noisy, and I can pick precise
spots to hit with it. I love the way using it makes my body feel. The
stroke starts in the soles of my feet and rises up my body like a wave of
sexual tension. When it lands and snaps, I feel as if I'm going to come
in my pants. I use this beauty on his shoulders, butt, and thighs until
my arm starts to ache.

Now his breathing is harsh and ragged, and there are a few red
stripes, but no broken skin. I use the long, unbraided flogger to bring
more blood into the tissue and start breaking it down. When somebody is this muscular, it takes a lot of effort to mark them. Mostly

this part will just feel good to him. It's like getting a massage. By the time I'm done, I'm panting, and his toes are curled. Both fists are wrapped around the chains, and I'm impressed. I didn't think I'd left enough slack for him to be able to do that. I love girls who can stretch chain.

"Are you trying to get away?" I ask softly. I prefer not to raise my voice in a scene. It forces the bottom to keep paying attention to me. I don't like it when they space out and start imagining they're all alone in a world of disembodied sensation.

"No!" she spits.

"Liar. I saw you try to get away. What else was it I said I would do?" Her balkiness makes me angry, so now I shout. "Answer me!"

"You said—" (rattle, rattle) "—you would make me scream."

"I told you I would make you do something else too."

"No!"

Making him think about it is, for now, every bit as effective as getting the forbidden words to come out of his mouth. I look to my weapons. The braided cat is next. I have several of these, too, in different widths. The thinner the braid, the faster they move, and the more they cut and burn. The authority is in the knots. They are like tiny fists. I try to remember all the rules about pacing and buildup, but I'm getting so excited that I want to take that motherfucking whip in both hands and go up on my toes and just bring it down as hard as I can until the walls are spattered with blood.

"This is how we get high together," I say. "You're getting me very stoned. Do you know how much I like to hurt you? When I hurt you I feel like I'm getting fucked. All I want to do is hurt you until my head explodes."

"Do that," she snarls, clawing at my jacket. "Do it harder. Do it some more. I thought you were going to make me scream."

"Sounds almost as if you want to scream," I reply. She laughs and shakes her head, tries to muffle it in my jacket. Striped and bruised, shaken and battered, she laughs at me. This is a good moment. We are in this together. It makes me laugh too.

I use my belt, another quirt, an assortment of implements. But I'm delaying the grand finale, and we both know that. I finally draw a cane out of the stand.

Women who can take the cane are an elite group. If somebody has a genuine enthusiasm for the cane, she will not have much trouble persuading me to pick one up. I don't care what she looks like, who she is, or why she wants it, as long as she can hold her butt up and wait for my stroke. The first time I was handed one of these supple, wicked scepters, it immediately became an extension of my arm and my libido. I've never had a bad time caning somebody, and, no matter what emotional price I've had to pay for it later, I've never been sorry.

But to do this with somebody I love—well, that's a very different thing. Normally I run off my own narcissistic energy within a scene. Voyeurizing, watching myself is the hottest part for me. But this is someone who has me by the short hairs. I want her to like this. I want him to tell me he needs it.

"Tell me you want to be beaten," I say. "Boy," I add.

There's no hesitation. His head comes up, the lips move. "Please—I want to be beaten." The voice is definite and clear, even though the eyes are glazed. It's impressive.

"Tell me who I am."

"You are my master. I belong to you. Please hurt me."

It's not exactly what I want to hear. But it's close enough. So I do what she tells me.

The cane eventually breaks the skin. I know I am going too fast, but I don't care. I can't stop. I know my lips are drawn back in a snarl, and my arm is a blur of motion. If anybody tried to stop me now, I would rip their throat out. I have to have this. Somewhere in the middle of this, I have taken off my boots and chaps so I can move more freely. This is what makes masochists dangerous. They get to see this part of me. They know how much I need to raven, rend, and ravage them. It gives them quite a hook to twist.

But this woman will not punish me for being a sadist. She never will. We may come to hate everything else about each other, but I really believe we will always honor this exchange, and be proud of ourselves for going this far with each other.

My boy is twisted on his side. His face is full of tears, his mouth stretched open in an O of disbelief. I go to my dresser, take a bandana out of the top drawer, tie a knot in it, then dunk the knot in the glass of water I keep by the bed. I shove the wet bundle into his mouth and tie the bandana behind his head. He shakes his head no, no, but right now it is my job to say yes, yes. "I thought you didn't want to scream," I snicker. "I'm just helping you to keep quiet. I don't want you to embarrass yourself. Besides, if you scream now, I'll have to stop, and you'll be so disappointed."

This is why he keeps coming back to me, because I know better than to quit when he thinks he's had enough. If I unchained his feet, knelt between his legs, and rode his ass right now, he'd come within minutes, but he'd be disappointed. This isn't about good sex. I'm not sure how to describe the place that lies beyond that. You have to use the body to get there, but it's a state that seems extraphysical.

I pick up the short quirt and move closer, wrap my arm around his hips so I put him back on his stomach, and hold him in place. Then I strap his butt without mercy, lacing into flesh that has already been cut by the cane. I do not spare the thighs. Only the back I ignore, because it doesn't have enough padding to withstand this assault. Besides, it doesn't have the same psychological impact, hitting somebody on their shoulders. They are used to carrying the burdens and tensions of their life there. It feels good to get some of that weight beaten off your back. But being struck across the buttocks makes someone feel younger and more frightened. It is more sexual. It is a breaking point.

It's hard to scream with a mouth full of wet cloth. I spare a look over my shoulder so I can relish the outraged expression that's common to all gagged faces. The cheeks are strained, the eyes are wide, the throat is tight. But I do not stop until my arm has gone dead and numb, and several strangled screams have died against the gag. They don't count.

So I take off the gag. My next-door neighbor is a pervert, and the apartment downstairs is vacant. I reach for the cane again. When he sees it, his body slumps. He knows I am going to win, but it has not yet occurred to him that this means he wins too. "Try not to cry out before the last stroke," I tell him. "Because there will be six of them, no matter how much noise you make." Despite my big talk, a tiny part of me is afraid he may be able to tough it out and keep still. So I aim for the sorest part of his butt, and I pile all six strokes on top of the same quarter-inch-wide ribbon of scored flesh. It bleeds as freely as he screams, for mercy and for joy.

I unchain his hands and feet and get myself a drink of water and a hit of my asthma inhaler. The straps of my harness are cutting into my ass. My pubic mound is sore from having the rubber base of the dildo pressed against it, and underneath my cock I am wet to my thighs. I offer him water, and he has a little, but doesn't really want to be bothered with it. His ass keeps coming off the bed. Some of this is a shock reaction to all the pain, but most of it is heat.

I understand that. We've waited long enough. "Jack off for your dad," I say, unchaining his hands. Both paws immediately slide under his belly and get busy. He doesn't even think about the tacit agreement he's just made. He has been hurt enough, and now he is hurting to come. Standing close to the bed, I slap his swollen and bloody ass. "You're gonna let me in here," I snarl. "Isn't that right? You're going to let your daddy fuck you."

He is licking my jacket, biting the collar. That alone is almost as good as sex. "Uh-huh," he says. "Uh-huh." He reaches for me, frees my cock from the elastic pouch of the jockstrap, wraps his fist around it, and swallows it whole. Nobody else has ever gotten my entire cock in their throat this fast. I swear I can see the shape of my shaft below his jawline, a swollen line along his trachea, the head of it wedged far past his soft palate. I can't help it, my hips jerk, and he has to cough up a little of my cock so he can breathe.

"I'm going to fuck your face," I say, and he grabs my butt and hangs on to it as hard as I hang on to the back of his head. I repeatedly tell him he is sucking his daddy's dick, and right now he can't argue with me. We move like the pieces of an engine, and I know it is not physically possible, but I come that way, come so hard I think I might tip over. Only his hands, clamped around my thighs, keep me on my feet. My cock comes out of his face, looking slippery and a little mauled.

"Did you get hurt enough?" I ask, climbing onto the bed.

"I don't know, I don't know anything anymore, just put it in, please sir, put it in."

I lube up my cock, rolling my fist up the crack of his ass. I love the dark fur that grows thick all over these long legs, the thighs, and lines the cleft I am about to pummel. With two fingers I press down on the head, angling it toward the sphincter's lower lip. There is a brief catch. I can't tell which one of us moans, as if in protest. Then— "Daddy, please!" he sobs, and all resistance dissolves. There's a smooth descent, and the heat from that opened asshole warms my belly, too. I am where I want to be, physically, emotionally, psychologically. This is home.

I have a looped choke chain in my left hand. It's got lube all over it now, but I don't think I'll stop and wipe it off. I throw the loop over his head. The long end is in my fist, and I yank. Instantly his entire rectum contracts, compressing me, just like I'm compressing his throat. I laugh, delighted to have this much control over something so important. Can I be trusted? Maybe. Probably. Maybe not.

My sadism has been fed, so now I feed his ass. I pack that butt, moving slow, lost in the ozone until some curses remind me that there's a person connected to that asshole. "Can I come now?" he screams, meaning, "Fuck me harder, you dipshit!"

"Tell me what I want to hear," I insist, panting so hard I am not sure he will be able to understand what I am saying.

"Let me come, please, Daddy!"

I change gears abruptly from a waltz to a slam-dance. The hand that isn't keeping the choke chain taut is clamped over his hipbone, and I'm using it to keep him from sliding off my cock in his frenzy to be penetrated. I feel myself coming seconds before I hear the harsh noises that mean my boy is losing it, and somehow make myself keep moving even though my thighs have turned to rubber. For a split second, I feel sorry for him. It's so hard to come when you can't really catch your breath. It makes the orgasm last longer, but in some ways you feel like you didn't really get to come.

Now the choke chain comes off her neck. I grease it up. I roll my boy onto his back. There's more. There has to be more. One fuck can't possibly use up all the energy we've generated. One link at a time, I push the chain up his ass, leaving the two large rings at either end of it dangling outside the sphincter. The chain is very smooth, but each link pinches a bit as it goes in. I remove my harness. My boy doesn't like being dick-fucked in the cunt. The leather straps are slimy and there's shit on the condom, but I don't want to bother with cleaning it up now. It goes somewhere, off the edge of the bed into never-never land with all the other discarded toys.

Finally, I touch her cunt. "I love to fuck the come out of you," I smile. "I love it when you can't help it, when you have to come." I separate the inner lips. There's so much juice, they are plastered together. Even the hair on her cunt is wringing wet, and has broken up into little curls. Her clit, always large, is rigid and outrageously big. The shaft and hood are two inches long, the glans the size of my little fingertip. "Can you take Daddy's fist? I have to be inside you now. I have to own you. Take you and use you. Fuck every single one

of your holes." This is classic dirty talk. I don't think I ever fuck
without saying this. But lust transforms cliches into poetry.

My hand slides in with very little trouble. I stroke the wall
between cunt and asshole. Links of chain move behind the thin mem-
brane. Every time I put my hand deeper into her or draw it out, I put
pressure on the heavy, metal mass in my boy's ass. I love fucking
someone on their back because I can see their face and watch their
nipples get hard. But he can't come this way, so eventually I have him
roll over, back on all fours.

"Fuck you from behind like a bitch in heat," I say. It's an old, reliable line, but it always works, like calling somebody a cocksucker. I
reach forward and pull on his nipples. "You get hard when I handle
your tits. You like being played with like a girl. Getting fucked like a
girl. Make your asshole my pussy, boy. Use every hole you've got.
Take your breath away and maybe I'll never give it back. Give it up,
now. Give me what I want or I swear I'll punch a hole in you."

Those long, slender hands are a blur over her clit. I feel contrac-
tions starting to flutter. It's time to draw out the chain. Link by link
it slides, each link making the asshole open and close and open and
close, and each link is another small orgasm, each small orgasm
becoming a slightly bigger orgasm, until somebody is shouting my
name, telling me I am a bastard, he loves me, he is my boy, his cunt
belongs to Daddy, and I know I'm going to have a bruised wrist in
the morning.

Except that it's morning already. One more day out of the precious few we have is gone. I can't help but ask myself if I've done
enough, if I've used each hour as completely as possible. I don't know
when I'll get to do this again.

I stagger into the bathroom and wash my hands, find the bottle
of rubbing alcohol and a handful of cotton balls. I go back into the
bedroom. She's curled up on one side, breathing lightly. Her face
looks peaceful. She stirs a little when I clean off her right shoulder.

The rubbing alcohol is cold, and its strong smell makes me feel a little sick to my stomach.

There's a number-fifteen scalpel by the bed. I peel it out of its sterile wrapper and snap the plastic backing off the blade. Slowly, carefully, biting my lip, I cut the runes into her shoulder that say, *We are of one blood, you and I, outlaws together, one folk with the same dream.*

Then I lick the blood from her shoulder, rub it on my face, smear it into my hair. It's not safe sex, but nobody lives forever, and I can't stand to deprive myself of this iron taste, her heart's fuel.

Like the stone butches who used to scare me so much when I was seventeen, I don't want to be touched right now. I came while I was making her come, and all I want is to be a peaceful witness to her satisfaction, a guardian of her slumbering body. We sleep tangled up, disowned children, and we do not dream our parents' dreams.

What Girls Are
Made Of

Bo (née Barbara, known as the Yeti in high school because of her
fondness for snow) had just shuttled her last set of papers from one
office to another. Not a moment too soon. Downtown traffic was
about to change from hellish to terminal. Instead of putting thousands of people who hated their jobs and hated each other in cages
and letting them race each other home, Bo thought they should just
give them loaded guns and let them duel it out at twenty paces. It sure
would thin out the freeway. It had been a very busy day, even for a
Friday. Every piece of paper she had delivered was an emergency,
although how anything that wasn't bleeding could constitute a crisis
was beyond her. The clerks and receptionists she'd dealt with today
weren't getting enough fiber in their diets. Cops were giving away
parking tickets like they got to put the fines in their own pockets.
And every taxi in the financial district seemed determined to eat a
motorcycle for lunch.

Before she went home to her microwave and a freezer full of
Stouffer's frozen entrées, Bo decided to detour through the Tender-
loin and visit one of the porn shops. She had a hot date this weekend.
Maybe she would buy a dick. The thought of putting it to somebody
else made her feel a little taller, a little meaner. Yeah. That was a

really good idea. Just walk into the porno shop and buy a dick, like it
was something she did every day. They were just lying there behind
glass, in a counter next to the cashier. A dozen of 'em, like big, pink,
deformed rubber hot dogs. The clerk didn't give a shit. Who cared
what he thought, anyway? Who cared what some jerk thought who
worked in a dirty bookstore? It would be easy, Bo told herself, and
backed her bike into the curb, between two cars that were far enough
apart to leave room for her soft-tail.

"What are you looking at?" she snarled at a lanky old wino who
had accidentally pointed his face in her direction. He blinked at her
but couldn't quite get her in focus. He mumbled, "Spare change?"
because that was about all he said to people anymore, other than,
"Gimme a pint of Thunderbird."

"I haven't got any," Bo said. "How about a cigarette?"

"Sure," he said, putting out a hand that shook so bad, Bo didn't
see how he ferried liquor from a brown-bagged bottle to his lips. She
took two cigarettes out of her pack, put one in his stiff shirt pocket,
lit the other one, and waited while he found it.

Now he could see her just fine. She was five-foot-six and well fed.
Her light brown hair was cut like a Marine's. But Uncle Sam would
never have put up with that ring in her nose. "Did that hurt?" he asked.

"No pain, no gain," Bo said, and backed away from the conversation and his bouquet.

"Be good," he admonished her, and let the building prop him up
again. The wall was freshly painted, which in this neighborhood
meant only one thing: it housed an adult bookstore. Bo glanced up at
the sign. The letters hanging on the marquee's wires spelled out
XXX SUGAR AND SPICE XXX. She pushed the heavy glass door
and went in, already wincing at the thought of her boots sticking to
the floor.

The shop was in the front. You had to walk past racks of hard-
core magazines in shrink-wrap covers and cases full of Hong Kong's

finest marital aids to get into the rest of the place, which featured REAL! LIVE! SEX! ACT! GIRLS! A big guy who looked like he might have been a biker before he lost one hand was there selling tokens, one for a dollar. Sometimes groups of women came through on "feminist tours of the red-light district." He always told them, "Ya can't go back there without an escort." Sometimes one of the customers would offer (with a leer) to provide that service. Bo wondered if he would tell her that. She imagined herself saying, "This is my escort," and whipping out a switchblade. That would make them all step back. She stuck one hand in her jacket pocket to make sure her Swiss Army knife was still there.

She loitered by the glass case full of dildos. It reminded her of a cage at the zoo. "See the wild, endangered, artificial phalli," the sign by the exhibit might read. They looked like dismembered organs in the fluorescent light. The bored clerk flicked a glance at her, said, "Back again?" in a bored tone of voice, and went back to his racing form. Bo blushed as red as the hanky in her back pocket. *Oh my God, he recognized me!* How could she possibly figure out what she wanted with this homophobic jerk cruising her? Well, he wasn't getting any money out of her today.

She turned away and walked toward the magazines. She touched some of the covers with the tips of her fingers, but what was the point in picking any of them up? You couldn't turn the pages and see what was in them. A small group of guys, including one man in a wheelchair and two men who were at least as old as her grandpa, were studying the racks anyway. One of them looked up, saw her, and edged away. *All I get from these straight assholes is constant harassment,* Bo thought bitterly, and headed for the bouncer guarding the turnstile. Just let him try to keep her out of the back. He'd find out pretty soon that he'd picked on the wrong kind of woman.

"Getcha tokens here," he said. "Hey, guy, how you doin'? Wanna spend some money on the foxy ladies? We got a red-hot trio today.

One blonde, one brunette, and a real exotic little Asian fox. You friends with summa the dancers?"

Bo had counted on being stopped. This geek obviously thought she was a man. She didn't know what to do. If she corrected him, he might throw her out, and that would be humiliating. She glared at him, daring him to hassle her.

"Getcha tokens here," he said, talking over her shoulder, addressing the entire room. "If you wanna see the show or watch a movie, you gotta getcha tokens here," he told her confidentially.

Bo felt as if everyone in the bookstore was waiting to see what she would do. She decided to just act casual, like this was something she did every day. She gave him a twenty. He wasn't impressed. "Getcha money's worth," he said, sliding four stacks of five tokens toward her, and motioned her through the turnstile. Looking at her back, he thought ruefully, *Why do all the cute ones have to be dykes?*

This part of the store was much darker. Bo was afraid to stop moving for fear she wouldn't be able to get herself going again. Why weren't her eyes getting used to the dark? She was going to bump into some guy, maybe some jerk who already had his dick out. Then she remembered she had her Ray Bans on and slipped them into the pocket of her overlay. The light was still dim, but she could see well enough now to know that she was in a maze of little booths with plywood walls. Most of the doors stood open. There were pictures on each door that looked like the photos on video boxes.

The temptation to cop a few minutes of privacy was too much. She went into one of the cubicles and shut the door. There was a machine on one wall of the booth. She stuck a token in it just to see what would happen. It made a sound like a coffee grinder, and then a square of color appeared on the opposite wall. A surprisingly attractive young woman was down on her knees, licking a surprisingly homely man's cock. The picture quality wasn't very good, but Bo could see enough to tell that he wasn't getting it up. Nevertheless, the sight of real people having actual sex right there in front of her was oddly arousing.

Then she noticed something moving around at the bottom of the screen that didn't seem to belong in the movie. Was that a couple of fingers, poking through a hole in the flimsy wall? "Hey, dude, put it through! Best suck job in town!" somebody whispered.

The guy on the screen was hard now, and the woman who was blowing him had wrapped her hand around the base of his dick to keep it from going all the way into her face. Bo wanted to kill him, but she also wanted to wrap her hands around that bitch's neck and shove her head—where? Meanwhile, there were those beckoning fingers, the brave and weird offer to give a stranger pleasure. She should probably break his fucking hand, but it wasn't like he knew who was in here.

"Uh—I'm resting," she said, pitching her voice as deep as possible.

"Maybe later," the voice said. The fingers slid out of sight faster than a vanilla dyke who had just found poopoo in her girlfriend's anxious rosebud.

Bo thought she'd better get out of there before he saw her. As she rattled the door, she became very aware of her cunt. It was pressing into the seam of her jeans like a cat that leans on your leg to let you know it's breakfast time. *Why,* she wondered, *is there no word in English to describe this? I can't exactly say I've got a hard-on, but I bet this is sort of like what it feels like to have your dick get hard. I don't know if I want somebody to suck on my clit or fuck me, but I sure don't feel passive or receptive. It's an aggressive kind of feeling, demanding, and it's not all in my head either. It's very physical.*

This was turning into quite a trip. Maybe she should have gone to the feminist vibrator shop and purchased a leaping purple silicone dolphin. Or a pink ear of vibrating corn. Or told her trick she'd have to bring her own damn treats! Bo staggered out of the peep show section and headed for the next attraction—a round, slightly elevated, glass-enclosed stage that was surrounded by more little booths, like one of those lazy-susan Plexiglas spice racks that yuppies bought at Macy's Cellar.

The public-address system burped (a sound that momentarily returned Bo to high school), and an unctuous female voice said, "Gentlemen, fill your pockets full of *tokens*. The performance starts *in five minutes*. Three of the hottest, *wettest,* sexiest girls on *earth* are about to *shake it* just for you. These ladies are uninhibited, they're *bad,* they're ready to cut *loose*. They also take *requests*. So *buy* those tokens *now!*"

Men started coming out of the peep shows and clustering around the bouncer. He made change really fast for a one-handed guy. Somebody tried to sneak under his arm and pilfer a token. The bouncer lifted him with one arm and shook him until his teeth rattled. "Don't do that. It upsets me," the big man said mildly, and handed over tokens for the five-dollar bill he was offered in lieu of an apology.

The P.A. system crackled again, and the female voice repeated exactly the same announcement, putting identical emphasis on the words "tokens," "five minutes," "wettest," "earth," "shake it," "bad," "loose," "requests," "buy," and "now." Bo shook her head. "Sucker born every minute," she said ruefully and headed for the nearest booth.

Backstage was a mess. Three dancers were supposed to get ready in a space that was only slightly bigger than a walk-in closet. There was only one chair and a small mirror that was losing its silver backing. The floor was cluttered with gym bags, carryalls, and discarded street clothes.

"My mascara came open in my lingerie!" Crash (née Lisa) wailed. Her blonde hair was only half teased-out, so she looked like a "before" ad for a PMS remedy. "Where's my hair spray?" She dug through her dancer's bag, throwing shoes, press-on nails, lace gloves, and anything else she needed over her shoulder.

"So wear black, Crash. Nobody will notice," Killer (née Brenda) said, rubbing lip gloss into her cheeks. She was already wearing a leather miniskirt and studded leather bra, but she hadn't finished zipping up her thigh-high boots. An asymmetrical, purple-streaked, black ponytail sprouted from one side of her mostly shaved head. "I have to make a lot of money today. The fucking manager's been harassing me about my eyebrow again. I think I'll get the other one pierced tomorrow. *And* my nipples. *And* my cheeks. *And* the spaces in between my fingers and toes!" She kicked the can of hair spray over to Crash.

"Toilet's stuffed up again," Poison (née Candy) announced, squeezing into the room. She wore only a gold G-string. The metallic fabric nearly blended into her old-ivory skin. She was shorter than the other dancers, but her body was solid from hours of dancing lessons and soccer. Her long, black hair had one eccentric platinum-blonde stripe. "Where is that boy, anyway? She's supposed to take care of this shit for us."

"Literally," Killer snickered, painting big Egyptian eyes around her own. She snapped on her favorite wristbands. Their large pyramid studs matched the ones on her bra. Then she reached for the high pit-bull collar that completed her outfit. "Come on, Poison, get dressed. We go on in five minutes."

"I'm really sick of Bad Dog's lame excuses," Crash said, shimmying into a cherry red merry widow without bothering to unhook the back. She'd left the stockings attached to the garters and crammed her feet into them like they were an old pair of jeans. Miraculously, they did not run. Poison lined up her scarlet patent pumps so Crash could step into them. "Are you trying to tell us you feel like being the victim today?" She grabbed a comb, elbowed Killer out of the way, and started flipping her hair back into a lacquered bouffant.

"Sure, I'll do it. Just don't get too rough. I wish they'd at least put a piece of carpet down on that stage. It's a hard place to fall."

Killer stood and zipped up her boots. "There are no easy places to fall," she said. "Where the fuck is your costume? I am not going to get docked again just because you like to wander around forever in your underwear."

"I don't have to dress up. I'm a China doll, a submissive geisha, every sailor's fantasy. It drives the white boys crazy." Poison sang, "Such a gentle way about you, Singapore girl." Killer shot her a nasty look. "I'm just going to wear my kimono," Poison said hastily, taking it off a hanger that dangled from a nail in the cracked, industrial green plaster wall. Hints of gold embroidery still glittered against the old, white silk. "Don't worry, Killer, I have a lot of toys in my pockets to keep the customers satisfied." She untangled her obi, printed with a green chrysanthemum pattern, from the mess on the floor, wrapped it around her waist, and then fished out her gold stiletto heels.

A knock on the dressing-room door shook the cubicle. "Ladies," the manager said, and came in before anybody gave her permission. Her name was Carole, but everybody just called her "the manager." She was a former dancer who always noticed when they were late and often failed to notify them that their time onstage was up. She was always pressuring them to do without a lunch break or work overtime on lame shifts. The dancers hated her even though she didn't demand sexual services like the men they'd worked for. "Where's your charming assistant?" she asked snidely.

"Flaked," Killer said briefly.

"Tell me about it later. You're on."

She closed the door, and Crash sent her a gesture that has been getting people killed in Sicily for hundreds of years. The three dancers filed into the hallway and opened the stage door. "We need some music!" Killer shouted, and their tape came on. Crash had made it. She called it "my tribute to popular culture's fascination with vicious bitches." The first song was the Waitresses, singing, "I know what boys like." The manager hated it.

They distributed themselves around the perimeter of the stage, dividing up the customers. If somebody started tipping, all of them clustered there, unless the customer indicated a preference for just one of them. The stage was about three feet higher than the floor, which put the customers' faces at a level with the dancers' knees. Sliding windows went up and down between the booth and the stage, and the men had to keep feeding tokens into a machine to keep the window up. There was also a little hole in the Plexiglas, to make it possible for folding money to get shoved through. Dancers got paid minimum wage because tipping was allowed. They put on two twenty-minute shows every hour, for eight hours, and on a really good night, they might each make $500. Usually, they made just enough money to make dancing seem a lot more attractive than being a secretary. They were supposed to receive a percentage of the token sales, but they all knew the manager shorted them.

The three of them had been working here for three months, three days a week. Nobody danced full-time. Theater owners were not about to dip into their profit margin for health insurance or other benefits. They had finally managed to get "promoted" to a weekend evening shift, when you made decent money, so they were probably about to get fired. Managers did that routinely to make room for new bodies and faces onstage. But they always found nasty, personal excuses—"You're late, you're on drugs, you can't dance, the customers don't like you, your tits sag, you're too fat." Smart dancers moved on to another theater before that happened, but nobody looked forward to working up another act or performing with strangers. Some of the straight dancers were uptight about dykes, and transsexuals were so competitive. It was unusual for three friends to get work together. The specter of dancers cooperating with or protecting one another made managers nervous.

You could make more money as a street hooker, but that was a lot more dangerous. There was no customer contact here. A girl on one of the other shifts had been followed to her car after work and raped, but that could happen to anybody. One of the adult theaters a few blocks away featured lap dancing, and the money was supposed to be fabulous, but it sounded like a very difficult job. How many different ways could you say, "Give me some more money or I'll go away" and make it sound flirtatious?

Killer had tried working as a dominatrix, but it was boring. "All I did was sit on my ass all day and wait for the phone to ring," she complained. "The other mistresses thought I was really strange, and most of the clients hated punks. It's so bogus. All the domination ads say, 'No sex,' right? But they all gave handjobs. I made the mistake of talking about it, and after that, the tacky comments about whores just kept coming. One day I had a slave down on the floor jacking off, and he came all over my shoe. I snapped. I took off my other shoe and went after him. I got him good a couple of times, too, before the woman who owned the place threw me out."

Today all the booths were busy. It was a Friday afternoon, and the working man was ready for some fun. Each of the girls danced, trading places onstage, for one more song. Poison had shed her kimono already, after taking some tit clamps and a small, battery-operated vibrator out of its pocket. Crash took some money from a guy who wanted to see her ass, turned around, took down her panties, and waved it in his face. He showed her a $50 bill and said, "Give me those hot little panties, honey." So she inched them down, bent over to take the $50 in her teeth, and pushed the scrap of red satin through the hole. *Baby gets new shoes tonight,* she thought.

Poison somehow managed to keep gyrating on her high heels while she worked the vibrator in and out of her pussy. Her other hand was busy yanking on the tit clamps. She didn't have a free hand to take tips. Crash danced over to her, started playing with her nipples, and used her free hand to collect the cash. "Honey, don't do that," one of the men said. "Don't hurt yourself like that."

"Fuck you," Poison said, sticking her tongue out at him. "This is the only part of this show that I like, asshole." He let his window come down and stay down.

"You just broke that piggy bank," Crash said, yanking on Poison's chain. "At this rate, you're never going to finish law school."

"Hey!" Killer said, tossing her head so her black-and-purple ponytail whipped through the air, "you're supposed to be *my* girl-friend!"

Poison snickered. You had to hand it to Killer, she always came up with an excuse for a little girl-wrestling onstage, and the boys loved it. "So what?" she yelled. "I want her to fuck me, and you can't stop us!" She did a little end-zone, in-your-face dance while Crash took over manipulation of the vibrator. Then she grabbed Crash and tried to smooch her.

"Get your hands out of my beehive," Crash said irritably, smooching her back. "It'll look like shit if it comes down over my face."

Killer stormed over to them, looking genuinely pissed off. The bright lights above the booth made it a hot box to work in. Crash and Poison could see the perspiration on her shoulders and breasts, above the leather bra. She pretended to slap Poison, who did a neat stage-dive onto the floor. While the customers shoved tokens into the machines like they were cops eating donuts, the blonde in her red corset and the brunette in her leather skirt struggled onstage, with Killer finally gaining the upper hand and administering a not-so-fake spanking.

"I'm sorry, I'm sorry!" Crash wailed, trying to protect her bee-hive. Poison floor-danced around the perimeter, running her obi back and forth between her legs and pretending to whip herself with it, picking up money, making sexy ooh-baby faces at the customers and feigning masturbation for the ones who gave her something bigger than a single. "Don't be so mad at me, lover girl," Crash said to Killer when she got tired of having her hair pulled. "We can both have her!"

Poison couldn't stop giggling as her two friends picked her up and tossed her back and forth between them. Even with an audience, it was a good time. "You don't scare me," she told Killer. Then it was Crash's turn to collect tolls as Killer "forced" Poison to her knees, slowly removed her studded leather bra and skirt, and "made" Poison go down on her.

Normally Crash didn't check out the booths too much. All she saw were hands and green paper. But one member of the audience had pissed her off. The window on his booth had been open since they came onstage, and he hadn't tipped once. So she stomped over to that cubicle and glared at its occupant. "What do you think this is, Catholic Charities?" she snapped. Then she saw the tits. "Hey, there's a girl over here!" she yelled. The click of spike heels told her that Killer and Poison were on their way.

There was just enough room in the booth to stand up and whack off. Bo wondered why there was a machine on one wall. Who wanted to watch movies if there was a live show? Then the three space tramps came onstage, and she thought she would die. They looked like the beautiful, come-fuck-me straight girls that she didn't dare talk to in the clubs. Because the stage was higher than the floor, she could look right up their dresses. But their shoes were even more intriguing than their pussies. Bo loved high-heeled shoes. The tall, thin spikes looked like they should punch holes in the floor. How could anybody do all those turns and kicks in them? Her heart was in her mouth, for fear one of the dancers would slip or fall. But they kept their balance. It was magic.

The first time her window came down, it scared her so bad she almost peed. What was she supposed to do, leave the booth and let somebody else have it? She opened the door a crack, but nobody else was exiting. "Are you going?" asked a hopeful onlooker who'd been too slow to get a booth.

"Well, I don't want to, but I can't see anything."

He gave her a strange look. Bo braced herself for a homophobic comment. But all he said was, "You gotta put a token in to make the window come up."

Feeling like a complete idiot, Bo muttered, "Oh. Thanks," and closed the door. It was warped, so she yanked it into place. With the window down, it was really dark in there. She had to feel for the token slot. When the window came up, it revealed something even more wonderful than solitary dancers. They were tussling with each other! She got out another token and held it over the slot, ready to drop it in the minute her view was threatened. The leather girl with the black ponytail sure had a hard hand. But her friend in the red corset seemed to like it. A lot of girls had hinted around about kinky stuff like that with Bo—like the one who was coming over on Saturday night. It made Bo happy to know she was projecting the right kind of tough image. But when it came down to actually tying somebody up or getting rough with them, somehow the timing was never quite right. Either they wanted it too much, or she wasn't sure they really wanted it after all. Too much pressure or something. Besides, she didn't *really* want to hurt anybody. Did she?

Meanwhile, all the hair-pulling and slapping onstage was making Bo's stomach feel funny. It was awfully hot in there. She reached for her right pocket to get her bandana, realized she was keeping it in the other pocket this week, fished it out, and wiped her face. She shouldn't let herself get conned like this. It was just an act, breeder chicks faking lesbian sex, but she pulled her T-shirt up anyway and pinched her own tits. Hard.

The window began to descend, and she dropped a token. As it came up, Bo's zipper went down. She had to work her jeans down over her hips to get her fingers in between her lips. She had a moment of panic, imagining cops barging in, but even the threat of being caught here with her pants down around her ankles made her cunt wetter and plumper. If she put one finger on her clit, it would take a little longer to come, but that would leave one hand free to work her tits. If only she knew why they'd put a glory hole in the Plexiglas. What was it for, kissing the dancers? Gross!

She was so close to coming. Of course, that little Asian girl wasn't really eating out the cat lady, but Bo knew what it would feel like. She knew what it would taste like. To be that helpless—to have all these people watching—

Her vision was blocked again, but not by the window. An angry blonde in red lingerie was plastered against the Plexiglas, looking like she might use her long red nails to claw right through it. "There's a girl in here!" she cried. Bo's arousal was swept away by a flood of shame and fear.

"Hey, what about us?" one of the guys yelled as the other dancers converged on Bo's window. *I have to get out of here,* she thought, dragging at her clothes. She pushed on the door, but it was stuck.

"Leaving so soon?" the brunette crooned. She had taken off everything except her boots, wristbands, and collar. "We were going to put on a special performance just for you. We don't see other dykes in here very often."

"Don't bother, I was just leaving!" Bo panted, wrestling with the door.

"Chicken," said the Asian girl, who was wearing only her gold spike heels.

"Enjoying the show?" the blonde jeered, rotating her hips. She had taken her breasts out of the cups of her merry widow. Bo couldn't stop staring at her bush. All this blatant female nudity and aggressive attitude were making her sweat.

"No," Bo lied, trying to sound defiant. "I'm not enjoying the show."

That offended all of them. "But we're working so hard," the blonde pouted. "Is there something special you'd like to see? Want me to stick that vibrator through the hole so you can lick it?"

"This is sick," Bo blustered. "How can you stand to do this? It's degrading, letting a bunch of men jack off while you squirm and wiggle around."

"Ooh, Crash, degrade me some more!" the Asian girl crooned. They started French-kissing, hands between each other's legs. The sight completely exasperated Bo.

"Cut it out! That's disgusting. You can't fool me. You're just a bunch of mercenary straight bitches. You don't know anything about making love to a woman."

The door shrieked as Killer forced it open. "Is that so?" she hissed, dragging Bo out by her belt. One minute, Bo was staring at the pissed-off vixen's pierced eyebrow, and the next minute she was on the floor, staring at her boot heels. Then her hands were being cuffed behind her back, and she was up on her feet again. The rapid changes in altitude made Bo dizzy. This girl ate her spinach.

The bouncer left his post by the turnstile. "Have we got a problem here, Killer?" he asked, eyeing Bo.

"Not anymore," Killer told him. "We just got a new whipping boy. Maybe this one will be a good dog instead of a bad dog. Are you a good dog, honey?" She punched Bo's upper arm. "Huh? Answer me!"

"Well, you'd better get her in back before the manager sees her," he said. "She just went out to get a prescription filled, and she'll be back any minute."

A buzzer sounded, signifying the end of the act. Bo thought about putting up a fight. But where was she going to go in these damned handcuffs? Killer shoved, and Bo went. Men were coming out of the stage booths, and most of them had hurt feelings. A few of them looked like they might complain, but Killer said clearly, "The first one of you bozos to whine at me is eighty-sixed. The show's over."

"You could do that to me," one of them said wistfully, ogling Bo's handcuffs.

"You'd like it too much," Killer said scornfully. Bo couldn't believe her ears. This girl was *naked*. How could she talk to a room full of men like that when they could see everything she had? Wasn't she afraid of anything?

Killer hustled Bo into the dressing room and tumbled her onto the floor. Bo's face was buried in a pile of nylon, spandex, lace, PVC, satin, and suede unmentionables. Something—probably a pair of high heels someone had left on the floor—dug into her stomach. The tiny room smelled like perfume, makeup, hair spray, girl sweat, and pussy. Bo thought she might suffocate. She much preferred the smell of motor oil and bourbon. All these filmy, stretchy, whispery, see-through, tight, gauzy, wispy, shiny, femmy things undid her. Clothing should be durable, comfortable, sturdy, and protect you from the elements. How did they get in and out of these rags? Where did they find the moxie to walk around half-naked? How could they trust garments that were held together with itsy-bitsy hooks and eyes or skinny pieces of elastic?

Then Killer kicked her lightly in the ribs. "Look at me, home boy."

"I am not your fucking home boy," Bo said hotly. But she refused to roll over.

"You're right," somebody else said, "but it's not very smart to argue with Killer. Hey, get off my torts textbook! Do you know how much that damn book cost me?"

The next kick was not so gentle. Bo gave up and rolled onto her side, just far enough to see all of them. God, they gave off a ferocious aura, like the three witches in *Macbeth*. "Take off these cuffs," she said, without much hope that they would.

Everybody laughed. Bo did not enjoy being their punch line. "You know my name," Killer said. "This is Poison, and the B-52 girl is Crash."

Bo refused to play along. She wasn't telling them anything.

"I guess we'll just have to call you shit head," Poison said.

"Or pig boy," Crash added.

"Or dead meat," Killer concluded.

Such lovely options. "Bo," the butch on the floor muttered. "My name is Bo."

"That must be Bo as in 'Boy, am I stupid,'" Crash said thoughtfully. "Don't you think it's rude to call a girl a tramp when she's only trying to show you a good time, baby boy?"

Killer snorted. "Baby boy is right. What are you, lover, all of seventeen?"

"I'm twenty-two," Bo snarled. "And you look old enough to be my mother."

"That's one," Killer said softly. "We'll just run a tab for you, shall we? Poison, what's she got on her?"

Poison knelt and rummaged through Bo's pockets. The Swiss Army knife drew gales of hilarity. "I'll take custody of this," Poison said, shaking it under Bo's nose. "This little toad-sticker won't protect you from us, sugar."

"Give me back my knife!" Bo shouted.

"Shut the fuck up!" Crash snarled, looking nervously over her shoulder. "The walls have ears."

Killer leaned down and spoke to Bo. Her lips were an inch from Bo's nose. "Don't be dumb, my little lamb. None of us happens to like your little toy, so when we're done with you, if you're a good boy, you'll get it all back. *Capeche?*"

"Look, this is getting completely out of hand," Bo said. "If you let me go *right now,* I won't call the cops. Okay?"

"Woojums," Crash said tenderly. "If you do absolutely every little thing we say, *we* won't call the cops and report you for breaking and entering. Okay?"

Bo muttered something under her breath.

"Was that an epithet?" Poison asked, her eyes wide. "I believe it was a sexist epithet, Killer." She took one step closer to Bo and slapped her across the face. The stinging blow brought tears to Bo's eyes. "This is a very small place. We simply don't have room for inflammatory hate rhetoric in here."

"I don't know about you girls, but dancing always makes me horny," Killer said, giving Bo a very unmotherly smile.

"Oh, yes, I feel almost compelled to have an orgasm," Crash affirmed. Poison didn't say anything, so Crash nudged her.

"Ouch! Definitely."

"So let's just fix our little boy toy up here so she has some back support," Killer said, and backed Bo into the corner. "No escape attempts," she warned her, and showed her the handcuff key. "Crash has got a gun in her purse. Don't you, dear?"

Crash obediently stuck her hand in her purse and pointed it at Bo. "Yeah. Don't move, sucker."

"Oh, bullshit, she does not have a—" Suddenly Bo was looking down the muzzle of a Beretta.

"It's licensed, too," Crash explained. "I used to be a security guard. If I ever get off the waiting list, I'm going to be one of the city's finest. Think I'll look good in blue?"

Killer took advantage of Bo's surprise to remove one of the cuffs and lock it around a water pipe. "Don't do any Samson imitations," she warned Bo. "It's a hot-water pipe. All you'll do is scald yourself. Now suck me off. And make it snappy. I have to be back onstage in five minutes."

They stared at each other for several long seconds—the triumphant bitch goddesses and their flustered, hijacked tourist. "Maybe she doesn't know how to eat cunt," Poison said helpfully. "Maybe she's one of those awful straight girls who gets a short haircut and hangs out in lesbian bars pretending she belongs there."

"Well?" Killer said impatiently. "What about it? Do you know what to do with a piece of cherry pie, stud, or is your tongue just for making rude comments to your betters?"

They were not going to let her go. It was no use fighting them. Whoever would have thought that girls in lipstick and pushup bras could be so mean? "No," Bo said finally, looking at the floor. "I'll do it."

It was hard to get her tongue all the way into Killer's silky inner lips. Handcuffed to the water pipe, she couldn't get her neck to bend at the right angle. But she did her best, and Killer's flexible dancer's hips and slender legs made it easier. Out of the corner of her eye, she noticed the other women changing clothes and refreshing their makeup. Geez, if Bo was going to humiliate herself this way, the least they could do was watch.

"You're good," Killer said, tugging one of her ears. "Do it faster. Not harder, idiot—just faster!"

Killer's inner lips were thin and long, like the two halves of a razorback clam. Her teardrop-shaped clit was very small, like a seed pearl. She seemed to like having Bo's tongue go around it without actually touching it. The thought of biting her was very tempting, but then she'd probably stay handcuffed to this pipe until she starved to death.

"Oh, yes, that's it. Do that!" Killer said, squeezing Bo's head. There was a knock on the dressing room door. One of the other girls told somebody they'd be right out. Killer came silently, biting her own hand. Bo was shaken by the sexual electricity that passed through her own body when Killer peaked. She barely noticed the dancers filing out and shutting the door behind them. They had left one of her hands free. It was the wrong hand, but nothing else was in sight. Wait—there was Poison's vibrator. She'd left it on the floor. Bo had to strain to reach it with her boot toes, but she managed to nudge it within reach.

There was no way she could come sitting down with her pants on. Bo somehow managed to pry her boots off, undo the jeans with one hand, and wiggle out of them. Lucky she didn't believe in underwear.

She closed her eyes and tried to remember the exact shape of Killer's clit, the way her palms fit over Bo's ears, the other girls breathing faster as Killer got more excited, how she couldn't escape, couldn't get away, and had no idea what would happen next.

The awkward fingers of her left hand kept rebelling and cramping up. Frustrated, Bo switched the vibrator on and held it against her outer lips. She was embarrassed to even touch the thing. She had seen them in porn shops often enough, in boxes that always had these dopey pictures of women running them over their faces. It felt good, but it kept getting caught in her pubic hair. She tried to point it at her clit, but she was so wet that the head of it somehow slipped down and went into her. It seemed content to stay there, purring away, while Bo stroked her clit.

It just wasn't enough. She needed more, something, anything, to push herself over the edge! She stared around the room, wild-eyed. Right by her left thigh was another love offering from Poison, the discarded pair of tit clamps. Bo could sometimes make herself come just by twisting her own nipples. It was hard to get them on one-handed. Her nipples kept wanting to slip out of the clips. But finally she got both sides to catch.

Oh, God, she was going to come. It was inevitable. Even if the building blew up or her hands fell off, so much pressure had accumulated, Bo knew she would explode. She didn't have Killer's self-control. She heard herself whining, panting, and then saying, "Please, please."

The door opened and Killer walked in. "Yes, you may," Killer said, and jammed her high-heeled shoe between Bo's legs, pinning her hand and the vibrator in place. Bo came with the sharp heel of the dancer's shoe against her perineum. "Come again," Killer said, and jerked on the chain that connected the clamps. She also rocked her heel into Bo's tender flesh. And Bo came again, in terror and shock. "Still want to call the cops?" Killer asked. "No, I didn't think so. Stick around. Pets always get smarter when you play with them."

"Good boy," Crash said, replacing Killer in front of Bo. "Now it's my turn to ride the pony."

Bo guessed it was kind of stupid, but she'd never really noticed before that women liked to come in so many different ways. Crash had coarse pubic hair that made her face burn. Instead of Killer's elegant Art Deco genital geometry, her cunt was built like a '50s diner. It was robust, with shorter, thicker inner lips. The head of her clit was perfectly round and the size of a pencil eraser. She didn't get wet as quickly as Killer. She wanted a lot of long, slow, light strokes with a teasing little flutter at the end. Nobody told Bo that she couldn't, so she kept masturbating while she tried to get Crash to come. For some reason, she kept thinking about the short porn clip she'd seen in the video booth. Was this exactly like that woman sucking cock, or was it completely different? Probably both, Bo decided, though she couldn't have explained why. She was too busy jamming her face into Crash's thighs, sucking her clit like it was a straw buried in a milkshake. The dancer had finally gotten really juicy, and Bo was afraid she'd have to go back onstage before she got off. Finally Crash started pulling her hair—quite a trick, since Bo's flattop was less than an inch long—and tilted her pelvis so Bo's tongue was moving in and out of her cunt. "Yesyesyes," she sang. "Good dog, good dog, good dog," and finally, "Sweet Jesus, yes, good boy!"

Bo felt quite pleased with herself. She leaned against the wall panting. But Crash was looking at her through narrow eyelids. Had she done something wrong? "I always have to tinkle after I come," Crash said delicately, and placed two fingers of her right hand on either side of her clit. The V-shaped fingers lifted her lips a little, and a golden arc of piss sprang through the air.

"Hey, don't pee on my clothes!" Poison snapped.

"Don't worry, I never miss," Crash said sweetly as the last few drops soaked into Bo's T-shirt. "Don't forget us while we're far from home," she smirked, and the dancers left to put on one more show.

"Here," Poison said before she walked out, and dropped a long, thick dildo in Bo's lap. "That teeny thing is only good for fooling around in front of the customers. A big, strong girl like you needs a substantial tool to fuck herself with. There's some lube in my dance bag—the pink one—if you need it."

Bo covered her face with her one free hand. How had she gotten into so much trouble? And why was she having so much fun? Poison was right, she probably didn't need any lube to get that truncheon in her cunt, but it was too embarrassing to go without it. So she wrapped her toes around the straps of Poison's hot pink carryall and dragged it over.

"Who says size doesn't matter?" Bo growled, and worked the head of the dildo in. It was wide enough to make her gasp. The wet T-shirt was going to give her a chill if she didn't keep moving. It sure was funny how things didn't feel the way they looked. Getting slapped looked like the worst thing in the world, but it was actually pretty exciting. It stung a lot, but it made her heart beat faster and her PC muscle jump. The thought of getting pissed on would have made her gag this morning, but now all she could smell was Crash's cunt and her own sex. The wet shirt was like a badge or a medal. She had something that belonged to Crash now. The dancer had given Bo a part of her. You couldn't just abandon somebody you'd pissed on, could you?

She jabbed the dildo in, remembering how it felt to have Killer kick her between the legs. The spike heel was like the point of a knife. It was cruel and relentless, like . . . like a woman, Bo realized. Cruelty was a feminine quality. The dancers' willful ways suddenly made sense. Of course they were bossy and nasty and liked to hurt people. Femmes always wanted to be in control. But you weren't supposed to notice it. No, that was one way to get yourself into shit up to your nose hairs. You were supposed to do everything they wanted, before they asked you, and make them think it was all your own idea. Nothing was ever their fault, it was always *your* fault because you were the butch and it was your job to make sure everything went smoothly.

Bo thought she preferred this up-front sexual assault to that silly game. The dildo hurt a little. The hurt made her want to come. But maybe she shouldn't come. Killer seemed to take it for granted that she would wait until she had permission. Maybe she was supposed to wait. Maybe if she waited, it would make Killer happy.

As soon as Bo thought about resisting orgasm, it became much more likely. Of course, she could just quit touching herself, but it was so boring being stuck here with nothing but a broken chair and a cracked mirror for company. She strained her ears, trying to see if the last song in the dancer's set was playing yet.

It was hard to wait. Hard to wait. Hard. Hard. So hard. So big. So—

"You *are* a pig," Killer said, amused. "Look at you, jacking off all covered with piss, just waiting for somebody to come and use you or hurt you or tell you what to do. Aren't you lucky that we bother to take an interest in you?" She stalked over to Bo and removed the tit clamps with one smooth jerk. Bo had forgotten they were there. Her nipples had gone numb while she was eating out Crash. She wanted to shriek, but Killer was waiting to slap her if she did. So she just whimpered a little.

"Well?" Killer said. "Answer me!"

"Well—what?" Bo stammered.

"Aren't you lucky that we're training you?"

Is that what's happening? Bo wondered. "Yes, I'm lucky, ma'am."

Killer looked even more amused. "Now I'm a ma'am. I suppose it's a step up from being your mama. Just call me mistress. I think Poison wants to check you out."

Poison was chewing a large wad of gum. She nonchalantly blew a bubble that was bigger than Bo's face, popped it, and sucked it back into her peony red mouth. "You betcha," she said, sticking the gum to one corner of the mirror. Crash peeled it off with the tips of her fingers and dropped it in the trash.

"Put some lube on your, hand," Poison told her. Bo managed, awkwardly. "Now put your fingers up my ass," the dancer ordered, and positioned Bo's head so her tongue was poised in just the right spot. She wanted a hard, flicking motion just above her clit, which was slightly pointed, and a lot of in-and-out work between the cheeks of her muscular behind. Bo's arm rapidly got tired, but Poison was not about to let her rest. "Come on, you can do anything for twenty minutes," she snapped at Bo. "Fuck me like you mean it, put your shoulder into it, and keep that tongue busy too. I want to come all over your face, I want to suck your arm into my ass, I want to eat you alive in little bloody chunks, slave boy, boy toy, bet you never really fucked a girl in your life. You're probably used to taking it up the ass, not dishing it out. Lowlife trash, you come sneaking in here thinking you can get your rocks off and then sneak out again, serves you right getting caught. Fuck me! Fuck me! More! More! More!"

She came briefly, but very hard. Bo's shoulder hit the wall. "Okay, stop it, I'm done now," Poison said, and walked off to change her G-string.

And that was how it went for the rest of the night. Killer eventually took the dildo away from Bo, saying, "We don't want our puppy to get spoiled." Bo gathered from the high energy the dancers brought into the dressing room that they were doing very well out there. She was startled when Killer took the handcuffs off, made her strip, and said, "Go in the bathroom and clean yourself up. Then come back here and we'll dress you up. Make it snappy. Poison already called the limousine."

"My bike—" Bo said weakly.

"I already had somebody take it home for you," Killer said.

Bo gave her a horrified look.

"Well, your keys were right in your jacket pocket," Killer said impatiently. "And you do live at the same address that's on your checks, right? So what's the problem? Eddy's wife knows from Harleys. She's been taking him to runs for years. She isn't going to fuck your bike up. Look, if you don't want to go out with us, you can always walk home. Naked."

Once again, doing as she was told seemed like much the best option. Bo tiptoed into the corridor, and hoped the only door she could see led to a bathroom. The toilet seemed to have indigestion, but a few minutes' work with the plunger fixed that. The sink wasn't very clean, and only the cold-water tap worked, but Bo doused some paper towels and sponged herself off. Shivering, she crept back into the room, and was astonished to see that all the mess that had covered the floor ankle-deep had vanished into three little bags.

Killer, Crash, and Poison looked ready to hit the streets of a sex zone on some perverted, faraway Amazon planet. Killer was wearing a strapless black leather dress with a studded bodice. The purple tips of her ponytail swept her white shoulders and back. Bo wanted to bite her, to leave a round red mark on that fair and very fragile-looking skin. The skirt was slit so high in the back, you could almost see Killer's buns. Her black stockings were decorated with a cobra on each ankle. The snakes had rhinestone eyes. And the heels of her pumps were even taller than the boots she'd worn onstage. Poison was wearing a body-harness made out of leather straps and fine silver chains. The carefully draped chains hid her nipples, and a tiny leather strap just barely concealed her sex. Her shoulders were covered with spiked leather pads, and she wore matching spiked gauntlets on each arm. She had traded in her gold pumps for a pair of knee-high engineer boots with steel toes. Bo wondered where the dancer got such butch footwear in tiny sizes. She had to wear three pairs of socks with *her* engineer boots. Crash was in a high-necked, long-sleeved PVC catsuit that had zippers in its crotch and over the nipples. She had combed out her beehive and had pulled her long, blonde hair through a hole in the back of a patent-leather helmet. Bo couldn't tell where the suit ended and Crash's boots began. Her outfit was a seamless piece of glossy midnight, except for the zippers that protected and flaunted her erogenous zones.

"You didn't have any underwear," Killer said, "so you'll have to wear these."

"These" were a pair of lilac tap pants with black lace around the waist and legs. Bo's whole body went rigid. "I will not!" she said.

Crash sighed and put her in a half nelson. Poison picked up Bo's feet, one at a time, and Killer smoothed the lingerie into place. "We can't have you running around with a bare butt," Killer soothed. "You'll catch your death of cold. Nobody will know what you have on under your jeans. Now get into your Levi's and your boots."

"You can wear my tank top," Poison said, tossing Bo six square inches of black spandex.

"I don't think that's big enough for me," Bo said weakly, tucking the cuffs of her jeans into her boots.

"Let's dress the baby," Killer said. "Put ooh widdle awms up, diddums. There we go."

Bo was afraid to look at herself in the mirror. But Crash turned her bodily to face it. "Nice delts and lats," she said approvingly. "How come butches have all the cleavage, Bo?"

"I hate you all," Bo said unhappily.

"Aren't we the lucky ones?" Killer said coldly. "Just for that, you can wear some lipstick on your way out. So everybody knows who you're with."

Bo tried to struggle, but Poison and Crash held her in place. How could they get so many muscles just dancing? With a firm and practiced hand, Killer made a bright red Cupid's-bow mouth on Bo's trembling lips. "They ought to be that red anyway, considering how much pussy you've chowed down today," Crash snickered.

The dancers hustled Bo to the front of the store. Bo noticed that Crash and Killer were taller than she was. Must be the shoes. A black stretch limousine was parked in the bus zone in front of the store. "Easy come, easy go," a middle-aged woman told them bitterly, staring at the luxurious car.

"Oh, you're welcome, we loved making all that money for you," Crash said, blowing her a kiss.

"She knows a hell of a lot more about going than she does about coming," Poison muttered. The chauffeur was opening their door. "Next time that'll be your job," she said, jabbing Bo in the ribs. *Next time?*

The seats in the back of the limo were so wide that the three dancers sat side by side. "Put her on the floor," they had told the chauffeur, and he did as they asked as if there was nothing unusual about their request. So Bo was lying on the carpeted floor, listening to the engine, watching Crash put a tape in the stereo while Poison uncorked a big, green bottle and Killer took three shrimp cocktails out of the little refrigerator.

"Where to first, ladies?" asked the chauffeur. He must be using an intercom. There was a pane of soundproof glass between him and the passenger compartment.

"Over the bridge and back again," Killer said. "We need to unwind. Then we'll visit the club."

"Very good, madam," he said, and did not speak again.

"Impressed?" Killer asked, nudging Bo with her toe.

"Yeah, I guess I am," Bo had to admit.

"Sex workers make a lot of money," Poison bragged. "Especially if they have somebody like Killer to invest it. You should see our coop. It's a nice place, but it's too big for us to keep up with. Too bad you aren't looking for a job. We need a new houseboy. Somebody who won't put my lingerie in the washing machine because they're too lazy to get out the Woolite."

"Somebody who can cook something besides pork chops and baked potatoes," Crash sighed, digging into her shrimp cocktail. "Somebody who dusts."

"Shut up," Killer said sharply. "This little asshole has to make it through the night without disgracing us first."

Bo couldn't see any higher than the ankles of the women who were taking her for this wild ride. Her eyes went back and forth between the poisonous snakes that sprang from Killer's six-inch heels; Poison's carefully polished engineer boots; and Crash's spike-heeled boots. She was mesmerized by the rhinestone eyes of the snakes, their enraged, inflated hoods; the hint of a reflection of her own face in Poison's steel toes; the spurs that Crash cheerfully dug into the carpeted floor of the limo. Inside her 501s, the lilac-colored tap pants bunched up and slid around. The lace scratched. What would her friends think if they could see her now?

"Hey, good dog," Killer said caustically, "want a shrimp?" She held out a piece of seafood, dripping red sauce. Bo opened her mouth and took it carefully from her fingers. "Don't muss your lipstick," Killer added. "What would your buddies think if they could see you now, Bo?"

Poison and Crash laughed. Bo startled like an animal that's been hit with a BB gun. "I think they'd laugh at me," Bo said slowly, "just like y'all do."

That shut them up. "Yeah, they probably would," Killer said judiciously. "But they'd be jealous too, honey, and don't you ever forget it. More shrimp?"

Bo let the dancers feed her crackers smeared with brie, pinches of caviar. Poison tilted some liquid from her glass into Bo's mouth, and she swallowed before realizing it was champagne. "Hey, I can't drink that," she protested.

"What are you, allergic to sulfites?" Crash asked. "You gonna keel over dead if we let you eat at the salad bar? No trips to the Sizzler for you, sissy boy."

"No, I—"

"She doesn't drink, asshole," Killer snapped. "Here, Bo, this is Calistoga. Wash your mouth out."

It seemed only appropriate to kiss Killer's shoe to thank her. Bo didn't think she could feel it through the finely crafted leather. But Killer rolled her foot to the side and pressed the toe into Bo's throat. "You have good instincts, baby," she said. "But you're supposed to ask permission."

Bo hesitated. "It's a great way to get the lipstick off your mouth," Poison pointed out. That kind of spoiled it.

"I wasn't thinking about that," Bo said. "I'm just not used to asking for things."

"Oh?" Crash said bitterly. "You think butch girls like you ought to just grab whatever they want, without asking?"

"No," Bo sighed. "Usually I don't grab anything, I just wait and hope whatever I want will come to me. If you don't want anything, you can't get hurt when you don't get it. It's dangerous to ask for things, Crash."

"That's Mistress Crash to you," the blonde said loftily, and rested her boot heels on Bo's legs.

"Aren't you the deep one," Poison said, cuddling the hard shells of her boot toes into Bo's stomach.

"Quit thinking so much," Killer advised, and stroked Bo's cheek with her soles.

"Can I kiss them?" Bo whispered.

"Honey, it's what you were born to do," Killer replied. "Just don't slobber on me. I hate it when my shoes get wet."

Once more, Bo lost track of time. She was busy creating new yoga positions to gain access to the footwear of all three women. She had never imagined doing anything like this. She had watched a leather boy set up a boot-shining stand at a benefit once, and wondered why the crowd of men who surrounded him seemed so intense, like a pack of coon hounds. The boy's daddy had made Bo get in front of the men who were waiting and ordered the kid, who was kneeling, wearing nothing but a jockstrap, his hands and face streaked with black polish, to make her cowboy boots shine. The boot boy had stoically done his job, but Bo didn't find it very exciting. She knew Daddy Rick from meetings, and he always greeted her with a smile, but they weren't exactly friends. She couldn't tell if he was doing this to let everybody know he thought she belonged in this bar, or to subtly punish his "son."

This act of worship was very different. It was like taking somebody's panties off with your teeth. You had to be delicate. Not biting—not tearing anything—was what made it erotic. If you were really lucky, the girl you were with got so excited that she forgot to take her underwear home with her. Bo blushed when she thought about the secret collection she kept tucked between her mattress and the box spring. She didn't think anybody would forget their shoes that easily. And who would have guessed that the smell of perfume and leather, mingled with a little sweat, could be such an aphrodisiac? It shouldn't be as exciting as smelling somebody's wet cunt and knowing you made it juicy. But above the foot (which might kick you away), there was the ankle, and above the ankle the muscular calf (which would feel so nice draped over your shoulder), then the knees, which might part, then the thighs, round and soft with promise, and after that—

Maybe after that came even more work, more personal service, for a good dog who had a careful, soft, and respectful mouth. Bo hoped so.

"Enough," Killer said firmly. "Stop it, Bo. We're here. We're getting out now. Oh, don't look so upset. We're taking you with us. Poison, would you do something with our guest?"

Bo had to force herself to stop staring at the two spots of color that decorated Killer's cheekbones and look at the other dancer. The two leather bands around Poison's upper arms came off, snapped together, and went around Bo's neck. "It'll have to do until we get our real collar back from the bad dog," Crash said, attaching a leash and extracting Bo from the limo.

Get what back from who? Bo wondered.

"We'll page you," Killer told the driver. "Why don't you go get dinner?"

"Certainly, madam," he replied, and the car floated away.

"Charley would kill to be in your place," Poison snickered, tapping Bo between the shoulder blades.

"Charley can go fuck himself," Killer said. "The last thing I want after I get off work is one more prick hanging around looking for a freebie."

This looked like an industrial zone. The streets were empty. But the block around the bar was crowded with motorcycles, parked so close they almost touched. The three dancers strolled into the club, which Bo recognized as one of those places that was always getting shut down by the city for violating the fire code or selling liquor to minors. What was it called, Jack's? Something like that. No, Jax! That was it. Bo's date for Saturday night had talked about coming down here for a drink, like it was some kind of big deal to walk into this joint.

The bouncer waved them through without asking for ID or a cover charge. The bartender—one of the biggest women Bo had ever seen—shouted, "God help us all, it's the Furies incarnate."

Bo's captors waved back, looking smug. "We're regulars here," Poison explained, adjusting her chain harness so her nipples showed. "Kat likes us because we're troublemakers."

"There's a table," Crash said, pointing somewhere into the crowd. Somebody snatched at one of the zippers on her catsuit, and she elbowed them in the face. "You're a bigger asshole than your asshole," she told the unlucky and unsuccessful woman who had dared touch her without permission. That poor soul was clutching her nose. "I'd put some ice on that if I were you," Crash sneered.

"Go save that table for us," Killer ordered, slapping her gloves against her palm. Crash put the end of the leash in Bo's mouth, and she went without thinking. A couple of the patrons barked at her, but she kept on going until she saw the vacant table. She stood behind one chair and put her hands on the backs of the other two.

"Perfect," Poison said, positioning her hard little rump on the seat. Her legs were too short for her feet to touch the floor, so she propped her engineer boots up on the legs of the table. Bo thought that was pretty cute. "I want more champagne."

"I am not holding your head while you puke all night," Killer said severely. She had seated herself like a grand duchess, and Bo was trying to figure out how she managed to sit down in that tight skirt without splitting it up the back.

"If you make me switch to something else, I'll get sick for sure," Poison replied. "Dom Perignon for me, Bo. Want to help me out, Crash?"

"Whatever," Crash said. She had not taken a seat. She remained standing, drumming her red claws on the back of a chair and scanning the crowd. Apparently she did not find the party she was looking for, because she suddenly blew air out of her nose, picked up the chair, turned it around, and sat on it backwards. "Champagne is as close as I'm going to get to Paris tonight, girl-friends."

"I'm sure Bo could take a few lessons in French," Killer said coldly. "A Virgin Mary, with extra Tabasco," she told Bo. "Go on! Don't *worry* about the *money*, Bo, we run a tab here."

Crash intercepted her before she left the table and unsnapped the leash. "Be prompt, or this goes back on," she warned.

More barking followed Bo to the bar. She wondered what that was all about. It didn't sound unfriendly. It was more like a cheer. The next time somebody howled at her, she howled back. This caused a moment or two of relative silence. She was still close enough to the table to hear the three dancers chortle. "Still think she's going to embarrass us, Killer?" Poison demanded.

Bo fought her way to the bar, where a short, redheaded dyke in a leather vest and jeans was arguing with the mountainous, blonde bartender. "You have to quit covering up for Lolly," the redhead said. "Look at this mess. How are you supposed to tend bar all by yourself on a Friday night?"

"Aw, Reid, ease up, I'm doing okay. You're just mad 'cause I can't take a break and sneak out to the patio and give you a blowjob. We weren't supposed to see each other tonight anyway. Why don't you go home and take a nap? I'll come over after I get off work."

"Fuck that," Reid said. "This is not the way friends treat one another, Kat."

"What do you want me to do, get her fired? In case you haven't heard, there's a recession out there. I am not going to be responsible for somebody getting laid off when there's no place else for them to go. Lolly's in love, and when she's in love, she's just not herself. She'll be back again as soon as the bitch dumps her or they run out of poppers."

"Codependents are a pain in the ass, aren't they?" Bo said sympathetically to the redhead. Reid turned around quick, like somebody had bitten her in the ass, and snapped, "Who asked you?" The keys on the left side of her belt jingled.

"Nobody had to," Bo replied. "It's a free country."

Reid snorted. She turned her back on Kat and her talkative customer and leaned against the bar, scanning the crowd like American radar looking for Russian jets. Kat shrugged, almost stuck her tongue out at the back of Reid's head, then thought better of it.

"You need a tray, right?" Kat asked. "Tell me what your keepers are drinking. No, I'll tell you. One bottle of champagne, two glasses, and a Virgin Mary, right?"

"Extra Tabasco," Bo added, trying to process the idea of these two women being in a relationship and the bartender being a bottom.

"You look like a Southern Comfort girl yourself," Kat suggested.

"Calistoga," Bo said, smiling.

"We don't have any more that's cold," Kat said, sounding harassed. She arranged other beverages on a tray. "We need some ice, but it doesn't look like anybody's going out for any."

"All right!" Reid shouted. "I will get on my friggin' bike and somehow find a place in this godforsaken neighborhood that has ice, and try to convince myself I don't look like a complete and total dweeb running errands for you because your coworker had to pick this week of all weeks to go out on a toot!"

"Don't do me any fucking favors!" Kat snarled. But Reid kept shoving through the crowd. "Don't let those hellcats get too riled up, now," the bartender told Bo, pushing the tray toward her. "I got enough on my hands tonight without them swingin' on the chandeliers and slashing people's tires."

Bo put the tray up high on one hand, the way real waiters did it, and bayed at the women in front of her. It didn't exactly sound like a wolf pack baying at a National Geographic film crew, but Bo figured she could refine her sound effects as time went on. The patrons of Jax let her cut through like the pointer on an Etch-A-Sketch.

"What took you so long?" Poison complained. "Don't let that cork fly—oh, you know how. Never mind."

Bo unwrapped the little, white towel from the neck of the green bottle, put the cork on the table, and poured two flutes of champagne without releasing all of the bubbles.

"Kat and Reid are having a fight, huh?" Crash said. "I knew it could never last. Butch-on-butch is such a joke."

"Shut up," Killer said. "What about your little fling with Belinda, huh? Surely you remember her—the girl who did the snake act at the Manslaughter Brothers' Cow Palace." She took a sip of her Virgin Mary. "Hot!" she sputtered. "Good," she added, biting on the celery stick. It snapped like a little bone.

"That was hardly butch-on-butch," Crash said, holding out her glass for some more champagne. Bo poured carefully. There was no chair for her, so she guessed she was supposed to just stand up and wait on everybody. She filched a bowl of peanuts from the closest table and offered them to Killer, who took a few but did not put them in her mouth because she was too busy hassling Crash.

"Yeah, well, how would you have responded to the suggestion that you get a crewcut if you were going to strap it on with her, huh?" she asked. "I mean, that *is* why you broke up, isn't it? Because one of you wasn't butch enough?"

"No," Crash snapped, putting her glass down almost hard enough to snap the stem. "We broke up because she gave me crabs, if you must know. Did I forget to mention the torrid night we spent in your bed, darling?"

"You're awful," Killer said, smiling happily.

"I think we're all pretty awful," Poison said contentedly. "Isn't it wonderful? Bo, do you smoke cigarettes?"

"No."

"No what?"

"No, uh, mistress. I don't smoke cigarettes. I do carry a few around with me, though, for the street people. So they'll leave my bike alone."

Poison gave Killer a significant glance.

"Stop that," Killer said irritably. "I know it would be nice to have a boy who doesn't smoke. I'm as sick of Donna's dirty ashtrays as you are. But for godsake, Poison, she can't even say the word 'mistress' without stammering. She doesn't know a single thing about the scene. Do you really want to clutter up our lives with a novice who will probably cut and run the first time somebody teases her about giving it up for a bunch of girls?"

Crash, still smarting from Killer's sarcastic remarks about her affair with another dancer, saw her chance to get even. "Well, I'm so glad you were born with a bullwhip in your hand," she said lightly. "I think Poison's right. If we ever see Bad Dog again, we ought to sic Bo on her. Winter's coming. It's time for indoor sports. And I can think of a lot worse ways to spend evenings in front of the fireplace than some training sessions with this little hunk. She knows enough to wear her red hanky on the left. That's all the etiquette I want out of my houseboy."

Bo looked from one woman to the other as they took turns talking. Nobody looked at her. That seemed a little weird. Shouldn't somebody ask her what she thought about all of this? Or explain it? "Hey," she finally interjected.

The silence was frosty. "Yes?" Killer finally said.

"Don't you think it would be a nice idea to ask me what I want before you all go dividing me up like a pizza?"

The three dancers exchanged amused and outraged glances. "No," Killer said firmly. "That would not be a nice idea. Shut up, Bo. We'll let you talk later."

Bo shrugged and let her mind wander while the bickering resumed.

"See that stool over there?" Crash asked her, reeling Bo in by her collar. She ran her fingernails down the skin between Bo's breasts. Even through the spandex, Bo's nipples became visibly more firm. "I want you to grab that empty bar stool and drag it over by this table. Do you understand me, butchy boy?"

Bo nodded. Her only fear was that Crash would keep hanging on to her collar so long that somebody would sit down on the bar stool. But Crash gave her a little shove, and she got to the only empty seat in the house just a split second before somebody's fanny descended upon it. The crowd hooted at her as she wrestled the awkward piece of furniture back to the table. *Why does everybody in this place seem to know somethin' I don't know?* Bo wondered. *Maybe 'cause they do. Shit.*

"Bend over it," Crash instructed Bo, speaking over her shoulder.

"I—I—what?" Bo sputtered.

"Bend over," Poison piped up. She pushed her chair back and walked over to Bo, who was trying to follow directions and feeling like a horse's neck. Poison stood by Bo's head and leaned forward, pinning her shoulders down. "Remember me?" she said. Her soft belly was plastered against the top of Bo's head, and the smell of her juicy, bossy little cunt made Bo's nose itch with lust.

"Just what do you think you're doing?" Killer said flatly, trying to make Crash back down.

"Come on, dearie, she already has one demerit. You said so yourself in the dressing room. So let me give her a spanking. That should make it pretty clear whether she's got the right qualifications for the job."

Bo could barely hear this conversation. Poison's thighs were partially blocking her ears. But she heard Killer and Crash's high heels clicking as the two friends came to stand beside her. Bo thought it was Killer who touched her on the small of her back, sliding her hand under Bo's spandex shirt and grazing the skin with her long fingernails. Then Poison moved away from her, and Bo could tell it was definitely Killer who was talking.

"You've had a very busy day," Killer said. "I'm sure when you walked into Sugar and Spice, you never expected to find yourself in this position."

"Butcha are, Blanche, ya are!" Poison crowed.

"Be quiet, please," Killer said severely. "Bo has some very serious thinking to do. When I gave you a demerit in the dressing room, I really had no right to do that. You have no agreement with us that gives us the right to discipline you or order you around. So now you have to choose. If you want to stay with us for the rest of the night, you have to let Crash spank you. Right here in the bar. If you'd like to go home, I'll give you some cab fare. No hard feelings, but if we run into you again, we probably won't remember who you are. There are so many butch bottoms who would give their eyeteeth to be where you are right now that I'm sure we won't have any trouble replacing the bad dog who currently calls itself our house-boy. If you can take the spanking without trying to get up off the bar stool, we can talk about a more permanent arrangement. If you find that you can't tolerate being paddled, I'm afraid we'll have to put an ad up on the bulletin board here and start interviewing applicants. Crash and Poison mostly care about your strong right arm, darlin', but I want to make sure your hide is tough enough to deal with my strong right arm."

Now Bo knew what that phrase "got your tit caught in a wringer" meant. What the hell was a butch bottom? She was so wet that she wasn't sure she could stand up and walk away from the bar stool. She would probably slip across the floor like somebody who just stepped on a bar of soap. She looked at Poison. The dancer gave her a wicked smile. No wonder she had a white stripe, that little skunk. She obviously didn't care if Bo succeeded or failed. Either outcome would entertain her. Bo sighed and glanced at Crash. The blonde's attention was focused on Killer. So Bo looked that way too. Both of Killer's eyebrows were raised. "Well?" she demanded. "All you have to do is choose."

"Then I choose to ask for a spanking," Bo said defiantly. "Please, ma'am. Uh, ladies."

Poison applauded and scampered over to the bar stool, where she once again pinned Bo's shoulders to the padded seat. Crash threw one arm across the small of Bo's back. She let her other hand rest on Bo's denim-clad butt.

"No," Killer said meanly, deliberately pitching her voice so that Bo and probably everybody else in the bar could hear her. "No pants."

Bo froze. That meant everybody would see the lingerie the dancers had forced her to wear. She was mortified. But her clammy fingers were already unbuttoning her jeans and pushing them down. "Fine," she said, and left it at that. If she made a longer speech, her voice would shake.

Crash ran her palm over the slippery, pastel purple cloth. God, she had big hands for a girl. "We'll do one soft, four medium, and one hard," she decided. "On each side, of course."

Bo kept her teeth together, anticipating the use of great force. She was surprised by the mildness of the blows. Was Crash going easy on her, or did she simply not hit people as hard as Killer had hit her? Could it be that she was actually disappointed that it didn't hurt more? Wasn't that a puzzle! It didn't occur to her that Crash was playing a little mistress game with Killer, making sure that the new boy didn't flunk out of class.

Bo's face was bright pink when she straightened up, but she figured that was only natural. She'd been hanging practically upside down. The three dancers were back at their table, sipping their drinks. Crash looked like a kitty with canary feathers up its nose, and Killer was obviously fuming. Bo tried not to look beyond that little table. But as she raised her britches, Bo came face-to-face with the big bartender. Kat's knowing eyes made Bo blush tomato red. To hell with those mean, if entertaining, bitches. Kat had seen the shameful undergarments. Another butch—a senior dyke— knew what she had let these femmes do to her. Bo wanted to run and hide.

"Hey, there, little dog," Kat said softly. "You're a good boy. Did you know that? Well, you are. You're being very good."

Bo squared her shoulders, took a deep breath, and whispered, "Thanks." But Kat was already at the other end of the bar, waiting on customers, and probably never even heard her. Bo took another deep breath and then dared to look around at the other dykes in the bar. Nobody seemed to be pointing or staring at her. Was that scorn she saw in the few faces that turned toward her—or was it envy?

"Did I pass your little test?" Bo demanded.

Killer looked ready to jump on her for that. But somebody rammed her from behind, and the table slid forward. Drinks slopped out of their glasses. "You!" Killer said angrily.

"Donna!" Kat called out warningly. "Don't go stirring shit in my bar!"

"What do they expect, dressed up like that?" Donna jeered. "They're a walking advertisement for sexual harassment! They just get me so excited, I can't help myself. I have to let them know how they really make me feel." And she grabbed her crotch.

Bo thought this must be the bad dog that the dancers had been complaining about ever since she met them. Donna was as tall as Killer and outweighed her by at least forty pounds. She had short hair that curled like black sheep's wool and liquid, dark brown collie eyes. Bo had last seen that look in the eyes of a dog that belonged to an uncle of hers. Whenever it came around to lick your hand and fawn on you, you could bet that it had killed another chicken. Bo wrinkled her nose at the smell of marijuana and gin. What an uncouth combination.

"Why all the long faces? It's not like I *raped* anybody," Donna jeered. "I'm just sayin' hello." She leaned into Killer's face. "Hello!" she shouted. "Where have you been? You're all *late*. I thought I'd have to take a doorknob home if I wanted to get laid tonight." She took the cigarette from behind her ear and held it under Poison's nose. "Gimme a light," she whined. "Who do I have to fuck to get a match around here?"

"You're fired," Killer said firmly, pushing her away. "So give us back our collar, Bad Dog, and get out."

"Fired? You can't fire me! I'll sue. Besides, who's going to pay my tab?" Donna blustered.

"From now on, you'll have to pay your own fucking way," Poison told her.

Donna took a simple leather dog collar out of her back pocket and threw it at Killer, who caught it in one hand. Then she pursed her lips and spit at her.

Kat was hustling down the bar with a sap in her hand. But Bo was faster. She reached out, grabbed the interloper by her earlobe, and twisted. Donna shrieked and fell to her knees.

"You're pulling out my earrings!" she yelled.

"I certainly hope so," Bo replied, and dug her fingernails in a little deeper. She took off toward the front door of the bar, and Donna followed her, duck-walking on her knees.

"You bastard," Donna swore. "I hate you. What did they do, promise to let you kiss their asses? Well, they're nothing but a bunch of dirty little whores, and you know what that makes you. Let me go! Stop it, stop it!"

Apparently Donna was well-known at Jax, because there was scattered applause as the patrons became aware of what Bo was doing. The clapping grew to standing-ovation proportions as Bo reached the door, hauled Donna to her feet, and sent her outside with a boot to her backside.

But the wretched Bad Dog wouldn't go quietly. "I bet you lick their assholes!" she shrieked, just outside the bar. "I hope they shit in your mouth! Whores! You run around with—"

Bo heard a roaring noise behind her head, and white light flashed at the edges of her vision. She took two steps forward, grabbed Donna by the front of her shirt, and punched her in the mouth. "Where I come from, we don't talk that way to ladies who are paying for our drinks," she said, letting her opponent crumple to the pavement. "You've lost. Go home."

Reid pulled up to the curb, three bags of ice held across the back of her seat with bungee cords. She undid the cords and threw a bag of ice at Bo. "Help me get these inside," she told her, stomping into the bar. She gave Donna one unpitying glance. "Have a little trouble, did we?"

"No trouble," said Bo. The ice felt good against the split knuckles of her right hand. She let Reid walk ahead of her, afraid Donna would rush both of them. But when the disgraced dog got up, she kept herself pointed in the opposite direction, as if Bo were a bad smell she was determined to ignore. She took some change out of her pocket and headed for a pay phone across the street.

Inside, Killer, Crash, and Poison took the bag of ice away from Bo and practically heaved it across the bar at Kat. "You're hurt!" Crash said, cradling Bo's battered fist.

"We could have taken care of that rowdy little jerk ourselves," Poison muttered.

"Yeah, but why should we have to?" Killer smiled. "We have a much bigger and better dog taking care of us now. A pit bull, I think. Do you feel like a pit bull, Bo?"

From behind the bar, Kat gave Bo a thumbs-up. "What the hell is going on here?" Reid grouched. "I leave you alone for twenty minutes and World War III breaks out. One of these days somebody in this lunatic asylum is going to hurt you, Kat, and I'm going to have to—"

"Page Charley," Killer told Poison. "Let's take our baby home."

"We'll find out how you like your red hanky when it's on the other side," Crash promised, pressing into Bo's side. Her perfume made Bo dizzy. She wished to hell she knew what that red hanky meant, but after finally getting this lucky, she wasn't about to ask.

Too Much Is Almost Enough

"What's your name, little slave?" Wolfe asked her. She stood motionless as a tree trunk, tall in front of her toy, and waited, quiet and patient as a piece of property could never be, for the response.

In the beginning, the girl on the floor would have thoughtlessly replied with the label that served her in the mundane world. In fact, she would not even have known that by the time she was asked such a question, she had better be on her knees. She bit her lips and stared at Wolfe's engineer boots, a man's size 12. The inside of the left boot was scarred slightly from maneuvering the gearshift of Wolfe's bike. Their toes were scuffed from the construction work that kept Wolfe's body and hands hard and strong. Wolfe was dressed for riding. Only her gloves had not yet been pulled on, over the hands that the girl adored. Adored because she knew what rewards they could mete out and also knew that any punishment dealt from Wolfe's hands was fair.

She was still naked, the girl on the floor, and feeling a little violated by the rare enema that had been prescribed for her, even though it had been self-administered and very small. It is hard to avoid such resentments when you are a slave. The costume that Wolfe had picked for her was neatly laid out on the bed, and she was nervous about the fact that she was apparently expected to wear this revealing outfit where someone besides Wolfe might see her. Still, her training held. She bent at the waist and leaned forward, stretched out her back parallel to the floor so Wolfe could see the twin ridges of dancer's muscle along her spine. She threw her hair forward also, so the brown waves that Wolfe had just brushed into shining perfection fell onto the battered toes of her owner's work boots.

"My name is whatever you choose to give me, master," she replied, pitching her voice to carry without making it shrill or excessively loud. Wolfe liked girls with musical voices, voices that were gentle without being inaudible. This ritual, she could not help but recall, was taken almost word for word from one of those dreadful books that Wolfe had made her read at the beginning of their association. Something by John Norman about a planet called Gor, where all the women were slaves and all the men were masters. "The guy's a total pig," Wolfe had said, "but he knows something about this master and slave business. I want a girl like the girls in these books. So you just imagine it's me he's talking about whenever he describes these conquering heroes. Because that is what I will be to you, if you please me. Your protector, your hero, and your owner. Don't ever think I am not completely serious about every part of that promise. And don't ever think I won't demand every privilege, no matter how small, that I am entitled to receive for giving you that much attention. I'm willing to die for you, girl, so you'd better be prepared to do just about that much for me."

Now Wolfe was considering her, so the girl raised her torso and spread her legs. She placed her hands palm up on her thighs. She looked at Wolfe briefly, and was both frightened and gratified by the intensity of the look that swept over her body. Imperceptibly, she tried to straighten her back, throw out her breasts, and flatten her stomach, push her pubic mound forward, spread her knees just a bit more until the sockets of her thighs protested. She willed her hands to become little poems of submission, things of beauty offered up to Wolfe's greater strength. It wasn't pleasant to walk around all day being known by a derisive title like "Arrogance" or "Unwilling."

"Your name is Jasmine," Wolfe decided.

The girl on the floor was surprised, but tried not to let it show. This was a new name. She wondered if Wolfe would give her any hints about what sort of baggage came with the name. Nothing that Wolfe said or did was accidental. She was not surprised to feel her inner lips moisten, as if they too had been christened. They had been separated by the position she had assumed, and the slight trace of wetness made her feel cold between the legs. It was a relief to feel the liquid of arousal begin to flow because it meant she had physiology on her side. A girl needed to be excited to cope with Wolfe.

"Jasmine looks delicate, but it is vigorous," Wolfe said. "So light on the evening air, but dramatic. Impossible to ignore. A very feminine scent. Today we will be putting some finishing touches on you, like the perfection created by selecting just the right perfume. I expect such a cloud of need and desire will surround you by the time this day is through that everyone will know who and what you are and why I think you are the most beautiful woman I have ever met." She moved closer, and Jasmine could smell her leather jacket, the slight tang that Wolfe's sweat acquired just before she slapped her property or possessed her. She moved closer still, and Jasmine gasped as Wolfe's boot made contact with her slippery, opened folds.

"Put a little of that perfume on the toe of my boot," Wolfe said, her voice low and lusty, and she wound her hand in Jasmine's hair. "Go ahead, touch yourself, spread your pussy open and put it right there. You know where I want it, honey. So that later if you lick my boots you'll be able to smell yourself and remember the first time you came today."

Wolfe had done this to her, made her so sensitive to a word or a touch that it sometimes took only a meaningful smile on Wolfe's lips to make Jasmine shudder with a brief climax. So Jasmine put her hands on her own wet fur and divided it. Now the tip of her clitoris was resting on rough leather, laid over steel. She moved her hips in small circles, and Wolfe helped her by pulling her hair slightly, just enough to make her nipples get hard. She spared one helpless glance up at Wolfe and got no mercy, just a raised eyebrow that said, *Do it now.* So she came, her thighs tensing and relaxing to heighten the sensation. Wolfe did not allow her any recovery time, just used her hair to tow her to the bed and show her the scandalous things that glittered there. "Dress," Wolfe said shortly.

So Jasmine put on the stockings, which had a spiral pattern of rhinestones over each ankle. There was a garter belt but no panties. She fought the impulse to cry. A girl could go out in public dressed in practically nothing as long as she had her panties on. Without panties, a wool pantsuit would have felt insecure, unsafe, as if every cowboy for a hundred square miles would somehow hear a siren and gather to ogle your naked ass and try to grab your cunt. She fastened the back hooks of a translucent black push-up bra (which matched the garter belt), turned it around, and pulled it up over her breasts. It had an underwire and some side panels that molded her ample cleavage into a whorish silhouette. Her full breasts were suspended in midair, the nipples offered up to any stranger's hand. And over this she was allowed to put a see-through dress made out of stretchy lace and gauze. The bodice was trimmed with a row of tiny rhinestones. It fit her like a second skin.

Jasmine felt as if she had been transformed into a piece of bait. Wolfe and her friends liked to talk about getting one of the femmes to go into redneck bars and lure men out for them to gut. It was one of their favorite fantasies. They would debate the merits of various girls they might use as pawns in this dangerous game, which ones had the courage and the class to be a part of a real manhunt. Most of the girls they considered were strippers, although Jasmine knew that one was a certified electrician and another was independently wealthy. They seemed to have a rough sort of admiration for the long-haired dykes who looked like straight bitches on the outside, but whose hearts were unswervingly loyal to the butches who spent their tips, kept their cars running, fumed about their regular clients, and shredded their stockings. Her position as Wolfe's property made her a silent witness to these raucous conversations, but she had never felt their speculative eyes fall on her or heard one of them clear her throat and say, "What about your piece, Wolfe? Ever think about sending her out to beat the bushes for us?" Some part of her resented that exclusion, but more of her was afraid. Was that what they were going to do today?

She turned to face Wolfe, who was examining three different pairs of shoes. Jasmine guessed that the pair with the rhinestone-studded bows would win, but she was wrong. Wolfe put the shoes down upon a shelf and carefully measured the heel height of each pair. The highest heels won. Fortunately, they had a platform sole, or Jasmine was not sure she could have walked in them at all. Wolfe forbade her to wear anything lower than a three-inch heel, and had promised that the height would go up a half-inch for each year of her servitude. Sometimes Jasmine studied the catalogs in Wolfe's library that showed women prancing in ballet slippers with eight-inch heels, and shook her head in amazement. Still, if you'd asked her a year ago if she would ever eschew Nikes for pumps and stiletto heels and spike-heeled boots, she would have laughed in your face. She could already do things in heels that some butches couldn't do in their boots or tennies, but this particular pair of shoes would be a challenge.

Wolfe drew a circle with her index finger, and Jasmine spun around, making sure the skirt of the dress flew up as she turned. That Marilyn Monroe thing, although Jasmine thought if Marilyn had ever had a good butch's strong arms around her, she wouldn't have drowned the hot and perfect flame of her life with booze and whatever passed for good drugs in the '50s. Privately, Jasmine thought of her as Saint Marilyn and often held imaginary conversations with her when she was confused about her life or unsure of her own impulses. Saint Marilyn had told her to go ahead and sign the contract that Wolfe had drawn up after their first date. "Take it from me, honey," she had said, her voice all breathy like she was scatterbrained, only you knew underneath it she was terribly wise. "You never know how much time you're going to have. And personally, I think getting to know people before you become intimate is overrated. If you like the way they kiss you, you might as well screw them. This is like a very big opportunity for you to star in your very own movie. Opportunity doesn't knock twice. If you say no you'll never forgive yourself. Damn the torpedoes, sign the silly piece of paper, and get ready for your close-up."

Seams aligned, dress smoothed over her breasts and hips, Jasmine sat on the edge of the bed. Wolfe knelt and fastened the slender straps of the shoes around her ankles. Then she pulled a chair up to the bed, put a towel around Jasmine's neck, and carefully applied her makeup.

It seemed to Jasmine that her face was being accentuated a little more than usual. The eyebrow pencil was black, not brown, and there were more than the usual number of strokes. She got two applications of mascara. The blush was darker, and the eye shadow had silver highlights. The lipstick Wolfe chose was a deep, true red, and she brushed it on with careful strokes that Jasmine knew would perfectly outline her mouth. She sat patiently with her lips parted slightly, to let the color dry. She remembered a passage in another awful book Wolfe had given her, *The Story of O*, where O was required to put rouge on her nipples and her sex before she saw her master. It made her blush, just remembering it.

There was something touching about Wolfe's big hands performing such meticulous work, making tiny and precise gestures. Jasmine supposed it was one of the things that enslaved her. The same hands that could dig ditches or lay a new roof could also do subtle things to her clitoris and her cervix that no one else could equal. Wolfe paid attention to girl things. Being a butch who liked femmes, she studied their ways and their wiles the same way she would study a microfiche schematic of an unfamiliar engine before she did a tune-up. Wolfe knew ten times more about lingerie, makeup, and women's bodies than Jasmine, who still didn't know the difference between a corset and a bustier or a teddy and a chemise. She just put on the frilly things that Wolfe gave her. They always fit, and the colors always worked. Jasmine had no idea why Wolfe had picked out a particular facial scrub; she just used it and enjoyed the fresh apricot scent. And she was so spoiled by the deep, long orgasms Wolfe gave her that she had practically given up on masturbation. Which was forbidden half the time anyway, so who cared?

Before meeting Wolfe, Jasmine supposed she had been more on the femme side of things, but Wolfe had remade her into something glamorous and tantalizing. Jasmine would have blushed to spend this much time on her own hair or clothing, but Wolfe insisted. Wolfe dressed her up, told her she was pretty as sin, and then fucked her senseless. Nobody could have resisted conditioning like that. So Jasmine relaxed, preened, and let Wolfe make her beautiful. Jasmine's little cunt got plumper and wetter as Wolfe plied tiny brushes and smoothed creamy unguents over her face. Wolfe noticed the change, of course, and gave her a knowing grin.

Finally, there was the perfume. Wolfe took the stopper from the bottle of a scent the slave girl had never seen before and touched it to the back of her ears, the hollows of her arms, the back of her knees. One burning drop she placed in the pelt above Jasmine's clitoris. She took Jasmine by the upper arm, stood her up, and turned her critically this way and that, evaluating her in different gradations of light and shadow. "You'll do," she said finally.

Wolfe abruptly bent Jasmine at the waist. The girl stifled a protesting gasp. But she was unable to hold back a moan that felt as if it had been pushed out of her by cold lubricant and the pointed tip of a glossy anal plug. "Hold that in," Wolfe warned her, as if she could get rid of it once her sphincter had closed around the narrow neck of the intruder. "Hold your skirt out of the way," Wolfe said impatiently, and Jasmine hastened to gather the frothy handfuls of fabric and draw them up away from her buttocks. A leather strap went around her waist, pulled tight enough to make her hiss. Another strap went between her legs, but before fastening it in front, Wolfe pushed something short but thick into her other opening. The crotch strap of the harness fit smoothly when it was buckled, and Jasmine flexed her sex muscles against the smooth surface. "Hey!" Wolfe said, smacking her on the butt hard enough to really sting. "Don't be getting yourself off now. You got one come already. Don't be greedy. You're going to have to ask for the rest of them."

She took her gloves out of her jacket pocket and made for the door, looking exceptionally pleased with herself. It was then that Jasmine broke the form of what had been a remarkably obedient morning. "Where's my coat?" she asked bravely, refusing to follow Wolfe out the door until she got an answer. The things that penetrated her were burning. Had Wolfe put mentholated ointment on them?

"Coat? You don't have a coat. You don't need one. It's warm outside, and we're not going far."

Oh, fuck. She had surprised Wolfe into giving her an explanation, and a rather lengthy one at that. There would be hell to pay, Jasmine knew. She watched anger slightly change the color of Wolfe's face. If she balked again, it was very possible she would be stripped completely and put on the back of Wolfe's bike in the nude. She put her wrists together and offered them to Wolfe, a silent way to say, *I belong to you. I forgot my place. Please let me apologize.*

Wolfe finished pulling on her gloves and indicated that Jasmine should precede her out the door. The girl threw her shoulders back and stalked out, playing the part of a bold hussy who doesn't care who sees her tits or watches the cheeks of her ass flex as she walks. If it pleased Wolfe to put her on display, so be it. She knew her owner by now well enough to trust that Wolfe was willing and able to deal with anyone who thought the visibility of all this female flesh was an invitation to trespass upon it. She waited with her nose in the air like a grand duchess while Wolfe started the bike.

As she settled behind Wolfe and wrapped her arms around her master, she felt the outlines of a shoulder holster through Wolfe's jacket. Her reaction to this was complex: arousal, frustration because she had no weapon of her own and could not have come to Wolfe's assistance if they were in danger, fear that she would not be able to help even if she were armed, a deep sense of respect for Wolfe's more violent talents, and a struggle to accept her own need to simply acquiesce and become the coveted object that Wolfe guarded.

"Put your right hand on my belt," Wolfe said, yelling to be heard over the bike's rumble. Jasmine did as she was told. Her hand came to rest on the bone hilt of a bowie knife that was almost big enough to be a short sword. "If the shit hits the fan," Wolfe said, "you have my permission to pull that and make yourself useful. Now stop fussing and enjoy the ride, honey. You look great, everybody wants you, and nobody has the balls to do anything about it. Foxy bitches like you scare the piss out of straight boys, darlin', honest they do. So mush your luscious tits up against my shoulder blades and let's see how big a hard-on you can give me before we get to Mack's house."

Jasmine let go of a breath that she didn't know she had been holding and settled into the place and the person she loved. The seat of the bike vibrated against the strap between her legs and made her orifices clench with excitement. It was going to be hard to keep herself from coming, and she was pretty sure Wolfe would not give her permission to get off. Not yet. Well, that's what you got for asking too many questions. It would be nice to know where they were going, and why she was so dressed up for a social event in the middle of the afternoon. But she wasn't about to make the same mistake twice and try to wheedle information out of Wolfe. She had been told as much as Wolfe thought she needed to know. Any more importuning might set her up for a truly rare piece of hell, a weekend of being subjected to Wolfe's expert teasing without any release.

Mack's house was on the outskirts of the city, a slightly shabby, two-story farmhouse that stood on three acres of ground that was all that was left of a farm that had existed since the city's founding. Mack kept chickens and a few goats, and had the biggest vegetable garden that Jasmine had ever seen. Her fences were in much better repair than the house itself, and a shotgun (loaded with rock salt) sat by the back door in case Mack had to take potshots at prowlers or a bad dog trying to sneak itself a chicken. Wolfe was fond of saying that Mack had bounced in and out of AA more often than Martina had bounced a tennis ball. Something really terrible was always going wrong in Mack's life. The IRS was after her, her latest girl-friend had taken refuge in the battered women's shelter, her bike went down under an 18-wheeler and took most of Mack's skin with it, stuff like that. Wolfe was always swearing at Mack and saying she should go back to the goddamned reservation if she couldn't keep her shit together in the city.

But Jasmine had noticed that the two of them loaned each other money, called each other when they were puzzled by mysterious noises in the many different vehicles (motorcycles, cars, snowmobiles, boats) that they worked on, and they were always cordial to one another's dates in public. In fact, Wolfe had asked Jasmine before agreeing to play with her, "Who you been fooling around with?" and taken pains to make sure she had not been with Mack. They seemed to divide up the novices in town, and if someone had come out into leather with Wolfe, they did not go from her into Mack's stable, and vice versa.

Jasmine thought Mack was a lot scarier than Wolfe, partly because her life just seemed so unstable. She was about six inches shorter than Wolfe, but lacked only a few of Wolfe's pounds. Jasmine already knew it was a mistake to write a big girl off as a fat or out-of-shape weakling. Muscle on women doesn't look the same as muscle on men. Fat or not, she had seen Mack knock an obnoxious bouncer down with a single punch, and was sure she could never have done anything like that. She gave Jasmine the same sense of calm, reassuring physical presence that Wolfe did. But Wolfe had a little more privilege, or maybe she had just been a little more lucky. Mack never seemed to be able to decide whether she wanted a traditional short butch haircut or a warrior's braid, so her hair (which was thick and very black) got combed back into a longish DA. Her clothes were often in poor repair, and Jasmine had once endeared herself to Wolfe by quietly taking Mack's sweater out of the closet, darning the holes and replacing a couple of buttons while the two butches had yet another argument about the relative merits of various models of Harleys.

"That was a nice thing for you to do," Wolfe had said. Mack had put the sweater back on under her leather jacket without seeming to notice any improvements. "It'll piss off that bitch Joanna, though. You better watch yourself around her. She'll probably think you're makin' a play for her daddy."

Jasmine nearly lost the points she had accrued by making a face. "Think you're too good for Mack?" Wolfe had said, sounding really angry. "Mack works 40, 50 hours a week in that warehouse to feed Joanna and her kids. Goes to night school, too. I better not catch you turning your nose up at her, girl. Not all of us have been to college."

Shortly after that, Jasmine found out that both Mack and Wolfe had been going to evening classes so they could take the GED. Both of them had been thrown out of their families' homes for being dykes before they turned 16. Wolfe stayed the course and eventually got her high school equivalency certificate. Mack had to drop out because they laid off some of the guys in the warehouse, and she suddenly had to work a lot of overtime. Jasmine felt a pang of guilt when she heard that news, as if her unthinking snobbery had somehow weakened Mack and made her waver.

Wolfe parked next to Mack's bike, which was leaking oil, and went to greet their host. Mack came banging out of the screen door with a couple of barking dogs escorting her. The two butches briefly clasped hands, and Wolfe lit a cigarette so she could have a quick smoke before going into the house. Joanna was enjoying a no-doubt brief reconciliation with her very strange family and had taken her kids to Europe to hang out with grandma. It wasn't clear whether she was coming back or not, but smoking was still not allowed in "her" house. Mack, as usual, ignored Jasmine. Jasmine attempted to slide by them both and go about her usual tasks in the household, clearing a place in the living room for them to talk, seeing what was available to drink. If she was very lucky, there would be crackers and cheese or something else she could turn into a snack. The dogs, however, remembered her from previous visits and fawned on her, hoping to get brushed or driven to a frenzy chasing a foam football down the hall. They were mutts who had never spent a day in obedience school, but they somehow knew who was Mack's friend and who shouldn't be allowed to set foot on the property. A new mailman or meter reader was bound to experience their version of DNA testing at least once before being given safe passage.

Today Wolfe would not let Jasmine pass. She gently hooked one big paw over Jasmine's forearm and drew her to her side. "What's your hurry, honey? Why don't you stand right here and give everybody on the highway a little thrill?"

The sardonic comment reminded Jasmine that she was half-naked and, to the knowledgeable eye, wearing something in at least one of her holes. Wolfe had definitely put something on the dildo and the plug; they were making her sweat. She could not look at the ground any longer, and was afraid to meet Wolfe's eye. So Jasmine inadvertently caught Mack staring at her. Mack's high cheekbones and big nose suddenly seemed aristocratic, and her expression was inscrutable. Jasmine shivered. Why wouldn't they let her go inside, where it was safe?

"If you knew what was inside, you might not be in such a hurry," Mack said, taking a cigarette and a light from Wolfe. Jasmine flinched at this intrusion into her thoughts, and Wolfe laughed. The master blew smoke at Jasmine and tightened her grip when the slave girl tried to get out of its way.

"What's the matter?" Wolfe asked lightly.

Jasmine tensed at the tone. They were making fun of her. She thought she might cry. Then Wolfe swept her into a one-armed hug, let her go, and fondled her front and back. "Just remember I love you, honey," Wolfe said. "All I ask is that you do the best you can."

They went in with Jasmine sandwiched between them. The dogs frisked along behind, convinced it was all some new jolly human game. Mack and Wolfe escorted Jasmine up the stairs and into a parlor that adjoined one of the bedrooms. She was startled to see three other women there, but not so surprised that she did not hear Mack turn a key and lock the door behind them. The dogs had been shut out, and she could faintly hear them whining and scratching at the door.

"Race, Del," she heard Wolfe say. "Damien. Thanks for coming." Everyone was standing up and formally shaking hands, as if this were some kind of business meeting. There were only five chairs, so she was obviously supposed to stand. There were some bottles and glasses out on a sideboard, so she tried to move over there, to take up the role of a bartender, but Mack blocked her and, without touching her, kept her on the periphery of the room, a ghost at the feast.

To distract herself, she tried to get interested in the room's furnishings. But the carpet on the floor was obviously a cheap American
factory-made approximation of a Persian rug. The couches and
chairs were overstuffed, upholstered in red, blue, or pink velveteen.
Some of the furniture was dressed up with draped pieces of old tat-
ting or big crocheted doilies, probably stuff Joanna had found at a flea
market. But Jasmine thought the tasseled brocade lamp shades might
be genuine pieces from the 1920s. And the silver tea service in a
breakfront cabinet could probably have covered another shot at night
school for Mack, if it was cleaned up. Jasmine thought unkindly that
Joanna had probably stolen the tea service the first time she ran away
from home, ostensibly to go to art school, but actually to smoke hash
in Morocco and gradually wend her way to this town where she could
trouble the sleep of decent dykes and make an open secret of her dis-
tinguished, if homophobic, heritage.

But she didn't really know if Joanna had ever run away from
home, and was there anything more predictable and boring than a
catfight between two femmes? Saint Marilyn shook her head in dis-
taste just at the thought of it. Besides, Jasmine knew something was
up. There was some reason why Wolfe had brought her here. The
slave girl knew all of these women. What was going on?

Race was a botanist who did environmental impact surveys. She
was of average height, had neatly cut, sandy hair, and wore round
wire-rim glasses. She was somewhat of an oddity in this community
since she rarely socialized with leatherdykes. She did not give demon-
strations of S/M technique at support group meetings, and she did not
appear as a judge or a spectator at women's contests. She rode with a
motorcycle club that was nominally mixed, but mostly gay men, and
served on the board of an AIDS charity. Del was her boy, an apple-
cheeked 25-year-old butch who had never acknowledged Jasmine's
existence. *Too bad for you Wolfe's not a faggot like Race,* Jasmine thought
meanly. She had gotten used to people flirting outrageously with

Wolfe in her presence. But Del had treated her like a dirty ashtray that the bartender should have picked up long ago. A girl liked to get at least a sheepish look and a shrug before the competition started throwing their underwear beneath Wolfe's boot heels.

She thought Del's problem was that she had come out just a couple years too late to realize that femmes were not some mad twist of dyke fashion that would go away in another six weeks. Del had no sense at all that she and Jasmine were members of the same tribe. She took her ability to bottom for other butches totally for granted. Jasmine wasn't that old, but when she came out, you just didn't acknowledge such goings-on in public. If two butches went to bed with each other, everybody knew one of them had to walk on the ceiling and play femme for a day. Somebody had to lose status, somebody had to come back to the bar shamefaced and angry, vowing not to make the same mistake again.

Jasmine didn't think that was right. She didn't think butches should feel bad for wanting to be with each other. But she didn't want to be overlooked or discounted. She had to admit she got a little panicky at the idea of butches who had no erotic response to silk stockings or dangly earrings. Because if butches did not want her, that left her in a world where no one but straight men would see her as attractive, and that was worse than being dead.

Of all the women who were here, Damien was the one who puzzled Jasmine the most. Damien was one of Wolfe's exes, a former slave who had torn up her contract and taken a hike. It had been five years, and as far as Jasmine knew, she and Wolfe had not spoken a civil word to each other since then. Damien was pretty much established as a top now, although her propensity for wearing lipstick with her tuxedo (as she was this afternoon) caused some muttering. She had also been seen around town in a sundress or two instead of the requisite cutoffs and tank tops. She was tanned, tall, and had a salt-and-pepper crewcut. Was she a butchy femme or a femmey butch?

Jasmine couldn't say. But Wolfe seemed very moved by her presence, holding on to her hand and bringing her close so they could exchange a few words that no one else in the room could hear.

Jasmine was surprised by the white-hot plume of jealousy that spouted out of the top of her head. Damien was so many things she was not. She would look like a fashion model in some of the clothes that Wolfe liked to see her girls wear. She had narrow hips and long legs and small breasts. And she had the capacity to be butch, to top, to leave the messy world of sexual craving and submission behind. Even when she was enraged with Wolfe, Jasmine could not imagine leaving her. She could only imagine their relationship ending at Wolfe's instigation. Well, elegance is all very well, but voluptuousness had to count for something. Jasmine decided Damien was simply a failed femme, and bottled up her hatred in a small, dark chamber at the bottom of her heart.

The gaze that she had been allowing to flit around the room landed on Mack. And Jasmine realized that Mack was cruising her. She was staring at her lips, then her breasts, her stomach, her thighs. Mack was assessing her legs, weighing the texture of her skin, thinking about what it would be like to kiss her . . . or spank her. Jasmine blushed so hard it was painful. Oh, this was awful, to be standing here with all these predatory women, not knowing what was going on, while somebody she was afraid of undressed her with her eyes and Wolfe didn't seem to notice or care.

Mack moved to one of the armchairs, and Jasmine noticed that everybody else, including Wolfe, was seated. "Come over here," her master said, and Jasmine's feet took her in the direction of the command before her brain could shriek, "Strangle Mack, steal the key, and flee!" She had to take small steps because of the unusually high heels. The only way to keep her balance was to sway from side to side, which made her hips move as if she were being penetrated. And, in fact, she was. Jasmine realized suddenly that all the butches in the room knew that Wolfe had dressed her in these indecent clothes, stuffed things into her cunt and ass, and brought her here for them to admire. This was the audience she had been groomed for. But these were all experienced butches who had seen more than one pair of boobs. Looking at hers wasn't going to be much of a show for them. What, then, was the afternoon's scheduled entertainment?

Wolfe drew a circle in the air, and Jasmine pirouetted, channeling Marilyn and feeling one thigh slip past the other. What traitors cunts were. No wonder calling somebody a cunt was like saying they were untrustworthy or faithless. Her own cunt couldn't even be persuaded to stop talking to strangers, much less these five experienced and ruthless women. *I am,* Jasmine thought, *fish in a barrel. Deer in the headlights.*

The quick turn had made her a little dizzy. Wolfe saw her confusion and indicated, with a curt wave, that she could stand a little closer. Jasmine scurried to obey. "Not so fast," Wolfe scowled. "Let's have a look at you. Let's all have a look at you. Take a promenade." Which way should she walk? Mack was behind her, so there was no way to see whether that face was welcoming or forbidding. Confused by potential trouble from so many directions, Jasmine went to Race and Del. They were wearing matching fatigues in a desert camouflage, with sand-colored T-shirts and very shiny combat boots. Del was sitting on the arm of Race's chair, and so she came to her first. The young butch regarded her with skepticism, as if to say, "What good are you?" Then Del reached out, tweaked one of her nipples, and laughed. Jasmine felt rage come up from her feet and grab her stomach. She came within a hairbreadth of slapping the boy. But behind her, Wolfe cleared her throat and said, "Jasmine, behave. You are to let my friends look at you and, if they like, they may handle you."

Race had a disgusted look on her face, and at first, Jasmine was afraid the daddy would be a mirror of the boy's contempt. But Race used her forearm to push Del off the arm of her chair. The upset boy was suddenly sitting on the floor, with his head below the hem of Jasmine's skirt. Race had Jasmine stand with her legs apart, and ran her hand up the inside of the slave girl's thigh. "Mmm," she said, finding no panties, but did not intrude. She simply let the edge of her hand rest against the strap that protected Jasmine's outer lips. She ran the fingers of the other hand inside the bodice of Jasmine's dress, found the bra, and scooped one of her breasts out of its confinement. It was the same nipple that Del had twisted like the knob on a stereo.

Race, knowing her boy was watching, lavished the skill of her palm upon the offended breast, soothing the skin around the slightly injured nipple until it hardened and welcomed her attentions. Race said something about girls with big breasts being more sensitive than flat-chested girls, and Jasmine had the brief satisfaction of seeing Del stiffen with the sort of resentment she knew only too well. It hurt to be compared unfavorably to another bottom, especially if your flaw was something you could not control. Then Race smashed Jasmine's smugness by bringing her fist up smartly into her crotch. The sudden pressure drove the butt plug and dildo into the slave girl, and her legs almost crumpled.

"Don't you come, now," Wolfe warned her. "I don't care if you get a few cheap thrills, baby, but don't you come."

Race got her clever fingers between the harness and the butt plug and manipulated it slightly. The water-based lubricant had dried until it was tacky, so Jasmine cried out as the plug first clung to the sensitive lining of her ass and then suddenly moved inside it. "Bet you could get something a lot bigger than this up her ass," Race said, and Jasmine knew she would have been pleased if she could have made the slave disobey Wolfe's orders and come. She clamped her lips together and tried not to respond.

But Wolfe would not let her be. "Well?" her master snapped. "What about it, Jasmine? Could we get something bigger than that up your ass?"

"Yes," she whispered, and Race put a hand under her chin and raised her head.

"I think you're going to have to say it louder than that," Race told her, not unkindly, and Jasmine complied, cheeks flaming. "Stand up," Race told Del, removing Jasmine's other breast from confinement. "Hold your tits up, sweetheart," she instructed the slave. "Del, let me see you artfully suck on these. Use your nicest, softest mouth, boy, because I want to see those nipples wrinkled and hard when you are done. Ah, ah, don't touch. Jasmine will hold them up for you. Just your mouth. That's the only part of you that gets to touch her. For now, anyway."

Perhaps it was because Del was under orders, but the calf-mouth that Jasmine felt sucking on her nipple was cunning. Her nipples rapidly hardened, and she could feel her pulse and breathing quicken. Del took more and more of her breast into her mouth, but that wicked little tongue continued to dance upon the point of her nipple. Jasmine heard herself begin to cry out, and then Race forcibly separated the two of them and sent her on her way with a slap on the bottom.

Damien was watching Jasmine with cool amusement. "So you're my little peace offering," she mused. "How does it feel, dear, to be a pawn in the big girls' games?" She made Jasmine turn, and ran her fingernails down the small of her back, the buttocks, the thighs. Jasmine found it increasingly difficult to stay on her high heels, to hold her skirt up and not react or push her aching cunt into the hand that touched her in other places. Damien also ran her fingernails down the front of her, digging their tips into her nipples, giving her goose bumps by dragging them down her upper arms and her shoulders. "You're very responsive," Damien said sadly. "It means a better time for us, but a worse time for you, I'm afraid." Then Damien stood up, took Jasmine's chin, and forced her to look her straight in the eye. "Don't think for a minute that I won't use you just as hard as Mack or Race or anyone except possibly your owner. Don't ever make that mistake with me, Jasmine."

"No, master," Jasmine whispered. "Thank you for touching me, master." Damien had drawn her firmly forward until their hips met, and along Damien's inner thigh, Jasmine felt a firm rod, which directed her to use the masculine honorific.

"Get along with you," Damien said, and gave her a little push toward Mack. Jasmine went, energized by the clues she was finally getting about what kind of evening this was going to be. She was past feeling nervous, past feeling hesitant or resentful. That brief and discreet contact with Damien's cock had set something free inside Jasmine. She was up on the pony and running full tilt, in the race at last.

Mack was seated in a pink overstuffed velveteen armchair that clashed in every possible way with the nubby red sweater (decorated with white reindeer) that she wore with her black leather pants. Her engineer boots had scuff marks identical to the motorcycle damage on Wolfe's boots. Mack had pushed up the sleeves of her sweater, exposing a six-inch long and two-inch wide burn mark on her forearm, a souvenir from the accident that had required her to lay her bike down last year. How many girls had those hands disciplined and loved into oblivion? Jasmine swallowed, visually tracing a line in Mack's forearm muscle that promised a great deal of sexual stamina. She imagined that the outside of Mack's leg probably looked worse than that burn on her arm. Mack was probably lucky she still had both of her legs. Then she forgot that extraneous crap, because Mack had caught her eye, and she was falling into two deep black pools of dangerous knowledge: butch wisdom about the guile of girls and how to defeat their automatic resistance to being roped and ridden home.

Saint Marilyn said something breathless about the eyes have it, honey, then giggled at her own pun, saying, "Aye, aye, sir." Jasmine thought it was true, that a top's eyes were really the key, more important than a studded belt, a thousand dollars' worth of whips, or knee-high boots. Because the eyes told you what that top knew, what she carried in her soul, and without that, all the accessories were just fakes, theatrical props for a turkey that was going to fold after opening night. Mack's eyes said, "I know you, little girl, I know where you came from, I know what you want, and I know how to give it to you. I know your past, and I am your present and your future." Once a butch had you, you could never take that back. It was like being in a porn shot, those images would live forever in both of your hearts, and you had no way to control how, where, or when they might turn up and change your life. You carried a piece of her in your soul forever, for better or for worse, just as she carried a snapshot of you flailing around dressed in sweat and torn-up stockings, panting like a racehorse and wailing for more cunt pumping, more face slapping, more shark-bite kisses.

Jasmine thought this encounter between her and Mack would probably have happened sooner or later. Better here and now, under Wolfe's eye and with the master's blessing, than sometime when Wolfe was out of town and they ran into each other when one of them was drunk or pissed off at Master W. Jasmine could not help but imagine herself and Mack clawing at each other, trying to get enough sweetness out of the clandestine encounter to ease the pain of paying for their betrayal later on. Saint Marilyn said, "Ouch! You might as well have sex with the Mafia, honey."

Moving to a music only she could hear, Jasmine sashayed over to Mack like a high-class dancer who expects to see hundred-dollar bills tucked into her G-string once a minute. She put herself through shimmies and whirls, dips and kicks, as if there were a pole that ran floor to ceiling eight inches away from Mack's knees. When something in those obsidian eyes shifted, got a little warmer and more accessible, she moved directly onto Mack's lap, hitching her skirt up in tantalizing increments before she landed, and finished with her breasts under Mack's chin, skinning the dress up and over her head and off. Still she moved, sinuous, shameless, as enticing as a gift sent from one king to another. If she was the only wealth that Mack would ever possess, let it be a king's ransom. She would pour herself out like gold for Mack to run her hands through, be a waterfall of shimmering pleasure. Those brown, square hands came to rest at the curve of Jasmine's waist, their light touch more provocative than a fist against the neck of her womb. The dancing girl lifted her tawny hair, let it fall in a glimmering haze, then grazed Mack's unforgiving cheekbones with the tips of her painted fingers, a pleading touch that said, "Use me as you will, as long as you know me completely."

The staccato sound of applause broke Jasmine's rapport with Mack, and she turned to see Del, sarcastically beating her hands together. Jasmine flushed kick-your-ass red, but then Race and the other tops joined in, turning the kid's bratty moment of envy into sincere appreciation. Was that a slight tightening at the corner of Race's mouth? *Just you wait till your father gets home!* Jasmine thought spitefully.

Wolfe motioned to her, and Jasmine extricated herself from the awkward position she was in, straddling Mack's substantial hips, and went to her master in style, on all fours, the doffed dress clasped as a peace offering in her mouth. Jasmine had actually been given extensive lessons on how to crawl beautifully. Wolfe had videotaped her first efforts and forced her to watch them while her moves were critiqued. Now she knew she was swimming forward as gracefully as a mermaid, the to-and-fro movements of her white buttocks hopefully engendering many dirty thoughts about fucking doggy-style. At Wolfe's feet, she knelt up, hands behind her back, hair thrown back, equally inviting slaps or kisses. She was deep into the freedom of slavery now, wearing her sensuality as proudly as a patriot raises the flag.

"Are you ready for your final exams?" Wolfe asked, her eyebrows knitted in a position that told Jasmine she was repressing a laugh.

"If it pleases you, Master," Jasmine said with a sly little wink, bat, bat of her painted eyes. On her knees, she did a vaudeville bump-and-grind.

Wolfe broke into a chuckle, and Jasmine felt a little more tension leave her body. She was never punished for making Wolfe laugh. "Then turn around and pay attention," Wolfe said. "Each one of my, um, colleagues has offered to test you in a key subject. If you pass every test, my wild child, you get to graduate today. The rules are very simple, Jasmine. You are to please each one of these, my associates, as much as you would try to please me. They are authorized to use you as fully as I would, to suit myself."

Perhaps to facilitate these examinations, Wolfe unbuckled the crotch strap that held the dildo and ass plug in place and removed them. Jasmine gasped as her orifices were smoothly but quickly emptied. She remembered the first time Wolfe had tried to take out her butt plug, and shuddered. Some control-queen hygiene-freak part of her had been outraged at the idea of letting someone else perform such an intimate operation. Thank Saint Marilyn, she'd never been that stupid again. She'd scrubbed Wolfe's bathroom three times with a toothbrush held between her teeth and still been in dutch for a week.

The empty holes behaved as if they were mouths that had just lost their gags, and talked to her in a rush of sensation and need. *Shut up,* she told them firmly. *There's no lack of trade here. You'll get all you can handle and more, I bet.*

Who would be first? Jasmine eyed each one of them in turn. The suspense built, and she could not tell from anyone's face what they would do next. Then Race stood up, having placed Del on a leash, and opened the door to the bedroom. Before Jasmine could enter, she cleared her throat and said, "The first precept is that of complete and prompt obedience. I will be the inquisitor of your obedience, Jasmine. Go in."

The high-ceilinged room was painted in a flaking cream-white. An ancient chandelier still swung from the center of the ceiling.

Against one wall there was a bed, covered in a sheet of black leather, with manacles and chains clearly displayed. Race ordered Del to kneel at the foot of the bed, then dropped the end of his leash over one of the posts. She intercepted Jasmine on her way to lie down upon the bed and brought her close, encircled her in strong arms. Jasmine tolerated the contact uneasily, made skittish by such an unfamiliar embrace.

"My first order is that you kiss me," Race said clearly.

Jasmine could hear the others filing into the room behind her. She had no doubt that Wolfe would get a prime vantage point. Why didn't Race simply chain her up and whip her severely? That would be easier than this. She wasn't allowed to kiss anybody but Wolfe. And yet . . . her orders were clear.

So she leaned forward and grazed Race's mouth with her own. There was no change in Race's facial expression, and her lips did not soften. Jasmine thought, *You look like such a science nerd,* and felt a fierce desire to melt Race's academic mien. So she went on tiptoe and leaned into the top, making sure her breasts were nipple-to-nipple with Race's chest, and placed her hands on the bare back of her neck. Jasmine had yet to meet a butch who did not come unglued when you played with the short hairs at the back of her head. She breathed gently on Race's mouth, then her lips landed on it like a fierce butterfly. She employed slight variations of pressure, then dared to insinuate the tip of her tongue, offering it as a treat if it was wanted or welcome. Race's mouth opened slowly, and Jasmine was lured inside. She felt a flush of arousal and triumph.

This ill-prepared her for what came next. Race seized her face with both hands and tipped it back, then administered a disciplinary kiss of shocking force and duration. Jasmine responded by reflex, crying out as her body melted under the instructional assault. But when Race drew away, Jasmine was pleased to see her wire-rim glasses fogged up like the windows of a car with a rockin' back seat.

"Now," Race said, bringing Del to her feet and unsnapping the leash, "I want you to kiss my boy."

Jasmine knew better than to hesitate for even a split second. She went toward Del like an ocean liner bearing down on a dinghy, determined to get through to her, throwing every bit of femme glamour she possessed at the flinty boy-bottom's macho little heart. Del actually rocked back on the heels of her combat boots, as if struck by friendly fire. Then Jasmine practically swarmed up her body, hand-over-hand, as if she were climbing a rope, and smothered Del with a sizzling screen-test-quality smooch. She put a little more steel into this one than she had dared to offer Race, letting the boy know the sex kitten had sharp little teeth. Maybe that was why Del softened in her arms and then stiffened again, having caught herself violating the butch-on-butch code by juicing up for a girly-girl.

Jasmine was, however, careful to erase any sign of amusement from her face before she went back to Race, asking humbly, "Will that do, master?"

"Get on the bed, on your stomach," Race said curtly, having seen more than Jasmine thought she had revealed. Quaking, Jasmine did as she was told, and displayed herself on the cold, smooth black background in an X of vulnerability that screamed, "Please! Don't! Stop!" She did not hear Race walk to the side of the bed, and jumped a little when the back strap of her bra was undone, the ends tucked beneath her chest. Race also sprang the clips on her back garters and stowed them out of the way. There was more dignity in complete nudity than in this half-stripped display of skin, Jasmine thought unkindly.

"You will take six strokes of the cane," Race said, "to display your obedience to me, as your master's proxy."

Jasmine had second thoughts about the relative difficulties of kisses and whippings. She calculated the odds of getting herself into even more hot water versus cajoling Race into going a little easier on her, and quipped, "What, no warm-up?"

No understanding chuckle acknowledged her sally.

"You will take 12 strokes of the cane," Race intoned, "to display your obedience to me, as your master's proxy, and to compensate me for the aggravation of being interrupted."

"Yes, sir," Jasmine said, soft but clear. "I apologize, sir."

She hated being caned. Hated it so much that Wolfe had considered using it as a punishment, then discarded physical pain in favor of the suffering engendered by good old neglect. She wasn't much of a masochist, that was the problem. She could go for hours with a heavy leather flogger, and if she was built up to it, enjoy a quirt or a cat, but canes were, she was convinced, a toy that had been placed on this earth for the enjoyment of only one half of the sadomasochistic duo. In other words, a top toy.

"I accept your apology," Race said. "You may grasp the chains by your wrists."

So she was going to have to do this without the solace of bondage. Jasmine tucked her head and wondered if she was going to be allowed to scream. She tried to calm herself down by adding up the time that a dozen cane strokes might take. Surely no more than 15 minutes, perhaps half an hour if Race had the patience of Job. Could she tolerate half an hour of severe pain? Why did that suddenly seem about as reassuring as an eternity of suffering?

"You may scream," Race said, with the damnable ability of all tops to read their victims' minds. "You may kick. However, you may not lift your torso from the bed or move from side to side. Would you like this quick or slow?"

Through gritted teeth, Jasmine said . . . nothing at all. The silence lengthened into a faux pas. "Whatever p-pleases you, sir," she finally stammered.

She could hear a rapping sound as Race impatiently struck the side of her leg with the cane. "What pleases me is for you to answer my question," Race said, enunciating clearly as if for one feebleminded.

"Slow," she almost shrieked. "Please, if it please you, sir."

The first blow came like lightning out of a clear sky, and Jasmine forced herself to let the cane drive her deeper into the bed, so she would not bolt. The second landed before the first stroke had gone through all the permutations of pain that the cane delivers, and it was high as well, so she could not repress a kick or two. This was slow? Then there was a wait for three, such a long wait that Jasmine repented her choice a dozen times, having forgotten how much agony can be meted out by anticipation. Four was cunning, five burned like a hot iron, six rolled over her like a tank. Seven and eight were a pair of lovers, tearing at her flesh so they could remain near to one another. Nine was a deep cut, ten was a rocket being launched across her backside, 11 severed her in half, and 12 was Judas Iscariot himself, doing all he could to persuade her to betray her lord and master.

"Such language," somebody murmured. Was it Damien? And Jasmine heard laughter. She had been giving Race a piece of her mind, then. That sometimes happened. She hoped it might be overlooked, and apparently it was. But when she tried to get up, Race pressed her back into the surface of the bed.

"You will now take six cane strokes from my boy Del," Race told her, and there was no pity in her voice, no hope of pardon.

It is one thing to take a thrashing from someone you like or respect. It is quite another to put up with being hurt by a pissant you despise. Jasmine bit the inside of her own cheek and did some fast and furious attitude adjusting. It didn't quite succeed. There was no way she could see Del as an honorable dominant who was entitled to her pain. *So let Del drop out of the picture,* she thought. *Instead of Del, let me think about Wolfe.* And she began to carefully build a mental portrait of Wolfe, from the boot soles up, lavishing attention on each buckle and zipper tooth, wanting each detail to be vibrant and perfect.

Then Del poked her with the end of the cane, and Jasmine's careful construct blew up in hot fragments of hatred. From the outline of the prod, Jasmine thought Del was not using the same thin, flexible cane that Race had wielded. This was a short, rigid rod of bamboo, half an inch in diameter, with sharp, raised joints that would leave distinctive marks. She was no shrink-wrapped hunk of rump roast to be poked by a cranky, hungover housewife in the supermarket! She was Jasmine, a treasured beauty, a delight, her master's pet and trophy.

Del swatted her, deliberately landing on preexisting marks, and Jasmine found that silence was the only suitable container for her hostility. She did not move. Nose to toes, she was a woman carved in ice. Disappointed and embarrassed, Del hit her again, much harder, on top of the first blow, and that pettiness was all the motivation Jasmine needed to maintain the barrier of her quiet disdain. Four more strokes followed in a flurry of impotent rage, and Jasmine cared less than the dead care if their headstones fall over.

Someone was trying to get her to stand up. She realized that someone was Race, and allowed herself to be pried up off the bed. The nipple of a sport bottle was between her teeth, and she drank the offering of cool water, which is so often administered as the sadist's apology. "Kiss me," Race murmured, and Jasmine went unthinking into her arms, drank in the strength and arousal of her imperious and impartial mouth. Saint Marilyn started singing, "She blinded me with science," and Jasmine had to slam an imaginary door on her guardian angel, not wanting to explode into a bluster of buffoonish laughter.

"You're steady on your feet," Race said, checking, and then handed Jasmine a coiled lash, braided to discipline a team of sled dogs, and largely sold in parts of the country where that mode of travel is not common. "You will now administer a half-dozen lashes to demonstrate your obedience to me as proxy for your master," Race said.

Jasmine's vision cleared immediately, along with her sinuses. She located Del in half no time, and gleefully moved in her direction. Or tried to. Race was in the way.

"No," Race said gently, motioning for Del to go and kneel by the far wall, with the rest of the spectators. "You are to whip me, Jasmine." She took off her T-shirt, slid out of her sport bra, and grabbed one of the posts at the foot of the bed, flexing her back. Then she waited, like a statue of patience. Her muscles were outlined, apparently by bodybuilding, grooves built for the tongue of an adoring bottom.

Jasmine did not think she could express in words the whirl of emotions that dizzied her. She had never even conceived of such a thing. *Whip Race?* That was like assassinating a king. In fact, killing a head of state would be easier. She knew there were femme tops, of course, duh! Sometimes Wolfe would threaten her, if she was sulky, with a weekend under the tutelage of one of the local Queens of Pain. It wasn't an experience that Jasmine would relish, she was sure of that. It would be too . . . homosexual, or something. And there were people who switched, switches, yes, OK, but in mid scene? If you did that to a car, wouldn't the transmission fall out and hit the street?

Then one word rang out, obliterating other thoughts like a comic Chinese gong. "Obedience," it said, spelling itself out in waves of imaginary black ink. Synonyms followed in lesser waves: "Compliance, submission, following orders, doing as you are told . . ."

Jasmine uncoiled the lash and took a practice shot at thin air. Maybe she had taken Wolfe's single-tail down off the wall a few times when she was pouty and supposed to be taking a time-out to clean up her attitude. Jasmine really hated it when Wolfe stomped out of the house and left her alone, supposedly to get all humble and penitent. Maybe she had wanted to see if she could get it to make that rifle-shot noise that made everybody's ears stand up if you heard it at a party. It hadn't looked that hard to her. Tops think they're so special. Well, they don't have a monopoly on hand-eye coordination. Or vicious-ness. Maybe she had even done a little target practice on nights when Wolfe was out with her butch buddies and Jasmine was supposed to be working on her slave journal. (One of the sofa cushions had split open, but Jasmine had fixed it with a safety pin and turned it around so the tear would not show. Wolfe never noticed the damaged pillow or the red ear Jasmine had gotten when she pulled the whip too close to her own head.)

Did she still have the knack? Jasmine frowned, and was rewarded with a clear snap. This whip was not as easy to manage as a cane, but it was not nearly as long as a bullwhip. She tried again, and it did as she wished, an extension of her eye and arm. Turning, she located Race, who waited still. Though Jasmine's entire world had shifted, only a moment had elapsed. Not even enough time for Race's back to grow cold. Willing herself to remain oblivious to the welts that wanted petting, Jasmine allocated the right amount of distance between herself and Race, and laid the first crack on between the daddy's shoulder blades. There was a surprising amount of satisfaction to be had in hurting the strapping butch body in front of her.

"No-o-o!" Jasmine heard Del bellow and stomp her feet. She was somehow able to keep herself from turning her head to see this tantrum. She had no doubt that Del had attempted to race over to the bed and throw herself at Jasmine. She also had no doubt that some-body else would restrain the rambunctious child. She told herself it was probably going to be a good long while before Del got a gradua-tion party that was half this good.

"One," Race said. "Thank you, madam."

That reminded Jasmine of the business at hand. She moved a little to her left and placed a star of pain alongside the original mark. Race counted it off in style, without a single quiver in her voice. Jas-mine wondered if anyone had ever looked at her and felt this weird sort of admiration. She went to her right and did her trick again. This time Race hesitated a bit, but the count came out good and strong, no sarcasm about the "madam" part either. Jasmine thought, *I could get to like this,* and decided she would make the six blows into a triangle shape of marks down Race's back. So she placed each of the remaining three, careful as could be, though the point of the triangle was a bit off center. Still, not bad for a novice.

Then Race turned around, and Jasmine dropped the whip and hit the deck, her incipient madamhood a tattered mist of fading memory. Maybe Race was pissed off. Maybe she was deliriously happy. Either way, Jasmine did not want to know any more than Moses had wanted to look at the burning bush. She was lifted off the floor and flung onto the foot of the bed, on her back, and entered roughly with a hand that did not doubt its mastery. Beneath the weight of her body, each cane mark introduced itself to Jasmine's consciousness in a way that could not be ignored.

"I want people in the next county to know you're coming," Race hissed, and Jasmine advertised her pleasure as ordered. It was not until after she collapsed, sweating and husky-voiced, that she wondered what Wolfe would think, to see her property so easily conquered by another top's possessive fingers. Race had smaller hands than Wolfe, which meant they went in farther, deeper. Race had a twisty, probing way of fucking that was distinct from Wolfe's battering-ram style. Jasmine blushed, recalling the way she had bellowed for more and pumped her hips until she got it.

But Wolfe did not shun her like a traitor. Wolfe came and got her, and straightened out her stockings and garters, and put her bra back on and fastened it in back. Wolfe took her into the parlor, poured her some lemonade, and after she drank it, sat her down and brushed her hair. As she collected her wits, Jasmine realized that Race's boy had been gagged, his hands cuffed behind his back. Furthermore, he was hog-tied neck to ankles next to Race's chair, under her close supervision. Race had not put her shirt back on, and Damien was with her, applying antibiotic ointment with the detached care of a veterinarian who is treating a fear-biter, and expressing purely aesthetic appreciation.

Wolfe looked at Race with a question in her big, honest face. Race at first looked puzzled, then laughed and waved her hands. "Pass," she choked out, through her laughter. "As if there could be any question, Wolfe. Pass, A plus, good fucking show."

Taking advantage of this moment of conviviality, Jasmine whispered a request to pee, which was granted, and left the room as quickly as possible. The dogs were overjoyed when she came out of the parlor and accompanied her to the bathroom to supervise her toilette. Privacy was a scarce commodity in Mack's home. Not for the first time, Jasmine was grateful that Wolfe had no pets save herself.

When she returned to the conference of the butch dyke deans of depravity, Jasmine noticed that Damien was sitting on the edge of her chair. Without being told to do so, she blew Wolfe a kiss, stalked over to Damien, and made her obeisance, kneeling with knees apart, hands upturned on her thighs like captive wild orchids. She had hoped that assuming the position would help her to hear the psychic vibration of Damien's dominance and tune her body to match it. When she was in the presence of someone she read as butch, Jasmine felt as if she were being snared by an invisible net. She could struggle against it, but this would only excite the person who had caught her. But between herself and Damien, she could not sense the polarity, the distance and difference that made her quiver with hope and dread. She might as well have been kneeling to a department store mannequin or a streetlight.

"A good slave is honest," Damien said, staring into Jasmine's eyes. "At your master's request, I will test your candor, little slave." Then she slipped a length of black silk over Jasmine's eyes and knotted it behind her head. The room disappeared. Jasmine was alone and reached out in a panic. Damien caught her hands and steadied her.

"Let's begin with just a little conversation," she said. Jasmine was instantly suspicious. That velvety and reassuring voice had to be up to something tricksy and sly. "Just answer my questions truthfully, yes or no."

When nothing else was said for a while, Jasmine answered grudgingly, "Yes, master."

"Do you like my lipstick, Jasmine?"

Criticizing the physical appearance of a top was not exactly one of Jasmine's habits. To her face, that is. It took a surprising amount of resolve for Jasmine to make herself say, "No, I don't."

Damien chuckled and took a tighter grip on her hands. "Do you find me attractive, Jasmine?"

This time it was marginally easier. "No," Jasmine whispered, embarrassed by her own truth.

"But you'll still do whatever I say, won't you?" Damien purred.

Jasmine hung her head. "Yes," she admitted, hating Damien almost as much as Del.

"Show me," Damien said, and took her supporting hands away. Damien's ringers touched her lips lightly, as if to say, "Farewell."

Abandoned, Jasmine was in danger of coming completely unglued. Then she remembered Damien pressing their bodies together, the brief but electric contact with her strapped-on dick, a seductive promise. She put her hands behind her back and fluttered them there, showing the entire room how beautifully she performed this symbol of helplessness. Then she went face first toward Damien, hoping that her sense of touch and smell would guide her to the fly of those expensive black tuxedo pants. She encountered Damien's thigh first and rubbed her face on it like a cat looking for skritches. Then she edged forward on her knees, trying to ignore some rather large particles of grit that made her kneecaps smart, and nibbled her way up. Her teeth encountered no evidence of a zipper. This must be a piece of retro fashion, or it was tailor-made with a button fly. Jasmine made short work of the top hook-and-eye.

"Before you go any further," Damien said, "I think you should put one of your pretty hands between your legs, and give us all a little show. Let's not have any furtive disobedient orgasms, however. In this county or the next."

If there was anything more embarrassing than the sound of one top laughing at you, it had to be the sound of four tops snickering at your expense. Jasmine visualized the caustic sound rolling off her back, like water off a duck, and kept her mouth soft and pliant around the top button. The fabric of the trousers was thick and scratchy, and left a dry coating on her tongue.

Fortunately, Damien was wearing only a plain cotton jockstrap beneath her pants. Fishing a cock out of a pair of Y-fronts with nothing but your mouth was an ungainly hassle, Jasmine knew. She got the elastic edge of the jock's pouch in her front teeth and lifted it up and over, enough to reveal the head of the object that she sought. She willed her salivary glands to speed up production of moisture, and slid her mouth down over the latex glans.

Sucking dyke dick has much in common with bio–cock sucking, but there are some important differences, Jasmine mused. She went too far down the shaft, deliberately, to make herself gag just a bit. The resulting mucus was a necessary and valuable lubricant for her efforts. Damien would be able to feel pressure on her labia and clit from the base of the dildo. So it was important to keep up a rhythm of motion that moved the toy just enough to provide stimulation. Slamming it around would only make a top sore and cranky. The rest of the stimulation was visual. So it was important to offer your face up to the top, so they could see the tears that fell from your eyes, the stretched-out O of your mouth, all the swirling and lapping that you did with your tongue.

Boys and butches had one thing in common, though, when it came to blow jobs: They all wanted to get it all the way in. A bisexual friend had once told Jasmine that it was actually easier to accommodate a phallus of flesh; "It bends," she said simply. Jasmine had no basis for comparison and didn't want one either. Damien's strap-on cock was different than many she had sampled. It seemed to have a slightly harder core within a very soft yet firm exterior. And it was getting warmer faster than an old-fashioned rubber dong. Jasmine still found it necessary to take a deep breath as she swallowed it down to the base, but it was much easier to keep there.

It was a lot to keep track of all at once—stroking herself and marveling at how the wetness from Wolfe combined with tribute to Race and now Damien in one seamless flow of excitement; letting Damien know that she was working hard to give good head; catching a sobbing breath in between bouts of smothered choking; and, with some part of her mind, trying to monitor everyone else in the room, despite the blindfold, which cut off all visual information and seemed to dull her hearing too. Eventually some of those tasks had to fall away, and Jasmine entered into a quiet place where there were really only two objects demanding her attention: a slippery clit that was standing out like the regal figurehead on a ship and an inanimate shaft that had taken on vicarious life because of her passion.

Damien was moved enough by Jasmine's display to put a hand on the back of her head, urging her forward and down. This gesture swept the girl into an even greater dedication to her task. Both of them were rocking together in a pattern of accelerating tension that could only lead to climax. Jasmine paused long enough to make an urgent request. She fondled Damien's wet rod as she spoke. "Please let me come," Jasmine whispered, just as the head of her clit disappeared, obliterated by the sexual swelling of the surrounding tissues. She filled her throat without waiting for an answer.

Damien did not reply. Instead, Jasmine heard Race say, "Look and learn, boy," and Del's sullen "Yes, sir." They were much closer than she had imagined. Startled, Jasmine stopped touching herself for a moment, only to feel a sharp pain across her shoulders. It was the dog lash, probably administered by Race at Damien's gesture of request.

"You can come if you can tell me what you are thinking," Damien said, and pushed Jasmine's mouth off her rod. There was another flash of pain, slightly to the right of her spine, and Damien added, "I want you to keep on stroking yourself while you answer my question."

Jasmine wasn't sure she had been thinking at all. This request seemed to contradict what she had been trying to do to please Damien—get her head to shut up, and allow her body and her desire to take over. Then she was struck again, and this time the snake of braided leather traced a short line of bright sensation below her left shoulder blade.

"You have till the count of three to start talking," Damien said in a cool voice that was without animosity and also without mercy. "Remember, it is your honesty that is being tested. If you continue your silence, I will have Race whip you across your breasts. You will know a great deal of pain and much dishonor. One."

A certain misunderstood and overexposed platinum blond came to Jasmine's rescue, like a rush of billowing skirts and Evening in Paris perfume. Might as well get the most shameful words out first, then the rest would follow more easily. "When I was sucking your cock, I was thinking about the difference between blowing a guy and blowing a butch," Jasmine confessed. "Then I was thinking about how I could look, what I could show you that would make it feel good for you. I was wondering what kind of dildo that was because it doesn't feel the same in my mouth as the other ones I've sucked on. It's easier to deep-throat than the dildo that Wolfe uses. I was hoping I wouldn't throw up. Giving head makes you cry when the dick goes past the back of your palate. So I was hoping that my makeup wasn't running. Then all I was thinking about was how wet I was, and how hard you were in my mouth, and I just wanted to come, that's all, I

couldn't think about anything else." Marilyn might have had a
problem speaking up for herself when she was alive, but as Jasmine's
alter ego, she was chatty.

Damien nodded. "You don't like me very much, do you,
Jasmine?"

"I don't even know you!" Jasmine made the mistake of protesting.
Damien spun her around, Jasmine was not quite sure how, since she
was on her knees, and to do so would seem to require paranormal
powers of levitation and rotation. Nevertheless, there she was, facing
Race and the dog whip, and one of her nipples felt as if it had just been
torn off. The sensation faded quickly to a fierce burning, as if the left
side of her bra had been stuffed with stinging nettles.

"The truth," Damien insisted.

"No, I don't like you at all," Jasmine shouted.

This seemed to gratify Damien no end. "Continue," she said
quietly.

"Because I don't understand you," Jasmine wept, and kept her
back to her tormenter. "I'm afraid you will take Wolfe away from
me, and I can't compete with you because I'm not like you; you try to
be so many things at once that you aren't anything at all that I can get
a handle on. And if you're a top I don't know what kind of top,
maybe you don't like femmes, I can't tell, so what's the point in even
trying? I wouldn't waste five minutes on you if Wolfe hadn't told me
I had to submit to everybody here."

Damien put a hand on each of Jasmine's shoulders, steadying her.
"Even her up," she told Race, who obliged with a snap-crack that told
the opinionated vixen exactly how many nerve endings she had in the
very tip of her right nipple. "And what do you think when you are
hit?" she asked, oblivious to Jasmine's gasp of pain, the involuntary
bow she made to its source.

"I think about how much I hate the person who is hitting me,
usually," Jasmine said, "and then I hate them so much I won't let

them know they are hurting me, so I bear it that way, but it's really none of your business; why do you even want to know these awful things?"

The blindfold came off with a flourish that sent a puff of cool air up Jasmine's nose. Instead effacing a room full of shock and dismay, Jasmine found herself confronted with a room full of quiet amusement. "That's OK, honey," Wolfe said, happily breaking Joanna's rule about no smoking in her house. Del was kneeling with an ashtray in one hand, looking way too pleased with her all-American–boy self. "I'm big enough to take it. You can hate me all you want. Long as I get to fuck you."

"This isn't fair," Jasmine said. "I never claimed to be a masochist. I'm just a submissive."

Race cleared her throat. "Del is a masochist," she said. "Or so I've been told. Del, get over here and take six on each nipple. Show Jasmine what you can do."

The bull's-eye did not materialize as ordered. Jasmine saw only the heels and toes of Del's boots, protruding from behind Wolfe's big armchair. A muffled voice said, "Oh, daddy, sir, please, no! Anything but that, sir. Anything!"

Race looked like a beleaguered parent who is beyond surprise or upset. "Anything?" she said, in a tone of voice that was so ominous it made Jasmine recoil.

"Anything!" Del sniveled, still hiding and apparently unaware of her great peril.

"Very well, then," Race said, and turned her attention back to Damien and the examinee.

"What would *you* do with Del?" Damien asked, as if the thought had just occurred to her.

Jasmine's answer poured out like a white-water rapid. "I'd teach him his manners," she snapped. "That kid has no respect for his elders and betters. I'd make sure he could be taken out in public without embarrassing his master. And I'd teach him not to take femmes for granted. That boy is a spoiled, self-centered little misogynist."

Race looked profoundly shocked. Apparently it had not occurred to her that things were quite that bad. *Well, what did she expect,* Jasmine thought impatiently, *taking her boy into an all-mule world where women were devalued or ignored?* Then Race looked very thoughtful, coiled up the dog lash, and sat down. Del came scurrying over in a crablike facsimile of Jasmine's puma-in-heat crawl, and got cuffed to one side. The boy lay where he fell, chagrined and uncertain what to do next. Jasmine obeyed a pressure on her shoulder from Damien that told her to face away from Race and the problem child.

"Well, Jasmine," Damien said, "your mind is not a pretty place. It's no garden of adoration and service, is it, my dear?" She had discreetly tucked her dick away.

Jasmine both hung her head and shook it, no.

"Then why do you let all these terrible things happen to you, sweetling?"

"Because it gets me off," Jasmine said, dreading this part of the confession especially. "And later, if it was really awful, I feel especially calm and peaceful inside."

"And if we are horrid . . ." Damien began.

"Then I'm good," Jasmine finished.

"And if I had you for six weeks, what would happen to your deep dislike of me?" Damien queried.

Jasmine threw her a hateful look. "I would bond with you and obey you," she admitted. "And the things about you that I don't like now would probably become turn-ons. They would become things that especially reminded me of you."

"And what did you think when you saw I had put my cock away and done up my fly?"

"I knew that meant you weren't going to fuck me, and I was disappointed," Jasmine cried, stung by her own hypocrisy.

How everyone howled at that, especially Wolfe.

"But that doesn't mean you won't get fucked," Mack said, coming out of the pink chair to stomp over to Jasmine's side. That square brown hand twined itself in Jasmine's hair, and took her into the bedroom in a duckwalk that hurt the back of her calves. She did not hear Damien tell Wolfe, in the other room, "Pass. With flying colors." At the side of the bed, Mack picked Jasmine up and threw her onto the leather coverlet. "The third precept is the precept of stamina," Mack said, sounding like she was reading a sentence that Wolfe had written down for her. "Let's see what you got, Missy. Is that a Teflon pussy, or will it cave in like a wet paper towel?"

Mack slapped a paw full of lubricant over Jasmine's vulva, and almost immediately worked three fingers into her opening. "You don't have to ask me for permission to come," Mack said, "but I do want to hear you say it when it happens. Is that a good spot?" She had found a sensitive place inside Jasmine and was manipulating it with devilish persistence. Jasmine nodded, wailed, "I'm comi-i-ing," and succumbed to the pent-up arousal that had accumulated during Damien's blow job and probing interrogation.

"First one hardly counts at all," Mack said. "Doubt that one had much to do with me anyway." She knelt between Jasmine's legs, unsnapped her leather pants, and took out an impressive implement. Without being asked, Jasmine bent her legs and picked up her own thighs, rocking back a little to present Mack with an easier target. Mack took a moment to peel off the red sweater, revealing a crumpled black T-shirt with a bleach stain at her belly button. She got the head of her cock lined up with Jasmine's notch and went in teasing and slow, back and forth, making sure there was plenty of room to proceed.

Jasmine kept her eyes resolutely fixed on Mack's warrior-handsome face. She did not want to know where the inevitable spectators had positioned themselves. To keep herself focused on Mack, she tightened her legs around the butch on top of her body and began to talk to her in a little-girl whisper of flirtatious protests. "Ooh, I don't think it will go all the way in, please don't hurt me," was just the opening salvo.

Jasmine had to throw this extra bit of effort into the sex because it was weird as hell to be getting balled by Mack. She had long ago accepted the dichotomy between Wolfe and her best friend's stables. Now she was realizing how very much her type Mack was. One by one, the things that Jasmine had told herself to hide Mack's body and keep herself from adulterous flirting were being blown up as falsities. Mack measured bigger around the waistline than Wolfe did, but she was at least as strong. She was capable of vulgarity, but the caresses she bestowed on Jasmine's trembling, sweaty skin were delicate and skillful. The hips that rammed into Jasmine's vulnerable flesh were rock-steady, keeping fuck-time as if they could keep it all day, all night, and most of the morning. She found herself touching Mack's face, trying to kiss her, wanting to move well so that Mack would know how good she was with that big stick.

Jasmine had no idea how many times she had climaxed when Mack slowly pulled out and put a thumb and forefinger on either side of her clit. She wasn't used to being manipulated this way. Wolfe would have sponged the lube off her pussy and fallen face first into what she liked to call "a piece of heavenly hair pie." Mack seemed to expect her to respond to the hand job, though, and so she did, doing her scales in an octave as high as Annapurna.

Panting, she begged Mack to fuck her some more, and her wish was granted, this time from behind. Jasmine had the contradictory sensation of being utterly safe with her tiny butt up against Mack's hips, Mack's arms holding her in place, and yet being helpless and threatened, with a spike of pleasure being driven into her softness. For a long time it seemed as if the only thing she could say was, "I'm coming!" or "More lube, please!"

Then Mack shifted position just a little, and the head of her cock hit a place inside Jasmine that she knew only too well. She knew that if Mack kept on going, hot jets of fluid would gush out of her. Wolfe was the only person who had ever made her ejaculate. But Wolfe had said she was to give in, allow these other hutches every privilege that Wolfe assumed. She explained, in halting monosyllables, what was about to happen to Mack, who thundered with laughter and told her to hurry up then and gush. "That's the only kind of baptism I'm interested in," Mack told her. The shameful jets came then, just like piss, except they smelled much sweeter, and Jasmine felt robbed of her secrets.

Mack gave her no time to recover from this experience, which was more draining than a regular orgasm. She just nipped Jasmine onto her back and kept going. Her hand, capable of more searching and exact motions, replaced the rubber length of her dick. For several moments, Jasmine was afraid she could not keep up with all this driving pressure and friction. There was too much discomfort. Then she opened her eyes and saw Mack's face, distorted by lust, intent on her defeat. Eye to eye, they egged each other on, and the flame of passion was relit between Jasmine's cervix and her perineum. Abrasion became provocation, then detonation.

Someone—Damien?—said, "Forty-two," as if she were keeping score, but Jasmine was too busy moaning to remember what numbers were for. Mack was twisting her hand back and forth, urging the broad palm past the drawstring sphincters that guarded the entrance to Jasmine's cunt. Encountering more resistance than she liked, Mack came out and walloped Jasmine across the butt, first with her hand and then with her belt, then climbed back onto the bed and tried again. The purse was open now, and Mack's hand changed from duck head to fist in the cookie jar. Jasmine shrieked like a band saw that has just lost its blade.

"Fifty," somebody said, and the bottle of lube was empty, useless, thrown across the room. Another one replaced it by Jasmine's upper arm. She looked at it glassy-eyed, not taking in its significance. Mack was panting, "More?" and for the first time the slave girl wondered if her answer would be an unqualified "Yes!" She could feel every ridge and fold of the vault between her legs; it had been outlined by constant stimulation and colored in with satiation.

Sensing Jasmine's ambivalence, Mack slid her hand out, and put the cock back in. But even with this decrease in stretch and friction, Jasmine could feel herself drying up inside. Pulling back into herself. Her throat was sore. Her parts were sore. Her legs ached, and her back hurt. She was very, very sleepy.

"Sixty-one," a voice said that was definitely Damien's, and a voice that might have been Saint Marilyn's added, "That's enough!"

"Oh, come on," Mack said, so out of breath she could barely be understood. Her hair stood up in spikes, and her T-shirt was torn in several places. Jasmine could see livid scratches on her upper arms and shoulders, and wondered angrily who had done such a thing when Mack ought to have been allowed to completely focus on her and her alone. Mack stuck her tongue all the way out and made it vibrate like an angry parrot's. "Just one more," Mack said. "One more, huh, honey? One more?"

"No," Jasmine said crossly. "I'm finished." She pulled away from Mack, curled up on her side, and was asleep in half a second, her thighs glued together with overworked lube and fuck juice.

But she was not allowed to rest. A host of hands lifted her from the bed, stripped the few remaining rags of finery from her body, and carried her into the next room. Jasmine pried her eyes open long enough to identify (barely) Wolfe, before she was placed on her knees before the author of her final exams.

"Had enough?" Wolfe asked gently.

Jasmine had just enough strength to nod once. She looked longingly at Wolfe's knees. It would be lovely to lean into them and take a nap.

"A good slave is loyal, Jasmine," Wolfe said, and then two things happened simultaneously. Wolfe slapped her and yelled, "Come!"

Something happened. Maybe it was an orgasm. Maybe it was just death by implosion. Jasmine couldn't tell. But suddenly she was wide awake and very, very hungry.

Wolfe made a little speech. Jasmine enjoyed the speech because it was all about her and complimentary, but she was even more appreciative of the ham sandwich that Mack handed her, from a platter of sandwiches that circulated around the room. What kind of mustard was that? Not Dijon. Something better. Something more basic. Probably that crappy yellow mustard Wolfe was always smearing on her salami sub to hold the peppers in place. There was also a hot cup of coffee with a lot of sugar and cream in it, "Indian coffee," Mack called it, and Jasmine wondered why she had ever drunk her coffee black. Damien came and got her and took her into the bathroom, where there was a tub of steaming water, and put her in it, then stayed to soap her, sponge her off, and dry her with a big soft towel that had Scooby-Doo on it. They had a nice little chat while Jasmine took her bath, and the slave girl wondered what she had ever found objectionable in Damien's style. She was a lovely person, perfectly lovely, and one of the best friends Jasmine had ever made. The dogs were there too, and they were just the darlingest dogs. So much spirit. So much life in them, and innocent joy.

When she got back to the parlor, naked except for her porn star shoes, everyone else had had something to eat and drink. They seemed to be very pleased with themselves. Wolfe was thanking everybody and passing out cigars. Jasmine supposed she ought to be self-conscious, but what was the point? Everybody here had seen everything she had, and some things she had not known she possessed. When Wolfe saw Jasmine come back into the room, she folded her in a full-length body hug that went on forever, almost long enough for Jasmine to fall asleep standing up against her master.

"Don't pass out just yet," Wolfe said. "Don't you want your graduation present?"

It was a full-length fur coat, black, lined with heavy satin, with two slash pockets and a big shawl collar. "Told you not to worry about your jacket," Wolfe said, and wrapped her in it. "Think that'll do to ride home in?"

Jasmine didn't know what to say. She kept opening her mouth to frame some grateful comments, but all that would come out was a squeak. Wolfe seemed to think that was more than adequate and patted her kindly.

Race came forward then, leading Del on the leash once more. "Here's the rest of your graduation present," she said. "I've already cleared this with Wolfe, Jasmine. Del is going to be staying with you for the next little while. We'll meet back here in six weeks to see if you've managed to get my boy to comply with your curriculum."

Even Saint Marilyn had nothing to say about this development. Jasmine took one look at the tearstained, stubborn face at the end of the leash and knew she was in for a heavy postgraduate colloquium.

Wolfe brought her back to earth by clipping a long silver chain around her waist. On the chain was a heart inscribed with both of their names, and four gems: a sapphire for obedience, a diamond for honesty, a ruby for stamina, and an emerald for loyalty. "I'll solder that on when we get home," she said. "Why don't you give Del back to Race temporarily? She can bring the boy over later tonight, after you and I have fixed him up a secure place to sleep."

So she would not be alone with this huge responsibility. That was a relief. But if Wolfe thought she was going to be in charge of this new toy . . . no, that was not going to happen. Tired as she was, Jasmine was making up a syllabus for Del's higher—and lower—education.

Jasmine handed Del's leash to Race and tried to make a grand exit but staggered in the tall shoes and had to lean on her owner.

Thank God tomorrow was Sunday. But the last thing she felt like
doing was grading 32 papers on "Collusion and Resistance: Women's
Oppression in the 20th Century."

Mercy

There it was, revealed at last: the exquisite white skin that had been pampered with milk baths and massage, the slim back that had been clothed in the most expensive silks and brocades, now stripped of the coarse linen prisoner's shift. Even without stays, her waist was still shapely, so tiny that it emphasized her round buttocks. Those haunches had bewitched a king (and a discreet handful of aristocratic admirers). It was whispered that the queen preferred the love of women to the love of men, for pregnancy would never betray the pleasures she took with another woman.

The prisoner made as if to turn around, and her jailer, Françoise, called out sharply, "No!" She meant to take the queen from behind, not to humiliate the fallen royal, but to conceal her own burning gaze, her shaking hands, the trembling fullness of her heart. But a glimpse of her breast, the nipple pink as a rose, made it impossible for Françoise to swallow, difficult for her to breathe. She would crush the frail beauty of those nipples so they would no longer disturb her dreams!

The passion that she felt for the enemy she should have despised was intolerable. Repugnant! Françoise began with blows instead of kisses, quickly bringing a blush to the porcelain skin that was the product of a hundred years of Austrian inbreeding. When the revolutionary did not immediately receive the satisfaction of a cry of pain, she struck harder.

Finally she jabbed her hand between the prisoner's creamy thighs, and discovered (twisting her fingers) the reason for this silence: The queen enjoyed being spanked. Enjoyed it as much as she enjoyed eating cake.

It was a hot summer afternoon, made even more uncomfortable by guilt. Theresa Barsini was vaguely aware of a little pain between her shoulder blades, mirrored by a thin trickle of sweat that ran down between her breasts as she typed faster and faster. She had no idea how hunched over she was or how much tension her body was carrying. Theresa was a short, round little dyke who hated her name almost as much as she hated her unruly dark hair, which had grown out to an uncomfortable length—too long to slick back in proper butch fashion, too short to tease out into big-haired femme glory.

Her lover Heather said that Theresa was an elegant name, and refused to shorten it to the masculine diminutive, Terry. Heather was like that. A tall, striking blond who had majored in community relations at Smith, she had strong opinions about a lot of things. She was fond of saying, "Your first impression is your last impression." She thought Theresa would make a much better first impression with longer hair. "Flattops and shaved heads are such a cliché," she sniffed whenever she saw someone who in her opinion looked a little too obvious. Not that there was anything wrong with being a lesbian, of course, but why did we all have to look the same? Wasn't that just a setup for not being heard, not getting what we wanted? Heather felt it was important to give people half a chance to give her what she wanted. Her trust-funded wardrobe guaranteed her a hearing at her job with a company that marketed E-mail greeting cards. And she was more than willing to share the benefits of her good taste with Theresa. After Theresa's half of the bills came out of her unemployment check, there wasn't much left over, so they went shopping at Goodwill for something appropriate for her to wear to job interviews. (One of Heather's favorite words was "appropriate.")

Theresa unconsciously shuddered at the memory of having Heather "do her colors." It had been a hellish three hours of having various colored fabrics flung under her chin. Heather would then view her under sunlight, incandescent light, fluorescent light, and halogen light, contemplate her visage, utter a disparaging verdict like, "That makes you look green," then make a note on a sheet of paper. At the moment, Theresa was not wearing the tones that were appropriate for a "summer," or for a job interview, for that matter. She was wearing a white tank top (with no bra), cutoffs with frayed edges, and red Converse sneakers with no socks and holes in their toes. On the desk to her left sat the Help Wanted ads, neatly folded and highlighted by Heather that morning. Theresa was supposed to be putting a résumé together and sending it out to those companies. Heather had suggested that since Theresa didn't have the kind of job experience that downtown was looking for, she should reframe her résumé and think of it as a list of job skills rather than a history of occupations.

Theresa knew it was important to call the ads and start the painful process of looking for a job. She had only two more weeks of unemployment left. But this morning she had woken up with a line of dialogue in her head. "I am worse than you, for you love the lash and pant for the touch of another woman, but I love someone who has crushed a nation beneath her satin slipper." She had a painful need to see who had said such an outrageous thing, and why. The idea had kept its vitality throughout Heather's breakfast routine (one half an organic pink grapefruit, sectioned and sprinkled with a hint of Nutrasweet, accompanied by half a plain bagel, toasted till it was ecru, no butter) and the inevitable tiny crises that erupted in sending Heather off to work. Theresa sighed, wondering how any woman could manage to communicate so much without speaking a word out loud. Just by the way she changed the battery in her cell phone, Heather could let Theresa know that her unemployed status was making Heather's high-pressure middle management job ever so much more difficult.

Heather would probably be home in about ten minutes, and she would want to know why dinner was not ready. She would also want to know why the dishes had not been done, and a host of other household chores. Theresa knew from bitter experience that if she started doing housework, she would not be able to do any writing that day. It had occurred to her more than once to ask Heather why they could not hire somebody to come in and clean once a week, but the question stuck in her craw. That was Heather's money, and Heather had explained more than once that it just wasn't "appropriate" for Theresa to control her finances.

This story had taken shape so nicely. A ragged revolutionary, now in charge of female prisoners at the Bastille, had fallen in love with the incarcerated queen. How was this perilous affection, this potentially tragic reversal of loyalty, to make itself known or play itself out? Theresa was so far into her characters' heads that she had made herself cry twice that day with poignant speeches they made to one another. She had no idea who would publish such a story, of course, given the fact that both characters were women, and their sexual proclivities were neither subdued nor vanilla. If she let herself, she would hear Heather saying, in her most maternal voice, "Sweetie, I just don't think your cute little stories have any commercial possibilities. When are you going to write some real fiction?" Lately, however, that honeymoon sentiment had changed to, "You know, you could always write in your spare time, after you became a network administrator and started bringing home a decent paycheck for a change. I want you to have abundance and prosperity, sweetie, don't you want that too?"

Hence the rush to drive as many words out of her head and onto the page as quickly as possible, as if she were herding steers away from the threat of mad cow disease. Mad cow disease, that was good.

"That's what I've got," Theresa said to herself, and winced as the front door opened and changed the air pressure just enough to make her ears ache. The guard was about to lay down her life in order to facilitate an escape attempt. Theresa was pretty sure the queen would perish as well, distraught at the loss of her tender captor. Telling herself that she could flesh out the ending tomorrow, Theresa forced herself away from the desk and into the foyer to take custody of Heather's undyed leather briefcase, laptop computer, camel-colored cardigan, the Hermes scarf with a tiny cigarette hole that was a present from her mother, navy blue thermal lunch bag, and Emporio Armani sunglasses. It was Theresa's job to put all these things in their preordained slots around the house. Otherwise, they would disappear forever, because Heather could not find her own Prada pumps two minutes after she'd kicked them off.

Fresh from her vicarious experience with utterly altruistic love, Theresa saw her lover with more compassionate eyes. It was the Friday before Father's Day, and the greeting card company was swamped. Heather had two new employees so the queue of service requests was scary. There were faint stress circles under her eyes. Theresa led her into the bedroom, where she carefully removed Heather's celery linen suit, cream camislip, high heels that Theresa privately thought were the color of stomach acid and cardboard, flesh-tone Safeway panty hose, champagne Wonderbra, and matching panties. Then she brought her a silk kimono. Heather sighed gratefully and seated herself at the vanity table. Theresa took a quick side trip to the kitchen for a tall glass of iced tea, then went back to the bedroom to remove Heather's makeup and put her hair up in a ponytail so she could feel a little cooler.

Heather's declawed lilac point Siamese cat jumped onto the vanity bench, perching as she had been trained to sit, beside Heather rather than on her lap. As Heather gave the cat a few gentle strokes, both of them closed their eyes, and Theresa was amused at their nearly identical facial expressions of self-satisfaction. She had wrung out a cloth in cool water, and applied it to Heather's neck, then dabbed at her eyes.

The two of them had met while they were in college. Heather had been at Smith for her master's degree while Theresa struggled to finish a BA in social studies at Columbia. Both of them had traveled to New York City for the big queer march that commemorated the 25th anniversary of the Stonewall riots. Theresa had attended the alternative march, which was organized by some boy lovers, transsexual activists, and other troublemakers who were angry about being excluded from the larger event. She figured everybody who rocked in queer theory would be there, and hauled a bunch of her books there in her backpack. Got a lot of them autographed too. Heather marched with PFLAG in the official event and later said she hadn't realized anything else was happening. She had, she said, planned to march with the leather contingent, but was put off by a swaggering uncouth six-foot-tall diesel dyke who was bullwhipping a couple of boys while angry leathermen with New York accents yelled at her to stop.

Both of them managed to make it to a dungeon party at the same time, a boisterous event held in a mildewed and cobwebby club that was normally populated by a few professional dominatrices and a lot of submissive men wandering around in grubby Y-fronts and laced-up business shoes. The battered Mafia-owned venue hardly knew what to do with such a diverse crowd of enthusiastic perverts. Theresa had been scared to death. Her only S/M experience, if you could call it that, was reading Trish Thomas's story "Wunnamyfantasies" out loud to a former girlfriend who had masturbated frantically, then scolded Theresa for "identifying with perpetrators." Heather was wearing a shiny latex dress that laced up the back. She looked like she had never been afraid of anything in her life. Her refined yet lush curves played hell with Theresa's young butch pulse. Theresa did not know until much, much later that this was the first time Heather had ever played too. At the time, she felt so underdressed, wearing the same jeans and rainbow suspenders that she'd worn to the march, that she just assumed Heather was leagues ahead of her in pervy experience.

There wasn't much space, so their scene consisted of Heather grabbing Theresa by the throat, saying mean things in her ear, letting her go to kiss her, twisting her nipples, then grabbing her throat again. Well, there were also a few strokes with a riding crop, borrowed from an amused, gray-haired dungeon monitor. This luminary's leather vest was thickly populated with enough motorcycle club run badges and pins to make her look like some sort of demented "Ride Hard, Live Free" Girl Scout. Theresa had known better, even then, to explain why it all gave her the giggles.

By the time they returned the riding crop, the crowd was thinning out, and they both got a little freaked out by the dank odor of the place and the guilt-ridden attitude and fuzzy paunches of late-arriving kinky suburban Johns. So they went back to Heather's hotel room and did a lot of body worship. Or rather, Theresa did a lot of body worship. Heather fell asleep right after she came, and could not return the favor in the morning since they had overslept and were in danger of staying past checkout time.

It had been difficult to keep their relationship going when they lived in two different states and attended different schools. When it was time for Heather to graduate and she announced her plan to move to California, Theresa didn't even think about leaving her degree program one semester short of graduation. It was just a bachelor's degree. She could always finish it later. Somehow, once she was caught up in the domestic routine of life with Heather, she never checked out local schools. The thought of sending for applications or transcripts just made her feel exhausted and blue.

"So what are we having for dinner?" Heather purred, opening her big green eyes, which were only slightly enhanced with colored contact lenses.

"I thought maybe we could order Chinese food," Theresa blurted without thinking. Heather abruptly pushed the cat off the bench and stood up. It meowed in the despondent and off-key way of its kind, then sped out of the room with its expensive ears pasted flat to its inbred narrow skull. *Uh-oh. Trouble in paradise.* Theresa was briefly afraid she might throw up.

What followed was not a fight as much as a lecture, weakly punctuated by Theresa's protestations, which were ignored much as a tractor ignores the weeds beneath its enormous tires. Later, Theresa could only remember certain key phrases that were like crescendos in a piece of music, bringing the heat of the argument to a series of peaks, uttered in Heather's merciless voice of pure calm rationality. "We had an agreement . . . fulfilling your obligations . . . necessary to merit my trust . . . our contract . . . you have certain obligations . . . responsibility is not inconsistent with creativity . . . you promised me . . . I have a right to expect . . . consistency . . . how hard I've worked . . . how patient I've been . . . laxness and unreliability . . . willful and provocative!"

The exclamation point after that last phrase brought Theresa up on her toes, her spine rigid and her eyes bulging with shock. She had an ugly feeling that she knew what was coming next. Heather was going to punish her. A year and a half into their relationship, this sort of scene was happening more frequently, but Theresa knew she would never get used to it. First there was a sense of injustice that she could not seem to quell, no matter how much she loved Heather as her mistress and wanted to please her. A rebellious part of her kept on asking, like a small child denied an outing, "Why must I be punished for working on my story? Don't you even want to read it? Why aren't you happy for me, that it turned out so well?"

Nevertheless, she bit her tongue and went to fetch wrist cuffs and riding crop. Heather had learned a great deal since Stonewall 25. For one thing, she had discovered that after the thrill of losing one's "flagellation virginity" dies down, very few masochists enjoy being lashed with a fiberglass stick, even if it is encased in black leather. Therefore, it was the appropriate choice for aversive conditioning. They could not have screw eyes in the doorway, since Heather's parents visited frequently. The brass bed was more than adequate for restraint. Theresa sighed, shrugged out of her clothes, folded them, put on the wrist cuffs, lay down on the bed, and clipped her chains around the nearest brass rail.

There was another lecture and a list of her shortcomings. Whenever Heather paused for breath, Theresa said one thing and one thing only: "Yes, Mistress." She pitched her voice low and quiet, to show as little emotion as possible. Perhaps Heather would think she was submerged in remorse. In fact, Theresa was on extreme-resentment autopilot, and barely caught herself in time to change her response to "Please, Mistress" when Heather told her she had to ask for her correction.

The narrow strokes that followed were nasty out of all proportion to their width. But for some reason, Theresa could not scream. The screams came up to a point just below her throat, and melted away like cotton candy in spit. Heather had a good ear for the difference between melodrama and genuine suffering. Like all tops, she wanted to know she was making an impact. Impressive sound effects would sometimes take the edge off her wrath. But Theresa just sent herself someplace else. For some reason, she remembered a play party they had attended, before Heather decided the local leatherdyke "support group" was run by downwardly mobile refugees from the '80s with serious personality disorders. Just the phrase "support group" gave Heather hives. "As if it's some kind of New Age halfway house," she said scornfully. "If everybody in a group is dysfunctional enough to need *support*, sweetie, it's going to be a short, fast ride into hell from there." They had left the party shortly after Heather observed one woman getting clobbered by four tops who left her ass a bloody mess. Theresa had wanted to stay. She wondered what it would feel like to get fucked in that many orifices simultaneously. Heather had been adamant. Her verdict: "This is about as entertaining as *America's Most Wanted*. I'm not ashamed to speak out when I think certain people have gone too far. What will you want to look at next, Theresa, monster truck racing?"

Now, in the part of her mind that was not off in the ozone layer, Theresa knew that her butt was getting pulpy. She visualized the slightly sick look of horrified fascination that Heather had fastened on the gang-bang bottom's black and blue cheeks. Heather usually did not mark her. Well, if she was doing it now and making herself sick, it was just deserts. Let Heather reap what she had sown.

Some instinct of self-preservation warned her to say "Yes, Mistress" when Heather, out of breath, intoned, "Do you think you have had enough?" Identical answers followed the questions, "Have you learned your lesson?" and "Will you endeavor to do better in the future?"

Then they got up and ordered Chinese food. Heather was being very affectionate, Theresa noticed, but she herself still felt far, far away. Using the pretext of obedience, she slipped away from Heather's embraces and left her on the blue-and-white striped sofa with the TV remote control while she went into the kitchen and washed dishes. The hot water and soapsuds were soothing. She had almost come back to herself when the deliveryman rang their doorbell, and she had to go ask Heather for cash or a credit card. Heather grimaced, then gave her permission to go into her briefcase and extract her wallet. That little moue of rosebud-frost disapproval sent Theresa's soul right back to a barren place that was the same temperature as Antarctica.

They ate together, chopsticks clicking, and Theresa submissively opened her mouth, chewed and swallowed anything that Heather deigned to feed her. *She really doesn't know that anything is wrong,* part of her said in amazement, while another voice said, *Am I going crazy?*

After *20/20* was done, Heather motioned for Theresa to kneel on the floor at her feet. "I think I know what the problem is," she said, speaking in the unctuous tones of an Evita or an Imelda.

"What, Mistress?" Theresa asked, not liking the way the Berber carpet felt to her bare knees and shins.

"We have a big piece of unfinished business," Heather said. Her pink mouth was crimped into a little circle of seriousness, and her thin eyebrows gathered up a pinch of white forehead between their dark bows.

No, Theresa groaned internally. *Don't go there! No-o-o.*

"I don't think you are going to be able to behave yourself until you feel that you really belong to me," Heather said self-righteously. "I blame myself, really. I made you a promise ages and ages ago. If we're going to do this at all, we should do it right. How would you like to get your hood ring tonight, my hot little one?"

I am not little. I do not belong to you, Theresa said inside, while her mouth went through the motions of, "Whatever pleases you, Mistress." Yes, she did want her clit hood pierced. She wanted it the way she had wanted a bicycle when she was 11, the way she wanted to play football when she was 14, the way she wanted to be a writer now. But there was nothing on earth that scared her worse than needles. They had tried to do this three times already, and Theresa had always safe-worded out of it, in hysterics.

Radiating generosity like Santa Claus, a student loan deferment, and a big refund from the IRS all rolled into one, Heather brought Theresa to her feet and escorted her to the bathroom. While Terry stood in the tub, Heather washed her labia with Betadine. The disinfectant stung a little, and Theresa had to grab the towel rack with both hands to keep herself upright. Her knuckles were white, and she wagered they matched her face. She made herself go into the bedroom, where Heather had laid out a surgical drape for her to lie upon. Then she was restrained, wrists and ankles, and this time Heather attached the chains herself. Heather brought a TV tray in by the bed and covered it with a sterile drape. There was some business about not having the right size of latex gloves; then those were discovered. As each implement hit the tray (piercing forceps, needle in a paper autoclave envelope, bead ring, packets of long, fat cotton swabs impregnated with more povidone iodine) a new wave of nausea hit Theresa. She swallowed over and over again, willing her stomach to stay down.

Heather took long strips of black latex and bound back her labia, wrapping the stretchy straps around her upper thigh. Theresa knew she would have to hold very still now, or the rubber would slip, and Heather would be plexed. The surgical marker descended, leaving two small dots to guide the needle. She kept her equilibrium when the soft grips of the piercing forceps descended upon her clitoral hood and lifted it slightly. She even remained calm when she spotted the sparkle of a descending needle out of the corner of her eye, and felt the bite of its point in the most sensitive part of her body. It would only take a few seconds of pressure for the needle to pass through, creating a passageway for the jewelry she coveted. Theresa wanted so badly to hang a little bell from her clit and go dancing. Let everybody wonder where the secret music that inspired her joy came from.

Whomp! It was as if the pain of the cropping had been bundled up and thrown into Theresa's central nervous system, like the biggest bowling ball in the world making a strike out of all 120 pins at once. Suddenly, the pressure of her own weight upon her injured buttocks was enough to squeeze cold tears from the corners of her eyes. The idea of taking even a single second of more agony, which was all the piercing would entail, was intolerable. Theresa screamed her safe word as if Satan himself were taking a venomous big greedy bite right out of her ass. "Griffindalydworkin! Griffindalydworkin! Griffindalydworkin!"

The bondage was gone, she could not remember when or how, and Heather was hugging her. The tray was gone too, like the fairy castle that will vanish if you tell the name of your immortal lover. "Sweetie, hush, hush, it's OK, stop screaming," Heather said over and over again, anxiously. Her hair, Theresa thought, smelled like too many different kinds of perfume all mixed together. Then she realized Heather was crying. "I know I'm a terrible mistress," she wept. "But I just can't do something to you if you hate it that much. I have to give in. I have to show you mercy."

Then Theresa began to cry too. She cried about being laid off at the printing company. *How could it hurt so much to lose a job you hated?* She cried about the rejection slip she had gotten from *Libido*. She wept for the way hope kept turning into bitterness in her relationship. She cried about not being allowed to go to her father's funeral. She sobbed about Sister Mary Andrew being expelled from the convent and about having to take the GED exam instead of being able to finish school. She cried about a dog that followed her home when she was six, only to be driven off by her father, who threw rocks at it and cursed, then slapped her for screaming at him to stop. This deluge of new grief linked to old in a continuous hot fountain of tears went on for two hours, until a fit of hiccups jolted Theresa out of it. Heather made her drink a glass of water upside down to stop the hiccups, then dosed her to sleep with a shot glass full of valerian extract.

After Theresa passed out on her back, Heather lay awake, kept open-eyed by her lover's snoring. But she felt far too guilty about this fourth episode of botched piercing to nudge Theresa and tell her to roll over and stop making such a racket. She had plenty of other things to keep her awake, anyway. Lots of problems that just seemed to keep adding up and adding up. Problems she couldn't even discuss with Theresa, much less get help with.

Rent on the town house had gone up again, and Heather was afraid the landlord would eventually try an owner move-in eviction. If she had not been living with Theresa, she was sure her parents would loan her the down payment to buy her own place, but they were not going to subsidize an "unsuitable arrangement." She'd dented another car in the parking lot this morning, her second fender bender in as many weeks. Car insurance premiums were already murder. She was over her head in credit card debt amassed while she was in school because Alex and Petra, Mummy and Daddy, had, without warning, stopped paying off her American Express card. All it would take is an extra hundred dollars in expenses every month and her student loans would go into default because the parental units weren't helping out with those either.

Theresa was always making deprecating comments about class privilege, but she had no idea what it was like to grow up with certain expectations and then get frozen out because Petra was not going to get to plan a white wedding and Alex was not going to get to bounce a grandson in a little sailor suit on his knee.

The job situation wasn't exactly peachy either. Gregory in sales kept asking her out, and she was running out of excuses. What was worse, dating a coworker or letting everybody you worked with know that you did not go out with guys? Theresa would have only two solutions: punch him in the nose or quit. As a middle manager who was female, overeducated, unmarried, and childless, Heather was already isolated from the other employees. People left the lunchroom when she came in for a cup of coffee.

At school she had not exactly envisioned herself working as the manager of technical support for a company that sold greeting cards. If there was a more embarrassing form of E-commerce, Heather was sure she did not know what that might be. What had happened to her commitment to social justice? What had happened to her creativity? But she couldn't drop down to part-time work or go back to school or look for a job at a nonprofit or take a year off and go to Europe and paint, not with a partner who was out of work. When was Terry— Theresa—going to get off her ass and start showing up with a paycheck again? Her COBRA conversion had almost run out, and nothing scared Heather more than the prospect of life without health insurance.

The fact that Terry had escaped from her Italian Catholic family of nine children and made it into college when neither of her parents had even finished high school amazed Heather, but also appalled her. Growing up in a tough neighborhood in the Bronx, a fireman's daughter, being out as a dyke in high school, having an affair with one of the nuns—Heather knew she would never have survived the first rock that was thrown at her or the scandal of being caught in bed with her gym teacher. Never could have forced herself to go on living if she had had to eat corned beef and cabbage or Spam or never wear anything that was new except underwear because (as Terry had explained to her) thrift stores do not sell underwear. Heather did not want to live like that, thank you very much. And she didn't understand why Terry seemed to be so feckless about money. She knew what it was like to be poor, really poor. So why wasn't she more motivated to better herself?

What had happened to the dapper young butch she had fallen in love with? If Heather had known that being a top was going to be so lonely, she might have insisted on interacting with the other end of that riding crop. She had read all the books, even gone online to ask advice from people in a B&D chat room. As far as she could tell, she was doing everything right—consent, negotiation, safety, limits, equality outside of the bedroom, never play when you are angry, and so on. Why, then, was she bored and resentful? Why did she feel burned out and overextended? She didn't know if she wanted to end their role-based relationship or make it more extreme. Would their life together be any easier if they never did S/M? Or if Terry became a real submissive and had to obey her for a change? What was the point in sticking out a tough ten-hour day with rude, stupid users and Goth computer geeks who would rather listen to Bauhaus than take calls from the rude, stupid users if you had to come home to a dirty kitchen and no hot meal?

"I sound like my father," Heather said, and there was no black pit of despair any deeper than that. So she too finally slept and was spared the indelicate knowledge that she snored even more loudly than Theresa.

To be continued . . .

Love Sees No Gender

Author's Note: The title of this story was the slogan for the 1994 celebration of the 25th anniversary of the Stonewall rebellion in New York City. Ironically, the organizers of Stonewall 25 refused to include trans-gendered people within the purview of their event.

I haven't seen you for ten days, and there are so many things I've forgotten—the shape of the bridge of your nose (there's a faint crease there), and the pattern of the fur on your knuckles and forearms. Was your black hair always this long? Were the strands of gray in exactly those places? Did I lose count of your earrings or incorrectly draw the shape of your beard on the face in my imagination? But I know it's you. My nose would recognize you even if every other sense I had told me there was a stranger at my door. This is the scent I look for in my bed every night, and now here it is all around me. My olfactory response makes any place you are feel like the center of the universe, home base, my place. Still, we are new to each other. I am not used to hearing you say "I love you" out loud instead of reading it in a piece of e-mail. It always makes me feel like a hand has been slipped between my bra and my breast: heart and sex fondled simultaneously.

I've been in an anxious sweat all day, cleaning house, putting things away, making compulsive lists of things I need to do to make this house (which an ex-lover recently vacated) my own. I've done everything except piss in the corners, and I'll probably do that before I can feel the process is complete. Now you're here, and I feel myself hovering around you like an anxious insect. Might as well wring my hands. You would think, hardened pervert that I am, I would not get this antsy just because I've asked a new crush to fuck me. Prior experience is of no use whatsoever. I am like Elizabeth Taylor on a hot tin roof.

You aren't hungry, don't want anything to drink, you sit on the couch and don't look as if you intend to move any time soon. Finally you tell me (out of pity, I suspect) that you will have a glass of water. I pour it for you but forget to bring it to you. I'm too busy fussing in the cupboards, checking on the cat's food, straightening dish towels. Finally I have to go in to see you sitting down because this is getting ridiculous.

Nothing ever seems to upset you. Whenever I get closer than a couple of feet to you, I feel an atmosphere of calm envelop me. It's rare to know exactly what you are thinking or feeling. This may be why I am driven to tie you up and hurt you. When I have complete control over your body and your surroundings, the odds of knowing what's happening inside you go up dramatically. And if I can make you scream, that's heaven. That's certain knowledge. And food for my predatory soul.

This is my couch, my living room, but it feels like you've taken possession of the territory. Anyway, I can't make myself sit close to you. Still, you can reach me well enough, and you put your hand on my thigh. I'm always surprised by your reach, your reflexes. You move quickly and neatly, with no wasted motions. The heat from your hand moves through my jeans to my skin within a split second. I am afraid to look at you, because if I meet your eye, I might start laughing hysterically or shriek. Still, I sneak a glance, and you are staring off in another direction. Yes, the spaces between your teeth are where I remember them. That's good. For some reason that makes my heart slow down.

By clamping my teeth together, I prevent myself from saying something inane. Once I start talking, I'll never be able to stop. You look at me and smile. "So, do you want to fuck?" you say quietly, evenly, directly, and I am up off the couch and back into the kitchen without touching the ground.

"I don't know, Mike," I say from the other room, "I don't think there's anything else in here that I can fiddle with."

"Good," you say firmly. And I realize you are probably nervous too. So I meet you in the hallway and we go into the bedroom, and this room that hasn't seen very much sex is suddenly full of nothing else.

This is what I want, but I still have to escape one more time, to go pee and clean my teeth and brush my hair and clean the bathroom mirror and rearrange the shower curtain and pick up the bath mat and shake stray kitty litter into the toilet. When I come back, you are stretched out on the bed, fully dressed except you have taken off your cowboy boots. They have fancy pointy lizard-skin toes, those boots, and they remind me of the boys I went to high school with—the blue-collar, redneck boys whose idea of living the wild life was to be rodeo cowboys or country music stars instead of inheriting their fathers' alfalfa fields, mink sheds, and dairy cows.

The sight of your naked feet makes my knees go weak. But wouldn't it be rude to just start sucking on your toes? Instead I stretch out beside you, putting my head where I can hear your heartbeat. It is strong and slow, like a runner's heart. Why does listening to this sound make me blush? It seems unbearably intimate.

Lying next to you, I feel the way I used to feel when I first came out and brought older butch women home with me. They always started out fully clothed and expected to remain that way the whole night. Until the evil hippie chick that I was plied them with marijuana and wild music and got them out of those goddamned flannel or Oxford shirts and jeans or chinos, boots or loafers. I wonder if young femmes have this conditioned response to feeling a woman's body behind fabric, pressed into their naked flesh. It still means sex to me. And when I touch you, slide my hands across your stomach, up to your nipples or down to your crotch, there is so much conflicting information, so many different images vying with one another that the world says can't coexist, can't simultaneously be true of the same person, that my consciousness falls into a kind of erotic stutter. Confusion only seems to turn me on even more.

You've been taking testosterone long enough to pass completely as a man. Nobody even looks at you twice, nobody wonders. On Castro Street I get evil looks from the gay men who resent a woman putting her hands on such a handsome biker dude. Your maleness, in some people's eyes, turns me into a straight girl. I remember admiring the triangle your torso made, from shoulders to waist. I touched you once between the shoulder blades and felt the elastic binder that preserved the illusion. Should I ignore it? Acknowledge it? It looks uncomfortable, and yet it makes you comfortable in the world. So I accept it as not being that different from my own need to wear a tank top to keep my tits from bouncing around when I fuck somebody.

Here in the privacy of my bedroom I can feel pecs that curve just a little too much, a little too softly, to be anything except female breasts. The nipples, though, look male, like those of a leatherman who has worked his tits hard with snakebite kits and vacuum pumps and clamps and coils of copper wire until they are swollen, exaggerated, long, and very sensitive. When I touch you here I am always careful not to cup my hand, in the gesture one makes to gather and caress a woman's breast. You haven't asked me to do this, and I don't know if you prefer to be touched that way or not. It is leftover training from making love to stone butches, who would sometimes let me pleasure them if I didn't ask permission and could somehow fathom the paths my hands and mouth should take between the mines. Very few things make me angrier than this, the harsh facts of life that plant traps that can suddenly explode and destroy the sexuality of dyke bodies.

The paradigm of the stone butch is like a stepladder. It gets me closer to understanding you, but it won't take me the whole way up. I sometimes think of you as a man with a lesbian history. You are female-to-male, FTM, but also Mike, yourself, an individual flavor of the category "transgendered." I study you, ask you so many questions that you sometimes look at me as if I were crazy. Do you understand that I interrogate you about these things because I see myself in you? Is it manipulative of me to court you in part to get closer to understanding myself?

When I put my hand inside your shirt, I am always shocked by the thickness and coarseness of the hair that covers your chest and belly. It makes me feel really wicked to enjoy the way it rasps on the palms of my hands, slightly abrades my face. And if I slide my hand down further, I will find . . . what? I think of your genitals, refer to them as your cock. You used the word "clit" once. Somehow I think this matters more to other people than it does to you. You are inside this body, which combines male and female in a whole that somehow makes sense, attracts me, suits you. In the process of getting to this place, I think you have decided to simply live with some contradictions because they are closest to being your true self. It's other people, folks who are less adventurous or rebellious about gender, who try to impose their own notions of consistency or propriety upon you.

The first time I topped you I wove you into one of those complicated body-hugging rope harnesses that I make when I want to impress somebody or hold them at bay. You had said you were an escape artist; liked bondage more than you liked pain. I was afraid to reach between your legs and adjust the ropes there. I probably hurt you because of my stupidity. When I finally handled you, I was pleased completely because I had everything: an ass that would admit my hand, wetness that signaled arousal to my lesbian consciousness, and a clitoral cock that could be touched more firmly and showed its response more clearly than one that had not been enlarged with male hormones.

There's no way to think about this coherently when you roll on top of me, and you weigh just the right amount, enough to anchor me and keep me in my own body, not enough to impede my breathing or make me tense my muscles to hold you up. I don't want to call on my physical strength now or struggle with you, although that's my usual habit when somebody wants me. I am afraid if I resist, you will back away. Despite your piratical good looks, you remain oddly gentle, gentlemanly. I can't count on your aggression overcoming my reluctance. I have to be more straightforward about what I want, and that carries its own excitement.

We don't talk. The agenda for this encounter was set in a two-line conversation a week ago, and we both know what's going to happen and are ready for it. Your hands are big, I expect calluses, but the inner surfaces are soft and warm. When you peel my shirt off my stomach and rub your face on my belly, I wrap my legs around you. It feels forbidden and dangerous for me to enjoy this. But haven't women, for hundreds of years, thousands of years, curled their toes with delight because a lover rubbed his beard across their exposed skin? It can't be wrong for me to like it too.

My back feels as if it is floating an inch off the surface of the bed. I'm not aware of holding myself up. Somehow there's just enough room for your hands to slide under me. There are three hooks on my bra strap, and it takes you three tiny motions to undo them. I have to admire your skill. Men, in my experience, can never do that so smoothly. You have your thigh pressed between my legs. I've had male partners who somehow figured out how quickly and easily that arouses most women. Giving a girl something to grind against is a much safer bet than dealing with a new clit, with its own unique and persnickety requirements, with your fingertips. But men don't position themselves to wring their own pleasure out of my thigh; they don't push into me the way you do or respond with a faster, harder motion when I tighten my muscles and shove back.

Then I feel you getting hard. Your genitals are suddenly there, changed, outlined against my skin, and I am once again in a realm of arousing ambivalence and ambiguity, a world where anything could happen. A world where the things I believe I know about men and women are useless and misleading.

From time to time as we perform this ancient yet strange and unique act upon my bed, I panic. You are too close, this is taking too long, I can't let you see me this way. You do not talk to me. Your mouth is set, you look like someone doing a careful piece of work. And I find I cannot talk to you. The usual stream of dirty talk has dried up. Somehow I am compelled to pay more attention than that. It's not that I'm not making any noise, I am, and sometimes I become irritated with my own sounds, the whine and neediness of it. Every time this happens, I reach up and wrap my hands around your upper arms or dig my fingers into your shoulders. The muscles I find there somehow make the fear subside. The power and strength of your body focuses me, sends my hips up into you.

Finally I wind up undressing myself, with some impatient assistance from you. We separate. I have to get under the covers, I can't bear to have you look at me. Why didn't I shower? I have to rub my feet, make a pretense of cleaning them, lower the light, and above all else, get under the damned blankets. While you put your harness on we make small talk, I don't remember what we say. I don't watch you struggle with the snaps and straps. When I put on my dick, I have learned to force myself to do it in front of the person I am about to fuck. I want them to deal with this transformation, I want it to be a natural part of sex. It isn't, of course, and never will be. But I refuse to hide while I am doing something we both want me to do. And yet on some level I am always angry that I've been seen putting on my tool, and I suppose that's just one more good reason to make sure at some point the person I am with is in delightful but very real pain.

It's not that I don't like my cunt. I've been through two decades of sex-positive feminist consciousness raising about the power and beauty of the female genitals. I have a first edition of Tee Corinne's *Cunt Coloring Book*, Honey Lee Cottrell's *I am my Lover*, Betty Dodson's cunt portraits in *Liberating Masturbation*, Joani Blank's *Femalia*, and a dozen other works of that ilk. These artists' sincere attempts to celebrate womanhood are a little too sentimental for me. I don't need to think about orchids, ocean tides, mandalas, driftwood, pearls, waterfalls, hollow trees, phases of the moon, or oysters to make my cunt seem spiritually meaningful or palatable. She has been a sturdy, if somewhat tetchy, companion, a reliable barometer of what I want (and an unreliable measure of what I should do about it). We have a relationship that is adversarial but companionable, like old married people who constantly grouse at one another but never question their mutual affection.

Fact is, I like other cunts a lot more than I like my own. How can I admit, even to myself, that it's not what I wish I was born with between my legs? I really like to fuck, and strapping it on is big fun. But it also makes me sad, because I would rather come that way, inside someone, mark them as mine. I am damned good at channeling psychic dick, making the experience so real for my partner that I've fooled biofags and pissed off women who discovered mid fuck that they wanted penetration without "all that male energy." I'm

tired of inferring the existence of my phallus by the sign of my
partner's orgasm. I want to feel myself working in, sliding out; I want
to watch my own come shot.

How can I admit all this, even to myself, without sounding like
a misogynist? (As if there's a man or woman alive in 20th-century
America who is not a misogynist of one sort or another.) But I can't
think of anything else I could do to make being a woman, having
female genitals, more acceptable. I've tried to be a different kind of
woman, unfettered by sexism, for so long that I'm exhausted and out
of new ideas. This is not about being ugly or a failure as a woman. I
can out-drag drag queens and out-femme femmes when the Spirit of
Cleavage and Spiked Heels moves me. And still I dissociate for a few
seconds when somebody touches my cunt, have to take deep,
cleansing breaths and give myself permission to accept those sensations. When I reach for my cock and squeeze it, there is a bizarre
absence of sensation that I can only call gender dysphoria. I live in
Women's Country, but I don't really like it there. Too many potlucks,
too much moralistic intrusiveness, too many ex-lovers. Men's
Country seems like an ugly place full of dirty socks and fistfights. I
wish there were someplace else to live, a third nation.

The difference between what I want and what I have makes sex
a treacherous experience for me. I do like getting fucked. It releases
tension that would otherwise build up in my body and become intolerable. I like coming that way. It's the easiest way to make me come.
But it takes a lot of mental gymnastics to get hooked up to my own
nerve endings and mucous membranes. It takes a lot of trust for me
to let myself be a girl. Maybe this would be easier if I could channel a
lusty boy-bottom fag persona, but that's never worked for me. I got
queer-bashed for being a sissy boy too much when I was growing up.
When someone comes on to me that way, I can't control my anger. I
feel as if my life is in danger, and I have to fight with every bit of
strength I have, or I will die.

Lost in this internal process, I miss my opportunity to undress
you. And you don't give me a chance to touch or go down on your
cock, you are just on top of me again, between my legs, smoothing
lube over yourself. The head of your cock rubs up and down, from
my clit to my asshole, and for a moment I am not sure what will
happen, where it will go. I haven't even seen what you are putting
in me.

But it feels just fine. I tend to use too much lubricant. It can make
things sloppy, make it hard for my partner to jack off while I rock
back and forth, in and out. But this thin sheet of Probe reminds me
that my own juices are in demand here, and there's plenty; I have
wanted this for a long time. You move my legs, raise them, then
lower them, and the sensation of being the one whose body is manipulated makes me a little queasy. I don't understand why I can't just
relax and let this happen. I trust you; it feels good. Whose dusty voice
from behind me tries to hinder my joy?

It's always hard to tell how many times I come when I'm fucked;
every movement feels like an orgasm. But there is one way that you
thrust into me that feels as if the head of your cock is rubbing up
against the most sensitive spot in my whole body, and for that motion
I find myself saying, "Yes, do that," instead of making incoherent
unbelieving sobs and moans. Sometimes a growl comes up in my
throat, but by the time it leaves my tongue it has turned into a sort of
purr, big happy kitty digging claws into the sheets. I want to kiss or
lick or bite your neck, but I can't get enough traction, you are too far
away. All I can hear is your breathing, it catches from time to time
because you are moving fast and hard. I feel you watching me,
gauging my response, waiting for the moment when it is enough.

And I feel a sudden rush of gratitude for all the butch women
who have been patient enough or mean enough to get me out of my
clothes and on my back or up on all fours, who have seen through me
and made me come like this, mouth open, blind, reaching for anything

and crushing what I find with both hands, crying for rescue while I experience the closest thing to salvation that mortals have on earth. Bioboys don't do this. There's too much direct pleasure for them in fucking. They lose touch, at some point, with the person around the cunt or the ass they are in, and they do what they need to do to come.

(Although there was one time, one man, who I think was tired of my using my vibrator every time we fucked. And he must have fucked me for an hour, in every possible position, until I literally could not come any more. I don't think he came at all that night. His face might have looked a little like yours does now, keeping watch, standing guard while I lost control. I can't remember; it was too long ago. And anyway I don't see that well without my glasses. But when we went to sleep he looked quite pleased with himself, quite satisfied. I tried to explain that the vibrator did not come out because I hadn't been fucked enough; I used it because I was turned on and felt safe enough to have both kinds of orgasms when he was in the room, the kind you have from fucking and the kind you have from buzzing off. He had no idea what I was talking about.)

"Please," I say. "Please!" It seems to me I have said this a hundred times. You respond only once. "What?" you say, sounding a little angry, meaning, *What do you want?* "Fuck me, please, this way, like that," I cry with no hesitation, one of the few honest moments in my life. You do, and I come even harder because I have said this is what I want, specified it, admitted it. As if it could possibly be a secret to anybody in this room.

My inner thighs are aching, and I want to put them together. But you are still on top of me, and I have quit thrashing around. Sweat is drying under my arms, making me feel cold. "Did I pop out?" you ask. I am confused because I can't tell for a moment. Then I realize yes, I'm empty. My cunt is still contracting, and it's sore; there's still so much happening in there that the absence of your cock hasn't been noticed. "I think I pushed you out when I came," I reply, and you nod

solemnly. There are tears welling up in my eyes; my chest is moving
the way it does when I cry, but I can't make a sound and the tears
won't flow. It's just been a long time, that's all, and I feel as if I have
partially exorcised the ghost of someone I have pined for, someone I
hate because she was incapable of loving another person as long as
there was dope to score anywhere in the known universe. You ask if
I am OK, and I say yes; then you roll away; and I can curl up on my
side and let one thigh comfort the other. I have a bruise on one arm,
and I don't remember how it got there.

Eventually I find you on the other side of the bed and press my
mouth into your armpit. Your hair is outrageously long there. It takes
a lot of spit and a strong tongue to burrow through it and find your
skin. From armpit to nipple is a short trip, but I hurry as if I'm running for a plane that might leave me behind. Now you put your
hands on me and hold my head there, grip me harder when I put the
edges of my teeth into you and pull back, stretching and indenting
the tissue. It's a bit of a struggle to get over to your other nipple, and
now your hands on me hurt a little, which is good. It makes it clear
you like what I am doing. More than anything I want my mouth
between your legs, but I tease myself (and probably tease you a little
too) by going after your other armpit, then back to your nipples. I
love tweaking these points of flesh; love how reliably they get your
attention.

You say you don't want chest surgery because it probably won't
leave the nerve endings intact. I don't believe you. You're not going
to wear that hot, annoying rubber undershirt for the rest of your life.
There's too much social pressure for you to get rid of your breasts.
You're already committed to being a butch fist-fucking leather bear
fag. I like these two connection points between me and your cock, but
would I vote to preserve them? I'm suspicious of my own desire to see
you with a flatter chest, sculpted male pecs, less gender ambiguity. I
have fantasies about running away to Amsterdam because the doctors

are supposed to be better there. But it's presumptuous and disrespectful for me to encourage you to have or not have top surgery. So much of our relationship relies on my supporting you for staying where you are right now, somewhere in between many, many dichotomies.

There's a place where I can go to get away from these conflicting thoughts, down, down there, where the fur is longer than your armpit hair and I have to part it with both hands, like British explorers in an old Tarzan movie trying to get through the jungle. There's always a little nausea for me in the second before my mouth makes contact with somebody else's sex. But the urge forward is greater than whatever qualms I have about safe sex or sodomy. What goes in my mouth looks like a small cock without a piss slit. The head is perfectly shaped; the hood is enlarged as well, so I can move it around like a foreskin. Your erection is constrained by two thin labial anchors. I use the side of my finger to bring moisture up from between them to supplement my saliva. Your hips lock whenever I touch you there; you stop moving for a split second, and I can't tell if that frozen motion means *go in* or *go away*.

I like sucking cock; I like eating cunt. Usually I try to duplicate the strokes that my partner uses when he or she beats off. But you like to press your fingers against the base of your clit and shake it hard until you come. I can't figure out how to do that with my mouth. I personally don't like receiving oral sex that much, usually. It seems to me that most people who put their faces in between my legs have no idea how their licking or sucking feels to me. They are lost in their fantasies about being used and abused, out of touch with my wincing, over-sensitive flesh. In my enthusiasm to taste you, I sometimes wonder if I am guilty of the same offense—enthusiastic but clueless cock sucking. With you I am never sure I am hitting the right stroke unless you hold my head and fuck my mouth. What seems to work best is making my mouth into a wet slit with a tongue in the middle of it, held rigid and still so it makes a convenient and slippery place to rub against. That way you can put your cock where it feels the best to you.

"I love it when you suck me," you say, your voice low and filthy, pitched to carry only to my ear, your hand on the back of my neck. This rare combination of verbal and physical affirmation makes my cunt close and open, a quick little inner motion that tugs on my clit. That brief, sharp feeling of joy makes my stomach jump. I am simultaneously breathless and a notch more excited than I was just a second ago. You are shy about talking dirty, or perhaps you just parcel it out, knowing a smutty sentence or two has more effect than a constant stream of gutter-gums rhetoric.

I am kneeling at right angles to your hip, bent over your body. The sheets smell like sex—a combination of sweat, artificial lube, and the come we're both making. My left hand is full of slippery stuff right now, the spit that is running from my mouth as I slowly pass my lips and tongue down the shaft and head of your cock, and the oily slick salty fluid that flows in a steady stream from your cunt. I have anchored my thumb inside, hooking it over the lip of muscle that guards this, your less friendly orifice. Two and sometimes three of my other fingers push thick sex juice into your ass. The muscle there is used to me; it would readily take my whole hand if I was wearing a glove and some grease. It has taken me surprisingly little time to get used to this unique sexual perfume: a woman's wetness with the acrid testosterone overtones of a man's armpits and balls.

Tonight I can't make you come with my mouth. But we've had a lewd, boisterous party trying, and you aren't angry. "Don't take that mouth of yours too far away, now," you say. Your hand comes down to the base of your clit, and you hold me in place with your other hand. It's like having someone jack off on my face. I like the contact with your pounding hand, the feeling of being held in place, and I pinch your nipples because I need to do something to be a part of what is happening to you. I want to fuck you, but this is no time to make a move in that direction. *After he comes,* I think to myself.

You come with your body bent in the middle, curved like a bow, and the noise you make in my ear is deep and a little scary. I like it that you are loud when you come. Your whole torso comes off the bed, and you make a bellowing noise full of pain and rut, a shocking noise that reminds me I have neighbors. Your face is a snarling mask of big white teeth and bushy black beard. But there's so much pleasure happening so close to me that I could not care less about noise. Sweat flies off your body, and I feel baptized by the spray. Let them listen. So they'll know I got laid. This is not a bad thing. I roll over on top of you to ground you while you shake.

All of a sudden, you are asleep. Snoring, even. Both hands on my upper arms, holding me in place, close to you. I try to move to get the blankets and cover you, and you will have none of it. Your lips move back in a snarl, and your grip tightens. So I stay that way, chilled, thinking to myself that only men can do this, get off and then fall instantly to sleep, while women can almost always be persuaded to try to get off just one more time.

Again I try to cover you, and you resist. And so I wait, listening to you snore, loving you with all my heart. Lube and come are slowly sliding out of my cunt. "Maybe it's your turn to get fucked," you had said. Apparently so.

Eventually you drift a little closer to consciousness, and I pry myself away, leave briefly to piss, and come back to bed. "Come here," you say, and I lay my head on your shoulder. My fucked-up neck won't permit me to stay there for long, but I remain in that position until I absolutely have to move. I'm the daddy, even though you won't call me that, reserving that title for your longtime boyfriend. My shoulder is normally the comforting hollow that soothes a lover's troubled mind to sleep. But I deserve to be the one whose head is cradled on a shoulder tonight. An aftershock like a tiny orgasm surprises me, and I fall asleep while I am running my tongue around the inside of my own mouth, finding the taste of you everywhere.

Am I tasting my future? I don't know, I don't think I can go to this place that you occupy, seemingly without ambivalence or fear. It's so much easier to be jealous of your other lover than it is to be jealous of your muscles, your facial hair, the ease with which you pass. Easier to imagine myself a magnanimous and broad-minded person who can tolerate having a bearded lover with an F on his driver's license. But simply loving you wrenches my identity out of shape as severely as a shot of testosterone. If I am going to back up your male identity, I have to think of myself as and call myself bisexual, not lesbian. I wish we could talk about this, but you don't want to go there. You aren't ready to cut your ties with the leatherdyke community, and you are puzzled when anybody points out the contradictions between your past and your future. If I stop calling myself a lesbian, that has implications for your identity that make you uneasy.

Nor do we talk much about my hermaphroditic tendencies. You simply follow the signals I broadcast, mean bitch or leatherman, and there are nights when we go back and forth across the gender frontier a couple of times. After one of our dates, there are more costumes to throw in the wash than there are trick towels. You have never suggested that we might be alike, of one kind. If we really are different, why do I feel shut out, excluded by that omission?

Battered by my own anxiety, I eventually sleep, and dream about pitching lit cigars into the Grand Canyon.

Incense for the Queen of Heaven

But since we left off to burn incense to the queen of heaven,
and to pour out drink offerings unto her, we have wanted all
things, and have been consumed by the sword and by the
famine.

—Jeremiah 44:18

It was a dark and stormy night when Ad set out for the bar, beaten down by a pain in his chest that would not abate. Still unaccustomed to the fact that he was no longer a chauffeur with the keys to a silver Citroen, he had no bus pass and chose to walk a mile and a half rather than dodge into a liquor store and ask for change. The drizzling rain did its best to make his wavy bleached-blond hair lie down, but Ad's hair product was wax-based and impervious to moisture. If Ad had been given to poetics, this would have seemed richly symbolic to him. Refusing to give way had been the source of much of his current misery.

It had been 42 days, 11 hours, and seven minutes since Cybil had dismissed Ad from her service. Ad had known that all was not well when he was summoned to his lady's drawing room and refused permission to kneel by her bentwood Art Nouveau chair. She was wearing

a dark blue Victorian day gown that had two dozen tiny buttons down
the front. He ought to recall the exact number; he had covered the
buttons in fabric and sewn them on himself. The dress was long-
sleeved and high-necked. Only Cybil's hands, an inch of throat, her
head, and the black tips of her ankle-high boots showed. Beneath the
gown (he recalled, salivating) was a corset and chemise, wave after
white wave of cotton eyelet petticoats, and drawers with eight-inch
cuffs of French lace. It was possible to hand-sew lace with such fine
stitches that the seam was invisible. The tips of Ad's fingers smarted,
recalling that lengthy lesson.

A hoop of embroidery, the interruption of which should have
signaled how insignificant this encounter was, sat on Cybil's knee.
She was decorating a matching set of pillowcases with forget-me-
nots. Ad was accustomed to being admitted to her inner sanctum,
which she always called "the bedchamber," never "the bedroom," so
this formal confrontation made him uneasy. In fewer words than it
takes to refuse a telemarketer but with a great deal more courtesy, she
notified him that his services would no longer be needed.

"What about this?" the boy demanded, made a little stupid by
sudden agony, tugging at the silver chain around his neck.

She wordlessly handed him the key. Still he tarried. His livery, a
black wool jacket and button-fly trousers with scarlet piping, suddenly seemed as tight as an iron maiden. Should he strip it off and
leave her side as naked as the day when he had taken his vows? She
did not seem to think his uniform was worth the trouble to ask for its
return, despite the fact that she had cut it out and fit it to his ribs and
thighs with her own two hands.

"What did I do?" Ad blubbered, humiliated by a sudden rush
of tears.

"If pointing out your flaws could mend this situation, you would
still have a position here," she deigned to explain to what was now an
interloper on her premises and a presumptuous one at that. Six

months of service were apparently a feather on the scale of her regard. The silverware Ad had polished (asparagus tongs! crab picks!), the shopping he had done clutching one of her alphabetized lists in minuscule spiderweb handwriting, all the driving (at five miles below the posted speed limit) and dusting (wearing a butler's apron), restoring antique furniture, cleaning out the rain gutters, adjusting his hat to the proper angle every time he passed a mirror, framing lithographs, keeping the red stripes on his trouser legs arrow-straight, melting her sealing wax, sprinkling sand on her correspondence to dry the ink from her fountain pen, standing for inspection with every buckle and button glittering—all that neurotic sweat, gone in a puff of feminine contempt.

Afraid that he lacked the coordination to remove the chain and fling it dramatically at her feet, Ad had fled, leaving behind sanity, dignity, and understanding. Or so it would seem. For in the weeks that followed, he could not gather his resources to look for a job, clean his apartment, call a friend, get a therapist, hire a whore, or go to a meeting. He could think of only one way to forget his troubles. A hangover and a forfeited two-year chip seemed like a cheap price to pay for even a few hours of belligerent amnesia.

At least his leather jacket still fit. In Cybil's retro world, motorcycle clothing was déclassé. Her fashion sense had stopped at the year 1914, along with the heart of Archduke Franz Ferdinand. Every closet in her house was crammed with medieval, Renaissance, and Victorian gowns, each of which used up at least 20 yards of fabric. Before meeting Cybil, Ad had never even *seen* a hatbox, much less been made responsible for their contents. In the first weeks of their relationship, Ad had made the mistake of giving his mistress a beaded 1920s flapper dress. She gave it away to a homeless shelter.

Cybil had told him once, "Living in the past is the only way I can cope with the present." She could not go everywhere she wanted to go in a coach-and-four or a period vehicle, but she could own a car that looked like nothing else on the road and refuse to touch its steering wheel. She could travel at a sedate speed calculated to infuriate other travelers. "I'm so glad that *we* left the house with sufficient time to accomplish all that we must," she would say severely as mad yuppies in Volvos, BMWs, and Lexuses swore, shook their fists, and swerved past them. There was just one room in her house where ugly modernity and its brutal pragmatism reigned. It was crammed with computer equipment in beige and off-white metal boxes that seemed to Ad's unschooled eye to be sufficiently powerful and complex enough to run the nation's defenses—or breach them.

He had no idea what it was that Cybil did to these machines that made her so much money. He was not allowed in the house on work days. Her single attempt to explain her labors sounded like "nawbing the tetch and gred the dweedle" and made him feel like an amiable and hopeful, panting dog that only recognizes the words "out," "treat," and "bath."

The rain had soaked through the thighs of his jeans, Ad noticed as he sighted the door of the Pearl and the Peacock, a faux English tavern that had become a dyke bar when its previous owner, an expatriate with a diagnosis of prostate cancer, gave up on capitalism and returned to the bony but reliable arms of the National Health Service. No redecorating had been deemed necessary; the place was a low-maintenance cash cow, like most gay bars. The cloying rain-clouds had prevented the night from becoming pitch-dark. It seemed as if the streetlights were trapped beneath a cup of gray fog. So a mellow glow surrounded the emblems on the bar's hand-painted sign. The pearl in the peacock's bill had a nacreous shimmer, and its prurient fan had a chatoyant luster. Then Ad remembered that he knew two of those esoteric adjectives because of Cybil's odious "Word for the Day" drills, and growled, "Useless!" The sound of his own voice startled him as he gripped the wet brass handle of the door, and that little jolt of adrenaline made him throw it open with a bit too much energy, so it banged loudly.

Cybil had once approved of this bar because no neon was visible from the street. But Ad doubted he would find her sipping sherry here tonight. That very day he had spotted her ad in the classified pages of *Buzz*. It was the same ad that had inspired his first phone call to his former, well, what the hell did you call her anyway? She certainly wasn't a girlfriend!

The ad said simply, "Goddess requires acolyte," and Ad was sure she was screening calls from dozens of hopeful new submissives, plus the batch of losers he had beaten out to win an interview with her on the spring equinox. Now it was fall, and like the red leaves of the oak trees and the yellow leaves of maple, he had tumbled from his place on the top bough into the slough of despond, where he could wilt and decay for all Cybil cared.

He pushed into the heated humidity and glare of the bar and had to stifle a cough as rancid tobacco smoke and the sour fumes of old beer assaulted his lungs. Despite his jealous fantasies about Cybil being besieged by new prospects, he nervously scanned the bar anyway, ready to bolt if he saw the scalloped hem of her 1892 riding habit or the violet fringe that edged her favorite shawl. What he found seated at the bar was almost as bad, but Ad shrugged his broad-enough shoulders and went down the steps into the main room to bump his chest against the mahogany rail that ran round the edge of the bar. Having both feet on the turf of lesbian longing abruptly pulled Ad out of the fantasy world of a great lady and her chivalrous squire, back into her real body, her identity as other women in the bar would see it.

There were two couples (one terse and monosyllabic, one tongue-entwined) and three single girls (one drunk, one dizzy from dancing, and one taut with rage at the presence of her ex-lover and former best friend) in between Ad and Tam. Tam resembled a mountain, bent over the bar with her weight on her elbows. She had a shock of black curly hair that made Ad think of Errol Flynn. Her hands were small and blunt, square as boxes, yet she neatly handled a cigarette and a tumbler full of clear liquid with only five fingers. A sense of menace came off her body the way nostalgia emanates from a sunset. She did not turn to acknowledge Ad, but the jilted boy knew his coordinates had been calculated and torpedoes locked on to that location, just in case.

Tam had been Cybil's lover Before. Before the classified ad, before she began to spell her name that way, before she spent half a decade in New York and then came back to this town. Everybody knew about them. The pyramid scheme that Tam pulled off to buy Cybil a huge diamond ring, which later was thrown into the bay during one of her rages about Tam's infidelity. The devotion Cybil displayed when Tam was at death's door from a motorcycle accident, forcing homophobic emergency room personnel to save her darling's life. The enormous settlement they got from the resulting lawsuit, which allowed them to purchase a building that Cybil refused to set foot in because of the way Tam had made it look inside. The mutual lover they had driven to madness and bankruptcy and traffic court. Their story was peppered with expensive dinners, exotic vehicles, fancy hotels, and emotion so intense it would have fried lesser mortals like a poodle in a microwave. Cybil and Tam were linked together in the legends of this city's dykes, inseparable as Abelard and Héloïse, Del and Phyllis, rugby and broken legs. Ad thought this was because they were both larger than life. Even though their breakup had taken place ages ago, they still seemed to belong in the same magical category, opposites that would forever attract, at least in other people's imaginations.

If there was anybody Ad hated more than she hated the next attendant at Cybil's shrine, it was Tam. Cybil never spoke of her, but Ad sensed her presence everywhere in Cybil's life, in the things she would not have or would not do, and could not ignore it any more than a proper dog can ignore the sight of a cat on the lam. Ad silently said some mean things about drunks who are active in their disease and held out a folded ten-spot to lure the bartender.

Is there such a thing as a dyke who is not psychic? There was something adversarial, almost toxic, in the air between Ad and Tam. It smelled like a thunderstorm, sounded like the track that bears two trains on a collision course, looked like nothing at all. One by one, the curt couple, the spooning couple, and singles one, two, and three melted away to find other places to perch. So Ad found five feet of clear space between herself and her hated rival, uncanny on such a busy night, and could not help but think of two Wild West gunslingers squaring off to settle all bets. "Bartender!" she called out testily.

With one abrupt gesture, Tam stopped the approaching barkeep in her tracks. The 50-something, rangy redhead sank her hands into a sink and began washing glasses while quietly whistling "Hello, Dolly." Ad drew in an angry breath and faced Tam full on, expecting to hear a taunt that would end with the two of them outside, butting heads like bighorn sheep. But Tam just said mildly, "Why don't you have some of what I'm drinking?" and pushed her glass down the bar. It slid smoothly like something in a movie and stopped an inch away from Ad's right hand.

The proposal that she actually drink from someone else's glass would normally be revolting to Ad, who worried a lot about germs. But it was such a weird suggestion that it got in under her radar, and she actually hoisted the sweating glass and took a swig. She expected the juniper bite of gin and tonic.

What she got was a mouthful of diluted ginger ale. Unadulterated except by melting ice cubes. Too surprised to mind her manners, Ad sprayed the floor with what was left in her mouth. "What the hell—" she sputtered and looked pleadingly at Tam.

The older butch was laughing, slapping her knee. When her amusement abated, she unclipped something from the zipper of her own leather jacket and threw it at Ad. Who caught it, for a wonder. (Ad was not particularly athletic.) It was a ten-year chip. Metal, anodized purple and silver. With a hole in it so it could be worn as a zipper pull. Ad's mouth was open, and she was about to shout something indiscreet to the whole bar. Tam's hand came down on her shoulder and pulled her close. "Cory," Tam snapped, and they had a bartender quicker than the man who rubbed the lamp got his genie. "Pour Adonis here a drink out of my bottle."

Cory complied briskly, and there they were, clicking big glasses full of secret soda, saying "Cheers," and there went Ad's big dream of a big messy relapse. She would *not* swill booze in front of Tam if Tam was in the Program. Though, come to think of it, she had never seen Tam at a meeting or heard her name mentioned. And no matter how often one recited, "What you hear here, who you see here, let it stay here," it was impossible to be ignorant of the identity of all the other 12-stepping dykes in such a small city. Ad began to get the paranoid idea that Tam must be playing some kind of trick on her.

It was into this atmosphere of suspicion that Tam's next remark, a question, fell. "So," Tam said, blowing smoke just past Ad's right shoulder, "you got the bum's rush. Tell me, little *acolyte,* aren't you going to miss having your goddess ejaculate all the way up to your elbow? I used to love the way she did that to me."

Ad's mouth fell open again. First, she was affronted by Tam's vulgar reference to Cybil's shell-like private parts and even more private sexual proclivities. Second, she was nonplussed because in fact Cybil had never rewarded her personal services with anything other than the usual quantity of sex-slickness. Long months of resentment and jealousy boiled within her already aching heart. More than once she had secretly blamed Tam for her inability to break through Cybil's reserve and win her undying love. Tam had broken Cybil's heart so thoroughly that only fine powder was left, sands of old pain that ran through Ad's fingers every time she tried to gather Cybil's affection and forge something to hang on to from it. Now, Ad realized, she could have her revenge on both of them—say something slanderous about Cybil's putative sluthood and one-up Tam as a ladies' man.

I'm weak, Ad said to herself and hung her head. She couldn't do it. "Actually, ah," she said, "um, well, that just never happened to me, Tammuz. I never got to that particular base with the lady. So I guess you have the advantage over me on that one."

A blow that was hard enough to rock her on the bar stool connected with Ad's right arm, but a look at Tam's face showed it was a friendly gesture. Ad wanted to rub her sore biceps but was afraid to look like a wuss.

"So you have a sense of honor," Tam said, stubbing out her cigarette. "Well, well. I wonder what else you have that I should know about?" She regarded Ad with the cold light of erotic appraisal, eyes wide, nostrils slightly flared, the fingers of one hand open and extended like a cat's claws.

Ad didn't know what to say. The odd sensation of being cruised by another butch went to her head harder and faster than liquor. She was suddenly transported to a new realm where the old rules did not apply. Were there any rules at all?

"You oughta oil that jaw of yours," Tam said easily, and put her hand inside Ad's jacket. Something happened to Ad's nipple that was weirdly arousing. Tam didn't play with her tit, she just went for the nipple like a gay man tweaking a boy's tiny brown nubs. "Shall we go?" Tam said, releasing her flesh, and Ad actually found herself leaning toward this . . . this oafish person, who had not even *asked* before laying hands upon her!

"Aw, come on," Tam said, seeming to read her mind. "Don't carry on like some stupid bitch in a miniskirt who's just gotten her ass pinched by a hard hat. We both miss her, neither one of us can have her, but that doesn't mean we're dead or gone to Jesus. Who else are we gonna go home with tonight but each other? It's kismet, bucko, get your ass up, and let's get the hell out of here."

Ad floated out of the bar in her rival's wake, dazed by the terrible logic of what that butch archetype had said about their fated tryst. As the door of the Pearl and the Peacock closed behind them, she swore she could hear the sound of a dozen quarters hitting pay phone slots. "You'll never believe what just happened!" she heard in a dozen variations from excited whispers to full-fledged shrieks. So Cybil would find out. BFD. What Ad did with her body was no longer any of Cybil's business, was it?

Tam was waiting, her battered black Chevy pickup truck idling at the curb. Ad got in and banged the door shut. "Don't slam the door," Tam said irritably. "This ain't a barn you're riding in, Fancypants. Light me a cigarette and watch the speedometer. I like it when the passenger does all the shifting."

Was this what had been missing from her life, Ad wondered— the grounding effect of a demanding and critical personality, clear orders, a definite hierarchy? Mmm, perhaps. But was there a hierarchy? Between the two of them, why should she automatically become Tam's underling? It was a question she pondered all the way up to fifth gear, when Tam used her free hand to investigate parts of Ad's body that turned her brain off when stimulated.

It was not a short drive. Tam headed for a part of town that Ad did not know very well, a rather industrial section near the airport. They slid into one of three whole parking places in front of a building that looked like a red brick warehouse. Ad wondered how long it had been since she had seen that many vacant parking spaces in a row in the part of the city where she lived. Tam let them in with a key that she fished from her pocket, and Ad had an uncharitable thought about the purely decorative function of the big bunch of keys that hung on her rival's left hip. They were otiose, is what those keys were, and damn Cybil again for the Word of the Day. It was as bad as trying to get the jingle from a

commercial out of your skull. Why did Tam live here? Was this where
she worked, doing something grubby with machines? Ad envisioned a
cot with stiff, gray sheets jammed between the carcasses of ailing auto-
mobiles and winced.

On the inside the building turned out to be not just a dwelling,
but one on a giant scale. Tam escorted her by now very nervous guest
into a huge loft and closed the door. Some lights had been left on
inside, just enough for Ad to glimpse a large studio. Two enormous
canvases dominated adjacent walls. The angry slashes of color hurt
Ad's eyes. The concrete floor was splattered with blobs and smears of
paint. In the middle of the room was a larger-than-life metal figure
of a woman tearing her way out of a snarl of barbed wire. The sculp-
ture was not complete. Welding equipment and pieces that had either
been discarded or awaited addition to the struggling figure littered
the floor and a worktable. The thought of Tam as a sculptor or a
painter—an artist, that *thug?*—blew out the few tiny fuses that Ad
had left.

Tam put a gentle hand on her upper arm and drew her into
another part of the space, which had been partitioned off. She got a
couple of kerosene heaters going in the living room, and Ad huddled
gratefully in front of one. The place was pretty fucking cold, actually.
The furniture was all shaped like cubes—wooden cubes for tables,
upholstered cubes in primary colors for chairs. "Are you hungry?"
Tam asked, going into the kitchen. Only a breakfast bar inlaid with
several different kinds of pale wood and three high-backed stools on
aluminum pedestals divided the kitchen alcove from the living room.
Tam switched on a coffeemaker, which immediately came to life,
grinding its own beans and heating water for brewing. Getting no
answer, she came back to where Ad was trying to thaw out her butt
without catching her clothes on fire, and asked again. Ad tackled her,
wearing the oddest look on her face, like someone whose actions are
being controlled by a remote and hostile power.

Not sure why she was finding this amusing, Tam rolled with the assault, pushing a coffee table out of the way with one hand so that Ad would not rap her head on it. They rolled on the carpeted floor for several minutes, giggling and gasping. There was no point at which Tam felt in any danger of losing the mock battle, but she was loath to humiliate the other butch just yet. Perhaps it was just the tenderness that an old scar shows to a new injury. But Ad did seem to be putting all she had into it, pushing with both of her hands to try to pin Tam to the floor. "Careful, now," she said, trying not to laugh. "If you flip me over, will you know what to do with me?"

It was exactly the same thing that Cybil had once said to Ad when a bout of puppy germs had infected her. Ergo, it must be something Tam and Cybil had said to each other—frequently. Ad took her hands off Tam as if she were a red-hot cast-iron stove and looked around for a phone. That would be the first step to getting a cab to take her home.

"Hey, hey," Tam said, "what bit you?"

"Do you think I'm *crazy?*" Ad spit. "I can't trust *you.* What the hell made you think I would ever let you tie me up?" She knew her ears were turning red. One wall of the living room had been turned into a fountain, built of fieldstones and rusting pieces of iron. She wondered how anyone could be in this room for more than five minutes without needing to pee, given the constant splashing and rushing sounds of circulating water.

"Tie you up?" Tam said, as if that were an unheard-of suggestion. "Who said anything about all that S/M shit, youngster? I just want to fuck."

"Oh," Ad said. After a long, lame pause, she could think of nothing else to say but "Where's the phone?"

"Come on, tell me the truth," Tam said, getting up and dusting off her knees. "You're disappointed."

"No," Ad said. Her lips were numb.

"Sit down," Tam said firmly. Ad's backside suddenly took over without consulting the rest of her, and hauled her down into one of the cubic chairs. Her hands parted to accept a white china diner cup of coffee. To drink it was to accept the premise that she would need it—intended to make a night of it. Ad bent her neck like a horse newly broken to the bridle and sipped. Her eyes lit upon the only anachronism in this ultramodern decor—a shadow box that contained a pair of dove-gray elbow-length silk gloves. The marcasite and onyx buttons were the size of a squirrel's eye. Recalling the process by which Cybil liked to have her accessories removed, Ad would have been willing to wager that some of Tam's spittle lingered on each button, and a few molecules of tooth enamel as well.

"Don't burn your tongue," Tam said, making a nasty joke of it.

"Do you always steal souvenirs from your exes?" Ad retorted. What a moment to remember the exact scent of Cybil's perfume, mixed with the odor of her body when she was a little aroused and determined to remain in complete control.

Tam knew exactly what Ad was talking about and did not deign to look at the item. "She can have them back any time she wants to ask for them," she said lightly, her voice as sharp-edged as a sword. Or a poignant memory.

Ad took refuge in the coffee, which was some delicious expensive brew that would have been ruined with milk or sugar. But halfway through the cup, she felt Tam's shadow approaching. The hand that she had envied and attempted to imitate fell on the back of her neck. If Tam had spoken to her then, she still might have bolted. But Tam simply drew her up, like a bucket from a well, and Ad allowed herself to be escorted into the bedroom, which was situated down a hallway, behind the kitchen.

They contemplated the room and its furnishings for a moment, Tam's body pressed against Ad's. The skittish boy tolerated the contact, needing the dumb human warmth of it. The room contained a huge bed built out of 4-by-4 lumber. Tam must have to get her sheets custom-made. Its head and foot were carved and curved to resemble the torii that guards the entrance to a Shinto shrine. But the hooks and eyes that broke up the smooth curves of the bed disrupted that aesthetic. In one corner there was a stand for a sling, made out of PVC pipe screwed together. The pipe had been meticulously painted in Mondrian colors and geometric shapes. Clothing was stashed into open storage cubes built into one wall.

Another wall held a few of the usual ominous implements that Ad had come to expect in the bedrooms of leatherdykes. The whips appeared to have titanium handles, and most of their lashes were made out of latex or plastic, not leather. There were some Plexiglas paddles and an aluminum umbrella stand full of black Teflon and brightly colored Delrin rods. None of the bamboo canes that Cybil favored. None of her beloved Victorian leather tawses or hand-carved wooden paddles. No riding crops, no hairbrushes. "A change is as good as a rest," Ad mouthed, not expecting Tam to overhear her.

It did not occur to the boy that hearing one of Cybil's favorite slogans on the lips of her successor might be as upsetting for Tam as the quip about flipping somebody over had been for Ad to hear. Tam said quietly, "It's hard for somebody who wants to live in the past to tolerate someone who wants to live in the future. We were both time travelers; we were just going in opposite directions." She put her hands on Ad's shoulders and squeezed gently, sending a wave of pleasure down the boy's spine.

But Ad could not relax into Tam's touch and let the games begin. She stepped away and plucked up a lacy garment that had fallen out of one of the wardrobe units. "This doesn't appear to be your size," she said in a fuck-you tone of voice. Her anger at Tam was fueled by a confusing sort of anger at herself. Why on earth should she be jealous at this evidence of the presence of yet another killer femme in Tam's boudoir and life?

"The demigoddess is in Key West for six months," Tam said, the very picture of ironic forbearance. "She is visiting her fiancé. Making plans for the wedding, I expect. Going over prenuptial agreements." To Ad's incredulous look, she replied with a shrug. "Just call me a big dumb straight boy, homey." Ad stuffed the offending bit of champagne-colored satin into the nearest bin, making a yuck-there's-a-bug-in-my-sandwich face. "Nobody ever *has* a girl," Tam patiently explained. "You just get to borrow them for a while."

Ad faced the older butch just in time to receive a slap in the face. It went through her frame like the vibrations of an engine, turning on some functions, shutting off others. "What I want to know," Tam said slowly and deliberately, "is what a candy-assed pansy boy like you is doing in my house. Faggot. Did you think I brought you back here to get all kissy, sissy boy?" He was a little hurt because his gender overtures had been rejected. *I'm not as young as I used to be,* Tam thought, growing weary of the way Ad's butch cadet image tugged him back toward his lesbian past. *Nostalgia is the enemy.*

He slapped Ad again. The boy changed colors but did not raise his fists. Ad was a churning mess within, trying to sort out this new game. What had he expected? More of Cybil's slow but relentless seduction? Tam was her virile counterpart. The butch was impatient where Cybil was cunning; harsh when the anachronistic mistress would have flattered or cajoled, speaking with honey in her mouth. Tam took what he wanted instead of waiting for it to come crawling to him, begging to be used. Ad resented being rushed into submission but had to admit there was a certain amount of relief to be found in buckling to Tam's bullying.

"Fucking queer," Tam snapped and punched Ad in the upper arm, pummeled his ribs and thighs. Ad stepped back under this assault and quickly found himself up against one of the four corner supports of the bed.

"Stop hitting me!" he cried out, on the brink of tears, and Tam laughed at him.

"Your mama can't help you now, little boy," Tam said, and forced him to his knees, then tied both of his wrists behind him, rope around the bedpost, knots professionally out of Ad's reach. He got slapped again for trying to locate them. "You stay where I put you, pussy boy," Tam snarled. "Don't worry, you're going to get what you came for. I've got you right where you belong. There's no skirts for you to hide behind here, nobody's apron strings to tug on 'cause you're a widdle fwightened tyke who needs his titty. Somebody has to toughen you up and smarten you up, boy, and I guess I'm just the mean son of a bitch to handle that very dirty job."

The last three words of this sentence were delivered very close to Ad's face and followed with a spray of spit. He was unable to wipe his face and had to feel it drying on his cheeks while he juggled his weight from knee to knee and watched Tam prepare for the next phase of his chastisement. Cybil would sometimes tie an ivory olisbos to her loins with a long silk scarf. But when she fucked Ad this way, she was never a boy; she was a girl, albeit a perverse one. Tam stripped out of his pants and strapped on a harness that looked as if it had been cut from a Michelin steel-belted radial and a big rubber dildo that could not possibly have been more realistic or more ugly.

As the head of this implement approached Ad's face, he became aware of some truly frightening new feelings. It was one thing to be Cybil's boy. He had enjoyed playing a male role with her because she protected him from certain expectations or responsibilities that would have made manhood too burdensome. When he passed as her son or boyfriend, he got to taste just a little bit of heterosexual privilege. Straight people responded to them as if they were a handsome and theatrical couple, queer only in the old-fashioned sense of being eccentric. That sort of approval can be quite heady when you are used to being ignored or stared at with hate and disdain. It made him happy to know that he made Cybil safer by appearing to be her male protector or escort. It was also deliciously naughty to have this big secret, their shared gender.

But this encounter with Tam was not nearly as safe. He wondered if Tam was right. Had he hidden behind Cybil's skirts? Were there parts of himself that he avoided or suppressed because she made his life too easy? Was he afraid to really be a boy because he did not want to be harassed or threatened like the handful of young faggots whose persecution he had witnessed with helpless fury in high school?

Tam petted his sore face. Rubbed and tweaked his nipples. Ad could not restrain a groan of arousal. "That's right," Tam said. "Give me that. That's what I want. Show me how much you want it, Adonis. Open that pretty little mouth of yours and lick your lips, and tell me what a fine greedy cocksucker you are, baby."

Tam's booted foot caressed him between the legs, and Ad rubbed himself against Tam's body, shamelessly wanting more of that good feeling, wanting to be touched. Wanting to be opened by those big hands, that big shaft. He said as much of this as he could, stammering it out, and Tam slapped him again, but it was different now. The blow was like a promise of pleasure to come. Ad opened his mouth and took in his reward, sucking like a calf at the bottle. Sucking to receive the nourishment he needed to live as well as to give pleasure.

Tam was a fierce master, alternating thrusts with scathing rhetoric that undressed Ad's pretensions and made him blush. Cybil knew how to do this too, make you naked and then undress your soul with her words. Tam was literally stripping Ad as well, easing open his shirt and pants, working his nipples again and again, shoving a hand down his fly to bring his wet hole to burning life with a few shallowly intruding fingers. His asshole was stroked as well, leaving him in a dither about where that big cock would go next. For the first time in many weeks, days, and hours, he felt something besides bitterness for Cybil. Those little butt plugs she was so fond of had made it possible for him to open up to Tam's questing hand and offer him one more place to take his pleasure. He was grateful to Cybil for that.

Tam untied Ad's wrists and picked him up by the upper arms. Ad felt like a rag doll who could be turned and manipulated, bent and crumpled, thrown down in any old position without being harmed. He was loose in every joint, giddy with this attention and sensation, swimming in an experience he thought he had lost forever when Cybil sent him away. So the magic ability to call forth his submissive self was not Cybil's alone. There was something sad about that. Ad felt a little innocence slipping away, like blood from a small hidden injury, and wanted to weep. But there was no time. There was someone large and smoky very close at hand, demanding all of his concentration.

"Kiss me," Tam said. "Show daddy what that pretty little mouth can do. Do you love your daddy, Ad? Did you like sucking a real man's cock? Kiss me like a good little faggot, kiss me now."

It was not the kind of kiss that Ad was used to giving girls, a kiss where you had to be careful not to crush their lips or leave spit on their faces. Tam's big face could take every bit of passion that Ad's mouth could give and still have room for more. While his mouth was being explored, Tam's hands removed the rest of his clothing and slapped him on the butt. It was hard to keep on kissing Tam when those heavy, hard hands fell on each cheek of his sensitive, downy ass, but Ad was brave and resolute. He was unbearably turned on, wetter than he'd ever been in his life, and crimson with guilt about enjoying Tam's homophobic ranting.

Tam put him facedown on the bed and anchored his wrists to the posts at its head. Without being asked, Ad put his ass up in the air, and Tam spanked him for that, for being a horny slut who could not think of anything else but getting some big stud to ream him out. Ad whimpered and begged for forgiveness but admitted it was all true and prayed that Tam would stop talking soon and fuck him.

The bed creaked as Tam put his weight on the platform, kneeling behind Ad and stroking his flanks with sweating hands. The big dick went slowly, slowly down Ad's vaginal funnel, wreaking havoc as it progressed. It was the kind of fuck that felt as if it were changing you internally, so you'd never be able to be satisfied with anything smaller. Ad had reason to believe in his own ability to spring back into virginal narrowness after such an experience but chose to ignore that history because the fantasy of being permanently altered was just too thrilling. As he started to come, Tam worked two thick fingers into his ass, then pulled the dick out slowly. The fuck proceeded in this syncopated fashion—withdrawal from one hole equaled dilation of the other. Tam was thorough and controlled for a very long time and allowed Ad to come again and again.

Between orgasms Ad tried not to think about how this looked to Tam. A face-to-face fuck was so much more civilized. You could pretend that nothing was going on below your waist. Or at least ignore the way it appeared, shut out the pornographic close-up of spread legs and impaled orifice. And you could read the face above or below you. It would tell the tale of pleasure, pain, or indifference. Tam had probably seen more of Ad's butt, the boy thought, for longer than anyone else. It was humiliating. Hard-core. But he kept shuddering with cresting pleasure and knew he would continue to do so as long as Tam intended that he should. It was a horrid sort of freedom.

Then Tam switched to a different technique. Now both holes were being filled simultaneously. Ad felt as if the bones of his pelvis were being spread apart. If he didn't actually have a prostate gland, you would not have been able to tell from the way his ass was feeling. This orifice had been able to tolerate penetration before but had never actually craved it. Now he waited for every thrust with a pure hunger that was in itself a pleasure. His butt was purring like a hungry cat that knows the big hand in the sky is about to lower a dish of chopped chicken liver.

Cybil was certainly not a bad fuck. She had narrow hands and a devilish amount of stamina, especially for a lady with no obvious muscle. So this was not better, the pistoning that Tam was giving him, but it was certainly different. Cybil liked to make Ad wait for what she called "gratification," and there was always something a little distant and deliberate about the way she gave it to him. Maybe that was just as well, because she refused to trim her nails. Ad got what he needed to get off from her, but no more; no extras and no seconds. Tam's relish and enthusiasm made Ad's spine go slack. He felt caught up in a passion that transcended his own. There was no doubt at all that Tam's ruthless body would give him everything he craved, and then some.

"Do you wanna be my bitch?" Tam drawled, dropping sweat on Ad's back, his hands sliding down to clamp over the boy's hips. This was the sort of language that Ad might have used when Cybil had one of her rare whimsies to be the flirtatious character she referred to as "the blowsy barmaid," but Ad knew Tam was not asking him to be his femme. It was boy talk, straight out of one of those 4M2M chat rooms on AOL that Ad sheepishly patronized under a virile ten-letter pseudonym. Ad never thought he would hear someone say something like that to him in person, and Tam's deep voice and direct challenge made him go a little crazy with candid lust.

"Pleaseplease pleaseplease please," Ad chanted, panting.

Tam dripped more lube on both of them and said, "I can't hold back any more." The fast and furious fucking that followed drove Ad right out of his skull. He couldn't talk, he could only have big big orgasms that left the muscles of his thighs, chest, and buttocks wasted. "Bitch," Tam said, sounding very distant, and made some bear-and-bull noises that persuaded Ad his top was undone by his own peaking pleasure. Ad knew what that felt like, coming partly because the base of a dildo had pulverized your clit beyond bearing, partly because the visuals were so intense that what you saw almost persuaded you that you did have a cock that could feel heat and friction and respond to the gripping of pelvic muscles.

Ad tipped over, and Tam rolled with him. They were spooned together on the bed, stuck together with lube, sweat, and come. Ad thought the world had never been such a grand and glorious place. Tam rubbed his face into Ad's shoulder, and Ad was too far gone to understand the significance of a distinct rasp on his delicate skin.

Eventually Tam recovered enough to go and fill a bicycle bottle from the tap in the bathroom, drink some of it, and come back to offer water to Ad. Ad drank absentmindedly, noting there was no door on the bathroom without being able to figure out what that might mean. Tam sat up in bed beside him, threw a sheet over him so he would not get the shakes, and lit a cigarette. "So why did she send you away?" Tam asked comfortably, as if asking for help with a cross-word puzzle.

Ad giggled. The euphoria that followed great sex often made him chatty. For some reason, this topic had temporarily lost the power to level him. "She told me I was too toppy. She told me I should burn that energy off with somebody else. She got mad at me any time I couldn't tell her yes. I wanted to go to the movies; she never wanted to go to the movies. Petty crap like that. But I got tired of staying home holding my hands up while she wound yarn around them."

"Mmm," Tam said and petted Ad's head. The hair product had left his blond schoolboy locks in lank disarray, yielding to the rigors of sex as it had not given in to foul weather.

"But really," Ad said, moved to be truthful, "and I don't understand this at all, she got extremely and terminally pissed off at me when I asked her to take me to a play party and top me in public. I really, really wanted to show off for everybody. I wanted them to know how great she was, see the depth of what we felt for one another. Prove to her that I would do anything for her. She told me no, and I couldn't leave it alone. I kept on asking. And I think that was the last straw."

There was a long silence, during which Ad admired the smoke rings that Tam blew and wondered (not for the first time) about taking up cigars. Or perhaps a pipe would be more stately.

"What about you?" Ad dared to ask, examining the fastenings at the sides of Tammuz's harness.

Tam's snort of laughter sounded as if it hurt him. "Well, I had a lot of trouble controlling my temper," Tam said judiciously. "And she really hated it when I'd go off like a hound dog and get under somebody else's skirts. She didn't seem to understand that I had to take back my power somehow, score with other girls because otherwise I could not stand the hold that she had over me. When I came out, you know, a butch's job was to make the femme happy. Whatever she wanted. Even if what she wanted was to tie you up and cut you to pieces with a cane."

Tam stubbed out his cigarette and opened the pack, then shook his head and put it down. "But what really tore it," he confessed, "is the fact that I refused to go to a play party with her. I wouldn't bottom for her in public. I could wear her marks, even wear her chain around my waist, but I could not get down on my knees for her in front of a room full of spectators."

The two regarded one another for long, precious moments, two chapters of Cybil's past, wondering if there was a new story to be written between them, testing and sampling what they had just done to see what portents it might hold.

Ad sat up and grabbed both sides of Tam's harness. It came apart with the ripping racket of unseated Velcro. "What the hell do you think you're doing, youngster?" Tam asked, but did not raise his hands.

"I worked pretty hard for this," Ad said. "Don't you think I deserve it?" The truth was, Ad had no idea how to make love to another butch, but he was going to die if he didn't try to figure it out. He bravely slid his hands under Tam's shirt and then froze. Tam held his gaze, not apologizing, not explaining. Ad cautiously explored the unexpectedly flat chest, then raised the hem of Tam's shirt a half an inch. "Can I look?" he asked.

Tam shrugged.

Ad shucked the thin, knitted cotton up and over Tam's head. His chest bore two anchor-shaped scars. There were small brown discs, facsimiles of nipples, higher up on his chest. Ad traced the thin silver lines, boundaries of breasts that had vanished. "Does this hurt?" he asked.

"Not anymore," Tam replied. "Is it hurting you?"

"I don't know," Ad said. He looked at Tam's face, really looked at it to inquire what was there, instead of confirming what he assumed should be there. Tam's cheeks were darkened with a five o'clock shadow that had been allowed to linger long past midnight. It was this slight abrasiveness he had felt across his upper back. "Did you do this for Cybil?" he asked, wondering if he was being far too familiar.

"I thought so, at first," Tam said slowly. "But it didn't please her the way that I thought it would. She wasn't angry with me, but she told me it wasn't necessary, that she would have been happy with my body the way it was. Then I realized that I did it for myself. *I* could not have been happy with my body the way it was."

"Are you happy now?"

Tam shrugged. "I've stopped thinking about it. I think that's better."

For some reason, tears began to smart in the corners of Ad's eyes. "Kiss me," he said, and took Tam's face between his palms. This was a third sort of kiss, one between equals, Adonis asserting his attraction to Tammuz in the absence of any role playing or fantasy. Gradually he persuaded Tam to lay down beside him, threw the sheet over them both, and let his hands wander over Tam's back and his arms. The muscles there were infused with a new meaning, and Adonis felt as if he were taking their strength in through his palms. Tam relaxed slowly, as if each part of his body had to be ordered to get down and stay down. Ad could tell that when he stroked Tam's body, he was providing a rare sort of ease or respite. From time to time Tam would put a hand on Ad's side or shoulder, and Ad accepted that contact without focusing his attention upon it. Eventually the hand would fall away, and Ad would continue to tickle Tam's skin, massage the tissues underneath it.

When he bent to put his mouth on Tam's genitals, Tam made room for him there and used his hands to show Ad where to go. Ad was not sure how to stimulate this new sort of sex organ, which had begun life as a clitoris and been enlarged with testosterone until it was two inches long and as thick as Ad's thumb. He wasn't even sure what you would call it. A dicklet? Tam gave him a few monosyllabic hints, minimal driving directions that assumed Ad had the basic smarts and ability to do his job. Mouth wrapped around Tam's sex flesh, Ad was surprised by his own level of contentment and excitement. He had been swept away by blowing Tam's proxy of a phallus, but this was a more direct route to pleasure, one more way to acknowledge Tam's masculinity. He felt more like a gay boy now than he had an hour ago, struggling to mouth Tam's latex shaft. This was flesh and blood in his mouth. It contained nerve endings that responded to his slightest touch. He was so turned on he wanted very badly to touch himself, beg for permission to jack off like a cock-sucking boy in a story in *Drummer* magazine. But he abstained, not wanting the distraction, figuring that the edge of need would drive him to be more skillful.

It became impossible to ignore the fact that Tam's crotch contained more possibilities than a bioboy's stiffie. Ad allowed his fingertips to graze these sensitive openings. The response he got was equivocal. He interpreted it to mean don't stop, but don't go any further, either. So he contented himself with stroking the rim of muscle that guarded the opening to Tam's cunt. There was a prominent little mound of tissue around the urethra that seemed especially sensitive, so when it sounded like Tam was about to come, Ad pressed on it fairly hard and was rewarded by having his air cut off and his neck adjusted by Tam's substantial and not exactly alabaster thighs. Despite the tight quarters, Ad felt a gush of sweet-smelling liquid that went halfway up his forearm. He hoped the bed had a plastic sheet on it. The honeyed reek of Tam's ejaculation made him giddy.

After that they reclined side by side, not looking at one another, as if they were a little abashed. Ad began to wonder if he should find some graceful way to make an exit. Dawn could not be far off. He really should go home and clean his flat, buy a Sunday paper, and fluff up his résumé. But he seemed incapacitated, unable to even get up and piss, or ask for another slurp of water.

"So if you're a guy now, what the hell were you doing at a dyke bar?" Ad was startled by how rude the question sounded. How could he move so quickly from wallowing in fantasies about sucking Tam off through a glory hole in a filthy gay sex club, fantasies in which he would do anything to take Tam's load in his mouth, to issuing such a belligerent challenge?

Tam, however, did not seem to be offended. "Well, for one thing, I own a third of the bar," Tam said mildly. "When you've been going to lesbian bars and courting femmes for as many years as I have, sissy boy, ask me that question again."

"But you're a man!" Ad insisted, not sure if he was truly scandalized or just sulky from a lack of sleep.

"If your definition of a man is somebody who has a penis, I'll never qualify. But I look male. I pass. Socially I live as a man, most of the time," Tam said in a calm, reassuring tone of voice. "But when you walked into the bar, you didn't see me that way, did you? You saw me as somebody like you. A butch into genderfuck. And that's why I was there, Ad. I shaved and greased my hair back because I thought you might need to spend a little time with somebody who was like you. It's really hard to manage all the contradictions, trying to be man enough to keep a high femme happy, but knowing if you go too far, it might threaten her lesbian identity. Sometimes I need to be with somebody like me so I don't have to watch my step every fucking minute. You'd just gotten your ass kicked in a big way, and it was such a nice ass, I thought maybe I could get myself a piece of it while you were on the rebound."

Did Tam also say: "My identity is a kaleidoscope"? Did he say, "Besides, you were the last person who touched her. And by touching you, I could get a little closer to her"? No, impossible. That must be Ad's imagination, creating a confession that was far too personal for somebody as tough as Tam to make to a trick.

The only way Ad knew he had fallen asleep was the fact that he woke up, to the jangling sound of an irate telephone. He had been dreaming about trying on men's shirts that fit him perfectly. Tam had grabbed the receiver and was sitting up in bed, listening intently. When he saw that Ad was awake, he dropped the ubiquitous pack of cigarettes and smoothed Ad's hair, stroked his cheek, and stuck a couple of fingers in his mouth. So it had been all right to pass out between these alien sheets. Ad relaxed, even regressed, sucking on someone else's thumb, which left his poor psyche open to shrapnel attack by the shocking news that Tam delivered in a flat, clipped voice.

"Get up, Fancy-pants. We need to choke down some aspirin and shit, shave, and shower. Looks like we're taking a goddess out to brunch in half an hour."

No Mercy

Heather didn't have much to say during their ride to Mad Medea's Body Art Salon. Theresa—no, *Terry*—supposed that was not such a bad thing. She couldn't remember the last time they'd had a civil conversation. In its place a fight had sprung up, a fight as long as a novel, and Terry felt as if she knew each chapter by heart, especially the one they had about her new name. Heather still refused to use it consistently, and the only way Terry had won even marginal acceptance was to claim it was a pseudonym for the movie review column she was writing for the local free queer paper, found on top of better jukeboxes in gay dives everywhere. The fight about her name was apt to segue into a fight about the column, which Heather thought was somehow both frivolous and dangerous. Then that would change into a fight about her job, since the column was the only thing she was doing right now that made any money, and her unemployment had run out three months ago. "We could move into a cheaper apartment," Terry had offered, to which Heather replied, "Since you are making a grand total of $100 a month, Theresa, where exactly do you propose we live? A shack in Bolivia?"

It had taken Terry 58 long days to persuade Heather to take the unfinished business of her clitoral hood ring to a professional piercer.

Like any bottom with a brain, Terry knew how to make a top think that something was actually *her* idea. Discovering this ability to manipulate within herself did make Terry feel a bit queasy. Now Heather viewed this excursion as a last-ditch attempt to save their relationship. Maybe if Theresa finally had the permanent piercing that symbolized Heather's ownership of her body, she would give up her rebellious ways and comply with Heather's very reasonable requests. Terry had gone along with this because she knew that she wanted the piercing, and there was no way that she would ever accept it from Heather. The core of her being had rejected that possibility emphatically. Letting someone other than Heather change her body in such an intimate way was, for Terry, a proclamation of independence, just one more wave in the tide that was carrying her away from her first dominatrix, her only live-in lover.

Medea's was located downtown, in the same block as the methadone clinic and a peep show, across the street from a run-down motor lodge. Within a four-block radius you could visit McDonald's, Wendy's, Burger King, Taco Bell, and Popeye's Chicken. Wrappers in the gutter vividly attested to this, withered blossoms that had fallen from the bough of capitalism's wealth of opportunities. Heather parked with the same look on her face that she wore when she had to clean hair out of the sink. When she got out of the Volvo, she looked at the tires, and Terry winced, remembering without being told that the car should have gotten new tires a month ago. She resolutely fixed her gaze on the shop instead. What could have been a dingy store front had been dressed up with a plywood facade painted in carnival colors. A wildly tattooed woman with a crown on her head was flying away in a chariot pulled by dragons, laughing. The dragons had pierced nipples. On the ground below, dismayed people wandered in the black-and-white wreckage she had left behind.

The sign on the door said, "If you do not have an appointment, do not knock or ring now." Below this stern warning was the drawing of a gargoyle chewing on a bone. Most of the windows had been covered by the ornamental false front of the shop, but through the chain-mail curtain that hung behind the glass of the door, Terry could barely glimpse a wall covered with tiny drawings—tattoo flash, she told herself, proud to know the term. On the opposite wall was a three-tiered shelf bearing an assortment of statues of women, weapons, and flowers. There was a White Tara, Athena, Kali, and many more figurines that Terry could not identify, nestled between a mace, knives of all sizes and varieties, a pair of nunchuks, throwing stars, and porcupine quills. While she hunted for the doorbell, her eyes came across another sign, higher on the door, which said simply, "Help Wanted. Grown-ups need not apply." This sign was decorated with a pen-and-ink sketch of very grown-up fairy girls doing pretty naughty things to one another with pussy-willow switches and mushrooms.

From behind her, Headier released an exasperated sigh, then sent out her hand, fingertips painted in a pale noncolor called Moonglow, and unerringly pressed the doorbell. It made a big "oo-gah" sound like the Addams Family doorbell, and Terry laughed out loud. She was still laughing when a woman who was almost as tall as Lurch opened the door and said, "Watch it, Terry Bear, somebody might take that open mouth of yours as an invitation." Heather was so scandalized, she hissed like a balloon that's just bounced off the point of a pin. Terry didn't care; she was too shocked by the odd familiarity of the woman's salutation.

This must be Metamorpheen, owner of Medea's, pointer of the piercing needle, brandisher of the tattoo gun, the artist who had covered the wall with mermaids, birds of paradise, Japanese carp, lilies, astrological symbols, dolphins, simpering '50s pinup girls, black pumas, spiderwebs, heavy metal band logos, snakes, geishas, gorgons, and goddesses. She was more than six feet tall, very solidly built, and had big, almost coarse features and a haircut that reminded Terry of

Elvis Presley. When Terry wandered out of the visual feast of flash, her imagination was working full blast. She immediately got lost in the feverish wilderness vision of Meta's cunt, which must look like a large, moist, scarlet carnivorous flower between her mighty thighs. Not at all like the meticulously clipped and bikini-waxed strip between Heather's catwalk legs. Gaugin as opposed to Erté. She blushed as red as the lining of Meta's black leather vest and suddenly could not take her eyes off the floor, which needed to be swept. Meta was 40 if she was a day. How could Terry be thinking such dirty thoughts about her?

Heather cleared her throat, a clear signal that the social dynamic needed to reshuffle itself and focus on her. "We have an appointment," she said when Meta did not take the cue.

The big woman walked over to Terry to ruffle her hair. "I know," she said, without turning to look at Heather. Terry watched with regret as her big, capable hands returned to her sides. "Come in the back."

When the three entered the large single room behind the waiting area, there was more art to distract Terry from the fearsome business at hand. The walls were decorated with an airbrushed Wonder Woman, textiles from Panama, antique '60s psychedelic rock posters, reproductions of prehistoric cave art. There was also a photo of Meta-morpheen in a copper silk corset and a top hat. "What do all these things have in common?" Heather said under her breath. The term "eclectic" could cover such a multitude of aesthetic sins.

Meta was all business, snapping a surgical drape over the gyne-cological table, turning on a big light, checking the implements on an adjoining surgical tray. But she must have ears like a cat, Terry thought, because she answered Heather's question by saying simply, "I like them all."

Terry regarded the medical-looking stuff arrayed on the tray. They were the same tools that Heather had tried to use, but for some reason, they did not look like sinister harbingers of doom in this setting. Instead, the steel surfaces seemed to twinkle with hidden messages of hope and optimism. "Well," Meta told her, "get your pants off. I can't pick the right gauge jewelry till I see your equipment, Terry Bear."

"Theresa," Heather said coolly, "do as the piercer instructs. Take off your clothes, fold them up, and put them over here on this, uh, *beanbag* chair." By the time she had finished her first sentence, Terry had already shucked her jeans and was up on the table, her feet in the stirrups. A little furrow of anger sprang up between the perfect curves of Heather's fawn-colored eyebrows.

Heather hoped that this gargantuan person was not some kind of hack. This entire place did not inspire confidence, although everything that was actually touching Theresa's body seemed to be sterile. The piercer was meant to be her proxy, nothing more than a glorified pair of forceps in Heather's hands. But whenever she tried to reassert control over the situation, it slipped away. What a rude person this . . . *behemoth* was. (Heather refused on principle to use a preposterous made-up name like "Metamorpheen.") She would never refer anyone she knew to Medea's, that was certain. Shouldn't she be shown a certain amount of respect as Terry's top, the person who had brought her here, the only one with a positive balance in her checkbook?

Let's get this over with. "Terry, do you have the rings?" she prompted, feeling unreasonably exasperated at having to ask her.

Terry presented Meta with two different rings. One was surgical stainless steel with a hematite bead. The other, slightly larger ring, was a circle of anodized blue metal with a faceted crystal bead. Meta took them in her thick fingers and held them up against Terry's— *Theresa's*—rosy and, to be perfectly honest, ungainly clit.

"Heather," Meta said, "which one do you like the best?"

Heather had averted her eyes. Shouldn't it bother her to see that big paw planted in such a proprietary fashion on Theresa's sex?

Somewhere down around her diaphragm, Heather got the choking feeling that her therapist had helped her to identify as repressed weeping. "Whatever you think best," she told the floor.

"Well, actually," Meta said, aware that she was probably stepping on toes that were already sore, "I don't think either one of these is very good for a clit piercing. The hematite bead is not going to hold up very well in a moist environment. And that anodized ring won't keep its color. As soon as piss hits it, it will start turning green. We're not even putting horizontal rings in clit hoods these days. They don't provide much sexual stimulation, which is what most women are looking for. So we do a vertical barbell, placed very carefully so it will stimulate the clitoral glans."

Heather looked dumbfounded. She clearly had no idea what to do next. Meta didn't particularly want to lose a client, even one who had her hair on way too tight. It had been a slow week. "Lemme pick something out for you," she said, rising from her stool, and lumbered over to a case of jewelry. She picked out the right size of jewelry and brought it back to the jumpy couple. Simultaneously, Heather said, "It's too big," and Terry said, "Oh, it's beautiful." Meta waited a heartbeat, then Heather said, sounding vicious, "Very well. Let's get *on* with this."

"Do you want to hold Terry's hand?" Meta asked, trying to make peace. "You won't be in my light if you stand right here." She began to clean Terry's labia with Technicare.

"Wait a minute," Heather said triumphantly, certain she had caught Meta doing something unsafe, "you have to disinfect that area. Why aren't you using Betadine? Water won't do."

"Uh, this isn't water," Meta explained. "I quit using Betadine. Too many people have shellfish allergies. This is a clear disinfectant that works more quickly. Don't worry, I'll keep this clean."

A glowering silence was her only response. "So you gals have tried this before?" she asked brightly, trying to get a little conversation started. This couple intrigued her. They were obviously leatherdykes, but Meta had not seen them around. Where (and why) had they been hiding themselves away? Maybe they needed to be put in touch with the rest of the community. They might not know about the support group or the contest that was coming up.

But the tight-faced femme simply said "Yes" in a gunslinger tone of voice that shot down that topic. She clearly was not looking for a friendly mentor or a liaison to the rest of the tribe. The other one, the bottom, seemed like a friendly person, albeit a little anxious. Not nearly so stuck-up.

"Your name is so familiar," Meta said, marking her entry and exit points. Then a light went on. (Meta literally saw a light being turned on whenever one piece of information collided with another to make a new idea.) She was pleased with herself for being able to retrieve a name, for a change. Tags were hard for her to remember. So many people, most of them women, came and went through her shop each day. "Hey, didn't you write that story that's in the latest issue of the newsletter?"

Terry felt Heather grip her hand painfully tight, then let it go. She clung to Heather's hand anyway, refused to be sent away. "Yes," she admitted, knowing there would be hell to pay.

"Well, that's quite a story," Meta said. "You must be real proud of your bottom, Heather. She's got quite a way with words. I can't wait to read part two."

Heather did not say anything for a long long time. Meta, sensing the chill in the air, stopped fussing with her paraphernalia and just sat looking at both of them, taking deep even breaths and waiting to see what would happen next. It wouldn't be the first time she had thrown a snarling pack of dyke drama out the front door to be resolved on the sidewalk, away from her face.

"You published a story in the *Bad Grrrls Are Better* newsletter?" Heather demanded, her voice a little shrill. "Without consulting me? Theresa, what if somebody from my job sees that?"

"Why would anybody from your job be reading a newsletter for leatherdykes?" Terry replied. "Besides, Heather, nobody at your job has ever met me. They don't even know you've *got* a girlfriend."

"We'll talk about this later," was Heather's reply. "But I don't see why you couldn't have waited to send it in until you had at least informed me."

Because if I told you about it you'd find a way to keep me from doing it, Terry thought bitterly, then let go of Heather's hand. But this time it was Heather who refused to release her.

It didn't look like anybody was going to hit anybody else or try to throw something. "Well, let's get on with things," Meta said cheerfully, picking up the piercing forceps. She gently gripped Terry's clitoral hood, lifted it, and swirled the piercing needle in a dab of antibiotic ointment. "Let me know when you're ready, little bear cub."

That was a new concept. Terry took a deep breath, let it out, and thought to herself, *What is the worst thing that could happen? It might be excruciating, but it won't last forever.* "Ready," she said.

But then the cutting edge of the needle made contact with her tender flesh, and she felt her shoulders go up and a shriek hit the back of her teeth. She began to say her safe word, but got stuck on the first consonant. "Grrrrrr—" was all she could get out.

"Stop, oh, stop!" Heather cried. "That's her safe word. This is what *always* happens to me. She gets to this point, and then she makes me stop."

Except that Meta did not stop. Before Terry could caterwaul, "Griffindalydworkin," something hot and thick went through her, unbearable brightness exploded in her chest, and the deed was done. Meta was patting her on the shoulder and telling Heather to hold up a mirror so she could see the needle pointing at the head of her clit like a rude "One Way" sign. It was a miracle, this change in her body that she had pined for, like watching a baby be born, or a blind man being given back his sight. Meta fit one end of the barbell into the back side of the needle and pushed it through. More heat, more light, and an intense need to get off filled the lower half of Terry's body. Then the bead was resting heavily on the most sensitive point in her body, subtly stimulating it, and she was a new woman, decorated like a warrior with a medal.

"You didn't stop!" Heather said. One strand of hair had freed itself from her ponytail and was curving out from her head at a ridiculous angle. She was a bright tomato color, and her cheeks were puffed out in rage. She looked like an umpire calling somebody out at home plate.

Meta replied, looking at her as if she was crazy, "Of course I didn't stop. Terry said she wanted this piercing. She told me she was ready. If I had stopped, she wouldn't have gotten what she wanted."

"Of all the unsafe, inconsiderate—"

But Terry had something really important to say. She pushed herself into a sitting position and began to talk. The words flowed out of her as if they were being carried by a river of honeyed eloquence. She spoke about her past, her present, her future, her hopes and dreams, the meaning of life and love and happiness. It was a long speech delivered with great passion, and at the end of it, she said, "Thank you very much," as if she had just accepted an Oscar, and lay down on the table again, feeling dizzy.

Heather's mouth was open in a perfect O, and she said anxiously, "Are you all right, Theresa?"

"She's fine," Meta said, laughing so hard her belly shook. "When you poke a hole in somebody, something frequently comes out. So what are you going to do to celebrate?" Maybe now that this ordeal was over, the two of them would loosen up a bit. People frequently got cranky before being tattooed or pierced. It was sort of like waiting to see the dentist, Meta thought. Performance anxiety.

Celebrate? That was another new concept to Terry. She was pale, and not just from the pain of the piercing.

"We have to go home and have a little talk," Heather said ominously.

"Oh, gee, that's too bad," Meta replied, finally getting pissed off, though you would not have been able to tell by looking at her that she was angry. Meta thought it was a bad idea to share your feelings with people you did not trust. But her Mother Bear aspect was irate. She had had about enough of this yuppie bitch's bad attitude and her headache-making cologne. A good (and pretty cute) bottom who had just allowed the most sensitive part of her body to be penetrated with a sharp piece of surgical steel deserved something better than an evening of stale wrangling and tearful accusations. "The Better Bad Grrrls are having a meeting tonight," she said smoothly, keeping her face poker-flat. "It's Bring Your Favorite Bedtime Story night. You could read your piece, Terry Bear Cub. Sure would make some of the girls frisky to hear it in your own voice. It's been one of our most popular issues of the newsletter, you know."

"I'm afraid she doesn't have a way to get there," Heather said. The thought of not being able to express her anger and disappointment to Theresa the moment they got out the door was creating an unbearable pressure behind her breastbone. It was like having an excruciating case of gas. But she was not about to dig into her handbag for Tagamet at a time like this.

Terry, reclining half naked, with a throbbing sensation beginning to ache between her legs, saw in a woozy sort of way that Heather and Meta were face to face on either side of the table, only two feet apart, practically spitting at each other.

"I can take her on my bike," Meta said. She had not had too many girls refuse to take that bait. It was better than showing somebody your etchings and almost as good as red wine and a prime rib dinner.

"It's not safe," Heather snapped.

"You can't fall off a Honda Goldwing," Meta rejoined amiably, thinking, *Safety Nazi. Buzz buster. You're too closeted to even be a lipstick lesbian!*

"No helmet." Heather could barely squeak out those two words.

"I've got an extra helmet." She did too, left behind by the last person who had worked as an apprentice in the shop. It was collateral for debt incurred by pilfering from the cash register. Meta would rather have an extra motorcycle helmet than a messy interaction with the cops.

"No . . . no protective clothing!" Heather's voice was rising in pitch, making her sound a little ridiculous.

"I've got an extra jacket," Meta said in a rich, placid alto that indicated she could do this forever without running out of comebacks or losing her temper. It was about time somebody wore Lark's jacket, which Meta had taken from her apartment the day after she killed herself. Along with anything else that might have upset her parents (or the coroner) to discover. What exactly did you do with 37 vials of blood, labeled neatly with the name of the donor and the date it was drawn? Or with three photo albums full of Polaroids of anonymous bruised tushies and tits distorted with fans of clothespins? But Heather was sputtering like a candle with a bad wick.

"Well—well—I have to be to work early tomorrow."

Terry finally roused herself enough to realize that she was the object of this contest and had better contribute something. "*I* don't have to be at work," was all she could think to say. Her tongue felt thick and furry, as if she were getting drunk. Meta got up from her station by the piercing table and ambled toward the front room. Heather followed her like an imprinted baby duck, intent on continuing their argument.

Instead of engaging in further debate, Meta opened the front door of the shop and waved Heather out of it. "Better not wait up for her," Meta said and closed it firmly, then snapped the dead bolt shut. From her recumbent position on the padded table, Terry heard the doorbell make that "oo-gah" sound again, and she winced. Heather would never forget or forgive the way it ruined her exit.

"Better put your pants back on," Meta said, coming back to the room. "You can't get fucked for a couple days, until that heals." Was that regret that Terry detected in her voice?

As she got dressed and tried on the leather jacket with the padded shoulders that Metamorpheen gave her, Terry knew that when she finally did go home, her punishment would be dire. As if she were reading her mind, Meta said, "Are you gonna be in trouble at home?"

"Yeah, probably. But I think it's worth it."

"You know," Meta said, "if somebody wants to punish you, and you don't want to be punished, you don't have to take it. There's rules about that sort of thing. Consensuality and all of that."

Terry looked at her openmouthed, as if she'd just heard from her guardian angel.

"There you go issuing that invitation again," Meta laughed. "Come on, Bear Cub, let's go get a burger before the meeting. Once I get you on the back of my bike with that fresh piercing, you won't miss getting fucked for a few days."

Terry followed Meta out of the shop, in a haze of stage fright about reading one of her stories out loud to real people, pain from her injured flesh, excitement about being on a motorcycle, and a surprising amount of hunger. She listened to Meta's instructions about how to be a proper passenger on the bike and found, as she got up behind this stranger who had taken an inexplicable interest in her affairs, that she was so scared all the fear just went away. It seemed there was room for only so much fear, and if you exceeded that amount, it spilled out of you like water. Still, she was grateful that they only needed to go a few blocks to the diner. It gave her a chance to practice leaning on the turns at a relatively low speed.

Terry knew about the diner, since it was in the gay part of town, but Heather didn't like greasy spoons, so she'd never been in the place. There was so much noise, so many faces, that it became a blur.

She hardly noticed that Meta had ordered for her. Heather disapproved of red meat, not because she opposed cruelty to animals, but (Terry suspected) because it was too primal a pleasure. Too messy and male. She also skimped on dairy, unless it was a cup of low-fat yogurt, which she was always telling Terry tasted much better than ice cream. As for onions . . . or fried food . . . well! Consuming both would be inconsiderate, and Terry was not sure which offense would be considered more serious in Heather's eyes, deliberately giving yourself bad breath or being fat in public, forcing other people to look at your gross excess and lack of self-control.

But Meta was ripping big, deeply satisfying bites out of a rare hamburger that was stacked up with oozing melted cheddar cheese, a slice of red onion, lettuce, tomatoes, and enough ketchup to drip back onto the plate. She was also consuming, with great relish, a plate of spicy curly fries, dipping them into a cup full of ranch dressing. Terry picked up her burger, wondering how she was going to get her mouth around something that barely fit in her hands; then the first taste of hot cheddar, blood, and grease hit her palate, and she turned into a shark. The next thing she knew, she was sitting in front of a plate full of crumbs, and Meta was saying, "You got ketchup on your chin, kid," and wiping it off for her.

It was in gestures like these that Meta revealed a tender part of herself that Terry recognized as the hallmark of femmedom. Most straight people, even some lesbians, would probably look at Meta and assume she was butch, given her height and short hair. She certainly didn't look like a femme next to Heather. But weren't there a lot of different ways to be a butch or a femme, a top or a bottom? If you could be a butch bottom couldn't you be a butchy femme? Meta was an earthy, dykey kind of femme, Terry felt sure, but wasn't quite confident enough to share her conclusion with Metamorpheen. Not yet, anyway. Maybe later. In the dark. A butch with good hands could get lucky in the dark even with a very big and kinda scary girl. Terry surreptitiously checked her jacket pocket for the Ziploc baggie that held a pair of gloves and a tiny bottle of lube.

On their way out of the diner, Meta was greeted by some of the gay waiters and customers. She waved to all of them and introduced her dining companion as "Terry Bear Cub." Some of the people they stopped to talk to were women who looked like they were probably going to the meeting, and Terry was hit by a paralyzing wave of shyness. All of these people were going to hear some of her most private thoughts. But the abashed, almost shameful, feeling went away once her thighs were wrapped around the bike again, and she wondered how much one of these things cost. Even an expensive motorcycle was probably cheaper than therapy, and it sure was a lot more fun.

The meeting was held at a queer community center that housed the offices for a rape crisis center, the gay switchboard, a food bank for indigent people with AIDS, and a public health clinic that devoted Tuesday nights to women only, Wednesday nights to gay or bisexual men, and Thursday nights to trannies. The face of the building was painted with a three-story mural of people of color (men harvesting crops, women having babies). Terry thought it looked like something commissioned by a bunch of middle-class leftists who felt really bad about being white. Awfully Earnest Early '80s Public Works Project Art.

"We had a hell of a time getting permission to meet here," Meta complained, backing into a parking space. "I think we must have done a year of arguing and fund-raising. Fucking feminist fags telling *me* that I couldn't be here because it would upset 'the women' at the rape crisis center, like I'm not a woman, and leatherdykes *never* get raped or *volunteer* at that agency. Vanilla queers don't like pervs very much, Bear Cub, but everybody will cash our checks. Money talks and bullshit walks."

They went into the lobby, then up in an ancient elevator that complained a little too much for Terry's comfort. On the second floor they disembarked and entered a conference room that was full of mismatched chairs. A big table had been pushed up against one wall to make more space in the middle of the room. Meta dumped her helmet in one chair and Terry did the same. It was a relief to have that weight off her neck and feel the air around her head again. "Do you have stage fright?" Meta asked, and Terry nodded mutely. "Well, let's piss, then," Meta said. "The world always seems brighter with an empty bladder."

Meta seemed to have a common-sense solution to everything. Terry thought, trotting after her, that it was nice to be with a femme who was calm and practical. It was OK, with Meta, to simply figure out what you wanted and then go get it. You didn't have to agonize about your desire, trying to figure out what it really meant, or be ambivalent about the consequences of having what you wanted. There was none of the emotional torture that Heather called "going through my process." Terry thought she must be surrounded with a little cloud of noxious vapor as years of anxiety and tension melted out of her system and evaporated away. Or maybe it was just the result of eating all that cheese.

Meta noticed, as she walked into the bathroom, that her level of arousal automatically increased. She was horny most of the time. Having a lot of sex made you want even more, she had found. And there was something about being in a bathroom that was just dirty and sexy, it was both public and private, girls only, so what was she gonna do about it? She pissed first, listening to Terry doing the same thing in an adjacent stall, grinning when she heard the muffled "Ouch!"

"Are you doing OK?" she asked, pushing open the door of the disabled stall. None of the locks on these stalls seemed to work very well (hee hee).

Terry had wiped herself and stood up, but she hadn't quite gotten her jeans zipped yet. Meta put her hand on the back of Terry's belt and hauled her closer, then bent over to smooch her. They were a pretty good fit, Meta thought. Terry was small enough to make her feel big and powerful, but not such a shrimp that it would hurt her back to neck with her. She pulled out of the kiss, which had been kind of slow, as if Terry weren't awake, and bit her on the neck. She gradually maneuvered Terry in the small space until she had her back up against the door, holding it shut.

She stuck her hand down the back of the bear cub's pants and hefted her ass. It was more than a handful. The skin was smooth; the flesh resilient. She sent her other hand down the front, careful not to bump into the fresh wound and the jewelry that held it open.

"Hey," Terry said, pulling on the front of Meta's jacket, "I thought you said I couldn't get fucked until that healed."

Meta took one of her hands out of Terry's pants and fished in her jacket pocket for a plastic bubble of lube. "I'm not going to mess with your cunt," she promised, dowsing her fingers with just enough slippery stuff to facilitate a quickie.

Terry hung on to her jacket then, more curious than afraid, thinking not at all (well, hardly very much) about her ostensibly non-monogamous relationship with Heather, which had yet to be put to the test of actual sex with anyone else. Either the time, the person, or the way she asked never suited Heather, and eventually Terry had stopped asking, to avoid the weeks of heightened scrutiny and insecurity that followed. Something about seeing Meta chase Heather out of her shop had given Terry a shot of courage. It was possible to get rid of Heather, it seemed, maybe even easy to get rid of Heather. Besides, Meta was doing some very nice and squishy things with her butt. And she wanted to come really bad, had wanted to come ever since she looked in the mirror to see the triumphant bloody needle wedged in place. Maybe it would be OK to touch her clit just a little.

Meta's fingers were nicely padded, and two of them seemed to fit perfectly. "Oh," Terry gasped, making the lightest of all possible circles at the top of her very tender hood. She couldn't tell if she was coming inside or out, the rhythm of fucking seemed to be radiating out from her ass until it made all of her sexual parts vibrate. She had a moment of panic when she remembered that she had not cleaned herself out first, but Meta seemed to know what was going on and said, "Everything's OK in here, honey, just relax and let me fuck you. Does that feel good?"

"Yeah!" Terry replied.

"Do you want some more?"

Pleasure was not like fear. There seemed to be no limit to how much of it you could contain. Terry gasped, riding her own hand and Meta's fingers to a new level of openness and squirming dirty joy. Was that another finger going up inside her? "Yes, more, please!" Terry gasped, remembering her manners.

Meta fucked her good and hard then, timing her movements to Terry's wildly circulating hand, and everything went off together, clit and ass and cunt. How weird it was, Terry thought, to feel your cunt contracting when there was nothing in it. How strange to want to keep something *inside* your ass.

Meta took her by the lapels and turned her around, then sat her down on the cold, white plastic toilet seat. She strolled out of the cubicle, washed her hands off, then came back with a handful of paper towels. "You'll never be able to get that lube off with toilet paper," she said matter-of-factly. "It'll just shred and stick to your bum."

Terry cleaned herself off, blushing, but Meta seemed perfectly at ease, lounging in the door of the stall. "Do you like public sex?" the tattoo artist asked.

"I guess so," Terry said. "I mean, that was what we just did, right?" "Mmm," said Meta, examining her fingernails, "more like *potentially* public sex."

The door of the bathroom swung open, making both of them jump. It hit the opposite wall with a metallic clunk, then swung shut behind a girl who weighed about 95 pounds at most. She had on a black leather pencil skirt that screamed "designer label," not "your local leather shop," and a thin, clinging gray silk-and-cotton yarn sweater, one of those simple little tops that cost $500. Over that was a Versace jacket in amusing colors that perfectly fit her little waist and hips. And if her shoes weren't Gucci, well, Terry had never spent hours and hours polishing all of Heather's expensive and uncomfortable imported shoes. The girl's hair had been carefully styled to look expensively mussed up. Her face was expertly made up, and Terry felt fairly certain that she didn't buy her cosmetics at the Mac counter. She probably had her own shade of powder (maybe even an individual blend of perfume) made up at a boutique.

She was so appalled at herself for knowing all this stuff that it did not occur to her to be embarrassed about sitting on the potty, practically naked from the waist down, in front of a total stranger.

"I thought it might be safe to come in here when all the grunting stopped," the new arrival said, giving Terry and Meta a haughty and disapproving stare. Her face seemed especially full of dislike when it contemplated Meta.

"Hey, Hadley," Meta said, looking amused.

"You know, Meta," Hadley said, looking at herself in the mirror and opening her raw silk clutch, "if you keep fucking people in this bathroom, we'll get thrown out of this building, and I don't know where we'll meet then." She was obviously not going to enter a stall as long as either of them were there.

Terry stood up, tucked in her shirt, and got her pants zipped up and her belt buckled. It seemed to be her day for watching Meta tussle with vituperative femmes. She felt better once she was prepared to make a hasty exit. Her bottom was still talking to her, making up nonsensical little poems and songs of childish happiness. She felt so alive, full of strength and goodness. Meta's haunches drew her eye, and she surreptitiously petted her hip. She wanted to lie down between Meta's legs and do that swimming thing with her tongue that Judy Grahn talked about, lay her tongue on the edge of the sea or however it went. She also wanted to put her knuckles up against Meta's cervix, but she didn't think Grahn (or Olga Broumas, for that matter) had forged any poetic metaphors about fisting.

"Yeah, and if we have any complaints from the building committee, I guess we'll know who tipped them off, won't we?" Meta said evenly. "By the way, how much did that ticket cost you, the one you got last month for parking your Ferrari in the disabled zone?"

Hadley flipped her hands as if she were chasing off a cloud of midges and said nothing at all. Meta nodded, satisfied by a job well done, and walked out of the bathroom with her arm around Terry's waist. Once they had turned the corner and were entering the conference room, she said, "Some people are a waste of oxygen, you know that?"

A woman who was Metamorpheen's age and about the same size, though not as tall, came bustling up to Terry with a clipboard and a box of name tags. She wore leather pants, a T-shirt with the group's name on it, and a tessellated leather vest that had been rendered rigid with pins and badges. It was the woman who had loaned Terry and Heather a riding crop at the party where they played for the first time! "Put your name badge on," she said officiously, as if Terry had been caught in front of her locker without a hall pass. "The admission charge is $5."

"Hello, Maxine," said Meta. "Bear Cub is going to read tonight. Don't people who are doing the program get in for free?"

"Well, nobody talked to me about that," Maxine said, peering nearsightedly at the piercer. She wore half-glasses, which made her look like somebody's demented and aberrant grandmother. Then she looked at Terry, and her bureaucratic mouth widened into a big, honest smile. "I remember you!" she said. "You've come up in the world. Hanging out with somebody who actually owns her own equipment, I see!" She wrote "Bear Cub" on a name tag and plastered it to Terry's jacket. "Go talk to Angela about reading. Welcome to the club."

"Don't I have to wear a name tag too?" Meta joked, handing over a $5 bill.

Maxine laughed and shook her gray head. "I'm not going to give you the free publicity," she said, and laughed again at her own joke. Then she was off to point her clipboard at somebody else.

Meta introduced Terry to Angela, who turned out to be a Latina bodybuilder and a whole lot butcher than her name. She had a hand-written list of names, and when Meta explained that "Bear Cub" would like to read, she was visibly relieved. "None of these girls are here yet," she said, waving the list under Terry's nose. "How would you like to go first?"

"I guess—well—ah—" As she stammered, Terry realized that she did not have a printout of the story. What a disaster! Then Meta flipped open her burgundy bike-messenger bag and handed Terry a copy of the newsletter. The cold sweat stopped seeping under her collar and armpits.

"That'll be just fine, Angela," Meta said and took Terry to the front row, where they both sat down, first putting their helmets under their chairs. Terry had a good view of Angela's muscles from that vantage point. She wore a latex tank top that outlined every bit of her hard-bodied anatomy. Terry had never seen a woman before who had pecs rather than tits. She liked the leather straps Angela wore around her upper arms but guessed you'd have to work out a lot to get your biceps to hold them up like that. They were kind of like butch arm garters, weren't they? She visualized little suspender clips holding up a pair of latex gloves and giggled.

"You sure are a funny one," Meta said, ruffling her hair. "You just keep yourself constantly amused, don't you?" She settled her big arm comfortably behind Terry's shoulders.

"Sometimes I get lucky and other people amuse me," Terry replied, giving Meta a quick grin.

"I was a little amused myself," Meta acknowledged. "Don't care if we get thrown out of the damn building. It was worth it."

The meeting got called to order, and Angela introduced Terry to the group. As she took her place at the head of the room, she saw Hadley taking over at the door from Maxine. If Hadley kept chewing out late arrivals like that, it would be hard to make herself heard. "Could we have a little quiet?" Maxine asked, rising a couple of inches out of her chair. Everybody settled down, and Terry got her first look at the audience. There was quite a bit of leather out there, but there were also several women in overalls or jeans and flannel shirts. A few femmes who had dolled themselves up. They looked like a room full of dykes, was all, and Terry couldn't understand why Heather had been so pissed off at this group. What was all that crap about personality disorders? Then she had an unpleasant memory of the Lesbigaytrans Student Union and decided it would be just as well if she never attended one of the Bad Grrrls' business meetings.

The pages in her shaking hands called to her like a second cousin once removed at a family reunion. She knew she had something to do with the words that appeared there, but the connection was a little mysterious. She took the first sentence into her mouth as if she were tasting it, and once it was out in the air, where other people could hear it, the next sentence followed as naturally as breathing. "It was more scandalous than the love of a priest for his parishioner, more forbidden than incest, this love that Citizen Françoise felt for the deposed queen. How could it be that her own hardships melted away when she saw that fragile beauty so despondent in her stony cell? A fine revolutionary she was!"

It was too late to be nervous; the words had taken over, and all she could do was allow them to swim through her mouth and out into the world. The slight tremor left Terry's voice, and she felt it becoming deeper and richer. The first time the audience laughed, she checked herself and waited until they stopped before reading again. *Timing,* she thought to herself. *I am developing my timing.* Things were going so well, she even dared to sneak a peek at Meta, who was beaming with approval. After years of hiding her fiction or getting lukewarm responses or hostility from friends and lovers, all this appreciation was heady and healing. *These women know what the hell I am talking about,* Terry realized.

Soon she was into the explicit part of the story. The queen had just explained that her marriage was loveless, a matter of policy. She had apologized, weeping, for the privations and tribulations of Françoise's underclass existence. "I did not know," she said. "I was a prisoner too, in my own way, and I did not understand how you suffered. How all of my people suffered."

"Still," Françoise murmured, "some reparations must be made. You must pay the penalty for your crimes against the people."

The queen stood and ripped her prison shift down to her waist. She turned to face the single window in her cell, an uncovered narrow opening in its thick stone walls, which admitted a stiff, chill breeze. "Then punish me," she said. "If you love me, Françoise, let me feel the pain that my subjects have suffered while I lost my soul to luxury."

Françoise lifted the lash that she always carried to clear prisoners away from the doors of their cells. With her heart breaking, with every cell of her body protesting that she must not hurt her darling, justice nevertheless must be served. Her arm descended once, then a dozen times, and crimson stripes lay across the aristocratic white shoulders that hitherto had borne nothing heavier than silk or lace. Sobbing with frustration, she drove her hand between her former sovereign's graceful thighs, knowing that nothing the two of them did in this dark room could alter the course of history. With her work-hardened hands, she brought joy to a pampered body that she should have despised; she made the queen cry out more loudly than the bells that had announced the storming of the Bastille.

Then Marie Antoinette put her dainty hands on Françoise's strong hips and said, "Let me serve you as I should have served the citizens of France." Her tongue lapped at the jailer's sex, and she laughed triumphantly when she discovered it was wet with excitement. "Perhaps love can grow in the same garden as hatred," she ventured before her head disappeared between Françoise's legs, spread—

Heather walked into the room, wearing the same latex dress that she had worn to the party in New York years ago. Hadley didn't greet Heather with the same scorn that she'd been heaping on other late arrivals. She whispered a quiet and polite request for money and offered to put Heather's name tag on for her. To Terry's way of thinking, Hadley took far too long to adjust the stupid sticker on Heather's small but very shapely bosom. Heather took the only chair that was still vacant, an avocado-green plastic monstrosity at the very back of the room. Terry forced herself to keep on reading. Heather refused to meet her gaze, and Terry found herself reading a little louder, getting more provocative. Let Heather hear every single four-letter word, vicariously experience every drop of cunt juice and every stroke of the whip. Let Heather experience the commoner's simulacrum of revenge upon royalty.

Hadley shut the door, put down her Magic Marker, and slithered over to where Heather was sitting. With sign language, she asked for and received permission to sit next to Heather. On the floor. While Terry toiled through a blazing description of subverted class warfare, Heather allowed one of her dovelike hands to settle on Hadley's head and caress it. Hadley pressed against Heather's shapely legs like a stray cat begging to be taken indoors.

Finally the damn story was done. "Look what you have done to me. I am reduced to beggary by the unnatural lust you have kindled in me. I am lower than any whore on the Champs Elysées, panting and pining after you," Marie Antoinette had said. And the author had added, "To be continued." Terry made herself look away from Heather into Meta's rueful smile and nodded thanks to everyone before sitting down.

Angela was moving to the podium, trying to compose an explanation or apology for the lack of other readers, racking her brains for something else to occupy the last hour and a half of the meeting. But Hadley raised her voice, managing to make herself heard without rising from the floor, and said, "I'd like to read something!" Was that trick of projecting your voice something you learned in prep school? Terry had seen Heather do it to waiters, salesgirls, and ushers. She could make her voice carry to the kitchen, dressing rooms, or balcony without sounding shrill or shrewish.

"Well, OK," Angela said, a little nettled at having her speech derailed, and sat back down.

Casting a winsome look at Heather, Hadley put her hands on the floor, her ass in the air, and crawled on all fours to the front of the room. She took her own sweet time doing it too, making everyone aware of her subservient yet arrogant position. Every sixth step or so, she paused and cast a glance back over her shoulder at Heather, who was sitting bolt upright with two little spots of color highlighting her cheekbones. Even from the front of the room, Terry swore that Heather's nipples were hard, damn it.

Hadley deigned to kneel in front of the room, which made her pretty difficult to see from the second row on back. She must have realized that would also make it hard for Heather to see her, because she shook her hair back and rose to her feet. How femmes got up and down in those shoes, Terry would never understand. It was one of the things that separated the girly-girls from the butches, for sure.

"This is a poem I wrote in high school for the first girl I ever loved," Hadley said dramatically. Her voice was dry and a little deep, reminding Terry of Tallulah Bankhead. Then she began to declaim in French:

Tu veux que je te fasse un amoureux poème.
Econte done plutôt si mon silence t'aime!

She went on for seven more couplets while Terry twisted, furious, on her uncomfortable, high-backed wooden chair. "She didn't write that!" she hissed at last to Meta, who was regarding Hadley with the displeasure of Diogenes, lamp lit during broad daylight and still unable to find an honest man.

"Such a show-off," Metamorpheen agreed, shaking her head.

It wasn't quite enough to still Terry's indignation. She could not help herself. She turned around almost 180 degrees, enough to see Heather listening with her eyes closed, face carefully composed into a look of rapture. From time to time, Heather would nod her head as if she were especially moved. "She doesn't know any *French!*" Terry protested to Meta, sounding even to herself like a hysterical shrieking teakettle.

"Oh, is that what it is?" Meta asked in sincere innocence.

Hadley fell silent, but her performance was apparently not finished. She raked her hands dramatically through her hair and said contemptuously, "For the rest of you, I'll translate."

You asked me for a love poem.
Listen, rather, to the love my silence speaks!

Terry mouthed the words silently, lingering fondly over her favorite phrase, "if my mouth, / Mute eloquence, still touches you," and was filled with the same ardent and subtle fire that she had experienced when she first came across these words, the first lesbian love poem she had ever read. She grabbed Meta by the epaulet and pulled her head to her mouth. "It's Natalie Clifford Barney!" she whispered. "How dare Hadley plagiarize Natalie Clifford Barney?"

Meta clearly had no idea who she was talking about, but sensed that she was upset. "Don't be too hasty, now," she said, touching Terry's mouth. "Let's talk this out." Plagiarism sounded serious to

Meta. Was it anything like pedophilia? Whatever. Terry was
unhappy, and she found herself being riled up as well.

Angela was asking if there were any announcements, and
women were standing up to put in a plug for various 12-step groups,
bake sales and other benefits for causes like the gay marching band
and a day-care center for lesbian mothers; somebody was looking for
a home for six kittens, and somebody else wanted to form a caucus for
cigar aficionados. Meta took Terry out of the room, steering her like
a forklift, ready to pounce and gag her if her indignation boiled over.
A few women said things like "Hot story, Bear Cub," and Terry gave
them an absent little wave, hoping she was not being too rude. Her
attention was being absorbed by the tableau of Hadley and Heather's
rapidly unfolding infatuation.

After finishing the poem, Hadley had walked slowly, head
down, back to Heather, and knelt with a flourish at her feet. Terry
knew if she had to look at that charade of submission for one more
second, she was going to shriek and do the same things with a folding
chair that created bitter feuds in the World Wrestling Federation.
Instead of stealing Hadley's championship belt, she could just rip off
her false eyelashes, Terry supposed.

While Hadley was speaking, Heather could not look away from
her. She had never seen anyone so wild and rebellious and yet so elegant and cultured. This was someone she had to get to know much,
much better. She didn't feel too bad about faking her understanding
of that lovely, languorous foreign language. There were tapes you
could listen to. You could learn French during your commute, for
heaven's sake. What would it be like to spend time with someone
who appreciated classical music, someone who had been to Europe,
someone who could be introduced to her family and her landlord
without embarrassment? Someone who would not hand her a coral
lipstick when she wanted tangerine, someone who would understand
that happiness could depend on having the right moisturizer?

Someone who did not sweat too much, who did not have too much pubic hair or hair on her legs, who did not follow sports or pick her teeth, a pretty girl with long hair and a good education?

Heather took Hadley's face between her hands and kissed her with the delicate passion of a girl who does not want to mess up another girl's lipstick. She felt a glorious melting sensation that had been missing from her life and her loins for far too long.

When they hit the street, Terry tried to tell Meta what was bugging her. It was very difficult to get it all out. Finally she settled for a buzz phrase that every lesbian understands: "We have a lot of class issues, OK?" Meta nodded wisely.

"Look, do you really want this chick?" she asked. "Do you guys have kids or something? Do you own a business together? Are you married?"

"No, we're not married. And I think our relationship is as dead as Renée Vivien. But Hadley *lied*. She lied about *literature*. You can't just steal somebody else's work and—"

"Settle down, Beavis," Meta said firmly. "I've known Hadley for about as long as you've known Heather. She's bad news, but it sounds to me like she's exactly what Heather deserves. Heather made you feel like shit for being a working-class dyke from a poor family, right? Well, let me tell you, as far as Hadley is concerned, Heather is rough trade. Got it? Hadley has more money than the Rockefellers. Don't you think it's about time for Heather to find out what it feels like when your supposed girlfriend is actually just slumming?"

Terry stared at Meta with her eyebrows knitted together. "But . . . but that's so mean," she said, looking aghast.

"Take it from me," Meta said, tapping her nose and looking wise. "Rich people are always mean. Sometimes the best thing you can do is show no mercy."

Terry thought long and hard about that. She saw a montage of the many botched attempts that Heather made to pierce her, all aborted when that damned safe word came out of hiding, everything done by the book, safe, sane, and consensual. As Heather had said, she had shown Terry mercy, undone by the depth of her fear and pain. Yet none of Terry's other sexual misadventures had made her feel worse than not being able to go through with getting that damned hood piercing. In a split second Meta had cut through all that crap and solved the problem. If she'd guessed wrong, Terry could have been pissed off, but she didn't guess wrong. She just did what Terry asked her to do. Metamorpheen followed through. You should never ask her for something unless you were sure you wanted it.

Meta heard someone coming out of the building and put her arm out, forcing both of them to lean back into the shadow of the wall. It was Heather, stalking toward the street with one of her hands wound in Hadley's tousled Sassoon hairdo. "You're hurting me," Hadley said, making it sound like a very sexy compliment. When Heather saw the red Ferrari, she didn't hesitate for a second. She just snapped, "Give me the keys, bitch," and threw Hadley up against the car until she got them. Then she stuffed her nymphette into the passenger seat, clicked over to the driver's side in her platform spike-heeled boots, and took the wheel. Meta allowed Terry to follow the departing vehicle with her eyes for a few moments, then drew her face to the side for their first real, serious, "Who the hell are you?" kiss.

"OK," Terry said when she could catch her breath. She straightened her shoulders and turned in the direction of Meta's bike. "What you said. No mercy. If I go home with you, can I interview for that job?"

"Oh, you already got the damn job," Metamorpheen drawled, pulling on her gloves. "Get your helmet on, little space dyke. Come home with me, and I'll show you the last frontier. You *will* be assimilated, Bear Cub."

Punching each other and giggling, they raced for the bike.

Blood and Silver

Once upon a time (and still), there was a young woman who was very tired of being treated like a little girl. Her name was Sylvia Rufina. Like most female persons in her predicament, the only available avenue of rebellion was for her to pretend to obey the commandments of others while protecting a secret world within which she was both empress and impresario. Having frequently been told, "Go out and play," more and more, that was what she did. Her family lived in a small farmhouse that felt smaller still because of the vast wilderness that surrounded it. She was at home in this untamed and complex landscape, if only because there was nothing false or sentimental about it.

One of the games she played was "holding still." This was a game learned under confusing and painful circumstances at home. But hidden within a stand of birches or scrub oak, she was not molested. Instead, if she learned to let her thoughts turn green and her breath slow to the pace of sap, she became privy to an endless variety of fascinating events: how beavers felled trees, how mice raised their children, the way a fox twitched its nose when it spotted a vole.

One day, when she was studying the spots on a fawn that dozed in a copse just a few dozen yards from where she held her breath, the wolf appeared. He (for there was no mistaking the meaning of his big face, thick shoulders, and long legs, even if she had not espied his genitals) was an amazing silver color, with dark black at the root of his stippled fur. His teeth were as white as the moon, and his eyes were an intelligent and fearless brown. They studied each other for long minutes, wolf and woman, until he lost interest in her silence and relaxed limbs, and went away.

The next time he came, he walked right up to her and put his nose up, making it clear that he expected a greeting of some sort. So she carefully, slowly, bonelessly lowered her body and allowed him to examine her face and breasts. His breath was very hot, perhaps because it was autumn and the day was chilly. His fur smelled of earth and the snow that was to come, and the air he expelled was slightly rank, an aroma she finally identified as blood.

Satisfied with her obeisance, he went away again, tail wagging a little, as if he were pleased with himself. This was the only undignified thing she had seen him do, but it did not make her think less of him. She appreciated the fact that the wolf did not caper, bow down, yelp, or slaver on her, in the slavish and inconsiderate way of dogs. The wolf was no whore for man's approval. He fed himself.

She did not see the wolf again for nearly a week. But when he returned, he brought the others: two males and three females, one of them his mate. This female was nearly as large as her spouse and as dark as he was metallic, the eclipse to his moon. Some instinct told Sylvia Rufina that she must greet them on all fours and then roll over upon her back. This seemed to excite everyone no end. She was nosed a good deal, fairly hard, licked three or four times, and nipped once. The surprisingly painful little bite came from the leader of the pack, who was letting her know it was time to get up and come away with them. It was later in the day than she usually stayed out-of-doors, and as she fled, lights came on in the little house, dimming the prettier lights that bloomed in the deep black sky.

Racing with the wolves was like a dream, or perhaps it was normal life that was a dream, for the long run with the wolf pack was a flight through vivid sensations that made everything that had happened to her indoors seem drained of color and meaning. She never questioned her ability to keep up with them any more than she questioned the new shape she seemed to wear. Her legs were tireless; running was a joy. Even hunger was a song in her belly. And when the group cut off and cornered a deer, she knew her place in the attack as if she had read and memorized a part in a play.

After they ate, most of them slept, yawning from the effort it took to digest that much raw, red meat. Unaccustomed to so much exercise and the rich diet, she slept also.

And woke up miles from home, alone, in harsh daylight. Every muscle in her body hurt, and her clothing was ripped, her hair full of twigs, leaves, and burrs. Her shoes were gone, and her stockings a ruin. Somehow she made her way home, hobbling painfully, trying to think of a story that would excuse her absence without triggering a proscription against hikes in the mountains.

There was no need for an alibi. Her family had already decided what must have happened to her. She had followed a butterfly or a bluejay or a white hart and gotten lost in the woods. When she crossed the threshold and heard inklings of this story, she saw that each of her family members had picked a role, just as the wolves had memorized their dance of death with one another. And she gave herself up, too exhausted to fight back, letting them exclaim over and handle and hurt her with their stupidity and melodrama. Though a part of her sputtered indignantly, silently: *Lost! In the woods! Where I've roamed for three-and-twenty years? I'm more likely to get lost on my way to the privy!*

Unfortunately, when she had gone missing, they had called upon the Hunter and asked him to search for her. He was someone she avoided. His barn was covered with the nailed-up, tanning hides of

animals and thatched with the antlers of deer he had slain. Sylvia
Rufina thought it grotesque. Her father had taught her to recognize
certain signals of an unhealthy interest. After having finally grown
old enough to no longer be doted upon by her incestuous sire, she
could not tolerate a stranger whose appetites felt revoltingly familiar.
When the Hunter lit his pipe, waved his hand, and put a stop to the
whining voices so glad of their opportunity to rein her in, she gaped
at him, hoping against her own judgment that he would have something sensible to say.

He had brought something that would solve the problem. No
need to restrict the young woman's love of nature, her little hobbies.
No doubt it gave her much pleasure to add new leaves and ferns to
her collection. (In fact, she did not have such a collection, but she was
aware that many proper young ladies did, and so she bit her tongue,
thinking it would make a good excuse for future rambling.) The
Hunter shook out a red garment and handed it to her.

It was a scarlet sueded leather cloak with a hood, heavy enough
to keep her warm well into winter. The lining was a slippery fabric
that made her slightly sick to touch. He had kept hold of the garment
as he handed it to her, so their hands touched when she took it from
him, and her eyes involuntarily met his. The predatory desire she saw
there made her bow her head, as if in modesty, but in fact to hide her
rage. Even during a killing strike, the wolves knew nothing as
shameful and destructive as the Hunter's desire. She knew, then, that
he had bought this red hooded cloak for her some time ago and often
sat studying it, dreaming of how she would look laid down upon it.
If she wore it in the forest, she would be visible for miles. It would be
easy for a hunter, this Hunter, to target and track her then.

She was poked and prodded and prompted to say thank you, but
would not. Instead she feigned sleep, or a faint. And so she was borne
up to bed, feeling the Hunter's hard-done-by scowl following her
supine body up the stairs like an oft-refused man on his wedding night.

It was weeks before she was deemed well enough to let out of the house. The red cloak hung in her closet in the meantime, its shout of color reducing all her other clothes to drab rags. It would snow soon, and she did not think she would survive being stranded behind the pack, in human form, to find her way home in a winter storm. But she must encounter them again, if only to prove to herself that the entire adventure had not been a fevered dream.

Her chance finally came. A neighbor whom nobody liked much, a widowed old woman with much knowledge about the right way to do everything, was in bed with a broken leg. This was Granny Gosling. As a little girl, Sylvia Rufina had gone to Granny Gosling with her secret troubles, mistaking gray hair and myopia for signs of kindness and wisdom. Her hope to be rescued or at least comforted was scalded out of existence when the old woman called her many of the same names she had heard in a deeper voice, with a mustache and tongue scouring her ear and her long flannel nightgown bunched up painfully in her armpits. The child's hot sense of betrayal was quickly replaced with stoicism. We can bear the things that cannot be altered, and now she knew better than to struggle against the inevitable.

Other neighbors, a prosperous married couple with a bumper crop of daughters overripe for the harvest of marriage, were hosting a dance with an orchestra. People were to come early to an afternoon supper, dance in the evening, and spend the night. Mother and father had their own marketing of nubile damsels to attend to, but their house stood closer to Granny Gosling's than anyone else's. They were expected to go and lend a hand. What a relief it was to everyone when Sylvia Rufina said quietly at breakfast that she thought it might do her soul a great deal of good to visit the sick and unfortunate that day. She was young. There would be other cotillions.

As the other women in the household bustled around curling their hair and pressing the ruffles on their dresses, she made up a basket of victuals. She picked things she herself was especially fond of because she knew anything she brought would be found unpalatable by the injured granny. She helped everyone into their frocks, found missing evening bags and hair ribbons, sewed a buckle on a patent leather shoe, and kissed her mother and her sisters as they went off, consciences relieved, to the dance. Her father, realizing no embrace would be offered, avoided the opportunity to receive one. As soon as their carriage disappeared around a bend in the road, she set off in the red cloak and kept the hateful thing on until she had gone over a rise and down the other side and was out of her family's sight.

Then she took off the cloak, bundled it up as small as she could, and put it inside a hollow tree, heartily hoping that birds and squirrels would find it, rip it to shreds, and use it to make their winter nests. At the foot of this tree she sat, snug in the nut-brown cloak she had worn underneath the hunter's gift, and ate every single thing she had packed into the basket. By the time she finished her feast, it was nearly dark. Cheerful beyond measure to be free at last from human society, she went rambling in quest of her soul mates, the four-footed brothers and sisters of the wind.

Faster and faster she went as her need for them became more desperate, and the world streamed by in a blur of gaudy fall colors. The cold air cut her lungs like a knife, and she found herself pressing the little scar the wolf had left on her collarbone, using that pang to keep herself moving forward. The sun plunged below the hills, and she ran on four legs now, chasing hints among the delicious odors that flooded her nose and mouth. At last she found a place where they had been, a trail that led to their present whereabouts, and the reunion was a glad occasion. There was a happy but orderly circle of obeisances and blessings—smelling, licking, and tail wagging—and favorite sticks and bones were tossed into the air and tugged back and forth.

Then they hunted, and all was right with the world. She was happy to be the least among them, the anchor of their hierarchy. Despite her status as a novice, she knew a thing or two that could be of value to the pack. The crotchety neighbor would never be in pain again nor have occasion to complain about the disrespect of young folk or the indecency of current ladies' fashions.

But this time, forewarned that dawn would put an end to her four-footed guise, the young woman took precautions. While everyone else turned in the direction of the den, where they could doze, meat-drunk, she bid them farewell with heartbroken nudges of her nose, and retraced her footsteps, back to the hollow tree. There, she slept a little, until dawn forced her to put on the hateful red cloak again, and return home. She was lucky this time and arrived well before her hungover, overfed, and overheated relations.

She thought perhaps, with what she now knew, she could endure the rest of her life. She would have two lives, one within this cottage and the other in the rest of the world. Knowing herself to be dangerous, she could perhaps tolerate infantilization. And so she made herself agreeable to her mother and her sisters, helped them divest themselves of their ballroom finery, and put out a cold lunch for them. She herself was not hungry. The smell of cooked meat made her nauseous.

She had not planned to go out again that night. She knew that if her excursions became too frequent, she would risk being discovered missing from her bed. But when the moon came up, it was as if a fever possessed her. She could not stay indoors. She pined for the soothing sensation of earth beneath clawed toes, the gallop after game, the sweet reassuring smell of her pack mates as they acknowledged her place among them. And so she slipped out, knowing it was unwise. The only concession she made to human notions of decorum was to take the hated red cloak with her.

And that was how he found her, in the full moon, catching her just before she took off the red leather garment. "Quite the little woodsman, aren't you?" he drawled, toying with his knife.

Sylvia Rufina would not answer him.

"Cat got your tongue? Or is it perhaps a wolf that has it, I wonder? Damn your cold looks. I have something that will melt your ice, you arrogant and unnatural bitch." He took her by the wrist and forced her, struggling, to go with him along the path that led to his house. She could have slipped his grasp if she had taken her wolf form, but something told her she must keep her human wits to deal with what he had to show her.

There was something new nailed up to his barn, a huge pelt that shone in the full moonlight like a well-polished curse. It was the skin of her master, the lord of her nighttime world, the blessed creature whose nip had transformed her into something that could not be contained by human expectations. The Hunter was sneering and gloating, telling her about the murder, how easy she had made it for him to find their den, and he was promising to return and take another wolf's life for every night that she withheld her favors.

His lewd fantasies about her wolfish activities showed, she thought, considerable ignorance of both wolves and women. The wolves were lusty only once a year. The king and queen of the pack would mate; no others. The big silver male had loved her, but there was nothing sexual in his passion. He had been drawn by her misery and decided out of his animal generosity to set her wild heart free. And her desire had been for the wilderness, for running as hard and fast and long as she could, for thirst slaked in a cold mountain stream, and hunger appeased nose-down in the hot red mess of another, weaker creature's belly. She craved autonomy, not the sweaty invasion of her offended and violated womanhood. But the Hunter slurred on with his coarse fancies of bestial orgies, concluding, "After all this time I pined for you, and thought you were above me. Too refined and delicate and sensitive to notice my mean self. Now I find you're just another bitch in heat. How dare you refuse me?"

"Refuse you?" she cried, finding her voice at last. "Why, all you had to do was ask me. It never occurred to me that such a clever and handsome man would take an interest in someone as inexperienced and plain as me. I am only a simple girl, a farmer's daughter, but you are a man of the world." Where this nonsense came from, she did not know, but he lifted his hands from his belt to wrap his arms around her, and that was when she yanked his knife from his belt and buried it to the hilt in the middle of his back.

He died astonished, dribbling blood. She thought it was a small enough penance for the many lives he had taken in his manly pride and hatred of the feral. She took back the knife, planning to keep it, and let him fall.

By his heels, she dragged him back into his own house. Then she took the hide of her beloved down from the barn wall, shivering as she did so. It fell into her arms like a lover, and she wept to catch traces of his scent, which lingered still upon his lifeless fur like a memory of pine trees and sagebrush, rabbit-fear and the froth from the muzzle of a red-tailed deer, the perfume of snow shaken off a raven's back. It was easy to saddle the Hunter's horse, take food and money from his house, and then set fire to what remained. The horse did not like her mounting up with a wolf's skin clasped to her bosom, but with knees and heels she made it mind, and turned its nose to the city.

Since a human male had taken what was dearest to her, she determined, the rest of the Hunter's kind now owed her reparations. She would no longer suffer under a mother's dictates about propriety and virtue. She would no longer keep silence and let a man, too sure of his strength, back her into a corner. The wolves had taught her much about wildness, about hunters and prey, power and pursuit. One human or a thousand, she hated them all equally, so she would go where they clustered together, in fear of the forest, and take them for all they were worth.

In the city, the hunter's coins obtained lodging in a once-fashionable quarter of town. Down the street, she had the red cloak made into a whip with an obscene handle, cuffs, and a close-fitting hood. For herself, she had tall red boots and a corset fashioned. The next day, she placed an advertisement for riding lessons in the daily newspaper. Soon, a man rang her bell to see if she had anything to teach him. He wore a gray suit instead of the Hunter's doeskin and bear fur, but he had the same aura of barely controlled fury. He was wealthy, but his privilege had not set him free. It had instead deepened his resentment of anything he did not own and made him a harsh master over the things that he did possess.

Since he despised the animal within himself, she forced him to manifest it: stripped of anything but his own hide, on all fours, forbidden to utter anything other than a wordless howl. He could not be trusted to govern himself, beast that he was, so she fettered him. And because he believed the animal was inferior to the man, made to be used violently, she beat him the way a drunkard who has lost at cards will beat his own dog. He forgot her injunction against speech when it became clear how the "riding lesson" was to proceed, but she had no mercy. Like most men, he thought of women as cows or brood mares, so if he wanted to experience servitude and degradation, he would have to experience sexual violation as well as bondage and the lash. Bent over a chair, wrists lashed to ankles, he bellowed like a gored bull when the wooden handle of the whip took his male maidenhead.

In the end, he proved her judgment of his character was correct— he knelt, swore his allegiance to her, and tried to lick her, like a servile mutt who wants a table scrap. She took his money and kicked him out with a warning to avoid attempts to sully her in the future. He went away happy, his anger temporarily at bay, his soul a little lighter for the silver that he discarded in a bowl on the foyer table.

Soon Sylvia Rufina's sitting room was occupied by a series of men who arrived full of lust and shame and left poorer but wiser about their own natures. But their pain was no balm for the wounds the Red

Mistress, as she came to be called, carried in her psyche. Her self-styled slaves might prate about worship and call her a goddess, but the only thing they worshiped was their own pleasure. She knew, even as she crushed their balls, that they remained the real masters of the world.

Her consolations were private: the occasional meal of raw meat, and nightly slumber beneath a blanket of silver fur. For one whole year, she tolerated the overcrowding, bad smells, and disgusting scorched food of the city. Her fame spread, and gossip about her imperious beauty and cruelty brought her paying customers from as far away as other countries. The notion that one could buy a little freedom, pay for only a limited amount of wildness, bored and amused the Red Mistress. But she kept her thoughts to herself and kept her money in an iron-bound chest. She lived like a monk, but the tools of her trade were not cheap, and she chafed to see how long it took for her hoard of wealth to simply cover the bottom of the box, then inch toward its lid.

When spring came, at first it simply made the city stink even worse than usual, as thawing snow deposited a season's worth of offal upon the streets. There was a tree near Sylvia Rufina's house, and she was painfully reminded of how beautiful and busy the forest would seem now, with sap rising and pushing new green leaves into the warming air. Her own blood seemed to have heated as well, and it grew more difficult to curb her temper with the pretense of submission that fed her treasure chest. An inhuman strength would come upon her without warning. More than one of her slaves left with the unwanted mark of her teeth upon their aging bodies and thought perhaps they should consider visiting a riding mistress who did not take her craft quite so seriously.

The full moon of April caught her unawares, standing naked by her bedroom window, and before she willed it, she was herself again, four-footed and calm. After so many months of despicable hard work and monkish living, she was unable to deny herself the pleasure of keeping this form for just a little while. The wolf was fearless and went out the front door as if she owned it. Prowling packs of stray dogs were just one of the many hazards on this city's nighttime streets. Few pedestrians would be bold enough to confront a canid of her size and apparent ferocity. When she heard the sound of a conflict, she went toward it, unfettered by a woman's timidity, ruled by the wolf's confident assumption that wherever there is battle, there may be victuals.

Down a street more racked by poverty than the one on which the Red Mistress plied her trade, outside a tenement, a man in a moth-eaten overcoat and a shabby top hat held a woman by the upper arms and shook her like a rattle. She was being handled so roughly that her hair had begun to come down from where it was pinned on top of her head, so her face and chest were surrounded by a blond cloud. She wore a low-cut black dress that left her arms indecently bare, and it was slit up the back to display her calves and even a glimpse of her thighs. "Damn you!" the man screamed. "Where's my money?"

The wolf did not like his grating, hysterical voice, and her appetite was piqued by the fat tips of the man's fingers, which protruded from his ruined gloves, white as veal sausages. He smelled like gin and mothballs, like something that ought never to have lived. When he let go of one of the woman's arms so he could take out a pocket handkerchief and mop his brow, the wolf came out of the shadows and greeted him with a barely audible warning and a peek at the teeth for which her kind was named. He was astonished and frightened. The same pocket that had held his handkerchief also contained a straight razor, but before he could fumble it out, the wolf landed in the center of his chest and planted him on his back in the mud. A yellow silk cravat, darned and stained, outlined his throat and was no obstacle.

The wolf disdained to devour him. He was more tender than the querulous granny, but dissolute living had contaminated his flesh.

She did not want to digest his sickness. Licking her muzzle clean, she was surprised to see the disheveled woman waiting calmly downwind, her bosom and face marked by the pimp's assault. "Thank you," the woman said softly. She knew her savior was no domesticated pet who had slipped its leash. Her life had been very hard, but she would not have lived at all if she had not been able to see what was actually in front of her and work with the truth.

Human speech made the wolf uneasy. She did not want to be reminded of her other form, her other life. She brushed past the woman, eager to sample the evening air and determine if this city held a park where she could ramble.

"Wild thing," said the woman, "let me come with you," and ardent footsteps pattered in the wake of the wolf's silent tread. The wolf could have left her behind in a second but perversely chose not to do so. They came to the outskirts of a wealthy man's estate. His mansion was in the center of a tract of land that was huge by the city's standards and stocked with game birds and deer. A tall wrought-iron fence surrounded this land, and the golden one made herself useful, discovering a place where the rivets holding several spears of iron in place had rusted through. She bent three of them upward so the two of them could squeeze beneath the metal barrier. The scent of crushed vegetation and freshly disturbed earth made the wolf delirious with joy.

Through the park they chased one another, faster and faster, until the girl's shoddy shoes were worn paper-thin and had to be discarded. The game of tag got rougher and rougher until the wolf forgot it was not tumbling about with one of its own, and nipped the girl on her forearm. The triangular wound bled enough to be visible even by moonlight, scarlet and silver. Then there were two of a kind, one with fur tinged auburn, another with underfur of gold, and what would be more delicious than a hunt for a brace of hares? One hid while the other flushed out their quarry.

Knowing the potentially deadly sleep that would attack after feeding, Sylvia Rufina urged her new changeling to keep moving, back to the fence and under it. The two of them approached her house from the rear, entering through the garden. The golden one was loath to go back, did not want to take up human ways again. But Sylvia Rufina herded her relentlessly, forced her up the stairs and into the chamber where they both became mud-spattered women howling with laughter.

"You are a strange dream," the child of the streets murmured as the Red Mistress drew her to the bed.

"No dream except a dream of freedom," Sylvia Rufina replied and pinned her prey to the sheets just as she had taken down the hapless male bawd. The wolf-strength was still vibrant within her, and she ravished the girl with her mouth and hand, her kisses flavored with the heart's blood of the feast they had shared. Goldie was no stranger to the comfort of another woman's caresses, but this was no melancholy gentle solace. This was the pain of hope and need. She struggled against this new knowledge, but the Red Mistress was relentless and showed her so much happiness and pleasure that she knew her life was ruined and changed forever.

The bruised girl could not remember how many times she had relied on the stupor that disarms a man who has emptied his loins. No matter how bitterly they complained about the price she demanded for her attentions, there was always ten times that amount or more in their purses. But instead of falling into a snoring deaf-and-blind state, she felt as awake as she had during the change, when a wolf's keen senses had supplanted her poor blunted human perceptions. The hunger to be tongued, bitten, kissed, and fucked by Sylvia Rufina had not been appeased; it drove her toward the small perfect breasts and well-muscled thighs of her assailant and initiator.

Goldie did not rest until she had claimed a place for herself in the core of her lover's being. It was the first time in her life that Sylvia

Rufina had known anything but humiliation and disgust from another human being's touch. Her capacity to take pleasure was shocking, and yet nothing in the world seemed more natural than seizing this cherub by her gold locks and demanding another kiss, on one mouth and then upon and within the other. They fell asleep on top of the covers, with nothing but a shared mantle of sweat to keep them warm. But that was sufficient.

Dawn brought a less forgiving mood. The Red Mistress was angry that someone had breached her solitude. She had not planned to share her secret with another living soul, and now she had not only revealed her alter ego but made herself a shape-shifting sister.

Goldie would not take money. She would not be sent away. And so the Red Mistress put her suitor to the severest of tests. Rather than imprisoning her with irons or cordage, Sylvia Rufina bade the blond postulant to pick up her skirts, assume a vulnerable position bent well over, and keep it until she was ordered to rise. With birch, tawse, and cane, she meted out the harshest treatment possible, unwilling to believe the golden one's fealty until it was written in welts upon her body. The severest blows were accepted without a murmur, with no response other than silent weeping. When her rage was vented, Sylvia Rufina made the girl kiss the scarlet proof of her ambition that lingered upon the cane. And the two of them wept together until they were empty of grief and could feel only the quiet reassurance of the other's presence.

That night the refugee from the streets, who had been put to sleep upon the floor, crept into the bed and under the wolf hide that covered the Red Mistress and made love to her so slowly and carefully that she did not fully awaken until her moment of ultimate pleasure. It was clear that they would never sleep apart again as long as either one of them should live.

They became mates, a pack of two, hunter and prey with one another, paired predators with the customers who were prepared to pay extra. With the comfort and challenge of one another's company, the work was much less onerous. The Red Mistress's income doubled, and by the time another year had gone by, she had enough money to proceed with her plan.

On a day in the autumn, a month or so before the fall of snow was certain, she locked up her house for the last time, leaving everything behind except the trunk of coins and gems, the maid, and warm clothing for their journey. They went off in a coach, with a large silver fur thrown across their knees, headed toward the mountains, and no one in the city ever saw them again. On the way out of the city, they stopped to take a few things with them: a raven that had been chained to a post in front of an inn; a bear that was dancing, muzzled, for a gypsy fiddler; a caged pair of otters that were about to be sold to a furrier.

They had purchased wild and mountainous country, land no sane person would ever have a use for, too steep and rocky to farm, and so it was very cheap. There was plenty of money left to mark the boundaries of their territory, warning hunters away. There was a cabin, suitable for primitive living, and a stable that had already been stocked with a season's worth of feed for the horses. Once safe upon their own precincts, they let the raven loose in the shade of an oak tree, freed the old bear from his cumbersome and painful muzzle in a patch of blackberries, and turned the otters out into the nearest minnow-purling stream.

And that night, amid the trees, with a benevolent round-faced moon to keep their secrets, Sylvia Rufina took the form she had longed for during two impossible years of bondage to human society. The golden-haired girl she loved set her wild (and wise) self free as well. Then they were off to meet the ambassadors of their own kind.

They lived ever after more happily than you or me.

I've told you this story for a reason. If your woman has gone missing, and you go walking in dark places to try to find her, you may find Sylvia and Goldie instead. If they ask you a question, be sure to tell them the truth. And do not make the mistake of assuming that the wolf is more dangerous than the woman.